A PROWLER IN THE DARK

The creature leans its head back, opens its jaws wide, and *screams*. And never before has Queen Wealthow or any of Hrothgar's thanes heard such a foul utterance. The world's ruin sewn up in that dreadful cry, the fall of
very eart

The ve
and fury
fires flare
the rafte
white-hot flame, showering bright cinders in all directions. From the throne dais, neither the doorway nor the monster standing there remains visible, the view obscured by the blaze. The hall, which but moments before was filled with song and laughter and the s
screa
gry s
scran
the c
the r

Th
beast
the m
other
into
less
throu
head
fore
Hrot

Beowulf

CAITLÍN R. KIERNAN
Based on the screenplay by
NEIL GAIMAN & ROGER AVARY
With an introduction by NEIL GAIMAN

HarperEntertainment
An Imprint of HarperCollins*Publishers*

HarperEntertainment
An Imprint of HarperCollins*Publishers*
10 East 53rd Street
New York, New York 10022–5299

ISBN: 978-0-06-134128-1
ISBN-10: 0-06-134128-2

First HarperEntertainment paperback printing: October 2007

Printed in the United States of America

Visit HarperEntertainment on the World Wide Web at
www.harpercollins.com

10 9 8 7 6 5 4 3 2 1

For Grendel

Talibus laboribus lupos defendimus.

Introduction

Sometimes I think of stories as animals. Some common, some rare, some endangered. There are stories that are old, like sharks, and stories as new on this earth as people or cats.

Cinderella, for example, is a story which, in its variants, has spread across the world as successfully as rats or crows. You'll find it in every culture. Then there are stories like the *Iliad*, which remind me more of giraffes—uncommon, but instantly recognized whenever they appear or are retold. There are—there must be—stories that have become extinct, like the mastodon or the sabre-toothed tiger, leaving not even bones behind; stories that died when the people who told them died and could tell them no longer or stories that, long forgotten, have left only fossil fragments of themselves in other tales. We have a handful of chapters of the *Satyricon*, no more.

Beowulf could, so easily, have been one of those.

Because once upon a time, well over a thousand years ago, people told the story of *Beowulf*. And then time passed and it was forgotten. It was like an animal that no one had noticed had gone extinct, or almost extinct. Forgotten in oral lore, it was preserved by only one manuscript. Manuscripts are fragile and easily destroyed by time or by fire. The *Beowulf* manuscript has scorch marks on it.

But it survived . . .

And when it was rediscovered it slowly began to breed, like an endangered species being nurtured back to life.

My first exposure to the story three hundred years after the only manuscript was acquired by the British Museum came from an English magazine article pinned to a classroom wall. That was where I first read about them, Beowulf and Grendel and Grendel's even more terrible mother.

My second encounter was probably in the short-lived *Beowulf* from DC Comics. He wore a metal jockstrap and a helmet, with horns so big he could not have made it through a door, and he fought enormous snakes and suchlike. It didn't do much for me, although it sent me in search of the original in the shape of a Penguin Classics edition, which I re-read years later when Roger Avary and I came to retell the story in movie form.

The wheel keeps turning. *Beowulf* has long since left the endangered species list and begun to breed its many variants. There have been numerous accounts of *Beowulf* on the screen already, ranging from a science fiction version to a retelling in which Grendel is a tribe of surviving Neanderthals. It's all good: different retellings, recombining story DNA. The ones that work will be remembered and retold, the others will be forgotten.

When Roger Avary and I were first asked if we thought there should be a novel inspired by the film we had written, we said no and suggested that people simply read the original poem instead. I'm glad that the powers that be ignored us, and just as glad that they found Caitlín R. Kiernan to retell this version of the story.

Because she did. She took the tale of *Beowulf* and the script to the film and she told a tale that pounds in your head, a mead and blood-scented saga that should be chanted at midnight in swamps and on lonely hilltops.

She tells a tale of heroism and firelight and gold, punctuated with love and secrets and moments of extreme violence. It's an old tale, one that deserves to be retold as long as people care about heroes and monsters and the dark. It's a story for each of us.

We all have our demons.

Beowulf thought his was Grendel . . .

Neil Gaiman
2007

Prologue

There was a time *before* men, a time before even the world existed, when all the cosmos was only the black void of Ginnunga gap. To the farthest north lay the frozen wastes of Niflheim, and to the farthest south, the lands of bright, sparking furnaces belonging to the giant Muspéll and so named Muspellsheim. In the great emptiness of Ginnunga, the cold northern winds met the warm breezes blown out from the south, and the whirling gales of sleet and snow melted and dripped down into the nothingness to form Ymir, father of all the Frost Giants. The giants called him Aurgelmir, the gravel-yeller. Also formed from these drips of rime was the first cow, Audhumla. With her milk she fed Ymir, and with her tongue she licked the first of the gods, Búri, from a block of salt. In later times, Búri's son, Bur, had three sons by the giantess Bestla. They were Odin, Vili, and Vé, and it was they who slew great Ymir and then carried his corpse to the dead heart of Ginnunga gap. From his blood they fashioned the lakes and rivers and seas, and from his bones they carved mountains. From his massive teeth they made all the stones and gravel, from his brain the clouds, and from his skull they constructed the sky and laid it high above the land. And so it was that the sons of Búri built the world, which would be the home of the sons of men. Last of all, they used Ymir's eyebrows to build an enormous wall, which they named Midgard, which was raised up beyond the seas, all around the edges of the world's disk, that it might always protect men from the enmity of the giants who had not been drowned in the terrible deluge of Ymir's blood.

And here, under the sanctuary of Midgard, would all the innumerable lives of men be lived. Here would they rise and struggle and fall. Here would they be born and die. Here would the greatest among them find glory in mighty deeds and, having died the deaths of heroes, be escorted by the Valkyries through the gates of Odin's hall, Valhalla, where they feast and drink and await Ragnarök, the final battle between the gods and the giants, where they will fight at Odin All-Father's side. The great wolf, Fenrir, will be at last set loose upon the world, and in the oceans, the Midgard serpent will be unbound. Yggdrasil, the world tree, will shudder, its foundations weakened by the gnawing jaws of the dragon Nidhögg. An ax age, an age of clashing swords and broken shields, when brothers will fight and murder one another; a wind age, a wolf age, there at the twilight of the gods when all the cosmos will dissolve, finally, into chaos.

But *before* the coming of that end, which not even the gods may forestall, there would be all the generations of men and women. All the countless wars and treacheries, loves and triumphs and sacrifices. And the greatest of these might be remembered and repeated in the songs and poetry of skalds, for a time.

There, under Midgard, would be an age of heroes.

PART ONE

Grendel

1

A Prowler in the Dark

The land of the Danes ends here, at this great wedge of granite cliffs jutting out high above the freezing sea. The foam of icy waves lashes the cruel shingle, narrow beaches of ragged bedrock and fallen boulders, polished cobbles and the stingy strands of ice- and snow-scabbed sand. This is no fit place for men, these barren, wind-scoured shores in this hungry, sun-shunned time of the year. By day, there are few enough *wild* things—only seals and walrus and the beached and rotting carcass of a whale, only the gulls and eagles soaring against the mottled, leaden sky. During the long nights, the shore becomes an even more forsaken and forbidding realm, unlit but for the furtive glimpses of the moon's single pale eye as it slips in and out of the clouds and fog.

But even here there is refuge. Perched like a beacon shining out to all those lost and wandering in the cold stands the tower of the Scylding king Hrothgar, son of Healfdene, grandson of Beow, great-grandson of Shield Sheafson. The tower throws specks of warm yellow against the gloom, and tonight, in the shadow of the tower, there is a celebration, revelry even on an evening so bleak as this.

Within the sturdy walls of the king's new mead hall, which he has named Heorot, the hall of harts, his thanes and their ladies have assembled. The fires burn bright beneath thatch and timber, driving back the chill and filling the air with delicious cooking smells and the comforting aroma of woodsmoke. Here, high above the reach of the angry sea, the king has at last made good his promise, the gift of this mighty hall to his loyal subjects. In all the lands of the Northmen, there is no other to equal its size and grandeur, and on this night it is awash with drunken laughter and the clatter of plates and knives, the rise and fall of a hundred voices speaking all at once, not so very different from the rise and fall of the sea outside, except there is no ice to be found here anywhere, and one might only drown in the endless cups of mead. Above the wide fire pits, pigs and deer, rabbit and geese roast on iron spits, and the flames leap and dance, throwing dizzying shadows across the walls and laughing faces and the massive oak timbers carved with scenes of warfare and the hunt, with the graven images of gods and monsters.

"Have I not kept my oath?" howls fat King Hrothgar from the alcove set into the farther end of the long hall. He is an old man, and his battle days are behind him now, his long beard and the braids in his hair gone white as the winter snow. Wrapped only in a bedsheet, he rises slowly from the cradle of his throne, moving as quickly as age and his considerable girth will permit. "One year ago . . . I, Hrothgar, your king, swore that we would soon celebrate our victories in a new hall, a hall both mighty *and* beautiful. Now, you tell me, *have I not kept my oath*?"

Momentarily distracted from their drink, from their feasting and happy debaucheries, the king's men raise their cups and raise their voices, too, drunkenly cheering on old Hrothgar, and never mind that only a handful among them are sober enough to know *why* they are cheering. At the sound of their voices, Hrothgar grins drunkenly and rubs at his belly, then turns to gaze down at his queen, the beautiful lady Wealthow. Though hardly more than a child, this violet-eyed girl adorned in gold and furs and glittering jewels, Wealthow is neither burdened with nor blinded by childish illusions about her husband's fidelity. She knows, for example, of the two giggling maidens whom he bedded this very night, farm girls or perhaps daughters of his own warriors, with whom the king was still occupied when four thanes came to bear him from his bedchamber out into the crowded hall. Hrothgar has never made the least effort to hide his whores and mistresses, so she has never seen the point in pretending not to see them.

"Ah, mead!" he grunts, and grabs the gilded drinking horn from the queen's hands. "Thank you, my lovely Wealthow!" She glares up at him, though Hrothgar has already turned away, raising the horn to his lips, spilling mead down his chin and into the tangle of his beard.

The drinking horn is a breathtaking thing, and she has often spoken aloud of her wonder of it. Surely, it was made either in remote and elder days, when such fine craftsmanship was not uncommon to this land, or it was fashioned in some distant kingdom by a people who'd not yet forgotten that artistry. It is a mystery and a marvelous sight, this relic rescued from a dragon's hoard; even clutched in the meaty hands of a man so crude as her husband, the drinking horn does not cease to please her eyes. The finest gold etched with strange runes the likes of which she's never seen before, and there are two clawed feet mounted on one side so that the horn may be set down without tipping over and spilling. For the handle, there's a winged dragon, also of wrought gold, with a single perfect ruby set into its throat. Horns and fangs and the jagged trace of its sinuous, razor spine, a terrible worm summoned from some forgotten tale, or perhaps the artisan meant this dragon to recall the serpent Nidhögg Rootnibbler, who lies coiled in the darkness at the base of the World Ash.

Hrothgar belches, wipes at his mouth, then raises the empty horn as though to toast all those assembled before him. "And *in* this hall," he bellows, "we shall divide the spoils of our conquests, all the gold and the treasure. This shall ever be a place of merrymaking and of joy and *fornication* . . . from now until the end of time. I name this hall *Heorot*!"

And again the thanes and their women and everyone else in the hall cheer, and Hrothgar turns once more to face Wealthow. Droplets of mead cling to his mustache and beard like some strange amber dew.

"Let's hand out some treasure, shall we, my beauty?"

Wealthow shrugs and keeps her seat, as the king dips one hand into a wooden chest that has been placed on the dais between their thrones. It is filled almost to overflowing with gold and silver, with coins minted in a dozen foreign lands and jewel-encrusted brooches. The king tosses a handful out into the waiting crowd. Some of it is snatched directly from the air, and other pieces rain down noisily upon tabletops and dirt floors, prompting a greedy, reckless scramble.

Now the king selects a single gold torque from the chest and holds it above his head, and again the crowd cheers. But this time the king shakes his head and holds the torque still higher.

"No, no, this one is not for *you* lot. *This* is for Unferth, my wisest man, unrivaled violator of virgins and boldest of all brave brawlers—where the fuck *are* you, Unferth, you weasel-faced bastard! *Unferth*—"

Across the long hall, at the edge of a deep pit dug

directly into the floor, so that men will not have to brave the cold wind and risk frostbite just to take a piss, Unferth is busy relieving himself and arguing with another of the king's advisors, Aesher. Unferth hasn't yet heard Hrothgar calling out his name, the old man's voice diminished by the endless clatter and din of the hall, and he stares into the dark pit, a great soggy mouth opening wide to drink its own share of mead, once the thanes have done with it. There is a hardness about this man, something grim and bitter in his gaunt face and braids as black as raven feathers, something calculating in the dull glint of his green eyes.

"Do not be so quick to laugh," he says to Aesher. "I'm telling you, we have to start taking this matter seriously. I've heard the believers now extend from Rome all the way north to the land of the Franks."

Aesher scowls and stares down at the yellow stream of his own urine. "Well, then answer me this. Who do you think would win a *knife fight*, Odin or this Christ Jesus?"

"*Unferth!*" Hrothgar roars again, and this time Unferth does hear him. "Oh, what now?" he sighs. "Can I not even be left in peace long enough to piss?"

Aesher shakes his head and snickers. "Best hurry it up," he says, laughing. "You'll not want to keep him waiting. What is a man's full bladder when placed alongside the will of his king?"

"Unferth, bastard son of that bastard Ecglaf! Where *are* you, you ungrateful lout!?"

Unferth hastily tucks himself back into his breeches, then turns reluctantly to push his way through the drunken mob. Some of them step aside to let him pass, while others do not even seem to notice him. But soon Unferth has reached the edge of the king's dais, and he forces a smile onto his face and raises his hand so that Hrothgar will see him standing there.

"I'm here, my king!" he says, and Hrothgar, catching sight of him, grins even wider and leans down, placing the golden torque about Unferth's thin neck.

"You are too kind, my liege. Your generosity—"

"No, no, no. It's nothing less than you deserve, nothing less, good and faithful Unferth," and then Hrothgar gazes out upon his subjects once again. And once again an enthusiastic cheer rises from the crowd. The king's herald, Wulfgar, steps forward from the shadows of the throne to lead the drunken thanes and their women in a familiar chant, and soon enough most of the hall has joined him. Warriors bang their fists and cups against tabletops or leap onto the tables and stomp their feet as Heorot rings out with song:

Hrothgar, Hrothgar!
Hrothgar, Hrothgar!
He faced the demon dragon
When other men would freeze.
And then my lords,
He took his sword
And brought it to its knees!

Now Hrothgar's musicians have all joined in, taking up the song with their harps and flutes and drums. Even Unferth sings, but the king's gift lies cold and heavy about his throat, and there is considerably less enthusiasm and sincerity in his voice.

Hrothgar, Hrothgar!
The greatest of our kings.
Hrothgar, Hrothgar!
He broke the dragon's wings!

But the torrents of joyous noise spilling forth from Heorot—the laughter and the fervent songs, the jangle of gold and silver coins—these are not a welcome sound to all things that dwell in this land by the sea. There are creatures in the night that are neither man nor beast, ancient beings descended from giantkind, the trolls and worse things still, who keep themselves always to the watches, to dank fens and forbidding marshlands. Past the mighty walls and pikes of Hrothgar's fortifications, beyond gate and bridge and chasm, where farmland and pasture turn suddenly to wilderness, there stands a forest older than the memory of man, a wood that has stood since before the coming of the Danes. And in the vales that lie on the far side of these gnarled trees, are frozen bogs and bottomless lakes leading back down to the sea, and there are rocky hillocks riddled with caves, tunnels bored deep into the stone even as maggots bore into the flesh of the dead.

And in one of these caverns something huge and, to the eyes of man, ghastly crouches in the muck and gravel and a bright pool of moonlight leaking in through the cave's entrance. It moans pitifully and clutches at its diseased and malformed skull, covering misshapen ears in an effort to shut out the torturous sounds of revelry drifting down like a thunderous, hammering snow from Heorot. For even though the mead hall and the tower on the sea cliff are only a distant glow, there is a peculiar magic to the walls and spaces of this cave, a singular quality that magnifies those far-off noises and makes of them a deafening clamor. And so the troll thing's ears ring and ache, battered mercilessly by the song of Hrothgar's men even as the shore is battered into sand by the waves.

He offered us protection
When monsters roamed the land!
And one by one
He took them on —
They perished *at his hand!*

The creature wails—a keening cry that is at once sorrow and anger, fear and pain—as the ache inside its head becomes almost unbearable. It claws madly at its own face, then snatches in vain at the darkness and moonlight, as if its claws might somehow pluck the noise from out of the air and crush it flat, making of it something silent and broken and dead. Surely, its ears must soon burst, and this agony finally end. But its ears do not burst, and the pain does not end, and the thanes' song swells and redoubles, becoming even louder than before.

Hrothgar, Hrothgar!
We honor with this feast,
Hrothgar, Hrothgar!
He killed *the fiery beast!*

"No more, Mother," the creature groans, rolling its eyes and grinding its teeth against the song. "Mother, I can't bear this. Only so much, and I can bear *no more*!"

Tonight we sing his praises,
The bravest of the thanes.
So raise you spears!
We'll have no fears,
As long as Hrothgar reigns!

The creature clenches its great fists together and gazes up into the frigid night sky from the entrance of the cave, wordlessly begging Máni, the white moon, son of the giant Mundilfæri, to end the awful noise once and for all. "I *cannot* do it myself," the creature explains to the sky. "I am *forbidden*. My mother . . . she has *told* me that they are too *dangerous*." And then it imagines a hail of stone and silver flame cast down by the moon giant, falling from the sky to obliterate the hateful, taunting voices of the men forever. But the singing continues, and the unresponsive moon seems only to mock the creature's torment.

"No more," it says again, knowing now what must be done, what *he* must do for *himself*, since none other will ever end this racket—not the giants, not his mother. If there is to be peace again, then he must make it for himself. And gathering all his anger and suffering like a shield, battening it close about him, the monster steps quickly from the safety of shadows, slipping from the cave and out into the shimmering, unhelpful moonlight.

From his place behind the king's throne, Unferth watches as the mead hall sinks ever deeper into drunken pandemonium. His own cup is empty and has been empty now for some time, and he glances about in vain for the slave who should have long since come to refill it. There is no sign of the boy anywhere, only the faces of the singing, laughing, oblivious thanes. There does not seem to be a single thought remaining anywhere among them, but for the drink and their women, the feasting and the baying of old Hrothgar's praises.

Hrothgar, Hrothgar!
As every demon fell —
Hrothgar, Hrothgar!
He dragged them back to Hel!

Wulfgar sits nearby on the edge of the dais, a red-haired maiden camped upon his lap. He lifts his cup to her lips and dribbles mead between her breasts, then she giggles and squeals as he licks it off her chest. Unferth frowns and goes back to scanning the crowd for his slave, that lazy, crippled whelp named Cain. At last he spots the boy limping through the crowd, clutching a large goblet in both hands.

"*Boy!*" shouts Unferth. "Where's my mead?!"

"Here, my lord, I have it right here," the slave replies, then slips in a smear of cooling vomit on the dais steps, and mead sloshes over the rim of the cup and spatters on the floor.

"You're *spilling* it!" Unferth growls, and he grabs a walking stick from Aesher, a sturdy, knotted length of birch wood, and strikes Cain hard across the forehead. The boy reels from the blow, almost falls, and spills more mead on the dais steps.

"You clumsy idiot," sneers Unferth and hits Cain again. "How *dare* you waste the king's mead!"

The boy opens his mouth to reply, to apologize, but Unferth continues to beat him viciously with the stick. Some of the thanes have turned to watch, and they chuckle at the slave's predicament. At last, Cain gives up and drops the goblet, which is empty now, anyway, and he runs away as quickly as his crooked leg will allow, taking shelter beneath one of the long tables.

"Useless worm," Unferth calls out after him. "I *should* feed you to the pigs and be done with it!"

Hrothgar has been looking on from his throne, and he leans to one side and farts loudly, earning a smattering of applause from the thanes. "I fear you'd only poison the poor swine," he says to Unferth, and farts again. "Doesn't this damned song have an end?" And as if to answer his question, the crowd begins yet another verse.

He rose up like a savior,
When hope was almost gone.
The beast was gored
And peace restored!
His legend will live on!

Hrothgar grunts a very satisfied sort of grunt and smiles, surveying the glorious, wild confusion of Heorot Hall.

"I ask you, are we not now the most powerful men in all the world?" he mumbles, turning toward Aesher. "Are we not the *richest*? Do we not merrymake with the best of them? Can we not do as we *damn well please*?"

"We can," Aesher replies.

"Unferth?" asks King Hrothgar, but Unferth is still peering angrily at the spot where his slave vanished beneath the table, and doesn't answer.

"Have you gone deaf now, Unferth?"

Unferth sighs and hands the birch walking stick back to Aesher. "We do," he says halfheartedly. "We do."

"Damn straight we do," mutters Hrothgar, as perfectly and completely content in this moment as he has ever dared hope to be, as pleased with himself and with his deeds as he can imagine any living man has ever been. He starts to ask Wealthow—who is seated nearby with her handmaidens—to refill his golden horn, but then his eyelids flutter and close, and only a few seconds later the King of the Danes is fast asleep and snoring loudly.

Through the winter night, the creature comes striding toward Heorot Hall, and all things flee before him, all birds and beasts, all fish and serpents, all other phantoms and the lesser haunters of the darkness. He clambers up from the mire and tangle of the icy bogs, easily hauling his twisted bulk from the peat mud out into the deep shadows of the ancient forest. And though his skull still rings and echoes with the song of the thanes, he's relieved to be free for a time of the moon's ceaseless stare, shaded now by those thick, hoary limbs and branches that are almost as good as the roof of his cave.

"I will show them the *meaning* of silence!" he roars, and with one gigantic fist shatters the trunk of a tree, reducing it in an instant to no more than splinters and sap. *How much easier it will be to crush the bones of men, to spill* their *blood*, he thinks. And so another tree falls, and then another, and yet another after that, the violence of each blow only fueling his rage and driving him nearer the true object of his spite. The creature's long strides carry him quickly through the forest and back out again into the moonlight. Now he races across the moorlands, grinding bracken and shrub underfoot, trampling whatever cannot move quickly enough to get out of his way, flushing grouse and rabbit from their sleeping places. Soon, he has reached the rocky chasm dividing Hrothgar's battlements from the hinterlands. He pauses here, but only a moment or two, hardly long enough to catch his breath, before spying a lone sentry keeping watch upon the wall. The man sees him, as well, and at once the creature recognizes and relishes the horror and disbelief in the sentry's eyes.

He does not believe me real, the monster thinks, *and yet neither can he doubt the truth of me.* And then, before the man can cry out or raise an alarm, the thing from the cave has vaulted across the ravine . . .

"Did you hear that?" Unferth asks Aesher.

"Did I hear *what*?"

"Like thunder, almost," Unferth tells him, and glances down at the fat hound lying on the dais near Hrothgar's feet. The dog has pricked its ears and is staring intently across the hall at the great wooden door. Its lips curl back to show its teeth, and a low snarl issues from its throat.

"Truth be told, I can't hear shit but for these damn fools singing," says Aesher. "Ah, and the snoring of our brave king here."

Unferth reaches for the hilt of his sword.

"You are serious?" asks Aesher, and his hand goes to his own weapon.

"*Listen*," hisses Unferth.

"Listen for *what*?"

The dog gets up slowly, hackles raised, and begins to back away, putting more distance between itself and the entrance to the hall. Between the throne and the door to Heorot, the thanes and their women continue their drunken revelries—

Hrothgar, Hrothgar!
Let every cup be raised!
Hrothgar, Hrothgar!
NOW AND FOREVER PRAISED!

"Whatever's gotten into him?" Queen Wealthow asks, pointing to the snarling, retreating dog, its tail tucked between its legs. Unferth only spares her a quick glance before turning back toward the door. He realizes that it isn't barred.

"Aesher," he says. "See to the door—"

But then something throws itself against the outside of the mead-hall door, hitting with enough force that the frame groans and splinters with a deafening *crack*. The huge iron hinges bow and buckle inward, and the door is rent by numerous long splits—but for now it holds.

On his throne, King Hrothgar stirs, and in an instant more he's sitting up, wide-awake and bewildered. The thanes have stopped singing, and all eyes have turned toward the door. Women and children and some of the slaves begin to move away, backing toward the throne and the far end of the hall, and most of the warriors are reaching for their swords and daggers, their axes and spears. Unferth draws his blade, and Aesher follows suit. And then a terrible, breathless quiet settles over Heorot Hall, like the stunned, hollow space left after lightning strikes a tree.

"Unferth," whispers Hrothgar. "Are we being attacked?"

And then, before his advisor can reply, the door is assaulted a second time. It holds for barely even another moment, then gives way all at once, thrown free of its hinges, sundered into a thousand razor shards that rain down like deadly arrows across the floor and tabletops and bury themselves in the faces and bodies of those standing closest to the entrance. Some men are crushed to death or lie dying beneath the larger fragments of the broken door as a concussion rolls along the length of the hall, a wave of sound that seems solid as an avalanche, and the air blown out before it snuffs out the cooking fires and every candle burning in Heorot, plunging all into darkness.

Wealthow stands, ordering her handmaidens to seek shelter, then she looks to the doorway and the monstrous thing standing there, silhouetted in silver moonlight. Its chest heaves, and its breath wheezes like steam from its black lips and flaring nostrils. Surely, this must be some ancient terror, she thinks, some elder evil come down from olden times, from the days before the gods bound Loki Skywalker and all his foul children.

"My sire," she says, but then the creature leans its head back, opens its jaws wide, and *screams*. And never before has Queen Wealthow or any of Hrothgar's thanes heard such a foul utterance. The world's ruin sewn up in that dreadful cry, the fall of kingdoms, death rattles and pain and the very earth opening wide on the last day of all.

The very walls of Heorot shudder from the force and fury of that cry, and the extinguished cooking fires flare suddenly, violently back to life. Rising to the rafters, they have become whirling pillars of white-hot flame, showering bright cinders in all directions. From the throne dais, neither the doorway nor the monster standing there remains visible, the view obscured by the blaze. The hall, which but moments before was filled with song and laughter and the sounds of joyous celebration, erupts with the screams of the terrified and the maimed, with the angry shouts and curses of inebriated warriors as they scramble for their weapons. Behind the wall of fire, the creature advances, roaming freely now beneath the roof of Heorot.

The four thanes nearest to the door charge the beast, and it immediately seizes one of them and uses the man as a living cudgel with which to pummel the other three, sending two of them crashing backward into chairs and tables. The third is flung high, helpless as a doll, and sails the full length of the hall, through the swirling tower of flame and over the heads of those still seated or huddled on the dais before his body smashes limply against the wall behind Hrothgar's and Wealthow's thrones.

"My sword!" the king shouts, tottering to his feet. "Bring me my sword!"

Still gripping the fourth warrior by a broken ankle, the monster pauses only long enough to gaze down at his half-conscious, blood-slicked face, only long enough that the man may, in turn, look up into *its* face and fully comprehend his doom and the grave consequences of his bravery. Then, having no further use of the man, the creature tosses him into the inferno of the fire pit. And the flames shine even brighter than before, seeming grateful as they devour the screaming warrior. Again the monster cries out, assaulting the air and the ears of everyone trapped in Heorot Hall with that booming, doomsday voice.

Aesher takes Queen Wealthow's hand and leads her quickly from the dais. When they come to an overturned table, he pushes her onto the floor behind it.

"Stay down, my lady," he says. "Hide here and do not move. Do not look."

But she *does* look, as she has never been one to cower or shy away from the countenance of terrible things. As soon as Aesher releases his grip on her, Wealthow peers over the edge of the table, squinting painfully through the glare from the pit. But she cannot see the beast or the thanes struggling against it, only their distorted shadows stretched across the firelit walls. Their forms move to and fro like some grisly parody of the bedtime shadow plays her mother once performed for her. She watches in horror as men are thrown aside and broken like playthings, their bodies ripped apart, skewered, impaled on their own weapons.

"What evil . . ." she whispers. "What misfortune has brought this upon our house?"

"*Stay down*," Aesher says again, but at that moment another body is hurled through the roaring flames, igniting and passing mere inches above the queen's head. She ducks as the dead and burning man lands in the midst of a group of women crouched together against the wall. The fire leaps eagerly from the corpse to the clothes and hair of the screaming women, and before Aesher can move to stop her, Wealthow grabs a pitcher of mead and hurries over to them, dousing the flames. Aesher curses and shouts her name, but as she turns back toward the sheltering table, a battle-ax slices the air between them, so close she can feel the wind off the blade. The empty pitcher slips from the queen's fingers and shatters upon the floor. Then Aesher has her by the wrists and is pulling her roughly down, shoving her into the lee of the overturned table.

"Did you *see* that?" she says. "The ax . . ."

"Yes, my lady, the ax. I saw that it almost took your damned head off."

"No, not that. Did you see it hit the *monster*? It just . . . it *bounced off*. How can that *be*?"

But now the creature has turned toward the table where she and Aesher are hiding, and toward the throne, as well, distracted from its attacks upon the thanes by the hurled ax. In one long stride it steps past the halo of the fire pit, and finally Wealthow can see it clearly, the thing itself and not merely its shadow or silhouette. The monster stops to inspect the unscathed patch of skin where the steel blade struck it, then narrows its furious blue-gray eyes and bares fangs grown almost as long as the tusks of a full-grown bull walrus. It moves with a speed Wealthow would never have thought possible for anything so large, rushing forward and seizing Aesher in its talons, raising him high above its head.

"Run, my lady. *Run*," he cries out, but she cannot move, much less run. She can only watch helplessly as the creature sinks its claws deep into Aesher's body and tears him in two as easily as a child might tear apart a bundle of twigs. His blood falls around her like rain, drenching the head and shoulders of the beast and spattering Queen Wealthow's upturned face, sizzling and hissing as it spills into the fire pit.

"My sword!" Hrothgar bellows, and at that the monster hurls Aesher's legs and lower torso at the king. The gruesome missile misses its target and strikes Unferth, instead, knocking him sprawling to the floor. Disappointed, the beast drops the rest of Aesher's body onto the overturned table, and the lifeless thane's eyes stare up at Wealthow.

Now I will scream, she thinks. *Now I won't ever be able to* stop *screaming*. But she covers her mouth with both hands, forcing back the shrill voice of her own fear, certain enough that she'll be the creature's next victim without screaming and attracting its attention.

And then she sees her husband, stumbling down from his throne, his body wrapped in no more armor than what a bedsheet might offer, his broadsword clenched tightly in his fists and gleaming dully in the firelight. She also sees Unferth, who does not rise to come to the aid of his king, but scrambles away on his hands and knees, fleeing into the shadows beyond the dais.

"No!" Wealthow shouts at her husband, and the monster turns toward her, snatching away the protective barrier of the table with one enormous, knobby hand. The same claws that ripped Aesher apart sink into solid oak as though it were no more substantial than flesh and blood. It lifts the table above her, wielding it like a club.

"Fight me!" howls King Hrothgar, trembling violently and waving his sword at the invader's back. "Leave her *alone*, damn you! Fight *me*!"

And all around them, the hall seems to grow still, no fight left in the surviving thanes, more terror gathered in this hall now than heroes. The beast bares its teeth again and glares triumphantly down at Queen Wealthow, but *still* she cannot move. Still she can only stand, watching her husband and waiting for the blow that will crush her and release her from this world where such demons may freely roam the night.

"I said fight *me*, you son of a bitch," Hrothgar yells,

and strikes the creature, but his blade glances harmlessly off and does not even break its skin. "Surely, you did not come all this way to murder *women. Fight me*!"

And now Wealthow can see that there are tears streaming down Hrothgar's cheeks, and the monster turns slowly away from her and toward the king. Suddenly, facing Hrothgar, the thing begins to wail and moan, shrieking in pain as its whole body is wracked by some strange convulsion. Its muscles twitch and spasm, and its joints pop loud as the limbs of great trees caught in a fierce Mörsugur gale.

"*Yes*," roars Hrothgar. "That's it. Fight me."

The creature takes two faltering steps backward, retreating from the king of Heorot Hall, from a fat old man, drunk and tangled in his bedclothes. Now it stands directly over Wealthow, its legs forming an archway high above her head. It whimpers, and drool the color of pus drips from its lips and forms a puddle at her feet. Again the monster roars, but this time there is more hurt and dismay than anything else in that appalling sound.

"Me," Hrothgar says, brandishing his sword, and he closes half the distance between himself and the monster, between himself and Lady Wealthow.

"NNNNAAAAaaaaaaaaaay!" the beast cries out, its foul breath hurling that one word with enough force that Hrothgar is pushed backward and falls, losing his sheet and landing naked on his ass, his sword clattering to the floor. And then with its right hand, the creature seizes two of the fallen thanes and leaps into the air, vanishing up the chimney above the fire pit. In its wake, there is a terrific gust of wind, and for an instant, the fire flares yet more brightly—a blinding, blistering flash of heat and light—and then the wind snuffs it out, and the hall goes dark, the winter night rushing in to fill the emptiness left behind.

The darkness brings with it a shocked silence, broken only by frightened sobs and the sounds that dying men make. Someone lights a torch, and then another. Soon, the night is broken by flickering pools of yellow light, and Wealthow sees that the mead hall lies in ruin around her. Unferth emerges from the gloom, clutching his sword like someone who is not a coward. The glow of the torches is reflected faintly in the golden torque about his neck. Wealthow goes to her shivering, weeping husband and kneels at his side, gathering up the sheet and covering him with it. She cannot yet quite believe she is still alive and breathing.

"What *was* that?" she asks Hrothgar, and he shakes his head and stares up at the black hole of the chimney.

"Grendel," he replies. "That was Grendel."

2

Alien Spirits

Slick with the drying blood of murdered thanes and grimy with the soot of Heorot's chimney, Grendel returns to his cave beyond the forest. Standing in the entrance, he feels the moon's eye watching him, has felt its gaze pricking at his skin since the moment he emerged from the mead hall. It watched him all the way home, following his slow trek back across the moors and through the sleeping forest and over the bogs. He glances over his shoulder and up into the sky. Already, Máni has started sinking toward the western horizon and soon will be lost in the tops of the old trees.

"Did you think I could not do it for myself?" Grendel asks the moon. "Did you think I *wouldn't*?"

But the moon doesn't answer him. Grendel did not expect that it would. For all he knows, the son of Mundilfæri is a mute and has never spoken a single word in all his long life, hanging there in the night sky. Grendel sighs and looks down at the two corpses he's carried all the way back from Heorot, then he slips out of the moonlight and into the comforting darkness of the cave.

He cannot recall a time before this cave was his home. Sometimes he thinks he must have been born here. Not far from its entrance, there is a pool of still, clear water, framed in drooping, dripstone stalactites and sharp stalagmites jutting up from the cave's floor. They have always seemed to him like teeth, and so the pool is the cave's throat—maybe the throat of all the earth—and so perhaps he is only something that the world coughed up, some indigestible bit of a bad meal, perhaps.

Grendel drops the dead thanes onto a great mound of bones heaped high in a corner of the cave, not far from the pool's edge. Here, the bleached bones of men lie jumbled together with the remains of other animals—the antlered skulls of mighty harts, the crumbling skeletons of bears and seals, wolves and wild boar. Whatever he can catch and kill, and in all his life Grendel has not yet encountered anything that he *cannot* kill. Relieved of his burden, he turns back to the pool and gazes down at his reflection there in the still water. In the darkness, his eyes glitter faintly, his irises flecked with gold.

"Grendel?" his mother asks. "*Hwæt oa him weas?*"

Surprised and startled by her voice, the melodic crystal music of her words, he turns quickly about, spinning around much too suddenly and almost losing his balance.

"What have you done? Grendel?"

"Mother?" he asks, searching the gloom of the cavern for some evidence of her beyond her voice. "Where are you?" He glances up at the ceiling, thinking her voice might have come from somewhere overhead.

"Men? Grendel . . . I thought we had an agreement concerning *men*."

Yes, she *must* be on the ceiling, watching from some secret, shadowed spot almost directly above him. But then there's a loud splash from the pool, and Grendel is drenched with freezing water.

"Fish, Grendel. Fish, and wolves, and bear. Sometimes a sheep or two. But not *men*."

He turns slowly back to the pool, and she's there, waiting for him.

"You *like* men," he tells her. "Here . . ." and he retrieves one of the dead thanes, the least gnawed of the two, and offers it to her.

"No," she says sternly. "Not these fragile things, my darling. Remember, they will *hurt* us. They have killed so many of us . . . of our kind . . . the giants, the dragonkind. They have hunted us until there are almost none of us left to hunt. They will hunt *you*, too, if you make a habit of killing them."

"But they were making so much noise. They were making so much *merry* . . . and it hurt me. It hurt my head. I couldn't even think for the noise and the pain." And Grendel holds the dead thane out to her again. "Here, Mother, this one is sweet. I have peeled away all the hard metal parts."

"Just put it down, Grendel."

And so he does, dropping it into the pool, where it sinks for a moment, then bobs back to the surface. Immediately, blood begins to stain the clear water. Grendel has started crying now, and he wants to turn away, wants to run back out into the night where only the moon can see him.

"Was Hrothgar there?" his mother asks, and now there's an edge in her voice.

"I did not touch him."

"You *saw* him? *He* saw you?"

"Yes, but I didn't hurt him."

His mother blinks her wide, brilliant eyes, then stares at him a few seconds more, and Grendel knows that she's looking for any sign that he's lied to her. When she finds none, she slides gracefully up from the pool, moving as easily as water flowing across stone, or as blood spilling over the blade of an ax. She reaches out, her scaly flesh damp and strong and even more soothing than the dark haven of his cave. She wipes away some of the gore and grime from his cheeks and forehead.

"I did not touch him, Mother," Grendel tells her a third time.

"I know," she replies. "You're a good boy."

"I couldn't stand it any longer."

"My poor, sensitive boy," she purrs. "Promise me you will not go there again," but Grendel only closes his eyes and tries not to think about shattered trees or the broken bodies, tries not to let his mind linger on the noise of men or his hatred or the beautiful, golden-haired woman he would have killed, there at the last, had Hrothgar not stayed his hand.

3

Raids in the Night

Grendel's attacks did not end after the first assault upon Heorot. Some hatreds are too old and run far too deep to be satisfied by a single night of bloodshed and terror. Night after night he returned, his hatred and loathing for the Danes driving him from his cave again and again, intent that the noise of Hrothgar's hall would be silenced once and for all. There would be no more deafening, painful nights. There would be no more merrymaking. And as winter closed ever tighter about the land, until the snow had gone to an icy crust and the warm sun was only a dim memory of summers that might never come again, Hrothgar's great gift to his people became a haunted, fearful place. But Grendel did not restrict his attacks to the hall alone, taking young and old alike, men and women and children, the weak and the strong, wherever he might come upon them. He held Heorot, coming and going as pleased him and making it the most prized trophy in his lonely war, but he also roamed the old woods and the moors, the farms and homesteads, and took all those who crossed his path.

And word spread, in the songs of skalds, in the whispered tales told by travelers and traders, of the lurking doom that had fallen upon Hrothgar's kingdom.

On a freezing morning when the frost might as well be steel and the sun has not yet seen fit to show itself, the king lies with his queen on soft pallets of straw bound with woolen cloth and deer hide. Hrothgar opens his eyes, uncertain at first what has awakened him, but then he sees Unferth standing beside the bed.

"My lord?" Unferth asks, whispering so as not to disturb Lady Wealthow. "My lord, it has happened again."

And Hrothgar would shut his eyes and fight his way back down to sleep, back to dreams of warm sunlight and nights without monsters, but Unferth would still be there when he opened them again. He dresses quickly and as quietly as he might, managing not to wake his wife, and then he follows Unferth to Heorot. Soon, he is standing in the cold with Unferth and Wulfgar and a number of thanes outside the mead-hall doors, the hall's *new* doors, reinforced with wide iron bands and easily twice as thick as those that Grendel burst asunder.

"How many this time?" asks Hrothgar, his breath fogging like smoke.

Unferth takes a deep breath and swallows before he replies. "In truth, I could not say. The bodies were not whole. Five. Ten, perhaps. It was Nykvest's daughter's wedding feast."

"Grendel's coming more frequently," Hrothgar sighs and tugs at his beard. "Why does not this demon simply make my hall his home and save himself the trouble of stalking back and forth each night across the moorlands?"

Hrothgar looks down and sees the red-pink stain leaking from beneath the door.

"The new door hasn't even been touched," he says, and angrily smacks the wood hard with one open palm.

"Nay," Unferth replies. "The Grendel devil obviously came and went through the skorsten." And he points up at the chimney vent in the roof of Heorot Hall. Hrothgar sees the blood right away, spattered across the thatched roof, then on the snow below the eaves, dappling the monster's splayed footprints. The trail leads away across the compound grounds and vanishes in the mist.

Hrothgar takes a deep breath and puffs out more steam, then rubs at his bleary eyes. "When I was young I killed a dragon, in the Northern Moors," he says, and Unferth hears a hint of sadness or regret in the king's voice. "But now I am an old man, Unferth. Too old for demon slaying. We need a hero, a cunning *young* hero, to rid us of this curse upon our hall."

"I wish you had a son, my lord," Wulfgar says, and takes a step back from the door and the spreading bloodstain on the threshold. His boots crunch loudly on the frozen ground.

Hrothgar grunts and glares at him. "You can wish in one hand, Wulfgar, and shit into the other—see which fills up first."

Hrothgar turns his back on the door, on Heorot and this latest butchery, and faces the small group of people that has gathered outside the hall.

"Men," he says, "build another pyre. There's dry wood behind the stables. Burn the dead. And then close this hall. Seal the doors and windows. And by the king's order, there shall be no further music, singing, or merrymaking of any kind." He takes another gulp of the frigid air and turns away. "This place reeks of death," he murmurs, then shuffles off through the snow, heading back toward his bed and sleeping Wealthow. After a moment, Unferth and Wulfgar follow him and have soon caught up.

"The scops are singing the shame of Heorot," Hrothgar says, speaking softly and keeping his eyes on the snow at his feet. "As far south as the middle sea, as far north as the ice-lands. Our cows no longer calf, our fields lie fallow, and the very fish flee from our nets, knowing that we are cursed. I have let it be known that I will give half the gold in my kingdom to any man who can rid us of Grendel."

Unferth glances at Wulfgar, then back to Hrothgar. "My king," he says. "For deliverance our people sacrifice goats and sheep to Odin and Heimdall. With your permission, might we also pray to the new Roman god, Christ Jesus? Maybe . . . maybe *he* can lift this affliction."

"You may pray as it best pleases you, son of Ecglaf. But know you this. The gods will not do for us that we will not do for ourselves. No, Unferth. We need a *man* to do this thing, a *hero*."

"But surely," persists Unferth, "praying cannot *hurt*."

"Yes, well, that which cannot hurt also cannot *help* us. Where was Odin Hel-binder—or this Christ Jesus of the Romans—when the demon took poor Nykvest's daughter? Answer that question or bother me no more with this pointless talk of prayers and sacrifices and new gods."

"Yes, my liege," Unferth replies, then follows Hrothgar and his herald across the snow.

4

The Coming of Beowulf

The storm-lashed Jótlandshaf heaves and rages around the tiny, dragon-prowed ship as though all the nine daughters of the sea giant Ægir have been given the task this day of building a new range of mountains from mere salt water. Towering waves lift the vessel until its mast might almost scrape the low-slung belly of the sky, only to let go and send it plunging down, down, down into troughs so deep the coils of the World Serpent cannot possibly lie very far below the hull. Overhead are banks of clouds as black as pitch, spilling blinding sheets of rain and lightning, and deafening thunder to rend a man's soul wide. There are fourteen thanes at the oars, their backs aching as they strain and struggle against the storm, their hands cold and bloodied and pierced with splinters.

A fifteenth man stands braced against the oaken mast, and the wild wind tugs at his cape of heavy black wool and animal skins, and the icy rain stings his face. The ship lurches forward, then back, teetering on the crest of a wave, and he almost loses his footing. He squints into the sheeting rain, unable to turn loose of the mast to shield his eyes, searching the gray blur where the horizon ought to be. But the storm has stolen it away, has sewn sea to sky and sky to sea. The ship lurches violently forward once more and begins racing down the face of the wave. When it's finally level again, one of the thanes leaves his place at the oars and makes his way slowly along the slippery deck to stand with the man leaning against the mast.

"Can you see the coast?" he asks, shouting to be heard above the din of the storm. "Do you see the Danes' guide-fire?"

The ship rolls suddenly to port, but rights itself before the sea can rush in and swamp the craft.

"I see *nothing*, Wiglaf! Unless you count the wind and rain!"

"No fire? No sun or stars by which to navigate? We're *lost*, Beowulf! Given to the sea, gifts to the Urdines!"

Beowulf laughs, getting a mouthful of rain and sea spray in the bargain. He spits and wipes his lips, grinning back at Wiglaf. He takes his right hand from the mast beam and thumps his chest hard, pounding at the iron-studded leather armor he wears.

"The sea is my *mother*! She spat me up years ago and will never take me back into her murky womb!"

Wiglaf scowls and blinks against the rain. "Well," he says, "that's fine for *you*. But *my* mother's a fishwife in Uppland, and I was rather hoping to die in *battle*, as a warrior *should*—"

The boat rolls again, this time listing sharply to port, and Wiglaf curses and clutches at Beowulf's cape to keep from falling.

"Beowulf, the men are worried this storm has no end!"

Beowulf nods and wraps his right arm tightly about Wiglaf's shoulders, helping him to steady himself as the ship begins to climb the next great wave.

"This is no earthly storm! That much we *can* be sure. But this demon's tempest won't hold us out! No, Wiglaf, not if we *really* want in! There is no power under Midgard that will turn me back!"

"But the *gods*—" Wiglaf begins.

"The gods be damned and drowned!" Beowulf howls into the storm, sneering up at the low black clouds. "If they have yet to learn I cannot be frightened away with a little wind and water, then they are foolish beings, indeed!"

Wiglaf wants to ask Beowulf if he's finally lost his mind, a question he's almost asked a hundred times before. But he knows that the answer hardly matters. He will follow wherever Beowulf leads, even through this storm, and whether he is mad or not. He shrugs free of his captain and kinsman and turns to face his nervous, exhausted companions, still seated wrestling with the oars.

"Who wants to *live*?" he shouts, and not one among them replies that he does not. "A good thing, then! For we do not die *this* day!"

And then he glances back at Beowulf, who is still grinning defiantly up at the storm.

"*Pull* your oars!" Wiglaf commands. "Pull for *Beowulf*! Pull for *gold*! Pull for *glory*! *Heave*!"

From his post along the sheer granite sea cliffs, the Scylding king's watch sits alone, save for the company of his horse, tending to his guttering campfire. He has speared a field mouse on a stick and is now busy trying to keep the rain away until dinner's cooked to his liking.

"What I want to know," he says, frowning up at the dripping, unhappy-looking horse, "is just who or what old Hrothgar has got himself thinking is going to be about in this foul weather? Have you even stopped to think on *that*, horse?"

The fire hisses and spits, and the watch goes back to fanning it. But there's much more smoke than flame, and the mouse is almost as pink as when he skinned it. He's just about to give up and eat the thing cold and bloody when the gloom is parted by a particularly bright flash of lightning and, glancing down at the beach, he catches signs of movement and the unexpected glint of metal along the shore.

"Did *you* see that?" he asks the horse, which snorts, but otherwise doesn't bother to reply. Another flash of lightning follows almost immediately on the heels of the first, and this time there can be no mistake about what he sees on the shore. A tiny ship with bright shields hung along its sides, its carved prow like a sinuous golden serpent rising gracefully from the crashing surf.

The watch curses and reaches for his spear, and a few moments later—the fire and his empty belly forgotten—the horse is carrying him along the steep path leading down to the beach.

When Beowulf and his thanes have finally hauled their ship out of the sea and onto the sand, when the whale's-road is safe behind them, Wiglaf sighs a relieved sigh and spits into the water lapping at his ankles.

"I'll wager old Ægir's gnashing his teeth over *that* one," he laughs, and then to Beowulf, "You are *sure* this is Denmark?"

"Denmark or Hel," Beowulf replies. "I expect we'll know which soon enough."

The rain is still falling hard, and lightning still crackles and jabs at the world, but the worst of the storm seems to have passed them by.

"What's that then?" Wiglaf asks Beowulf and points down the length of the rocky beach. A man on horseback is galloping swiftly toward them, his mount throwing up a spray of sand and small pebbles as they come. The man holds a long spear gripped at the ready, as though he means to impale them one and all.

"Well, I'm guessing it's Hel, then," Wiglaf sighs, and Beowulf nods his head and steps away from Wiglaf and his men, moving out to meet the rider.

"If you get yourself skewered," Wiglaf shouts after him, "can I have your boots?"

"Aye," Beowulf calls back. "Take the boat, as well."

"You know, I think he *means* it," Wiglaf says, pointing once more at the approaching rider, but Beowulf only nods and stands his ground. Wiglaf reaches for his sword, but at the last possible moment, the horseman pulls back on the reins. When he stops, the point of his spear is mere inches from Beowulf's face.

"Who are you?" the rider demands. "By your dress, you are warriors."

"Yes, as a matter of fact," Wiglaf replies. "We—"

"*Speak!*" the rider growls at Beowulf. "Tell me why I should not run you through right now. Who *are* you? *Where* do come from?"

"We are Geats," Beowulf replies calmly, ignoring the spearpoint aimed at the space between his eyes. "I am Beowulf, son of Ecgtheow. We have come seeking your prince, Hrothgar, in friendship. They say you have a monster here. They say your land is cursed."

The man on the horse narrows his eyes and glances at Wiglaf and the others, but doesn't lower his spear.

"Is *that* what they say?" he asks.

"That and worse," Wiglaf answers. "Bards sing of Hrothgar's shame from the frozen north to the shores of Vinland."

The watch sits up a little straighter on his horse and glares defiantly back at Wiglaf. "It is no shame to be accursed by demons," he says.

Wiglaf takes a step nearer to Beowulf. "And neither is it a shame to accept aid that is freely given."

Beowulf glances quickly at Wiglaf, then back to the watch and his horse. "I am Beowulf," he says again. "I have come here to kill your monster."

"Unless you'd rather we not," adds Wiglaf, earning a scowl from Beowulf.

"You should ignore him," Beowulf says. "He was very seasick this morning, and I fear he might have puked his wits overboard."

The watch lowers his spear, staring past Beowulf and Wiglaf to the other men standing beside the beached ship.

"You'll need horses," he says.

The storm has gone, and the terrible, driving wind has died away—the wrath of Hræsvelg Corpse-swallower, the giant eagle whose wings send all winds blowing across the world, choosing some other target for a time. But the sky is hardly any lighter than before, still crowded with portentous clouds that hide the sun and hold the land in perpetual twilight. Beowulf and his men follow close behind the Scylding watch, riding the sturdy, shaggy ponies that have been provided for them. They have left the sea cliffs and the shore and move now along a narrow road paved with dark shale cobbles. The road is lined on either side by tall, craggy standing stones, menhirs engraved with runes and erected to mark the ashes of the dead. Whenever the fog shifts, the thanes catch fleeting glimpses of King Hrothgar's tower in the distance. When they reach a wooden bridge spanning a deep ravine, the watch reins his horse and turns to Beowulf.

"This is as far as I go," he says. "I must return to the cliffs. The sea cannot be left unguarded. This stone path is the king's road." He smiles then, and adds, "It was built in better times. Follow it to Heorot, where my lord awaits."

Beowulf nods. "I thank you for your aid," he says.

"Geat, you should know that our monster is fast and strong."

"I, too, am fast and strong," Beowulf tells him.

"Yes, well, so were the others who came to fight it. And they're all dead. *All of them*. I thought no more heroes remained who were foolhardy enough to come here and die for our gold."

Beowulf looks over his shoulder at Wiglaf, then back to the watch. "If we die, then it shall be for glory, not for gold."

With that, the watch gives his horse a kick and gallops quickly past the Geats, heading back the way they've just come, toward his dreary camp above the sea. But then he stops, and calls out to Beowulf, "The creature took my brother. Kill the bastard for me."

"Your brother will be avenged," Beowulf calls back. "I swear it."

And then the Scylding watch turns and rides away, his horse's iron-shod hooves clopping loudly against the cobblestones, and Beowulf leads his men across the bridge.

This day is the color of the grave, King Hrothgar thinks, gazing miserably out at the angry sea and imagining Hel's gray robes, the flat gray gleam of her eyes that awaits every man who does not die in battle or by some other brave deed, every man who allows himself to grow weak and waste away in stone towers. For even brave men who slay dragons in their youth may yet die *old* men and so find themselves guests in Éljudnir, Hel's rain-damp hall. Behind him, Unferth sits at a table, absorbed in the task of counting gold coins and other pieces of treasure. And Hrothgar wonders which shadowy corner of Niflheim has been prepared for both of them. He has begun to see Hel's gates in his dreams, nightmares in which he hunts down and faces the monster Grendel time again and time again, but always the fiend refuses to fight him, refusing him even the kindness of a hero's death.

These cheerless thoughts are interrupted by footsteps and the sound of Wulfgar's voice, and the king turns away from the window.

"My lord," Wulfgar says. "There are warriors outside. Geats. For certain, they are no beggars—and their leader, Beowulf, is a—"

"*Beowulf*?" Hrothgar asks, interrupting his herald. "Ecgtheow's little boy?"

At the sound of Beowulf's name, Unferth stops counting the gold coins and glances up at Wulfgar.

"Well, surely not a boy any longer," Hrothgar continues, hardly believing what he's heard. "But I knew him when he *was* a boy. Already strong as a grown man he was, back then. Yes! Beowulf is here! Send him to me! Bring him in, Wulfgar!"

Beowulf and his men wait together, only a little distance inside the gates of Hrothgar's stockade. None of them have yet dismounted, as Beowulf has not yet bidden them to do so, and their ponies restlessly stamp their hooves in a gummy mire of mud and hay, manure and human filth. The thanes are at least as restless as their mounts, and they watch uneasily as villagers begin to gather around and whisper to one another and gawk at these strange men from the east, these warriors come among them from Geatland far across the sea.

"It may be, Beowulf," says Wiglaf, "that they really *don't* want us to kill their monster."

The thane to Wiglaf's left is named Hondshew, an ugly brute of a man almost as imposing as Beowulf himself. Hondshew wears an enormous broadsword sheathed and slung across his wide back—a weapon he's claimed, in less sober moments, to have stolen from a giant whom he found sleeping in the Tivenden woods. Only, sometimes he says it was a giant, and other times it was merely a troll, and still other times, it was only a drunken Swede.

"Or," says Hondshew, "perhaps this is what serves as hospitality among these Danes." Then he notices a beautiful young woman standing close by, eating a piece of ripe red fruit. She's watching him, too, and when next she bites through the skin of the fruit, purplish nectar runs down her chin and disappears between her ample breasts. The woman, whose name is Yrsa, smiles up at Hondshew.

"Then again," he says, returning Yrsa's smile and showing off his wide, uneven teeth, "possibly we should find our *own* hospitality among these poor, beleaguered people." Hondshew licks his lips, and Yrsa takes another bite of the fruit, spilling still more juice.

And then the king's herald arrives, riding up on a large gray mare, accompanied by two of Hrothgar's guard who have followed behind on foot. The herald silently eyes Beowulf and the thanes for a moment, then clears his throat, and says "Hrothgar, Master of Battles, Lord of the North Danes, bids me say that he knows you, Beowulf, son of Ecgtheow. He knows your ancestry and bids you welcome. You, and your men, will follow me. You may keep your helmets and your armor, but your shields and weapons will remain here until further notice."

Wiglaf glances apprehensively at Beowulf.

"I assure you, they won't be disturbed," says Wulfgar.

Beowulf turns and surveys his fourteen men, catching the wariness in their tired faces, their many hands hovering uncertainly above the hilts of their swords. Then he tosses his own spear to one of the guards standing alongside Wulfgar's gray mare.

"We are here as *guests* of King Hrothgar," he says, staring now directly into the herald's eyes. "He is our host, even as we seek to serve him, and we will not be disagreeable guests." And then Beowulf pulls a dagger from his belt and hands it over to Wulfgar, and then his sword, as well. "Let it not be said by the Danes that there is no trust to be found among the warriors of Lord Hygelac."

Reluctantly, Beowulf's thanes follow suit, turning their many weapons over to the two royal guards who have accompanied Wulfgar to the gate. Last of all, Hondshew draws his enormous broadsword and drops it to the ground, where the blade buries itself deeply in the muck.

"My, that's a *big* one you've got there, outlander," Yrsa smiles and takes another bite of fruit.

"*That* little thing?" replies Hondshew. "That's only my spare. Maybe later, when we've sorted out our business with this fiend of yours—"

"Hondshew," Beowulf says firmly, still watching Wulfgar. "Have you already forgotten why we're here?"

"Didn't I say *after* the fiend is slain?"

Yrsa watches and says not another word to Beowulf's thane. But with a pinkie finger, she wipes a smear of nectar from her left breast and slowly licks it from her finger.

"Woman!" Wiglaf snaps at Yrsa. "Have you naught else to be doing this day but teasing men who've not seen womanflesh for many trying days and nights?"

"Come, Wiglaf," says Beowulf, and together they follow Wulfgar through the narrow, smoky streets and up to Hrothgar's mead hall.

By the time they reach the steps of Heorot Hall, most of King Hrothgar's court has gathered there. Overhead, there are a few ragged gaps in the clouds and cold sunlight leaks down and falls upon the queen and her maids, on the assembly of guards and courtiers. The stone steps are dark and damp from the rain, and there are small puddles here and there, twinkling weakly in the day. Beowulf and his thanes have left their ponies behind and stand at the foot of the steps, staring up at the barred and shuttered mead hall that has brought them here.

"Beowulf!" bellows King Hrothgar, as he staggers and weaves his way down the steps to embrace the Geat. "How is your father? How is Ecgtheow?"

"He died in battle with sea-raiders," Beowulf replies. "Two winters back."

"Ahhhh, but he was a *brave* man. He sits now at Odin's table. Need I ask why you've come to us?"

Beowulf nods toward the shuttered hall above them. "I've come to kill your monster," he replies.

A murmur passes through the crowd on the steps, equal parts surprise and incredulity, and even Hrothgar seems uncomfortable at hearing Beowulf's boast.

"They all think you're daft," whispers Wiglaf, and, indeed, Beowulf sees the many shades of chagrin and doubt clouding the faces of the king's court. He takes a deep breath and smiles, flashing the warmest smile he can muster standing so near the scene of such bloody horrors as he's heard told of Heorot Hall.

"And, of course," he says to Hrothgar, "to taste that famous mead of yours, my lord."

Hrothgar grins, visibly relieved, then laughs a laugh that is almost a roar, laughing the way a bear might laugh. "And indeed you *shall* taste it, my boy, and soon!" And the crowd on the steps stops murmuring amongst themselves, reassured now by the hearty thunder of Hrothgar's laughter, and already Beowulf can feel their tension draining away.

But then Queen Wealthow steps forward, descending the stairs, the weak sunlight catching in her honey hair.

"There have been many brave men who have come here," she says, "and they have all drunk deeply of my lord's mead, and sworn to rid his hall of our nightmare."

Hrothgar frowns and glances from his wife to Beowulf, but doesn't speak.

"And the next morning," Queen Wealthow continues, "there was nothing left of any of them but blood and gore to be mopped from the floor . . . and from the benches . . . and walls."

For a long, lingering moment, Beowulf and Wealthow gaze into one another's eyes. He sees a storm there in her, a storm no less dangerous, perhaps, than the one he has so recently navigated. And he sees fear and grief, as well, and bitterness.

"My lady, I have drunk nothing," Beowulf tells her, at last. "Not yet. But I *will* kill your monster."

And again Hrothgar laughs, but this time it seems hollow, forced, somehow insincere. "Hear that? He *will* kill the monster!" Hrothgar roars. "The demon Grendel *will* die and at this brave young man's hands!"

"Grendel?" Beowulf asks, still watching the queen.

"What? Did you not *know* our monster has a name?" asks Wealthow. "The scops who sing of our shame and defeat, have they left that part out?"

"Yes, the monster is called Grendel," Hrothgar says, speaking much more quietly now, and he begins wringing his hands together. "Yes, yes. It *is* called Grendel."

"Then I shall kill your Grendel," says Beowulf, speaking directly to Wealthow. "It does not seem so very daunting a task. I slew a tribe of giants in the Orkneys. I have crushed the skulls of mighty sea serpents. So what's one troll? Soon, my lady, he shall trouble you no longer."

The queen starts to reply, opens her mouth, and

Beowulf can feel the awful weight of the words lying there on her tongue. But Hrothgar is already speaking again, addressing his court, filled once more with false bravado.

"A *hero*!" shouts the king. "I knew that the sea would bring to us a hero! Unferth, have I not said to look ever to the sea for our salvation?"

There's a halfhearted cheer from the people on the steps, then, but Wealthow does not join in, and Unferth glares suspiciously at Beowulf and does not answer his king.

Then Hrothgar leans near to Beowulf and cocks an eyebrow. "Will you go up to the moors, then, and through the forest to the cave by the dark mere?" he asks Beowulf. "Will you fight the monster there in its den?"

Beowulf nods toward Wiglaf and Hondshew and his other thanes. "I have fourteen brave men with me," he says. "But we have been long at sea. I think, my lord, that it is high time to break open your golden mead—famed across the world—and to feast together in your legendary hall"

At this, Unferth steps forward, past Lady Wealthow, to stand before Beowulf.

"Do you not *know*, great Beowulf, Geat lord and son of Ecgtheow? The hall has been *sealed* . . . by order of the king. Merrymaking in the hall always brings the devil Grendel down upon us."

"And has closing the hall stopped the slaughter?" Beowulf asks him.

"Nay," Hrothgar replies. " It has not. The demon-murderer killed three horses and a slave in the stables, not a fortnight past."

Beowulf glances beyond Unferth and Wealthow, looking to the high, barred doors of Heorot. "Well then," he says, and smiles at Hrothgar, who nods and grins back at him.

"If closing the hall has not so profited my lord," Beowulf continues, "and if, regardless of this wise precaution, the beast still comes to do his wicked murder, it seems a pity to waste such a magnificent hall, does it not?"

"Oh, it does, indeed," Hrothgar agrees. "It seems a most *terrible* waste. It seems a *pity*."

Unferth exchanges glances with Wealthow, then, turning to Hrothgar, says, "But, my liege . . . by your own *command*—"

"Exactly," Hrothgar interrupts. "By *my* own command. A command which I do hereby rescind, loyal Unferth. So, open the mead hall. Open it *now*."

By dusk—which seems hardly more than a gentle deepening of the gloom that loitered above the land in the wake of the storm—Heorot Hall *has* been reopened. The doors and windows have all been thrown wide to draw in fresh, clean air. New hay covers the floors, and the feasting tables have all been scrubbed clean. Old women clear away cobwebs and tend to embers that will soon enough become cooking fires to roast venison and fowl and fat hogs. And in the midst of all this, Beowulf's men sit together at a round table in one corner of the hall. Wulfgar, true to his word, has returned their weapons to them, and now they are busy sharpening steel blades, tightening straps and harnesses, oiling leather sheaths and scabbards. Beowulf wanders through the hall, examining its architecture with a warrior's keen eye, sizing up its strengths and weaknesses. Here and there are signs of the monster's handiwork—deep gouges in the wooden beams, claw marks in tabletops, a patch of wood so bloodstained that water cannot ever wipe it clean again. Beowulf pauses before the huge door, inspecting its massive bar and the wide reinforcing bands of iron.

Hondshew glances up from the blade of his broadsword and sees Yrsa, the girl from the gate, who's busy scrubbing a table not too far from where the thanes are seated.

"Ah, now *there's* a beast I'd love to slay this very night," he snickers, then stands and jabs his sword in her direction. "Not with *this* blade, mind you. I've another, better suited to *that* pricking."

Wiglaf kicks him in the rump, and Hondshew stumbles and almost falls.

"Listen to me," Wiglaf says, addressing all the thanes. "We don't want any trouble with the locals, you hear. So, just for tonight, no fighting, and no *swifan*. Do you understand me?"

Hondshew rubs at his backside but hasn't stopped staring at Yrsa, who looks up, sees him watching her, and sticks out her tongue at him. Another of the thanes, Olaf, a lean but muscle-bound man with a wide white scar across his left cheek, draws his dagger and brandishes it at all the shadows lurking in all the corners of Heorot Hall.

"I wa . . . wa . . . wasn't p . . . p . . . planning on doing any swi . . . swi . . . swi . . . *swifan*," he stutters.

Hondshew sits down again and goes back to sharpening his sword. "Well, I wa . . . wa . . . *was*!" he declares, mocking Olaf.

Wiglaf frowns and tries not to notice the way that Yrsa's breasts strain the fabric of her dress when she bends over the table she's cleaning. "Hondshew," he says. "Just this once, make me feel like you're *pretending* to listen to me. It's only been five days since you waved your wife good-bye."

"Five days!" exclaims Hondshew. "By Odin's swollen testicles . . . no wonder my loins are burning!"

The thanes laugh loudly, and Yrsa pauses in her work to listen to them. To her ears, the bawdy laughter of men is a welcome sound, here beneath the roof timbers of Heorot Hall, and it gives her strength and cause to hope. She steals a quick look at Beowulf, who's still inspecting the door, and Yrsa prays that even *half* the bold, fantastic stories she's heard told about him are true and that, soon now, Grendel's grip upon the night will be at an end.

5

Misbegotten

And far across the moorlands, shrouded now with evening mist, out behind the forest's ancient palisade, the creature Grendel crouches at the edge of the black pool inside his cave. The rotting corpse of one of Hrothgar's slaughtered thanes lies nearby, and Grendel carefully picks choice scraps of flesh from the body and drops them into the water. There are many strange things that dwell within the lightless depths of the pool, and sometimes when Grendel is lonely, he lures hungry mouths to the surface with bits of his kills. Tonight, the water teems with a school of blind albino eels, each of them easily as long as a grown man is tall—or longer still—and big around as fence posts. Their long jaws are lined with needle-sharp teeth, and they greedily devour the morsels Grendel has given up to the pool and fight among themselves for the largest pieces. Grendel watches the foaming water and the snow-colored eels, comforted by their company, amused at their ferocity. He rocks backward and forward, absently humming a slow, sad, tuneless sort of song to himself, something he either made up or has heard men singing on some night or another. He can't remember which.

In his left hand, the creature clutches a broken lance, and impaled upon its spiked tip is the decomposing head of yet another fallen thane. The eyes have been eaten away by such worms and maggots as thrive in dung and decay and the muddy earth of the cave. The jaw bone hangs crookedly from the thane's skull, and most of his front teeth are broken out. Grendel leans the decapitated head out over the frothing pool and pitches his voice high, imitating the speech of men.

"Da-dee-da!" he cries out. "Da-dee-da! Oh, such horrible, horrible things! They'll eat me all up, they will!"

And then Grendel chuckles to himself and leans close to the dead thane's right ear. "Who's laughing now?" he asks to head. "Eh? Just *who's* laughing now? Me—Grendel—*that's* who."

Suddenly, one of the huge eels leaps free of the pool; hissing like a serpent, it strikes at the head, tearing away the crooked jaw and much of what was left of the thane's face before falling back into the water with a loud *plop*. Grendel cackles with delight and shakes the mutilated head back and forth above the pool. The cave echoes with the creature's laughter.

"Oh me, oh my!" he wails. "It has eaten my poor, pretty face *all up*! What *ever* shall I do now? The beautiful women will not *love* me now!"

Another of the eels leaps for the head, but this time Grendel yanks it quickly away before the fish's jaws can latch on.

"No more," he scolds the eels. "No more tonight. You'll get fat. Fat fish sink all the way down to the bottom and get eaten by *other* fish. More tomorrow."

Abruptly, the dark water seethes with some new and far more terrible presence, and all the eels slither away quietly into their holes. There is a wheezing, wet sound, like spray blown out from the spout of a whale, and the water bubbles.

Startled, Grendel jumps to his feet, and in his panic, his body begins to change—his nails suddenly becoming long and curving claws, claws to shame the mightiest bear. The bones and muscles of his twisted, deformed frame begin to shift and expand, and his round, rheumy eyes start to narrow, sparking now with a predatory glint. Where only a moment before the eels fought viciously over mouthfuls of putrid flesh, now Grendel's mother watches him from the surface of the pool. Her full, wet lips shimmer, their golden scales gleaming with some secret, inner fire that is all her own.

"Grrrrendellllllll," she purls.

Recognizing her voice, Grendel grows calmer. Talons become only ragged fingernails again. His expanding, shifting skeleton begins to reverse its violent metamorphosis so that he seems to draw back into himself. He looks into his mother's bright reptilian eyes and sees himself reflected there.

"*Modor?*" he asks softly, falling back upon the old tongue. "Is something wrong?"

She rises slowly from the pool, then, her long, webbed fingers gripping the travertine edges and pulling herself nearer to her son.

"I had an evil dream, my child," she says, and the beauty of her voice soothes Grendel, and he wishes she would never leave him. "You were *hurt*," she continues. "I dreamed you were calling out for me, and I could not come to you. And then, Grendel, then they *butchered* you."

Grendel watches her, floating there, half-submerged, then he smiles and laughs and shakes the lance and the thane's head staked upon it.

"I am not dead. See? I am happy. Look, Modor. *Happy* Grendel," and in an effort to convince his mother that his words are true, Grendel does an awkward sort of shuffling dance about his cave, a clumsy parody of the dancing he's glimpsed in the mead hall of King Hrothgar. From time to time, he stops to shake the thane's head at the sky, hidden beyond the cavern's roof, and to hoot and howl in the most carefree, joyous way he can manage.

From the pool, his mother whispers, "You must

not go to them tonight. You have killed too many of them."

"But I am *strong*, Mother. I am *big*, and I am *strong*. None of them are a match for me. I will eat their flesh and drink their sweet blood and grind their frail bones between my teeth."

"*Please*, my son," his mother implores. "Do not go to them."

Grendel stops dancing and lets the thane's head and the broken spear clatter to the floor of the cave. He shuts his eyes and makes a disappointed, whining sound.

"Please," his mother says from the pool. "Please promise me this one thing. Not *this* night, Grendel. Stay here with *me* this night. Stay by the pool and be content to feed your pets."

Grendel sits down on the ground a few feet from the edge of the water. He doesn't meet his mother's eyes, but stares disconsolately at the dirt and rocks and his own bare feet.

"I swear," he sulks. "I shall not go to them."

"Even if they make the noises? Even if the noises make your poor head ache?"

Grendel hesitates, considering her question, remembering the pain, but then he nods reluctantly.

"*Gut. Man medo*," she whispers, satisfied, then slips once more beneath the surface of the black pool. Ripples spread out across it, and small waves lap against its stony edges.

"They are only men," Grendel whispers sullenly to

himself and also to the head of the dead thane. "They are only men, and it was only a dream she had. Many times have I had bad dreams. But they were all *only* dreams."

In his cave, Grendel watches the water in the pool grow calm once more, and he thinks about the concealing night and the conspiring fog waiting outside the cave, and he tries not to remember the hurting noise of men.

6

Light from the East

By sunset, the clouds above Heorot Hall have broken apart, becoming only scattered, burning islands in a wide winter sky. The goddess Sól, sister of the moon, is sinking low in the west, rolling away toward the sea in her chariot as the hungry wolf Skoll pursues close behind. Her light glimmers on the water and paints the world orange.

In Hrothgar's mead hall, his people are gathering for a feast in honor of Beowulf, who has promised to deliver them from the fiend Grendel. An enormous copper vat, filled to the brim with mead, is carried in, and a cheer rises from Beowulf's thanes. But the others, the king's men and women, those who have seen too many nights haunted by the monster, do not join in the cheer. From the cast of their faces, the gathering might seem more a funeral than a feast, more mourning than a reception for the Geats, who have promised to deliver them from their plight. But there is music, and soon enough the mead begins to flow.

Beowulf stands on the steps of the throne dais with Queen Wealthow, examining a curious carving set into the wall there, a circular design that reminds Beowulf of a wagon wheel. A mirror, placed some distance away in Hrothgar's anteroom, redirects the fading sunlight from a window onto the wall and the carving.

"It can measure the length of the day," Wealthow explains, and she points at the sundial. "When the sun touches the lowest line, soon the day will be finished."

"And Grendel will arrive?" asks Beowulf, turning from the carving to look into the queen's face, her violet eyes, the likes of which he has never seen before. Indeed, Beowulf doubts he has ever seen a woman half so beautiful as the bride of Hrothgar, and he silently marvels at her.

Wealthow sighs. "I hope that Odin and Heimdall are kind to you, Beowulf. It would be a great shame on this house to have one so brave and noble die beneath its roof."

Beowulf shakes his head, trying to concentrate more on what she's saying to him than on the sight of her.

"There is no shame to die in battle with evil," he tells her. "Only honor and a seat in Valhalla."

"And *if* you die?"

"Then there will be no corpse to weep over, my lady, no funeral pyre to prepare, and none to mourn me. Grendel will dispose of my carcass in a bloody animal feast, cracking my bones and sucking the flesh from them, swallowing me down."

"*I* would mourn you, my lord. Your men would mourn you, also."

"Nay, my men would join me in the monster's belly," Beowulf laughs.

"You shouldn't jest about such things," Queen Wealthow says, frowning now. "Aren't you afraid?"

"Afraid? And where's the reason in that? The three Norns sit at the foot of Yggdrasil, spinning *all* our lives. I am but another string in their loom, as are you, my Lady Wealthow. Our fates were already woven into that tapestry when the world was young. There's nothing to be gained in worrying over that which we cannot change."

"You are so sure this is the way of things?" she asks him, still frowning and glancing down at the dais steps.

"I've heard no better story," he replies. "Have you?"

She looks back up at him but doesn't answer.

"Ah, Beowulf . . . *there* you are!" And Wealthow and Beowulf turn to see four thanes bearing King Hrothgar toward the dais. Straining, they carefully set his litter onto the floor of the hall. "I was thinking about your father," says the king, as one of the thanes helps him from his seat upon the litter.

"My father?" asks Beowulf.

"Yes. Your father. Good Ecgtheow. There was a feud, I believe. He came here fleeing the Wylfings. As I recall, he'd killed one of them with his bare hands."

"Heatholaf," Beowulf says. "That was the name of the Wylfing my father slew."

"Yes! *That* was him!" exclaims Hrothgar, starting up the steps toward Beowulf and Wealthow. The thanes have already carried the litter away, and the king's court is assembling behind him. "I paid the blood debt for your father, and so he swore an oath to me. Long ago, that was. My kingship was still in its youth. Heorogar—my elder brother *and* the better man, I'd wager—had died. And here comes Ecgtheow, on the run, and so I sent wergeld to the Wylfings and ended the feud then and there. Ah . . . but no good deed goes unrewarded. I saved *his* skin, and now you're here to save *ours*, eh?" He slaps Beowulf on the back, and Wealthow flinches.

"I am thankful for the kindness you showed my father," Beowulf replies. "And thankful too for this opportunity to repay his debt to my lord."

"Well," says Hrothgar, "truth be told, it weighs heavy on my old heart, having to burden another with the grief this beast Grendel has visited upon my house. But the guards of Heorot—the demon has carried the best of them away. My following, those loyal to me, has *dwindled*, Beowulf. But you are here now. You *will* kill this monster. I have no *doubt* of it."

And now there is the sound of laughter, low and

bitter, from the shadows behind the king's throne. Unferth emerges from the gloom, slowly clapping his hands.

"All hail the great Beowulf!" he sneers. "Here to save our pathetic Danish skins, yes? And we are so *damned* . . . ah, now what *is* the word? . . . grateful? Yes. We are so damned *grateful*, mighty Beowulf. But might I now ask a question, speaking as a great admirer of yours."

Beowulf does not reply but only stares, unblinking, back at Unferth's green eyes.

"Yes, then? Very good. For you see, there was *another* Beowulf I heard tell of, who challenged Brecca the Mighty to a swimming race, out on the open sea. Is it possible, was that man the same as *you*?"

Beowulf nods. "Aye, I swam against Brecca," he says.

Unferth scowls and scratches at his black beard a moment. "I thought surely it must have been a *different* Beowulf," he says, furrowing his brow. "For, you see," and now Unferth raises his voice so it will be heard beyond the dais, "the Beowulf I heard of swam against Brecca and *lost*. He risked his life and Brecca's on the whale's-road, to serve his own vanity and pride. A boastful fool. *And he lost.* So, you see the source of my confusion. I thought it had to be someone else, surely."

Beowulf climbs the last few steps, approaching Unferth, and now the mead hall falls silent.

"I swam against Brecca," he tells Unferth again.

"Yes, so you've said. But the victory was *his*, not yours. You swam for seven nights, but in the end he outswam you. He reached the shore early one morning, cast up among the Heathoreams. He returned to the country of the Bronding clan, and boasted of *his* victory—as was his *right*. But you, Beowulf . . . a mighty warrior who cannot even win a *swimming match*?" Unferth pauses long enough to accept a cup of mead from his slave boy, Cain. He takes a long drink, wipes his mouth, then continues.

"Speaking only for myself, of course, I not only doubt that you will be able to stand for one *moment* against Grendel—I doubt that you'll even have the nerve to *stay in the hall* the full night. No one has yet lasted a night against Grendel." Unferth grins and takes another drink from his cup.

"I find it difficult to argue with a drunk," Beowulf tells him.

"My lord," says Queen Wealthow, glaring at Unferth. "You do not have to bandy words with the son of Ecglaf—"

"And it is true," Beowulf continues, "that I did not win the race with Brecca," and he closes his eyes, so vivid are the memories of the contest, carrying him at once back to that day—he against Brecca, both of them pitted against the sea . . .

. . . the freezing swells of Gandvik, the Bay of Serpents, rise and fall, bearing the two swimmers aloft so that they might, from time to time, glimpse the rugged, distant coastline of the land of the Finns. But then the water falls suddenly away beneath them, and the men can hardly even see the sky for the towering walls of the sea. The currents here are deadly, feared by fishermen and sailors alike, but Beowulf and Brecca are strong, stronger even than the cold fingers of the Urdines that would drag them under, stronger than the will of Ægir Wavefather. They are making slow but steady progress toward the eastern shore, swimming neck and neck, seeming an even match. And so it has been for the last five days, neither man holding a lead over the other for very long. Brecca carries a dagger gripped between his teeth, while Beowulf swims with a sword held tight in his right hand. One does not venture unarmed out upon the Gandvik. To the north, there are purple-black clouds tinged with gray, and lightning has begun to lick at the waves.

"You look *tired*!" Brecca calls out to Beowulf, then gets a mouthful of salt water.

"Funny . . . I was only just now . . . thinking the same of you!" Beowulf shouts back. Then a wave pushes them farther apart, raising Beowulf up even as Brecca slips into its yawning trough. And finally the Geat presses his advantage, for he is the stronger man, truly, and the better swimmer, and he has waited these five long days, conserving his strength for this last stretch before land. With only a little effort, he pulls ahead of Brecca.

But it may yet be that the sea giant and his daughters will have the final say, proving neither man a fit match for their domain. For the approaching storm brings more than wind and rain and lightning. It stirs the very depths, reaching down into the abyss where fearful creatures dwell, great snakes and unnameable brutes that crawl the slimy bottom and may live out their entire lives without once breaching or coming near to the surface. But angered by these gales and by the cracking hammer falls of Thor Giantkiller, they are distracted and drawn upward from their burrows in the mud of secret trenches and grottoes, moving swiftly through forests of kelp and midnight, and soon enough they find the swimmers. These are serpents beside which even mighty whales would seem as mackerel, the ravenous children of great Jörmungand, who holds all Midgard in his coils. The spawn of matings between Loki's dragon child and all manner of eels and sharks and hideous sea worms, these monsters, and no man gazes upon their faces and lives to tell another.

From his vantage point high atop the wave, Beowulf looks back down toward Brecca, spotting him there amid the chop and spray in the same instant that one of the monstrous serpents bursts forth from the sea. At first, Brecca does not seem to see it, looming there above him, its vast jaws dripping with brine and ooze and weeds, its single red eye peering down at the swimmer. Beowulf glances longingly toward the shore, and he knows it is within his grasp, surely, both dry land *and* victory. A lesser man might have looked upon the arrival of this beast as a blessing from the gods, but Brecca has been Beowulf's friend since their childhood, and so he sets his back to the shore. He shouts a warning, but already there are dark tentacles winding themselves about Brecca's body, driving the breath from his lungs and threatening to crush his ribs. He gasps, and the dagger slips from his teeth and vanishes in the sea.

"*No!*" Beowulf screams. "You will *not* have him!" And he swims as quickly as he can, moving against the current, back to the place where his friend struggles with the serpent. Distracted, the creature turns toward Beowulf, who slashes at its face with his sword, plunging the blade through the crimson eye and deep into its skull. Blood the color of the angry, storm-wracked sky gushes from the wound and stains the sea. But already a second serpent is rising from the water, and a third follows close behind it.

Brecca escapes from the dying monster's coils, and Beowulf tells him to go, *go now*, to swim if he's still able. Then something below twines itself about Beowulf's legs and hauls him under. Air rushes from his mouth and nostrils, silver bubbles trailing about his face as he hacks madly at the tentacle with his sword, severing it and wriggling free of its loosening grip. He breaks the surface a second later, only to find another of the creatures bearing down on him, its jaws open wide and bristling with teeth as long a warrior's lance. But Beowulf takes its head off with a single blow, slicing through scaly hide, through sinew and bone, cleaving its spine in two. And the third beast, sensing its imminent fate at the hands of the Geat, only watches him for a moment—hissing and leering hungrily—before it sinks once more beneath the sea, returning to whatever foul black pit birthed it.

Exhausted, bleeding, still clutching his heavy sword, Beowulf turns and begins to swim again and has soon caught up with Brecca. The waves have carried them much nearer the shoreline than before, and now Beowulf spies men scattered out along the rocky beach, all of them cheering the brave swimmers on. His spirits buoyed by the shouts and glad noise of the Geats and Finns, and also by the sight of Brecca alive and well and by his own victory over the serpents, Beowulf forgets his pain and pushes on. He passes Brecca and is ahead by a full length, and how much sweeter will be his victory, that it will have been gained *despite* the decision to go to Brecca aid, despite the Ægir's hounds.

"A good race!" he calls back to Brecca. "A shame that one of us must lose it," but then Beowulf is seized about the waist and pulled underwater for a *second* time. Again, wreathed in the shimmer of his own escaping breath, he whirls about to confront his attacker, his sword held at the ready . . . but then he sees clearly *what* has dragged him down. And this time it is no serpent, not one of the sea giant's fiends nor some other nameless abomination come stealing up from the lightless plains of silt and shipwrecks.

Instead, it is a being so beautiful that he might almost believe he has died defending Brecca and now this is some strange, fair herald of the Valkyries. Not a woman, no, not a *human* woman, but so alike in form that he at first makes that mistake. As his breath leaks away, Beowulf can only believe that he has been haled by an impossibly beautiful maiden, or some elf spirit that has taken the form of such a maiden. Her long hair, streaming about her face, is like the warm sun of a summer's afternoon falling across still waters, then flashing back twice as bright, and he squints at its brilliance. Her skin might be sunlight as well, or newly minted gold, the way it glints and shines.

So, perhaps this *is* a hero's death, and so a hero's reward, as well. He stops struggling and lowers his weapon, ready to follow this vision on to paradise and whatever banquet Odin has already prepared in his honor. And then Beowulf glances down, past the fullness of her breasts, and where the gentle curves of her belly and hips ought be, the golden skin is replaced by golden *scales* and by chitinous plates like the shell of a gilded crab. Worse still, where her legs should be, there is a long and tapering tail ending in a broad lancet fin. She smiles and clutches at him, and now Beowulf sees the webbing between her fingers and the hooked claws where a human woman would have nails. She does not speak, but he can plainly hear her voice inside his mind, beckoning him to follow her deeper. An image comes to him, then, of the two of them locked together in a lover's embrace, her lips pressed to his as they drift farther from the sun's rays and all the world above.

And he kicks free . . .

* * *

. . . "I killed the monster with my own blade," Beowulf tells Unferth and anyone else there beneath the roof of Heorot who is listening to his tale. "Plunging it again and again into its heart, I killed it. But I did *not* win the race."

"You do not have to prove yourself to him," Wealthow says, drawing a smirk from Unferth.

But Beowulf continues. "They sing of my battle with the sea monsters to this day, my *friend*. And they sing no such songs about Brecca. But I *braved* their hot jaws , making those lanes safe for seamen. And I survived the nightmare."

"Of course," Unferth says, and fakes a tremendous yawn. "The sea monsters. And you killed, what, twenty was it?"

"Three, all told. But . . . will you do me the honor of telling me your name."

Unferth shrugs and passes his empty cup back to his slave. "I am Unferth, son of Ecglaf, son of—"

"Unferth?" Beowulf asks, and before Hrothgar's man can reply, the Geat has turned to address his own thanes. "Unferth, son of Ecglaf? Well, then your fame has crossed the ocean ahead of you. I *know* who you are . . ."

Unferth manages to look both proud of himself and uncertain at the same time.

"Let's see," Beowulf says. "They say that you are clever. Not wise, mind you, but sharp. And they say, too, that you killed your brothers when you caught them bedding your own mother. In Geatland, they name you 'Unferth Kinslayer,' I believe," and Beowulf laughs.

Unferth stares back at him, speechless, his mossy eyes burning bright with hatred and spite. And then he lunges at Beowulf, growling like a dog. The Geat steps to one side, and Unferth trips, landing in a drunken heap at Beowulf's feet. The Geat crouches beside him, grinning.

"I'll tell you another true thing, Unferth Kinslayer. If your strength and heart had been as strong and as fierce as your *words*, then Grendel would never feel free to murder and gorge on your people, with no fear of retaliation. But tonight, *friend*, tonight *will* be different. Tonight he will find the Geats waiting for him. Not frightened sheep, like you."

Suddenly, several of the Danish thanes advance and draw their weapons, rushing to the aid of their king's most favored and trusted advisor. Seeing this, Beowulf's own men reach for their swords and daggers—

"*Well done!*" shouts King Hrothgar. "That's the spirit, young Beowulf!" and he begins clapping his hands together enthusiastically. The thanes on either side look confused, but slowly they begin to return blades to sheaths and back away from one another.

"Yes," continues Hrothgar. "That's the spirit we need! You'll kill my Grendel for me. Let us all drink and make merry celebration for the kill to come! Eh?"

The slave, Cain, helps Unferth to his feet and begins

dusting off his clothes. "Get *away* from me," Unferth snaps, and pushes the boy roughly aside.

Beowulf smiles a bold, victorious smile, his eyes still on Unferth as he places a hand on old Hrothgar's frail shoulder.

"Yes, my lord," says Beowulf. "I will drink and make merry, and *then* I will show this Grendel of yours how the Geats do battle with our enemies. How we kill. When we're done here, before the sun rises again, the Danes will no longer have cause to fear the comforts of your hall or any lurking demon come skulking from the moorland mists."

And now that those assembled in the hall have seen Beowulf's confidence and heard for themselves his pledge to slay Grendel this very night, their dampened spirits are at last revived. Soon, all Heorot is awash in the joyful, unfettered sounds of celebration and revelry.

"My king," says Queen Wealthow, as she offers him a large cup of mead, "drink deeply tonight and enjoy the fruits and bounty of your land. And know that you are dear to us." And when he has finished, she refills the cup, and the Helming maiden moves among the ranks—both Dane and Geat, the members of the royal household and the fighting men—offering it to each in his turn. Only Unferth refuses her hospitality. At the last, she offers the cup to Beowulf, welcoming him and offering thanks to the gods that her wish for deliverance has been granted. He accepts the cup gladly, still enchanted by the beauty of her. When he has finished drinking and the cup is empty, he bows before Hrothgar and his lady.

"When I left my homeland and put to sea with my men, I had but one purpose before me—to come to the aid of your people or die in the attempt. Before you, I vow once more that I shall fulfill that purpose. I will slay Grendel and prove myself, or I will find my undoing here tonight in Heorot."

Wealthow smiles a grateful smile for him, then leaves the dais and moves again through the crowded mead hall, until she comes to the corner where the musicians have gathered. One of the harpists stands, surrendering his instrument, and she takes his place. Her long, graceful fingers pluck the strings, beginning a ballad that is both lovely and melancholy, a song of elder days, of great deeds and of loss. Her voice rises clearly above the din, and the other musicians accompany her.

Hrothgar sits up straight on his throne and points to his wife. "Is she not a wonder?" he asks Beowulf.

"Oh, she is indeed," Beowulf replies. "I have never gazed upon anything half so wondrous." He thinks that perhaps the king is near to tears, the way his old eyes sparkle wetly in the firelight.

Then Beowulf raises his cup to toast Wealthow, who, seeing the gesture, smiles warmly and nods to him from her place at the harp. And it seems to the Geat that there is something much more to her smile than mere gratitude, something not so very far removed from desire and invitation. But if Hrothgar sees it, too, he makes no sign that he has seen it. Instead, he orders Unferth to stand and give up his seat to Beowulf, and Hrothgar pulls the empty chair next to his throne and tells Beowulf to sit. He motions to his herald, Wulfgar, who leaves and soon returns with an elaborately carved and decorated wooden box.

"Beowulf," says Hrothgar. "Son of Ecgtheow . . . I want to show you something." And with that the king opens the wooden box, and the Geat beholds the golden horn inside.

"Here is another of my wonders for you to admire," the king tells him, and Hrothgar removes the horn from its cradle and carefully hands it to Beowulf.

"It's beautiful," Beowulf says, holding the horn up and marveling at its splendor, at its jewels and the bright luster of its gold.

"Isn't she magnificent? The prize of my treasury. I claimed it long ago, after my battle with old Fafnir, the dragon of the Northern Moors. It nearly cost me my life," and he leans closer to Beowulf, whispering loudly. "There's a soft spot just under the neck, you know." And Hrothgar jabs a finger at his own throat, then points out the large ruby set into the throat of the dragon on the horn. "You go in close with a knife or a dagger . . . it's the only way you can kill one of the bastards. I wonder, how many man have died for love of this beauty."

"Could you blame them?" asks Beowulf, passing the horn back to Hrothgar.

"If you take care of Grendel, she's yours forever."

"You do me a great honor," Beowulf says.

"As well I should. I only wish that I possessed an even greater prize to offer you as reward for such a mighty deed."

Beowulf turns then from Hrothgar and the splendid golden horn and listens as Queen Wealthow finishes her song. For the first time since his journey began, he feels an unwelcome twinge of doubt—that he might not vanquish this beast Grendel, that he may indeed find his death here in the shadows of Heorot. And watching Wealthow, hearing her, he knows that the dragon's horn is not the only thing precious to the king that he would have for his own. When she's finished and has returned the harp to the harpist, he stands and clambers from the dais onto the top of one of the long feasting tables. Wealthow watches, and Beowulf feels her eyes following him. He takes a goblet from one of his thanes and raises it high above his head.

"My lord! My lady! The people of Heorot!" he shouts, commanding the attention of everyone in the hall, and they all stop and look up at him. "Tonight, my men and I, we shall *live forever* in greatness and courage, or, forgotten and despised, we shall *die*!"

And a great and deafening cheer rises from his men and from the crowd, and Beowulf looks out across the hall, directly at Queen Wealthow. She smiles again, but this time there is uncertainty and sadness there, and a moment later she turns away.

7

The Walker in Darkness

In his dream, Grendel is sitting outside his cave watching the sunset. It isn't winter, in his dream, but midsummer, and the air is warm and smells sweet and green. And the sky above him is all ablaze with Sól's retreat, and to the east the dark shadows of a sky wolf chasing after her. And Grendel is trying to recall the names of the two horses who, each day, draw the chariot of the sun across the heavens, the names his mother taught him long ago. There is a terrible, burning pain inside his head, as though he has died in his sleep and his skull has filled with hungry maggots and gnawing beetles, as though gore crows pick greedily at his eyes and plunge sharp beaks into his ears. But he knows, even through the veil of this dream, that the pain is *not* the pain of biting worms and stabbing beaks.

No, this pain comes drifting across the land from the open windows and doors of Heorot Hall, fouling the wind and casting even deeper shadows than those that lie between the trees in the old forest. It is the hateful song sung by a cruel woman, a song he knows has been fashioned *just so* to burrow deep inside his head and hurt him and ruin the simple joy of a beautiful summer's evening. And Grendel knows, too, that it is not the slavering jaws of the wolf Skoll that the sun flees *this* day, but rather that song. That song which might yet break the sky apart and rend the stones and boil away the seas.

No greater calamity in all the world than the thoughtless, merry sounds that men and women make, no greater *pain* to prick at his soul than their joyful music and the fishhook voices of their delight. Grendel does not know why this should be so, only that it is. And he calls out for his mother, who is watching from the entrance of the cave, safe from the fading sunlight.

"Please, *Modor*," he asks her, "make them stop. Make her be quiet."

"How would I ever do that?" she replies and blinks at him with her golden eyes.

"Oh, I could *show* you," he says. "It is not so very hard to silence them. It is a simple thing. They *break*—"

"You promised," she hisses softly.

"To endure this agony, is that what I promised?"

"You *promised*," she says again, louder than before.

So, Grendel dreams that he shuts his eyes, hoping to find some deeper twilight there, a peaceful, painless dusk that cannot be ruined by the voice of a woman, by harps and flutes and drums, by the shouts of drunken men and the shrieks of drunken women. He shuts his eyes tightly as he can and drifts down to some time before this sunset outside his cave, a *silent* time, and he pretends that the ache in his ears and the din banging about inside his brain have yet to begin. Heorot Hall has not been built, and the king has not found his queen. Grendel is yet a child, playing alone in the murk of the cave, making some secret game from a handful of seashells and the backbone of a seal. Not a day he actually remembers, but a day that might have been, nonetheless.

"I will never let him find you," his mother whispers from her pool.

And Grendel stops playing and stares for a moment into the cold water, the uneasy, swirling place where she lies just beneath the surface.

"Who?" he asks. "Who will you not let find me?"

She answers him with a loud splash from the pool, and Grendel looks back down at the shells cupped in his right hand. A mussel shell, four sea snails, two cockles, and he tries hard to remember what that means by the rules of his secret game. He knew only a moment before.

"Is that a question I should not have asked, *Modor*?"

"I cannot always keep you safe," she tells him, and there's regret and a sort of sadness in her voice, and it doesn't suit her. "They are weak, yes, these men. But still they slay dragons, and they kill trolls, and they make wars and hold the fate of all the world in their small, soft hands, even as *you* hold those stray bits of shell in yours."

"Then I will stay away from them," he assures her. "I will hide here . . . with you. I won't let them see me. I won't ever let them see me."

"That is not the truth," she tells him. "Even in dreams, we should not lie to ourselves. You are a curious boy, and you will go to see them, and they will see you."

Grendel lays the shells down on the dirt and travertine floor of the cave next to the seal vertebra. He's forgotten the game now, because it's something he never invented.

"Why do they kill dragons?" he asks his mother, and she sighs and slithers about at the edge of her pool.

"Because they are not dragons themselves," she replies.

"And is this why they kill trolls, as well?"

"They are not trolls," she answers. "They have neither the fiery breath nor the wings of dragons, nor have they the strength of trolls. And they are ever jealous of those things, and fearful. They destroy,

Grendel. They despoil. They destroy for glory, and from jealousy and fear, to make the world safe for themselves. And I cannot hide you always, child. Your father—"

"*Mé fædyr*?" Grendel asks her, surprised, having never much dwelled upon the subject of his absent father and, perhaps, thinking himself somehow genuinely *fæderleás*—born somehow *only* of woman.

"*He* has slain a dragon," she hisses from the pool.

"That *weorm*, *Modor*, maybe it did not *know* to hide," Grendel insists, and he crushes the seal bone to white-gray dust between his fingers. "I will stay always here with you. They will *not* find me," he says again. "Not ever."

"That is a *promise*," she says, and the words float up from the icy water like a threat. "But we break our promises all too soon."

Grendel opens his eyes, tumbling back up and up from the cave and that lost, imagined day that never was, tumbling back to the place where his dream began—sitting outside his cave, watching the vanishing, wolf-harrowed sun, his ears aching with the song of King Hrothgar's keening, yellow-haired bitch.

"Why can I *not* bear these sounds, *Modor*?" Grendel moans and stares up at the burning sky. "They are *only* songs, yes? Only frivolities and merrymaking, not swords and axes and spears. They are only the thin voices of weak creatures crying out in the dark to hear themselves. How is it that such things do *me* harm?"

From the entrance of the cave, his mother grinds bones in her teeth, sucking out the marrow, and does not reply.

And the harp of Heorot Hall has become a cacophony, the tumult as the very walls of Midgard collapse on that last day of all. Sól has gone from the sky now, leaving it to night and the pursuing wolf, and Grendel digs his claws deep into the rocky soil. Blood drips from his nostrils and stains the ground at his feet.

"Árvak," he mutters, recalling finally the names of the horses leashed to the sun's chariot, the answer to a riddle no one has asked. "Árvak and Alsvin are their names." He grates his jaws against the song. But he is only Grendel, and he has never slain a dragon, and the song fells great trees and causes the earth beneath him to shudder. The song has frightened away even his mother, the merewife, giant-daughter and pool-haunter. In only another moment, his teeth will shatter and fall like dust from his mouth.

"I will wake up now," he growls through blood and crumbling fangs. *I am only dreaming this pain. I am only dreaming the noise . . .*

And when next Grendel opens his eyes, he *is* awake, awake and alone in his cave at sunset, curled into a corner beneath the hides of deer and bears. His mother is not with him, but the pain is, and the flood of those voices rushing over the land, crashing upon his ears like breakers at the edge of a stormy sea. And the flood will drown him. Grendel opens his jaws wide and howls, vomiting rage and torment and confusion into that hollow space beneath the hills. But his voice, even in this wild frenzy, seems hardly a whimper raised against the flood. He turns toward the pool, wishing she were there, wishing he could find his way down through the depths to her, where she would hold him to her bosom and calm him and soothe away the hurt and fear swallowing him alive.

Standing, shaking off the sleeping pelts, he howls again, and if his mother were there, she would hear the words lost and tangled within that animal scream. She would hear the grief and the despair at a promise soon to be broken. But she would also hear relief in equal measure, that shortly he will crush and squeeze and pound the life from these clamorous fools, and they will taste sweet on his tongue. And then, when he is done, the night will be silent again, save those comforting sounds which come from the old forest and the marshlands and the beach. Save the soft dripping of his cave, and the splash of white eels in his mother's pool.

8

Nightfall

"So, would that be your demon?" Beowulf asks the king, as the ghastly shriek from the moorlands quickly fades away and a sudden hush falls over Heorot Hall. The musicians have all stopped playing, and the Danes and their ladies sit or stand, frozen by the voice of Grendel, each one among them waiting to see if there will be another cry to split the twilight. Hrothgar rubs at his forehead, draws a deep breath and frowns. Glancing toward the sundial carved into the wall, he finds it gone completely dark. The day has ended.

"Indeed," the king sighs. "I see that the dreaded

hour is come upon us once again." And he motions toward the sundial.

"We should clear the hall," Beowulf says, but already Heorot has begun to empty on its own, the evening's revelry cut short by those two cries from the direction of the approaching night, and the king rises weary and drunken from his throne.

"Well, it's just as well. This old man needs his rest," he says, and looks about until he sets eyes upon his queen standing not far away, watching Beowulf. "My beauty," he says to her. "Will you be so kind as to help me find my way down to sleep? Sometimes, I think I have almost forgotten the path." And he holds out a withered, trembling hand to his young wife. She hesitates a moment, still looking at Beowulf.

"My dear?" the king asks her, thinking that perhaps she has not heard him. "Come along. I do not believe I am yet either so drunk or infirm that we might not take some small scrap of pleasure beneath the sheets."

"A moment more, please," she says. "You go along without me. I promise, I shall not be very far behind."

"She promises . . ." Hrothgar mutters, only half to himself. Then, speaking to the Geat, he says, "I hope to see you in the morning, Beowulf, son of Ecgtheow . . . Odin willing. It is a great service you do me and my household this night. Be sure your men secure the door."

"It will be done, my lord," Beowulf assures him. "We will take all possible precautions."

Four of the Danish thanes come bearing Hrothgar's litter, having threaded their way through the thinning, nervous crowd. When they've lowered it to the floor, the old king steps down from the throne dais—aided by Unferth—and he climbs into the seat mounted there upon the sturdy platform. The thanes groan and heave and lift him into the air, supporting his weight and the weight of the litter upon their strong shoulders, and Beowulf bows respectfully to the Lord of Heorot Hall.

"Good night, brave warrior, Hygelac's heir," the king says to Beowulf. "Show the fiend no mercy. Give no quarter. Remember all those he has so callously murdered."

"No mercy," answers Beowulf, and the king smiles and orders the thanes to bear him away to his bedchamber.

"Yes. Good night, *brave* Beowulf." Unferth sneers. "And I trust you'll keep a weather eye peeled for sea monsters. I'm sure that imagination of yours is fair teeming with them."

"I am disappointed, Unferth, that you will not be joining us tonight in our vigil," Beowulf replies, looking the Dane straight in his green eyes. "Surely Odin Allfather has prepared a place in his great hall for you, as well."

"I already have *my* duties," Unferth replies curtly. "You see to yours," and then he turns and follows the thanes as they ferry King Hrothgar from the hall.

"It's a grievous responsibility," says Wealthow, when Unferth has gone. She's still standing there beside Beowulf at the edge of the dais. "Cowering in the shadows and cleaning up after a sick old man. But at least it's a duty to which he's well suited."

"Your song was beautiful," Beowulf tells her, changing the subject, not wishing to speak any more of Unferth. "But you need to go now."

"Of course. Grendel. That demon is my husband's shame."

"Not a shame," Beowulf tells her, and he begins loosening the leather straps and buckles on his breastplate. "A *curse*."

"No, my lord, a *shame*," Wealthow says, and she furrows her brow and looks down at her feet "My husband has no . . ." but then she pauses, glancing back up at Beowulf. "He has no sons to fight this evil, no Danish son to restore honor to our house. And he will have none, for all his talk of bedding me."

Beowulf removes his heavy iron breastplate and lets it fall, clanging to the floor between them, and then he begins unfastening his belt. Behind him, Hondshew enters the hall, though Beowulf had not noticed his absence. Olaf and another of the Geats begin to laugh, making some joke at Hondshew's expense, and soon the hall rings with their shouts and profanity. Hondshew hurls himself at Olaf, and the two tumble over a table and onto the floor, where they roll about, wrestling and trading blows and curses and insults.

"Why don't you stop them?" Wealthow asks, and Beowulf looks over his shoulder at the commotion. The other thanes are cheering them on, some rooting for Hondshew, others for Olaf. Beowulf sees that all the Danes have gone, and only his men remain in the mead hall.

"They're only letting off steam," he tells the queen. "They've a long night ahead of them. It is good to laugh before a battle."

"But if they knock themselves senseless—"

"You really *do* need to go now, Your Majesty," and at that he tugs his tunic off over his head and drops it on the floor atop his breastplate.

"What exactly are you doing?" the queen asks, staring perplexed at the pile of clothing and armor. Beowulf has already begun shrugging off his chain mail.

"When Grendel comes, we will fight as equals," he tells her, and continues to undress. "As I understand it, the creature has no sword, no shield, no helmet. He does not know strategy nor the art of war. And I have been assured that I have no weapon capable of slaying this monster. But I have *my* teeth, and sinews of my own."

"But . . . my Lord Beowulf," Wealthow protests, and she stoops to retrieve his discarded breastplate. "Your *armor*."

"Armor forged of man will only slow me. No. We will fight tonight as equals, this Grendel and I. The Fates will decide. The Norns have already woven their skein, and I cannot undo it, not with leather or cold iron. Let the demon face me unarmed, if he so dares."

"Do not be foolish. Do not throw your life away, Beowulf. You may be our last hope in all the world."

"Go now, good queen," he tells her. "Go to your husband's bed, before I have my men remove you. Or before I am forced to do it myself." And now the Geat's long mail shirt falls nosily to the floor, and he stands before Wealthow, naked save the modesty of a loincloth.

"You would *not*!" she gasps.

"Aye, it would be my pleasure, though I doubt the king would much approve."

"Are all the men of your country so brazen?" she asks, and takes a step backward, putting more distance between herself and Beowulf.

"They do their best, though I am generally held to be the worst of the lot." And now Beowulf can see that Wealthow is blushing, though whether it is at the sight of him unclothed or at his words, he cannot say. "This is my final warning," he says, and takes a step toward her.

"Very well then, son of Ecgtheow. Do as you will, as I'm quite sure you ever have," and she hurries away, disappearing through the anteroom door, which she slams shut behind her. He listens while she bolts it from the other side.

And finally Beowulf stands alone, gazing down at the dull glint of his broadsword and mail lying discarded upon the floor of Heorot, thinking more on the queen's violet eyes than on the beast Grendel or his weapons or the trials awaiting him and his thanes. It is good, he thinks, to face the coming fray with such a beauty yet so fresh in one's mind. All good men fight for honor and to prove themselves worthy of a seat in Valhalla, but they might also justly fight to keep safe those too few beautiful sights that lie here beneath the wall of Midgard, below the path of sun and moon. And then there's a loud crash somewhere in the hall behind him, the sound of shattering wood, and Beowulf turns to see Hondshew helping a stunned Olaf to his feet, hauling him from the ruins of one of Hrothgar's banquet tables.

"Here now. Take care you do not break him entirely," Beowulf shouts at Hondshew. "It would be a shame to rob the poor beast of that simple pleasure."

"It's not going to hold," Wiglaf says, watching and shaking his head as the other thanes labor to secure the great main door of Heorot. "Right off, I can tell you that for nothing." He turns and finds Beowulf standing directly behind him, naked save his breechclout.

"You're mad, you know that?"

"Yes, Wiglaf," Beowulf replies. "You've brought it to my attention on more than one occasion."

"And this door here, then you know I'm right about that as well?"

Beowulf bites thoughtfully at his lower lip and watches as four of his men set the immense crossbar into its black iron brackets, barricading the door. Then he nods and spares a smile for Wiglaf.

"Of course you're right about the door," he says. "If this door, or any other, would keep our fiend at bay, do you think the Danes would have any need of us?"

"Then why bother with the blasted thing at all," Wiglaf sighs, squinting up into the gloom near the ceiling at the clumsy system of pulleys and chains that has been rigged to raise and lower the heavy crossbar. "Why not just leave it standing wide open as an invitation to the bastard and get this over with?"

"If we're lucky, it'll buy us a little time," Beowulf replies. "Think of it as an alarm."

"An alarm."

"Sure. Hrothgar's door here might not keep this Grendel beast out, Wiglaf, but it's bound to make an awful racket coming through, don't you think?"

"An alarm," Wiglaf says again and scratches at his beard, the worried expression not leaving his face.

"Something vexes you, Wiglaf."

"Aye, it does. I don't like the *smell* of this one, my lord. Look at them," and Wiglaf motions toward the thanes, Hondshew and Olaf and the rest.

"I admit," Beowulf says, "they've smelled better. Then again, on occasion they've smelled worse."

"Fine. Jest if it pleases you," Wiglaf frowns, and he kicks halfheartedly at the door with the toe of his right boot. "But the men are not *prepared*. They're still tired from the sea. They're distracted. Too many untended *women* about this place, and I do not have to tell you that abstinence prior to battle is essential. A warrior's mind must be unblurred . . . focused."

"Olaf!" Beowulf shouts, startling Wiglaf. "Tell me, Olaf, are you ready for this battle?"

The fat thane stops tugging at a thick length of rope reinforcing the mead-hall door and turns toward Beowulf. Olaf's left eye is already swelling shut from his brawl with Hondshew. He blinks and looks confused.

"Good choice," Wiglaf mutters.

Beowulf ignores him and points at Olaf. "I asked you a question, man. Are you ready, right now, to face the murderous demon that haunts this hall?"

Olaf tugs at an earlobe and glances toward Hondshew. "Huh-huh-huh," he starts, then stops and starts over again. "Hondshew, huh-huh-he started it."

Hondshew stops what he's doing and points a grubby finger at Olaf. "Wot? *You* implied that I have intimate relations with sheep and other livestock, so how do you figure *I* started it? Maybe you need another poke in the—"

"I'm not *asking* about the fight," Beowulf interrupts. "I'm asking Olaf here if he's ready for the night's battle. Wiglaf here, he's worried you're not *focused*, Olaf."

Olaf continues to tug at his earlobe, but looks considerably more confused than he did a moment earlier. He blinks both his eyes, one right after the other.

"I can see juh-juh-just fuh-fuh-fine, if that's what you muh-muh-mean," he tells Beowulf. "It's just a shuh-shuh-shiner, that's all. I can *see* just fuh-fuh-fine."

"And what about you, Hondshew?" Beowulf asks.

"Beowulf, that fat idjit there, he said I been off swifan sheeps and pigs and what not. You'd have hit him, too. Don't tell me you would have done different, 'cause I know better."

"I duh-duh-didn't say nuh-nuh-*nothing* about Beowulf swifan with puh-pigs," Olaf grumbles defensively, and tugs his ear.

"I think you just proved my point," Wiglaf says to Beowulf, and turns his back on the door, gazing out across the wide, deserted expanse of Heorot Hall. One of the big cooking fires is still burning brightly, and it throws strange, restless shadows across the high walls.

"You worry too much, Wiglaf," says Beowulf.

"Of course I do. That's my job, isn't it?" and then he looks over his shoulder to see Hondshew glaring menacingly at Olaf and the other thanes still milling about the door. "That's good," he tells them. "Now, tie it off with more chain. Hondshew, Olaf, you two ladies stop frican about and help them!"

"More chain?" asks Beowulf. "But you just said it's not going to hold."

"Aye, and *you* just agreed, but more chain means more noise. If it's an alarm you want, then we'll have a proper one."

"Where would I be without you, Wiglaf."

"Lost, my lord. Lost and wandering across the ice somewhere."

"Undoubtedly," Beowulf laughs and then strips away his breechclout.

"I already said you're mad, didn't I?"

"That you did," and now Beowulf retrieves his woolen cape from a nearby tabletop and wraps it into a tight bundle, then sits down on the floor, not too far distant from the door. He lies down, positioning the rolled-up cape beneath his head for a pillow. "Good night, dear Wiglaf," he says, and shuts his eyes.

"And while you're lying there sleeping, what are we meant to do?"

Beowulf opens his eyes again. Above him, the firelight dances ominously across the rafters of Heorot Hall. It's not hard to imagine the twisted form of something demonic in that interplay of flame and darkness. He glances at Wiglaf, still waiting for an answer. "While I sleep, you sing," says Beowulf.

"Sing?" asks Wiglaf, and he makes a show of digging about in his ears, as if they might be filled with dirt or fluff and he hasn't heard correctly.

"Sing loudly," adds Beowulf. "Sing as though you mean to shame the noise of Thor's hammer."

"Yuh-yuh-you want us to *suh-sing*?" stutters Olaf, who's standing just behind Wiglaf. "You mean a suh-song?"

"Yes, Olaf," replies Beowulf. "I think a song will probably do just fine."

Wiglaf looks from Beowulf to the barred entryway, then back to Beowulf again. "Okay," he says. "This is like that other business, with the door being an alarm, isn't it?"

"Do you not recall," asks Beowulf, "what that ferret Unferth said this afternoon?" And Beowulf pitches his voice up an octave or so, imitating Unferth. "'Merrymaking in the hall always brings the devil Grendel down upon us.' That's what he said."

"Ahhhh," laughs Wiglaf and taps at his left temple with an index finger. "Of course. We sing, and the doom that plagues Hrothgar's hall will be drawn out of whatever dank hole it calls home."

Beowulf nods and closes his eyes again. "Wiglaf, I do not yet comprehend the *meaning* of it, but the sound of merrymaking, it *harrows* this unhappy fiend. It causes him pain somehow, like salt poured into an open wound."

"I had a wife like that once," Hondshew says. He's finished with the winch that lifts and lowers the crossbar and sits down on the floor near Beowulf. "But then a bear carried her off."

"I thuh-thought it wuh-was a wuh-wuh-wolf," says Olaf. "You suh-suh-"

"Yeah, fine. Wolf, bear, whichever. This woman, I tell you, she *hated* to hear anyone having a good time, singing, what have you. Used to put her in the *foulest* mood. Still, she was good in the sack. I have to give her that much. I think she was a Vandal."

Beowulf opens one eye and glares doubtfully at

Hondshew. "You freely admit to swifan about with some Vandal wildcat, and yet you get offended when poor old Olaf brings up the matter of sheep?"

"She might have been a Swede," shrugs Hondshew.

"So," says Wiglaf, "you lie there on the floor, naked as the day you were born, and we lot, we serenade this bastard Grendel, right, 'cause he hates the sound of merrymaking. And then he comes for us."

"Absolutely," says Beowulf. "Unless I'm wrong."

"We won't hold it against you, should that prove to be the case," and then Wiglaf turns to face the other men. "You heard him. He wants us to sing."

Thirteen sets of thoroughly confused eyes stare blankly back at Wiglaf, and nobody moves a muscle or says a word.

"So . . . *sing*!" shouts Wiglaf.

"And sound *happy*, while you're at it," says Beowulf. "Like you *mean* it. And remember, all of you, sing *loud*."

"Right," replies Wiglaf, "loudly enough to shame the clang of Thor's hammer." Wiglaf clears his throat and spits out a yellowish glob of snot onto the floor of the mead hall. "I'll get it started then," he says.

Beowulf shuts his eyes a third time and shifts about on the hard floorboards, trying to get comfortable should they be in for a long wait. The image of Lady Wealthow is waiting there behind his eyelids, unbidden, her milky skin and golden hair, the haughtiness of a queen and the careless beauty of a girl.

So, what would Wiglaf make of my *focus?* he wonders. But the singing has already begun, some horrid bit of doggerel of Hondshew's invention, and Beowulf decides it's better if Wiglaf believes there's naught on his mind this night but gore and valor and slain monsters.

Olaf is busy murdering the first verse, but at least, thinks Beowulf, he doesn't stutter when he sings.

There were a dozen virgins,
Frisians, Danes, and Franks!
We took 'em for some swifan'
And all we got were wanks!

And now all the thanes join in for the chorus, making up in sheer volume all that they lack in pitch and melodiousness.

Ooooh, we are Beowulf's army,
Each a mighty thane,
We'll pummel your asses, and ravage
your lasses,
Then do it all over again!

"Damn good thing you can fight, Hondshew," mumbles Beowulf, smiling at the awful lyrics and the memory of Lady Wealthow. "Because, by Odin's long gray beard, you'd have starved by now as a scop." And he lies there, listening to the rowdy rise and fall of the song, to the comforting crackle from the fire pit, and alert to every night sound beyond the walls of the horned hall.

"Well, come on," he whispers, half to the luminous ghost of Wealthow floating there behind his eyes and half to unseen Grendel. "I don't mean to wait all night . . ."

9

The Coming of Grendel

Grendel sits alone at the place where the old forest ends and the scrubby land slopes away toward the deep, rocky chasm dividing the moors from the walls and gates of Hrothgar's fortifications. Overhead, the moon is playing a game of tag with stray shreds of cloud, but the creature has learned not to look to Máni for aid. There may yet be giant blood flowing somewhere in Grendel's veins, but he is a gnarled and mongrel thing, a curse, impure, and time and again the Jötnar have shown they have no love for him. Never have they spoken to him or answered his pleas, never once have they deigned to offer the smallest deliverance from his torment. He crouches beneath the trees, clutching his aching head, his pounding ears, wishing there were any way to drive the ruinous noise of men from his skull and yet not break the covenant with his mother. But he has come this far already, pain-wracked and driven from the safety of his cave beyond the fell marches. He has come so near the mead hall and the homes of men that he can smell them, can almost taste them, and so has he not already broken his promise?

And here below boughs and boles grown as rough and knotted as himself, the *change* begins again. And perhaps *this* is all he'll ever get from the giants, this hideous transformation that overtakes him when rage and hurt and hate are at last more than he can bear. No vow between mother and son the equal to a fury so great it can dissolve his will and warp muscle and reshape bone, so complete that it can finally make of him something yet *more* monstrous. A grotesque parody of his giant-kin, perhaps, some trollish joke between the gods who have warred always with the Jötnar.

"I would *keep* my word," he groans, wishing his mother were there to hear, wishing she were there to help and lead him safely back to the cave and the edge of her pool. "I *would* be true, *Modor*. I would . . ." but then the pain has become so great he can no longer think clearly enough to fashion words. And still their song jabs and cuts and mocks him from that mismatched scatter of stone and thatch perched upon the high sea cliffs.

Her sister was from Norway,
She cost me twenty groats!
She showed me there was more ways
Than one to sow my oats!

At the edge of the forest, Grendel gnashes his teeth and covers his ears as his skeleton creaks and his joints pop. The pain and rage fester inside him like pus beneath infected skin, and like an infection, his body bloats and swells, growing quickly to more than twice its size. Some magic he will never understand, some secret of his curse, and soon his head is scraping against the limbs that only a few minutes before hung so far above his head. If only it would not stop here, if only he might *keep on* growing until he stood so tall that he could snatch the disinterested moon from out the night sky and hurl it down upon the roof of Heorot. There would be silence then, silence that might last forever, as much of forever as he needs, and never again would the bright eye of the moon taunt him from its road between the clouds.

Very soon, the change is done with him, having made of Grendel something worthy of the fears and nightmares of the Danes, and he stands up straight, bruised and bleeding from the speed and violence with which he has assumed these new dimensions. He glances back toward home, his gray-blue eyes gone now all to a simmering, molten gold, and he peers through the highest branches and across the tops of trees. From this distance and through the mists, he cannot make out the entrance of his cave, but he knows well enough where it lies, where his mother sits coiled in her watery bed with eels and kelp to keep her company. And then Grendel turns back toward Heorot and the voices of the men and makes his way swiftly across the moors.

"Doesn't someone know some *other* song?" asks Hondshew, wishing now he'd bothered to think up a few more verses. He's seated at a bench with the other Geats, and though the singing has finally stopped, they're all still smacking their fists or empty cups against the tabletop, making as much racket as they can.

"Huh-how can huh-he suh-suh-*sleep* through this?" asks Olaf, and nods toward Beowulf, who hasn't moved from his spot on the floor.

"I don't think he's really asleep," whispers Hondshew.

Wiglaf stops banging his cup against the table. "Why don't you go *ask* him and see?" he asks Hondshew.

"You're not *singing*," mutters Beowulf. "And I don't recollect complaining that I'd had my fill of your pretty voices."

"We've been through the whole thing three times now," says Hondshew. "Maybe this Grendel beast, maybe he don't mind Geat singing as much as he minds Dane singing, eh?"

Wiglaf grins and points a finger at a wiry, gray-haired thane named Afvaldr, though no one ever calls him anything but Afi. "Don't you know a ballad or three?" he asks, and Afi shrugs his bony shoulders and keeps whacking his fist against the table.

"Not a one," answers Afi. "You must be thinking of Gunnlaugr. Now, *he* had a pair of lungs on him, old Laugi did. You could hear him all the way from Bornholm clear across the sea to the Fårö-strait when the mood struck him. Why, once I—"

"A shame the dumb bastard went and drowned in Iceland last winter," sighs Hondshew.

"Aye," says Afi. "A shame, that."

"Beowulf, I do not think the frican beast is falling for it," Wiglaf says. "Maybe—"

"—that's because *you've* stopped singing," replies Beowulf, not bothering to open his eyes.

"I think I've strained my damned windpipe already," says Hondshew. "What if Wiglaf's right? What if this Grendel demon's decided to sit this one out, eh? Here we sit, howling like a pack of she-wolves in heat, making complete asses of ourselves—"

"Shut up," Beowulf says, and he opens his eyes. "It's coming."

"Wot? I don't hear—" begins Hondshew, but then there's a deafening thud, and the great door of Heorot Hall shudders in its frame. And for a long moment, the Geats sit still and quiet, and there's no sound but the fire and the wind around the corners of the hall. All of them are watching the door now, and Wiglaf reaches for his sword.

"It's *here*," whispers Beowulf. "Draw your weapons."

But the silence continues, the stillness, the crackling from the fire pit.

"What the hell is he *waiting* for?" hisses Hondshew.

And then the mead-hall door is hammered thrice more in quick succession—*Thud! Thud! Thud!* Dust sifts down from the rafters, and chains rattle.

"Guh-guh-Grendel," stammers Olaf. "He nuh-nuh-knocks."

There's a smattering of nervous laughter at Olaf's grim joke. Beowulf is sitting upright now, watching the door intently, his entire world shrunk down to that great slab of wood and rope and iron.

"Ah, that is no monster," snorts Hondshew, getting to his feet and drawing his enormous broadsword from its scabbard on his back. "That must be my plum, Yrsa! She's ready for me to taste her sweet fruit!"

There is more laughter from the thanes, bolder than before, and Hondshew bows, then turns and stumbles across the hall until he is leaning against the barred door.

"Hondshew," says Beowulf, rising to one knee. "That might not be the wisest course of action."

"Ah, you'll see," laughs Hondshew, and then he calls out through the door, "Patience, my lovely! Give a poor fellow a chance to find his pecker!"

Now Wiglaf stands, his own sword drawn, and he

looks anxiously from Beowulf to the door. "Hond-shew. No—"

"You drunken idiot," mutters Beowulf.

"Nah, you just don't *know* her the way *I* do," chuckles Hondshew and then he raps three times on the door with his knuckles. "She's a demon all right. I'll grant you that. One of Loki's own whelps, I'd wager." And Hondshew presses one ear against the door. "Are you listening, my plum? Are you ready for another go?"

The thanes have all stopped laughing, and the hall of King Hrothgar has fallen silent and still again. There is a faint scrambling noise from the other side of the door, and then the wood creaks and pops and the hinges strain, and the whole thing bulges slowly inward as some titanic force presses upon it from without.

Beowulf is about to order Hondshew to move away from the doors, when the huge crossbar snaps like a twig. A rain of splinters and deadly shards of the fractured iron brackets are blown out into the hall, and Hondshew is thrown high into the air and sails by over Beowulf's head to land in a heap on the far side of the room. But there's no time to see whether or not he's been killed. The doors of Heorot have swung open wide and hang crooked now on buckled hinges, all those chains dangling broken and useless from their pulleys. Beowulf stares awestruck at the hideous thing standing in the doorway, framed by the night, its scarred hide glistening a wet and greenish gold in the firelight.

"Wiglaf," he says calmly, though his heart is racing in his chest.

"I suppose," says Wiglaf, "this means the old man wasn't exaggerating. Right about now, I bet you're wishing you'd left your armor *on*."

The monster roars and takes another step into the mead hall, advancing on the thanes. Steaming drool leaks from its mouth and spatters the floor. It swipes at the air with taloned hands and glares directly at Beowulf.

"I think it fancies you," Wiglaf says.

"Save your wit," Beowulf replies without taking his eyes off the beast. "I fear we'll have need of it when this is over."

And then Már, the thane standing on Wiglaf's left and the youngest in the party, lets out a piercing howl, a crazy whoop that comes out more terror than battle cry, and he charges the creature. Wiglaf grabs for his cape, but the boy is too fast for him. So is Grendel. Before Már's ax can land even a single blow, the creature is upon him, plucking Már up in one fist like a child's toy. The beast snarls, its thin lips folding back to expose sickly black gums and yellowed eye-teeth long as a man's forearm; Már barely has time to scream before he's bitten in two. There's a sudden spray of blood and gore, and the severed body falls twitching at Grendel's feet.

Meanwhile, Beowulf has climbed atop one of the long banquet tables and is moving very slowly and deliberately toward the creature. Wiglaf is shouting commands, and other thanes have begun to close in on the monster. But Grendel only sneers and laughs at them, a gurgling throaty laugh like the sea rushing in between two stones, then drawing quickly back again. It lunges forward and grabs hold of another of Beowulf's men, a heavyset Geat named Humli, clutching him in both its clawed hands. Humli makes to slash at its face with his sword, but Grendel slams him headfirst into one of the ceiling beams, then tosses the lifeless body into the fire pit. A third thane charges, but is simply swatted away with the back of Grendel's left hand and sent crashing into the mead vat. The vat spills and pours out into the fire pit, hissing violently and sending up a dense plume of steam and ash. The air stinks of mead and smoke and charred flesh.

And now Hondshew rushes screaming from the shadows of Heorot, bloody and battered, his armor hanging askew and his eyes bright and frenzied. He rushes toward Grendel, his heavy broadsword raised above his head. Hondshew vaults easily over one of the overturned tables, and the monster growls and stoops to meet its attacker. Hondshew's blade finds its mark, plunging into the creature's skull, but Grendel only snarls and grins furiously back at the Geat, still holding tight to the hilt of his sword and dangling several feet above the floor.

"Screw you, you ugly bastard," Hondshew snarls back. "Here I was expecting to meet a proper demon, and all we get is a wee hedge troll."

Then the monster seizes him about the chest with one hand and with its other reaches up and snaps the broadsword's blade cleanly in half, leaving seven or eight inches of steel embedded in its cranium. The broken sword clatters uselessly to the floor.

Hondshew gasps and spits in Grendel's face.

The beast laughs at him again, then squeezes, and the green-branch snap of Hondshew's collapsing rib cage is very loud in the hall. Then Grendel's jaws open and snap shut again, decapitating the thane.

"That's four good men you've killed this night," whispers Beowulf, still moving silent and unnoticed toward the monster. "By Heimdall, you'll not have another."

But Grendel is too busy gnawing at Hondshew's mangled, headless corpse to notice that the Geat stands now but an arm's length away. Beowulf glances at Wiglaf and points to the monster's groin, then makes a stabbing motion. Wiglaf nods, and Beowulf turns back toward Grendel.

"Enough!" Beowulf shouts, and Grendel looks up at him, its chin smeared dark and sticky with Hondshew's blood. It blinks and narrows its golden eyes, surprised to find that one of the men has managed to get so close.

"That one's dead," Beowulf says. "Put him down and have a go at me now."

Grendel casts aside what remains of Hondshew and, bellowing angrily, slams one gory fist down upon the table where Beowulf is standing. The Geat is fast and sidesteps the attack, but the impact sends him catapulting up into the rafters. Cheated and confused, Grendel roars and hurls the ruined table toward the smoldering, half-extinguished fire pit.

"My turn now," says Wiglaf, who has crept in close behind Grendel, and he slides quickly between the monster's legs and slashes at its groin with his sword. But the blade shatters harmlessly against the brute's leathery hide.

"Beowulf, the bastard has no bollocks!" exclaims Wiglaf, staring up at the jagged scar where a scrotum ought to be. "He's a fucking gelding!"

Now Grendel growls and pivots about, swatting at Wiglaf. But the thane manages to get his shield up in time to block the blow and is only sent tumbling backward across the floor toward the open doors of Heorot Hall and the cold, black night waiting beyond. The beast grunts and rubs at its crotch, then charges toward Wiglaf.

"So, is that why you're such an arsehole," Beowulf shouts down at Grendel from somewhere among the rafters. When the monster pauses to peer up into the gloom, Beowulf drops onto its back and immediately slips an arm around Grendel's throat and beneath its chin. Locked in the stranglehold, the beast shakes its head and gurgles breathlessly, then lurches forward, almost sending Beowulf toppling forward and over its scabrous head. But Beowulf holds on tight, pulling himself up until his face is near to one of Grendel's enormous deformed ears.

"Oh no!" shouts Beowulf. "No, it's time I finished what Hondshew started, you *filthy fucking cur*!"

And now Grendel screams and claws at its head, screaming not in anger but in pain, and Beowulf realizes that at last he's found the creature's weakness. Something he should have guessed before, the reason the merrymaking of the Danes never failed to bring its wrath down upon them.

"Oh, was that too *loud*!" he shouts directly into Grendel's right ear. "Should I perchance *whisper* from here on out?"

Grendel wails and shakes its head again in a desperate, futile attempt to dislodge the Geat. The monster spins blindly about and smashes headlong into a support column. But Beowulf hangs on, and with his free hand, he punches viciously at the creature's aching ear. Beowulf feels his chokehold loosening, and so he squeezes tighter.

"It's *shrinking*!" shouts Wiglaf from the doorway. "Beowulf, the bastard's getting *smaller*!"

"Full of surprises, aren't you," Beowulf growls loudly into Grendel's ear, then punches it again. And now Beowulf can feel the gigantic body contracting and convulsing beneath him, that throat growing the slightest bit smaller around so that he has to tighten his grip a second time. "Neat trick!" shouts Beowulf. "Do you do somersaults, as well, and juggle cabbages? Can you roll over and sit up and *fucking beg*?"

"Whatever it is you're doing," yells Wiglaf, "keep doing it!"

"Listen to me, *Grendel,*" Beowulf calls out into the monster's ear. "Your feud with Hrothgar ends *here*, this *night!*"

In a final, frantic attempt to dislodge Beowulf, Grendel hurls itself backward toward the smoky, hot maw of the fire pit. But Beowulf guesses the creature's intent and jumps clear, catching hold of one of the lengths of iron chain still hanging from the ceiling. Grendel goes down hard on the bed of soggy ash and red-hot embers, and it shrieks and rolls about as putrid clouds of yellow-green smoke rise in thick billows from off its searing skin.

"Guard the door!" Beowulf shouts to Wiglaf and the remaining thanes. "Don't let it past you!"

"And just how the hell do you propose we do *that*?" Wiglaf shouts back. "We couldn't keep it out. How do you think we're gonna keep it *in*?"

"I'm sure you'll think of something," Beowulf says, speaking half to himself now, and he hangs from the chain, watching as Grendel flails and rolls about in the spilled mead and sizzling coals and the stinking, moss-colored smoke. It's plain to see the creature's the worse for their encounter, but he knows it might yet escape Heorot alive and slink back through the mists to its den, only to heal and return some other night, and this fight will have served no end but to redouble its hatred and murderous resolve.

Beowulf climbs the chain, pulling himself up hand over hand, then clambers out onto a broad rafter beam and kneels there. Below him, Grendel howls and paws madly at the collapsing edges of the fire pit, managing at last to haul its scorched and blistered bulk free of the wide bed of glowing embers. And to Beowulf's amazement, he sees that its shrinking body has been so reduced that Grendel now stands not much taller than a very large bear. The beast shakes itself, sending up a sooty cloud of ash and sparks, and then it stops and rubs roughly at its eyes, glancing from the thanes to Wiglaf standing alone and unarmed before the open doors.

"I do apologize for the inconvenience, Sir Grendel," Wiglaf says nervously, speaking to the monster as he quickly scans the hall for Beowulf. There's no sign of him anywhere. "I'm afraid you'll just have to endure our hospitality a bit longer."

Grendel coughs, then snorts and bares his sharp yellow teeth at Wiglaf.

"My sentiments exactly," sighs Wiglaf.

And now Beowulf spies another length of chain, only a few feet to his right and swaying to and fro like a pendulum. One end is looped fast about the ceiling beam, and the other is still wrapped about a large section of the shattered crossbar from the doors.

The other thanes have joined Wiglaf at the entrance to Heorot Hall, but Grendel is advancing on them. Even at hardly more than half its former height, the snarling beast remains a formidable adversary.

"You will have to take that up with my master Beowulf," Wiglaf tells the monster, and accepts a spear from a thane named Oddvarr, replacing his lost sword. "You see, he makes the rules."

"That's right," Beowulf whispers, crawling farther out along the beam. "Just don't you *dare* let that fucker escape." When he reaches the swinging chain, Beowulf lowers his body over the side, grips the metal links, and slides down until he's standing on the suspended chunk of crossbar. Then he steadies himself and leans forward, setting all his weight against the swaying chain, increasing its arc and aiming it directly at Grendel's head.

"Over here!" Beowulf shouts, and so the monster turns away from the open doors and the thanes blocking his way, moving more quickly than Beowulf would have expected. It has just enough time to raise one clawed hand and ward off the missile hurtling toward it. When the piece of crossbar makes contact with Grendel's clenched fist, it explodes, reduced at once to mere slivers, and Beowulf dives for the floor and rolls away to safety.

No longer wrapped about the broken section of crossbar, the loop of chain slips unnoticed like a bracelet sliding over the creature's knotty wrist. Grendel turns back toward the doorway and its path to safety, roaring as it rushes suddenly toward Wiglaf and the others. But then the chain pulls taut, cinching itself tightly about the beast's wrist and jerking it backward.

"Glad you could drop in," Wiglaf says, nodding

toward Beowulf. "Will we be keeping it as a pet, then?"

And now Grendel, burned and frightened, weary of this battle that it's clearly losing, lets out an ear-splitting shriek and tugs fiercely at the chain, lashing it side to side like an iron whip. A second later, the ceiling beam splits and the chain pulls free. Grendel turns once more toward the open door, trailing the chain behind it. As the chain rattles past, Beowulf grabs hold of it, and so he too is dragged along by the retreating demon.

"Flank it!" shouts Wiglaf to the other thanes, and they move away to his left and right, leaving only him standing between Grendel and the sanctuary of darkness.

The chain bounces and catches about an iron post set into the floor of the mead hall, and for a second time, Grendel jolts to a stop, now only scant inches from the threshold of Heorot. Seeing their luck, Wiglaf presses his advantage and stabs at its face with his spear, aiming for those glistening golden eyes. But Grendel effortlessly bats the weapon away with his free right hand, knocking it from Wiglaf's hands.

"You are definitely starting to piss me off," grumbles Wiglaf. And now the four thanes on either side of the monster attack, but all their weapons prove equally useless against Grendel's impenetrable hide.

"Hold him there!" calls out Beowulf, pulling against the chain with all his strength.

"I might have been a fishmonger, you know that?"

Wiglaf calls back, right before he fails to duck one of the monster's punches and is sent sprawling out into the night. There's a loud and sickening pop, then, as Grendel's left shoulder is dislocated, and it turns back toward Beowulf.

Beowulf swings the free end of the chain up and over another support timber, lashing it fast. The monster roars in agony and clutches at its shoulder. It struggles so savagely against its fetters that the beam is jarred loose, and the roof of the hall groans as thatch and mud fill rain down upon the thanes.

"Beowulf, it's going to pull the whole place down upon our heads!" cries a thane named Bergr.

"That may well be," replies Beowulf, "but it'll *not* escape this hall! It will not survive another night to plague the Danes." And now Beowulf sprints past his warriors to the doors of Heorot, where Grendel still strains to cross the threshold. Only the creature's captured left arm is still trapped beneath King Hrothgar's roof, and it moans and pulls against the chain encircling its wrist. The Geat gets behind the enormous door and heaves it shut, slamming it with all his might onto Grendel's dislocated shoulder. The monster's arm is pinned between the door and the iron doorframe, and its howls of pain echo out across the village and the farmlands beyond.

"Your days of bloodletting are finished, demon," snarls Beowulf, and he leans hard against the door.

"No," moans Grendel. "Let . . . let Grendel . . . *free*!"

"It can *speak*!" gasps an astonished Oddvarr.

"Muh-maybe that wuh-was only Wu-wu-Wiglaf," says Olaf.

"*No!* It's only some new sorcery," Beowulf snaps back at them. "A demon's trickery that we might yet take pity on the foul beast."

"I'm not . . . I'm *not* a monster . . ." comes the coarse, gravelly voice from the other side of the door. "Not the monster *here*! No *man* can kill me. *No* mere man. Who . . . *what* thing *are* you?"

"What am *I*?" laughs Beowulf and shoves the door hard with his shoulder, eliciting fresh screams of anguish from Grendel. Then Beowulf puts his lips to the door, almost whispering when next he speaks.

"You would know who *I* am?" he asks. "Well, then. I am *ripper* and *tearer* and *slasher* and I am *gouger*. I am the teeth of the darkness and the talons of the night. I am all those things you believed *yourself* to be. My father, Ecgtheow, he named me *Beowulf*—wolf of the bees—if you like riddles, demon."

"*No*," Grendel pants and whimpers. "You . . . you are not the *wolf* . . . not the wolf of the bees. You are not . . . not the *bear*. No bear may stand against me."

"I've heard enough of this devil's nonsense," Beowulf says, speaking loudly enough that his men will hear, then hurls his whole body against the door. To his surprise, the iron frame cuts deeply into Grendel's flesh. "So," he says. "You *do* bleed after all."

Grendel shrieks again, and the tendons joining its shoulder to its arm begin to snap, the bones to crack.

"Fuh-finish it," says Olaf.

"Think you now, Grendel, on the thanes whose lives you've stolen," says Beowulf, and he slams the door once more and Grendel yelps. Rivulets of greenish black blood ooze down Grendel's snared arm and drip from its fingertips onto the floor.

"Think of them now . . . as you die," and then with all the force he can muster, with the strength that gods may grant mortal men, Beowulf pushes against the door, slamming it shut and severing the monster's arm. It falls to the floor at his feet, still twitching. The dark blood gushes from the ragged stump, and when Beowulf kicks at it, the hand closes weakly about his ankle. He curses and shakes it loose. The arm flops about on the mead-hall floor, reminding the thanes of nothing so much as some hideous fish drawn up from the sea and battering the deck with its death throes. And suddenly it goes stiff and shudders and is finally still. Beowulf leans against the door, out of breath, sweat and drops of the creature's thick blood rolling down his face and his bruised and naked body. Later, in the years to come, there will be those in his company who will say that never before or since have they seen such a look of horror on Beowulf's face. Cautiously, the thanes approach the arm, weapons drawn and at the ready.

And now there's a dull knock from the other side of the door.

Beowulf takes a deep breath and holds one finger up to his lips, silencing the thanes. Slowly, he turns to face the door. "Have you not had enough?" he asks and is answered by the voice of Wiglaf.

"Enough for this lifetime *and* the next, thank you very much" replies Wiglaf, and Beowulf leans forward, resting his forehead against the door a moment. He laughs softly to himself, an embarrassed, relieved sort of laugh, and pulls the door open again. There's a viscous smear of gore streaking the doorframe, and Wiglaf is standing there, shivering and staring back at him.

"It made for the moors," Wiglaf says, stepping past Beowulf, "but I don't imagine it will get very far. That was a *mortal* wound, even for such a demon." He stands staring down at the severed arm as an exhausted victory cheer rises from the surviving thanes.

"He spoke, Wiglaf," Beowulf says and steps out into the freezing winter night, wiping Grendel's blood from his face.

"Aye, I heard," Wiglaf replies. "There are tales of trolls and dragonkind that can speak. But I never thought I'd hear it for myself. You think old Hrothgar will keep his promise now you've slain his beast?" And when some moments have passed and Beowulf does not reply, Wiglaf turns and peers out the open doorway, but there is only the night and a few snow flurries blown about by the wind.

10

The Death of Grendel

The kindly night takes Grendel back, one of its own come wandering, broken and lost, and for a time there is only the pain and confusion. No direction or intent, no destination, but only the need to put distance between himself and the one who called itself a *bear*, though it was *not* a bear. The man who is not merely a man and claimed to be the wolf of the bees and so a *bear*. The one who answered him all in riddles.

For a time, Grendel thinks he might lie down in the mists and die alone on the moors. It would be a soft enough bed for death, and the mists seem to have become some integral part of him, a shroud unwinding from his shriveling soul even as it winds so tightly about him. It would release him, and yet also would it hold him together, these colorless wisps curling soundlessly up from the tall grass and bracken. It would conceal him, should the Bee Wolf come trailing hungrily after, still unsatisfied and following Grendel's meandering footprints and the blood he dribbles on leaves and stones. He would only be a phantom, there on the moorlands, nothing that could ever be wounded again, for even the sharpest swords pass straight through fog and empty air, doing no damage whatsoever, and no hateful human voice can injure that which cannot hear.

But then Grendel finds himself once more beneath the ancient trees, though he knows at once he is not welcomed by the forest. It wishes no part in his demise or decay and tells him so, muttering from the boughs of towering larches and oaks, beech and ash. *If you fall here,* say the trees, *our roots will not have you. We will not hide your bones. We will not taste you, nor will we offer any peace.* And they speak of some long-ago war with the giants, with the dragons, too, and to them Grendel's blood stinks of both. They remind him of the wood that he has so thoughtlessly splintered on other nights as he raged and made his way down to the dwellings of men. He will not now be forgiven those former violations.

"It is no matter," Grendel whispers, and he apologizes, and maybe the trees are listening and understand him, and maybe they aren't and don't. "I was on the moors and cannot even say how I came to be here. But I will not lie down among you, not if you won't have me." And so he stumbles on, grown so weak, so tired, that each step seems to take a lifetime or two, and there are whole hours laid in between his slow heartbeats.

A deer trail leads him away from the mumblesome, resentful trees and out into the wide gray swath of peat bog and still, deep ponds, the fell marches before the sea, this dank land that would never turn away a giant or a dragon or a troll. Or only dying Grendel. He sits down by a frozen tarn and stares at the patterns his blood makes on the ice. It's snowing harder now, fat wet flakes spiraling lazily from the moonless sky, and Grendel opens his dry mouth and catches a few of them on his tongue. There are mists here, too, but they are thin and steamy and would never hide his ghost. Still, he thinks how easily he might break through the rime and sink, falling slowly through weedy gardens tended by vipers and nicors and fat slate-colored fish. And he would lie there in the comforting slime, forgetting life and forgetting all hurt and, in time, forgetting even himself.

"The Wolf of the Bees, he would *never* find me down there," Grendel laughs, then coughs, and his breath fogs in the night. "Let him try, Mother. Let him drown here in the reeds and come to sleep beside my bones. I will gnaw him in dead dreams."

"You cannot lie down here," his mother replies, though he cannot see her anywhere. "Come back to me," she says. "I would have you here with me."

But Grendel sits a while longer there beside the frozen pool, tracing odd, uncertain shapes in the fresh snow and his cooling blood. The shapes would tell a story, if his thoughts were still clear enough for that, a happy story in which he killed the Beowulf, in which he took the horned hall for his own den and was never again plagued by the noise of men and their harps and flutes and drums. With an index finger, he tries to draw sharp teeth and a broken shield, but the falling snow erases everything almost as quickly as he can trace it on the ice.

It would cover me, too, he thinks, *if I only sit here a little longer.*

"Come home," his mother sighs, her voice woven somehow invisibly into the wind. "Come home, my Grendel."

And so Grendel remembers the cave, then, his mother's pool and her white eels, and dimly he realizes that he's been trying to find his way back there all along. But first the pain distracted him, and then the mists, and the spiteful trees, and the dark spatter of his blood across the ice. He gets slowly to his feet, and the unsteady world cracks and shifts beneath him. Grendel stands there clutching the damp stump where his stolen arm used to be, sniffing the familiar air, and he squints into the snowy night, struggling to recall the secret path. Where to tread, where not to tread, the shallow places where there are stepping-stones and the places where there are only holes filled with stagnant, tannin-stained water.

They will not have him, these haunted fens. He will not die here, beneath the sky where carrion crows and nibbling fish jaws and the Beowulf might find him. Become more than half a ghost already, Grendel takes a deep, chilling breath, gritting his teeth against the pain, and sets out across the bog.

"Come back," the mists call, but he ignores them.

"We have reconsidered and will have you, after all," mutters the old forest, but he ignores it, as well.

"We are the same, you and I," calls the moorlands from very far away. But Grendel knows he could never find his way back there, even if the jealous trees would deign to let him pass.

And before long he has reached the other side, only losing his way once or twice among the rushes and rotting spruce logs. Soon, there is solid ground beneath him again, and Grendel stumbles over the dry and stony earth and into the mouth of his cave. It does not seem so terribly cold here in the shadows, out of wind, sheltered from the falling snow. He staggers to the edge of his mother's pool and collapses there, his blood seeping into the water and staining it the way the peat moss stains the marshes. His mother is waiting, and she buoys him up in her strong arms and keeps the hungry eels and crabs at bay.

"Do not cry," she says, and kisses his fevered brow with cool lips.

"He hurt me, *Modor*," sobs Grendel, who had not known he was sobbing until she said so. "Mama, how can that *be*?"

"I warned you," she says. "Oh, Grendel, my son. My poor son. I *warned* you. You must not go to them . . ."

Grendel opens his eyes, which he'd not realized were shut, and gazes up at the dripstone formations hanging like jagged teeth from the ceiling of the cave.

"He killed me, *Modor*," Grendel sobs.

"Who killed you, Grendel my son. Who? Who was it did this awful thing to you?"

Those are the fangs of the world serpent, thinks Grendel, blinking away his tears and staring in wide-eyed wonder at the sparkling stalactites overhead. *I am lying now in the maw of the Midgard serpent, Jörmungand Loki-Son, and soon he will swallow me, and I will be finished, forever.*

"Who took your arm, Grendel?" asks his mother.

"The Wolf of the Bees," replies Grendel, and he shuts his eyes again. "He tore my arm away . . . it hurts so . . ."

"The Wolf of the Bees?"

"It is a riddle, Mother. Who is the Wolf of the Bees?"

"My son, there isn't time for riddles," she tells him, stroking his face with her graceful, long, webbed fingers, her golden nails.

"I am so cold," Grendel says very quietly.

"I know," she says.

"He was only a man . . . but so strong . . . so very, very strong. He hurt me, Mama."

"And he shall pay, my darling. Who was this man?"

"He told me his name in a riddle. He said, 'I am ripper and tearer and slasher and gouger. I'm the teeth of the darkness and talons of the night. I am *Beowulf*,' he said."

"Beowulf," she says, repeating the kenning. "Wolf of the bees."

"He was so strong," Grendel says again, and he wonders if it will be this cold in the serpent's belly at the bottom of the ocean. "I'm so cold," he says again.

"I know," his mother replies. "You are tired, my sweet son. You are so awfully tired. Sleep now," and she covers his eyes as the last shimmer of life escapes them. "I am here. I will not leave you."

And now his eyes are as empty as the eyes of any dead thing, and grieving, she bears him down along the roots of mountains and into the depths of her pool. The eels taste his blood, but wisely keep their distance. She drags his body along the spiraling course of that flooded granite throat, that sea tunnel scabbed with barnacles and fleshy anemones, blue starfish and mussels and clusters of blind, wriggling worms. Following some tidal pull ever, ever down into lightless halls where her son was born, chambers that have never known the sun's chariot nor the moon's white eye. And she carries the name of his killer on her pale lips, *Beowulf*, etched there like a scar.

11

The Trophy and the Prize

From the safety of their bedchamber, the king and queen have listened to the battle between the Geats and the monster Grendel. Wealthow standing alone at a window and Hrothgar lying alone in his bed, they have heard such sounds as may pass through wood and stone and thatch. Cries of anger and of pain, the shattering of enormous timbers and the sundering of iron, sudden silences, the shouts of men and the howls of a demon. They have not spoken nor thought of sleep, but have only listened, waiting for that final quiet or some *decisive* noise, and now they hear the glad voices of weary men—the victory cheer rising from Heorot. King Hrothgar sits up, only half-believing, wondering if perhaps he's fallen asleep and so is only dreaming these muffled cries from joyous, undefeated warriors.

"Is that a cheer?" he asks his wife. "Could that be a cry of victory?"

She doesn't make reply, but only stands there at the window, looking out on cold and darkness, anxiously clutching a scarf, nervously wringing the cloth in her hands. It was a gift from the king, a precious scrap of silk from some land far away to the south, some fabled, sun-drenched place where it is always summer and dark-skinned men ride strange animals.

And now the door bursts open, banging loudly against the wall, and the king's herald, Wulfgar, rushes into the room. Delight and relief glow in his eyes like a fever.

"My lord!" he gasps, winded and panting. "My lord Hrothgar! My lady! It is over! Beowulf has killed the demon! Grendel is dead!"

"Praise Odin." Hrothgar sighs and clutches at his chest, at his racing heart. "Call the scops, Wulfgar. Spread the word! Tomorrow will be a glorious day of rejoicing, the likes of which this house has never seen!"

"I will, my lord," answers Wulfgar, and he disappears again, leaving the door standing open.

Hrothgar stares at the empty doorway a moment, still waiting to awaken to the news of Beowulf's death, to the sight of Grendel crouching there above him. He climbs out of bed and slowly crosses the room to stand with Wealthow. She's stopped twisting the scarf, and there are tears in her eyes, but she's still gazing out the window at the night. He places a hand gently on her shoulder, and she flinches.

"Our nightmare is over," he says, and his hand moves from her shoulder and down toward her breast. "Come to bed, my sweet. Be with me in this hour of triumph."

"Do not *touch* me," she says and roughly pushes his hand aside. "Nothing is changed. *Nothing.*"

Hrothgar chews impatiently at his lower lip and glances back to their bed. "My kingdom *must* have an heir. I need a son, Wealthow." He turns back to her, and Wealthow takes a small step nearer the window. "The terror that haunted us is passed, and it is time to do your duty."

"My *duty?*" she scoffs, turning on him and letting the scarf slip through her fingers and fall to the floor between them. "Do not speak to me of duty, my lord. I will not *hear* it."

"You are my *wife*," Hrothgar begins, but she silences him with the wet glint of her eyes, with a cold smile and an expression of such utter contempt that he looks away again, down at the brightly colored swatch of silk where it has settled on the stone floor.

"You are a wicked old man," she hisses. "And now that fortune and the deeds of *greater* men have delivered you from this ordeal, this calamity, you would bed me and have me bear your child?"

Hrothgar walks back to their bed and sits down again, staring at the palms of his hands. "Wealthow, may I not even enjoy this moment, these good tidings after so much sorrow and darkness?"

She turns to the window, setting her back to him.

"You may take whatever joy you can find, my lord, so long as you find it without me."

"I should never have told you," he mutters, clenching his fat and wrinkled hands into feeble fists. "It should have ever stayed my secret alone to bear."

"My Lord Hrothgar is so awfully *wise* a man," laughs Wealthow, a sour and derisive laugh. And then there is another, different sort of sound from the direction of Heorot Hall—the heavy pounding of a hammer.

"What are you *doing*?" asks Wiglaf.

"I would think that's plain enough for anyone to see, dear Wiglaf," replies Beowulf, and he goes back to his grisly work. He's standing atop one of the long mead tables, using a blacksmith's hammer to nail the monster's severed arm up high on one of Heorot's ornately carved columns. An iron spike has been driven through the bones of its wrist, and every time the hammer strikes the spike, it throws orange sparks.

"Fine. Then let me ask you this," continues Wiglaf. "To what *end* are you doing it?"

Beowulf pauses and wipes sweat from his face. "They will want proof," he replies. "And I am *giving* them proof."

"Would it not have been proof enough it you'd left it lying on the floor where it fell?"

Beowulf laughs and pounds the nail in deeper. "Are you turning squeamish on me, Wiglaf? You are starting to sound like an old woman."

"I am only *wondering*, my lord, if King Hrothgar and Queen Wealthow will be pleased to find you have adorned the walls of their hall with the dismembered claw of that foul creature."

Beowulf stops hammering and steps back, admiring his handiwork hanging there upon the wooden beam. "I do not find it so unpleasant to look upon. How is it any different from the head of a boar, or the pelt of a bear, or, for that matter, the ivory tusks of a walrus?"

"My lord," says Wiglaf, exhausted and exasperated. "It is *hideous* to look upon, so like the arm of a man—"

Beowulf turns and glares down at him from the tabletop. "Wiglaf, you stood against the fiend yourself. It was no *man*."

"I did not say it *was* a man, only that in form it is not *unlike* the arm of a man."

Beowulf laughs, then wipes his face again and looks at the hammer in his hand, then back to the arm hanging limply from the beam. "I will have them *see* what I have done this night. I will have it known to them all, so there can be no mistake. Tonight, heroes fought beneath the eaves of this place . . . this Heorot . . . and a great evil was laid low. Four men died—"

"Yes, Beowulf. *Four men died,*" says Wiglaf, hearing the knife's edge of indignation in his voice and wishing it were not there. "And still they lie where they fell, because you are too busy with your . . . your trophy."

Beowulf laughs again, and this time there's something odd and brittle in that laugh, something Wiglaf has heard before in the laughter of madmen and warriors who have seen too much horror without the release of death.

"As I said, Wiglaf. You sound like a worrisome old woman. I do not hear Hondshew or Már complaining," and he uses the hammer to motion toward the corpses on the floor. "We will send them on their way soon enough. Odin Langbard shall not close the doors of his hall to them just yet, nor I have forfeited their seats at Allfather's table." And then Beowulf laughs that strange laugh again and goes back to hammering the spike deeper into the column.

The laugh pricks at the hairs on the back on Wiglaf's neck and arms, and he wonders if perhaps some darkness was released with Grendel's blood, some spirit or nixie that may now have found purchase in Beowulf's mind. Thick blood still leaks like pitch from the monster's arm, and who can say what poison might lie therein? What taint? The blood flows downward, tracing its way along the grooves and lines carved into the wood. Wiglaf recognizes the scene depicted in the carving—Odin hanging from the boughs of the World Ash, Yggdrasil, pierced through by his own lance. Nine nights and nine days of pain, to win the wisdom of nine songs that would grant him power throughout the nine realms, and the gift of the eighteen runes and a swallow of the precious mead of the giants. The blood of Grendel winds its way slowly about the limbs of the tree and the shoulders of a god.

"So be it. You have always known best," he tells Beowulf, and Beowulf nods and strikes the nail again, causing the entire arm to shudder and spit another gout of that lifeless ichor.

"You are tired, Wiglaf," says Beowulf. "And maybe you are disappointed that you have not this night found your own hero's death.

"As you say," Wiglaf replies and turns away from his lord's awful trophy to look instead upon the mutilated corpses of his four fallen countrymen. Olaf and the others have laid each man out on his shield and covered him over with his cape. And, in truth, he feels no disappointment at all that he is still among the living, and if he is ever to find his path to Valhalla, it will have to be upon some other battlefield. He glances back at Beowulf, busy with his hammering and still laughing to himself, and sees that Grendel's blood has reached all the way to the gnarled and twisted roots of Yggdrasil.

* * *

In the last hour before sunrise the snow changed to rain, a steady, drenching rain to turn the thoroughfares and commons of Hrothgar's stockade from thick and frozen muck to gray lakes and gray rivers divided one from another by stretches of even grayer mud. The water pours from off rooftops and gurgles through rainspouts, as though the sky has found some reason of its own to mourn this day. But Wiglaf and Beowulf and the other Geats built the funeral pyre before the rain began, stacking cords of cured pine soaked in pitch and drenched in whale oil, and the fire burns high and bright and hot despite the downpour. A white column of smoke rises up to meet the falling rain, and the wood crackles loudly, and the puddles hiss and steam where they meet the edges of the pyre. Beowulf and his ten remaining thanes, the survivors of their battle with Grendel, stand in the shadow of the blaze, the rain dripping from their woolen capes. A handful of curious villagers loiter farther out, watching as the flames consume the corpses of Hondshew and the others.

"They were great warriors," says Beowulf, and Wiglaf nods.

"And they suffered a most foul death," Wiglaf replies. His eyes have begun to tear, and he squints and pretends it's only from the smoke or only rain that's gotten into his eyes.

Beowulf doesn't look away from the pyre. "They have found the deaths that all brave men seek, and now they are *einherjar*. Together they have passed as heroes through Valgrind, welcomed by Bragi and the Valkyries. Today, they will ride the wide green plains of Ásgard, readying themselves for that time when they will join the gods and do battle against the giants in Ragnarök. And *this* night, while we are yet cold and weary and wet, *they* will feast at Odin's table in Valhalla, and on the morrow wake gladly to the call of the rooster Gullinkambi, then once more will they ride the fields of Idavoll. They will not die old men, sick and bedridden."

"Is that what you believe?" asks Wiglaf, glancing at his lord.

"It is what I know, Wiglaf," replies Beowulf. "I have heard no better story. Have you?"

Wiglaf watches the fire. The funeral scaffold collapses in a flurry of red-hot embers, and whatever remains of the dead men tumbles into the heart of the pyre. "I have not," he says.

"Then mourn the living," sighs Beowulf. "Mourn old men who cannot fight their own battles, not the glorious dead who have fallen victorious against so terrible a foe." And Beowulf glances toward the open door of the horned hall, still stained with Grendel's dark blood.

"I've got their knives," says Wiglaf, and he takes four daggers from his cloak. "We'll carry them home . . . for their widows."

Beowulf clenches his teeth together, looking for words that aren't there, remembering again the sound of the creature's voice, that it asked him to spare it.

"They will not be forgotten," he tells Wiglaf, and takes him by the shoulder. "The scops will sing their glory forever. Come, before we catch our death. Let us drink to their memory. I want you to raise the first cup."

Wiglaf tucks the daggers back into his cape and shakes his head. "Nay, I'm not in the mood for merrymaking. I'll ride down to the mooring, to prepare the boat," and then Wiglaf looks out from beneath his rain-soaked hood at Beowulf. "We still leave tomorrow, on the tide? Do we not?"

Above them, thunder rumbles off toward the beach.

Beowulf nods. "Aye," he says. "We do."

A rainy morning gives way to a drear and windy afternoon and a sky gone almost the same the color as the muddy earth. But in Heorot Hall, reclaimed from Grendel and once again amenable to celebration and rejoicing, a great number of King Hrothgar's people have gathered together to see the proof of Beowulf's heroic deed. Already, news of the monster's defeat has spread for many leagues up and down the coast of the kingdom and far inland, as well. Already, the scops are composing ballads, based on such hasty and incomplete accounts of the night's adventures as they have been told by the king's herald and have scrounged on their own. An evil shadow has at last been lifted from off the realm of the Danes, they sing, that creeping shade that for long months bedeviled the winter nights is finished.

But it is one thing to merely *hear* good tidings, and it is quite another thing to *see* with one's own eyes some undeniable evidence. And so King Hrothgar—son of Healfdene, grandson of Beow, great grandson of Shield Sheafson himself—stands before the arm of the beast, which the Geat has taken care to nail up that all men might look upon it and be assured of their deliverance and, also, of his glory. For what is a man but the sum of his glorious deeds and brave accomplishments? How also might he find his way to Ásgard or even to the scant rewards of *this* world?

The king stands at the edge of a wide pool of cooled and clotting blood that has over the hours oozed and dripped down to the floor of the hall, accumulating there beneath the graven image of Odin hanging upon the World Ash for the good of all men. Hrothgar has been standing there some time, drinking in the sight of the severed arm, a wound even the demon Grendel could not have long survived, and now he turns to face his subjects and his thanes, his advisors and his queen, the Geat warriors and Beowulf, who is standing close beside the king. Hrothgar stands as straight as his age and health will allow, and though even now his heart is not untroubled, his smile and the relief in his eyes are true and honest.

"Long did I suffer the harrowing of Grendel,"

he says. "Only a few days ago, I still believed that I would not ever again be granted release from torment or again find consolation. And, of course,"—and here Hrothgar pauses and motions to all those assembled before him—"of course, this burden was never mine alone. Few were the houses of my kingdom not stained with the blood spilled by Grendel. This has been a curse that has touched us all."

And there's a low murmur of agreement from the men and women. Hrothgar nods and waits a moment or two before continuing.

"But this is a *new* day. And before you, with your own eyes, you see the *proof* that there has come at last an end to our sorrow and our troubles with the demon Grendel. Today, the monster's reign has ended, thanks be to a man who has come among us from far across the sea, *one* man who has done what even the greatest among us could not manage. If the mother of this hero still draws breath, may she be evermore blessed for the fruit of her birth labor. Beowulf—" And now Hrothgar turns to Beowulf and puts an arm about him, pulling him close and speaking directly to him.

"I want everyone here, and everyone who might in time hear of this assembly, to know that in my heart I will love you like a son. With Grendel dead, you *are* a son to me."

Until now, Beowulf has kept his eyes trained on the floor of Heorot, listening to the words of the King of the Danes. They have worked some magic upon him, he thinks, for the grief that has dogged him since the funeral pyre has vanished. He looks up into the faces watching him, and he feels pride, for has he not earned this praise and whatever reward may yet await him?

I might never have come here, he thinks. *I might have left the lot of you to fend for yourselves against the fiend. It was not* my *trouble, but I made it mine.* And he remembers the things he said to Wiglaf during the funeral, and asks himself what other prize a man might ever seek, but the glory of his accomplishments. But for the capricious skein of life, the weave of the Fates, he, too, would rightly ride the fields of Idavoll this day.

At the least, I have made good upon my boast, he thinks, staring directly at Unferth, and the king's advisor immediately looks away.

"I have adopted you, my son, *here*, in my heart," says Hrothgar, and thumps himself upon the chest. "You shall not now want for anything. If there is something you desire, you have but to ask, and I shall make it so. Many times in my life I have honored warriors who were surely far less deserving, for achievements that must surely seem insignificant when placed next to what you consummated here last night. By those actions, you have made yourself immortal, and I say, may Odin always keep you near at hand and give what bounty is due a hero of men!"

And now there is a hearty cheer from the crowd,

and when it has at last subsided, Beowulf takes a step forward and speaks.

"I do not have the words due such an honor," he says, smiling at Hrothgar, then turning back to all the others. "I am only a *warrior*, not a scop or a poet. I have given my life to the sword and shield, not to spinning pretty words. But I will say that here, beneath the roof of Hrothgar, my men and I have been greatly favored in our clash with Grendel. I may tell the tale, but I would prefer that you might all have been here, you who have suffered his vile depredations, to see for *yourselves* the brute in the moment of his defeat. Aye, I would have been better pleased could that have been the case, that you might have *heard* his pain as recompense for the pain he visited upon you and yours." And Beowulf turns and stares up at the severed arm nailed upon the beam above him. He points to it, then turns back to the crowd.

"I was sleeping when he came," says Beowulf, "wishing to take him unawares. I'd hoped to leap upon the beast and wrestle him to the floor, to wring from him with naught but my bare hands whatever sinister life animates such a being and leave his whole corpse here as the wergild due you all for the lives he had greedily stolen. But at the last he slipped from out my grasp, for slick was his slimy hide. He broke from my hold and made a dash for the door. And yet, I will have you know, what a dear *price* did cruel Grendel *pay* for his flight," and again Beowulf points to the bloody, severed arm. "By this token may you know the truth of my words. If he is not yet dead, he is dying. That wound will be the last of him. Never again will he walk among you, good people of Heorot, and never again will you need fear the coming of night."

And for a third time a wild cheer rises up from the grateful crowd, and this time only the repeated shouts of Hrothgar are sufficient to quiet them again. Two of the king's thanes have brought forth a wooden chest and placed it in Hrothgar's hands. He opens the box and draws out the golden drinking horn, the treasure he wrested long ago from the fyrweorm Fafnir, his greatest treasure, and the king holds it up for all to see. Then he turns to his queen and places the horn in her hands.

"Why don't *you* do the honors, my queen?" And Beowulf catches the needle's prick of sarcasm in his voice. But Wealthow takes the horn, her reluctance hardly disguised, and she presents it to Beowulf.

"For you, my lord," she says. "You have earned it," and with a quick glance at her husband, she adds, "and anything else which my good King Hrothgar might yet claim as his own."

The gilded horn is even more beautiful than Beowulf remembers, and it glints wondrously in the light of the hall. He grins, betraying his delight at so mighty a gift, then holds it up, as Hrothgar has done, for all the hall to look upon. This time they do not cheer, but a murmur of awe washes through Heorot, at the sight of the horn and at their king's generosity.

Queen Wealthow, her part in this finished, withdraws and stands with two of her maidens, Yrsa and Gitte, gazing up at Grendel's arm. Though withered in death, it is still a fearsome thing. The warty, scaly flesh glimmers dully, like the skin of some awful fish or sea monster, and the claws are as sharp as daggers.

Yrsa leans close to the queen's ear and whispers, "They say Beowulf ripped it off with his bare hands."

"Mmmm," sighs Gitte thoughtfully. "I wonder if his strength is only in his arms, or in his legs as well . . . all *three* of them."

Yrsa laughs, and Gitte grins at her own jest.

"Well," says Wealthow, wishing only to return to her quarters and escape the noise and the crowd and the sight of that awful thing nailed upon the beam. "After the feasting tonight, perhaps you may have the opportunity to make a gift of *yourself* to good Lord Beowulf and find out the strength of his legs."

"Me?" asks Gitte, raising her eyebrows in a doubtful sort of way. "It is not *me* he wants, my queen."

And Wealthow looks from Gitte to Yrsa, then from Yrsa back to Gitte. They nod together, and she feels the hot, embarrassed blush on her cheeks, but says nothing. She glances back toward Beowulf and sees that her husband has placed a heavy golden chain around his throat. The Geat is talking about Grendel again and all are listening with rapt attention. Wealthow turns and slips away through the press of bodies, leaving Yrsa and Gitte giggling behind her.

* * *

Outside and across the muddy stockade, Wiglaf sits astride one of the strong Danish ponies, still watching the funeral pyre. It has been burning for many hours now, fresh wood fed to the flames from time to time to keep it stoked and hot. But already no recognizable signs remain of the bodies of the four thanes slain the night before nor of the scaffolding that held them, and it might be mistaken for any bonfire that was not built to ferry the souls of the dead to the span of Bilröst, the Rainbow Bridge between this world and the gods' judgment seat at Urdarbrunn. Wiglaf can clearly hear Beowulf's words, carried along on the north wind, as though Hrothgar's craftsmen have somehow designed the structure to project the words of anyone speaking within out across the compound.

He broke from my hold and made a dash for the door. And yet, I will have you know, what a dear price *did cruel Grendel* pay *for his flight . . .*

Wiglaf scratches the pony's shaggy, matted mane, and it shifts uneasily from foot to foot.

"Will their wives and children be comforted with thoughts of valiant deaths and glorious Ásgard?" asks Wiglaf, turning away from the fire and looking toward the open doors of the horned hall. The pony snorts loudly. "I wasn't asking you," says Wiglaf, and he goes back to watching the fire. Hrothgar has promised that the ashes will be buried out along the King's Road and marked by a tall menhir, with runes to tell how they fell in battle against the fiend Grendel.

"Perhaps *that* will comfort the grieving widows?" he sighs. "To know their husbands lie in fine graves so far across the sea."

. . . but I would prefer that you might all have been here, you who have suffered his vile depredations, to see for yourselves *the brute in the moment of his defeat.*

"He's right, you know," Wiglaf tells the pony, leaning forward and whispering in one of its twitching ears. "I *am* beginning to sound like an old woman." But then he sits up and glances once more toward Heorot and Beowulf's booming voice. "Be merciful, good Beowulf, and do not talk us straightaway into yet more glory. I would have mine in some other season."

The fire crackles and pops as the charred logs shift and crumble, sending another swirl of glowing brands skyward. And Wiglaf digs his heels into the pony's flanks, tightens his grip on the reins, and gallops away toward the stockade gates and the bridge beyond.

Long hours pass, and the chariot of Sól rolls once again into the west. The gray day dims, and after nightfall the clouds break apart at last to let the moon and stars shine coldly down upon the land. Inside the mead hall of King Hrothgar, his people and the Geats celebrate Beowulf's victory. After so many months of terror, Heorot is awash in the joyful noise and revelry of those who believe they have no just cause to fear the dark. Though damaged by the battle, the hall is fit enough for merrymaking; there will be time later to repair shattered timbers and smashed tables. This is why the hall was built, Hrothgar's gift to his kingdom, that men might drink and feast and fuck and forget the hardships of their lives, the cold breath of winter, the nearness of the grave.

Beowulf sits alone on the king's throne dais, drinking cup after cup of the king's potent mead and admiring the beautiful golden horn taken long ago from the hoard of the dragon Fafnir. It is *his* now, his hard-earned reward for a job no other man could do, and it gleams brightly by the flickering light of the fire pit. From time to time, he looks up, gazing contentedly about the hall for familiar faces. His men are all enjoying rewards of their own, as well they should. But he does not see Lord Hrothgar anywhere and thinks that the old man has probably been carried away to bed by now, either to sleep off his drunkenness or to busy himself with some maiden who is not his wife. Nor does he see the king's herald, Wulfgar, nor Unferth Kinslayer, nor Queen Wealthow. It would be easy enough to imagine *himself* crowned lord of this hall, a *fit* king to rule the Danes instead of a fat old man, too sick and more concerned with farm girls and mead than the welfare of his homeland.

The air in the hall has grown smoky and thick with too many odors, and so Beowulf takes the golden horn and leaves the dais, moving as quickly as he may through the crowd. He is waylaid many times by men who want to grasp the hand of the warrior who killed the monster, or by women who want to thank him for the salvation of their homes. But he comes, eventually, to a short passageway leading out onto a balcony overlooking the sea.

"You are not celebrating?" asks Wealthow, standing there with the moonlight spilling down upon her pale skin and golden hair. She is swaddled against the freezing wind in a heavy coat sewn from seal and bear pelts, and he is surprised to find her unescorted.

Beowulf glances down at the golden horn, and he might almost believe that the moonlight has worked some sorcery upon it, for it seems even more radiant than before. He stares at it a moment, then looks back up at Wealthow.

"I'll never let it go," he says, and raises the horn to her. "I'll die with this cup of yours at my side."

"It is nothing of *mine*," she replies. "It never was. That was only ever some gaudy bauble of my husband's pride. He murdered a dragon for it, they say."

Beowulf lowers the horn, feeling suddenly uncomfortable and oddly foolish. His fingers slide lovingly about its cold, glimmering curves. "My lady does not *hold* with the murder of dragons?" he asks the queen.

"I didn't say that," she replies. "Though one might wonder if perhaps a live dragon is worth something more than the self-importance of the son of Healfdene."

"Men must seek their glory," Beowulf says, trying to recall the authority and assurance with which he addressed the hall only a few hours before. "They must ever strive to find their way to Ásgard . . . and protect the lives and honor of those they cherish."

"I admit, it has always seemed an unjust arrangement to me," the queen says, and moves nearer the edge of the balcony. Below them the sea pounds itself against sand and shingle, the whitecaps tumbling in the moonlight.

"My lady?" asks Beowulf, uncertain what she means.

"That a man—like my husband—may in his youth slay a fearsome dragon, which most would count a glorious deed. Even the gods, I should think. And yet, if he is *unlucky* and survives that encounter, he may yet grow old and feeble and die in his bed. So—dragon or no—the bravest man may find himself before the gates of Hel. Or, in your own case, Lord Beowulf . . ." And here she trails off, shivering and hugging herself against the chill, staring down at the sea far below.

Beowulf waits a moment, then asks, "In my own case?"

She turns and looks at him, and at first her eyes seem distant and lost, like the eyes of a sleeper awakened from some frightful dream.

"Well," she says. "You are alive, though by your bravery Grendel is slain. You are not in Valhalla with your fallen warriors. You have, instead, what? A golden horn?"

"Perhaps I will find my luck, as you name it, on some other battlefield," Beowulf tells her, then glances back down at the horn. "And it *is* a fine and wondrous thing, this gaudy bauble of your husband's pride."

Wealthow takes a deep breath. "Nothing that is gold ever stays long. Is that *all* you wanted, Beowulf? A drinking horn that once belong to a worm? Would you have none of my husbands *other* treasures?"

And now he looks her directly in the eyes, those violet eyes that might seem almost as icy as the whale's-road on a long winter's night, as icy and as beautiful.

"My lord Hrothgar," he says, "has declared I shall not now want for anything." And he moves across the balcony to stand nearer to Wealthow. "I recall nothing he held exempt from that decree. Steal away from your husband. Come to me."

Wealthow smiles and laughs softly, a gentle sound almost lost beneath the noise of the wind and the breakers.

"I wonder," she says, "if my husband even begins to guess what thing he has let into his house? First driven by greed . . . now by lust," and she turns away from the sea to face Beowulf. "You may indeed be most beautiful, Lord Beowulf, son of Ecgtheow, and you may be brave, but I fear you have the heart of a monster." And then she smiles and kisses him lightly on the cheek. Their eyes meet again, briefly, and her bright gaze seems to rob him of words, and Beowulf's still searching for some reply after she's departed the balcony and returned once more to the noisy mead hall, and he's standing alone in the moonlight.

12

The Merewife

Beyond the moorlands and the forest and the bogs, in the cave *below* the cave, this deeper, more ancient abscess in the thin granite skin of the world, the mother of Grendel mourns alone. She has carried her son's mutilated body from the pool, the pool *below* the pool above, and has gently laid him out on a stone ledge near a wall of the immense cavern. Once, the ledge was an altar, a shrine built by men to honor a forgotten goddess of a forgotten people, and the charcoal-colored slate is encrusted with the refuse of long-ago offerings—jewels and bits of gold, silver, and bronze, the bones of animals and men. Whatever it might have been, now it is only her dead son's final bed. She bends low, her lips brushing his lifeless skin, her long claws caressing his withered corpse. She is *old*, even as the mountains and the seas mark time, even as the Æsir and Vanir and the giants of Jötunheimr count the passing of the ages, but the weight of time has not hardened her to loss. It has, if anything, made her more keenly aware of the emptiness left behind by that which has been taken away.

"Oh, my poor lost son," she whispers. "I asked you not to go. I warned you they were dangerous. And you promised . . ."

If any others of her race remain in all the wide, wide world, she does not know of them and so believes herself to be the last. Neither troll nor giant nor dragon-kin, and yet perhaps something of all three, some night race spawned in the first days of creation, when Midgard was still new, and then hunted, driven over uncountable millennia to the brink of oblivion. She had a mother, whom she almost remembers from time to time, waking from a dream or drifting down toward sleep. If she ever had a father, the memory of him has faded away forever.

Long before the coming of the Danes, there were men in this land who named her Hertha and Nerthus, and they worshipped her in sacred groves and still lakes and secret grottoes as the Earth's mother, as Nerpuz and sometimes as Njördr of the Ásynja, wife of Njörd and goddess of the sea. And always she welcomed their prayers and offerings, their tributes and their fear of her. For fear kept her safe, but never was she a goddess, only some thing more terrible and beautiful than mere men.

She is legend now, half-glimpsed by unfortunate travelers on stormy nights. Sailors and fisherman up and down the Danish coast trade fearful whispers of mermaids and sea trolls and *sahagin*. Those passing by the bog on midsummer nights may have glimpsed for themselves the *aglaec-wif*, *aeglaeca*, the *merewif* or demon wife. But she and all her vanished forebears would have surely long passed completely and permanently beyond the recollection of mankind, if not for Grendel.

In the cave below the cave, crouching there before the cold altar stone, she sings a song she *might* have first heard from her own mother, for she does not recall where and when she learned it. A dirge, a mourning song to give some dim voice to the inconsolable ache welling up inside her.

So much blood where so many have died
Washed ashore on a crimson tide.
Just as now there was no mercy then . .

But the song buckles and breaks apart in her throat, becoming suddenly a far more genuine expression of her grief, a wild and bestial wail to transcend any mournful poetry. It spills like fire from out her throat, and the walls of the cavern shudder with the force of it.

And then for a time she lies weeping at the foot

of the altar stone, her long, webbed fingers gouging muddy furrows into the soft earth, scraping at the stone beneath, snapping dry bones.

"I *will* avenge you, my poor son," she sobs. "He will come to me. I will see to it. He will come, and I will turn his own strength against him. He will *pay*, and *dearly* will he pay . . ." but then the capacity for speech deserts her again.

The merewife rises, coiling and uncoiling, her scales shining in the ghostly light of these moldering, phosphorescent walls, and she leans down over the altar and cradles her dead son in her arms again. Her long and spiny tail whips furiously about, madly lashing at thin air and stone and the treasures that have lain here undisturbed for a thousand years, and it crushes everything it strikes to dust and splinters. She holds the name of her son's murderer in her mind, the bold riddler of Hrothgar's hall, the champion of men and the wolf of the bees. And her sobs become a wail, and then her wail becomes a shriek that rises up and up, leaking out through every minute crevice and fissure, slithering finally from the gaping mouth of the cavern—the cave above her cave—and cracking apart the gaunt ribs of the night.

Something awakens Beowulf, who lies where he fell asleep hours before, wrapped in furs, on the floor not far from the fire pit. He opens his eyes and lies listening to the soft noises of the sleeping mead hall—a woman sighing in her dreams, the ragged snores of drunken men, the warm crackle of embers, someone rolling over in slumber. The faint creaking sound of settling timbers. All the lamps are out, and the hall is dark save a faint red glow from the dying fire. Nothing is out of place, no sound that should not be here. Outside the walls of Heorot, there is the chilling whistle of wind about the eaves, and far away, the faint thunder of waves falling against the shore. He thinks of Wiglaf, alone on the beach with the ship, and wonders if he's sleeping.

Beowulf peers into the gloom and spies Olaf lying nearby, snuggling with Yrsa beneath heavy sheepskins, a satisfied smile on his sleeping face.

"Are you awake, Beowulf?" and he looks up, startled, to find Wealthow smiling down at him. She stoops, then sits on the floor beside him.

"My queen . . ." he begins, but she places an index finger firmly across his lips.

"Shhhhhh," she whispers. "You'll wake the others," and then she moves her finger.

"I was dreaming of you," he says quietly, only just now remembering that he was. In the dream, Wealthow was traveling with him back across the sea to Geatland, and they were watching the gray-black backs of great whales breaking the surface of the sea, their misty spouts rising high into the winter sky.

"How sweet," she whispers, and Beowulf thinks there's something different about her voice, the barest hint of an unfamiliar accent he'd not noticed earlier. "I hope it was a *pleasant* dream."

"Of course it was," he smiles. "What other sort could you ever inspire?"

"I love you," Wealthow whispers, leaning closer to Beowulf, close enough that he can feel her breath warm against his face. "I want you, Beowulf Demonfeller, son of Ecgtheow. Only you, my king, my hero, and my love."

Wealthow puts her arms about his neck, drawing him close to her breasts, and she kisses him lightly on the cheek.

"Do you not think your husband might have something to say in the matter?" he asks, looking nervously past her at the others, still asleep.

"My husband," sighs Wealthow. "Do not trouble yourself over Hrothgar. He is dead. This very night, I have done it myself, as I should have done long ago."

Beowulf says nothing for a moment, confused and baffled at what he's hearing. Wealthow smiles wider and kisses him on the forehead.

"Surely you have heard of his infidelities," she says. "They certainly were no secret. Hrothgar never tried to hide his whores . . . or I should say he never tried *very* hard.

"Why would you say these things to me?"

She has slipped her hands beneath his tunic, and they are cold against his chest and belly. He feels her nails rasping almost painfully at his skin.

"My poor sleepy Beowulf," she smiles. "Too much mead, too little rest. You are exhausted and confused." And now she presses herself against him, straddling him, her strength taking him by surprise as she bears him flat against the floor.

"First greed," she says. "Then lust. Is this not what you would have, my lord? Is this not everything you yet desire?" And she kisses him again, and this time she tastes like the sea, like salt water rushing into the throat of a drowning man, like beached and rotting fish stranded under a summer sun. He gags and tries to push her away.

"Give me a child, Beowulf. Enter me, and give me a beautiful, beautiful son."

And the air around Wealthow seems to shimmer and bend back upon itself somehow. Beowulf blinks, trying hard to will himself awake from this nightmare, terrified he may not be sleeping. She smiles again, and now her lips pull back to reveal the razor teeth of hungry ocean things, and her eyes flash gold and green in the darkness of the hall. Her gown has become a tattered mat of kelp and sea moss entangling a sinuous, scaly body, and Beowulf opens his mouth to scream . . .

. . . and he gasps—one breath he cannot quite seem to draw, the space of a heartbeat that seems to go on forever, his pulse loud in his ears, the sea and all its horrors dragging him down—then he opens his eyes. And Beowulf knows that this time he is *truly* awake. His chest aches, and he squints into the brilliant morning sunlight pouring in through the open door of Heorot Hall, then shields his eyes with his right hand. He blinks, trying to clear his vision.

The frigid air around him smells like slaughter, like a battlefield when the fighting is done or a place where many animals have been butchered and bled. The drone of buzzing flies is very loud, and there's a steady dripping from all directions, as though the storm returned in the night and the roof has sprung many leaks.

And now there's a scream, the shrill and piercing scream of a frightened woman. Beowulf peers out from behind the shelter of his fingers, and Yrsa is sitting nearby, pointing one trembling hand up toward the ceiling. Dark blood streaks her upturned face. Beowulf's eyes follow her fingertips, and he sees that there are many dark shapes hanging from the rafters, indistinct silhouettes weeping a thick red rain.

And then he realizes what those dreadful, dangling forms are.

The bodies of Beowulf's men hang head down from the roof beams of Heorot—gutted, defiled in unspeakable ways, each and every one torn almost beyond recognition. Their blood drips steadily down upon the tabletops and floor and the upturned faces of horrified women. Beowulf gets slowly to his feet, drawing his sword as he stands, fighting nausea and the dizzying sense that he is yet dreaming.

If only I am, he thinks. *If this might be naught but some new and appalling apparition, only a phantasm of my weary mind . . .*

He moves slowly through the hall, and now there

are other screams and gasps as other women come awake around him and look upon what hangs there bleeding out above them. Soon the entire hall is filled with the sobs and curses of terrified women. And soon, too, Beowulf can see that *every* man who slept there has been slain, that among the men, he alone has been spared the massacre.

There are footsteps at the doorway, and Beowulf swings about, raising his sword and bracing himself for the attack. But it's only Wiglaf, returned from the beach. He stands framed in winter sunlight, gazing up at the ragged bodies. He has also drawn his sword.

"In the name of Odin . . ." he gasps.

"Wiglaf, what dismal misdeed is this?" Beowulf asks, and a fat drop of blood splashes at his feet.

Yrsa has gotten to her feet, and she's pointing toward Beowulf instead of the murdered men.

"*Liar*," she hisses. "You told us it was dead. You told us you had *killed* it."

"What? Is Grendel *not* dead?" asks Wiglaf, taking a hesitant step into the mead hall. "Has the fiend grown his arm *anew*?"

Beowulf does not answer them, but turns about to look at the place where he nailed up Grendel's severed arm. Nothing hangs there now, and his eyes find only the naked iron spike and the monster's black blood dried to a crust upon the wooden column and the floor below.

"He took it *back*, didn't he?" asks Yrsa, her voice becoming brittle and hysterical. "He came here in the night and took it back! He walked *among us* while we slept. The demon is not dead. You *lied*—"

"*Shut up, woman!*" growls Beowulf, watching a fat drop of blood that has landed on the blade of his sword as it runs slowly down toward the hilt.

"Are you not thinking the same damn thing?" asks Wiglaf from the doorway. "The men are *dead*, and the arm is gone, and we did not *see* the creature die."

"We did not ever *say* we saw it die," replies Beowulf, and he shuts his eyes, trying to think, trying to blot out all these atrocities, all the sights and sounds and smells. But she is still there in his head, waiting behind his eyelids, the grinning phantom from his dream, the thing that came disguised as Wealthow . . .

Give me a child, Beowulf. Enter me now and give me a beautiful, beautiful son.

A cold spatter of blood strikes Beowulf's forehead, and he opens his eyes again, then wipes it away and stands staring at the crimson smear on his palm.

"Find Hrothgar," he says. "If he still breathes."

"It was not Grendel," Hrothgar sighs heavily. He sits alone on the edge of his bed, wrapped in deer skins and frowning down at his bare feet, his crooked yellow toenails. His sword is gripped uselessly in both hands, the tip of the blade resting against the stone floor. There are four guards standing at the entrance to the bedchamber, and Queen Wealthow, wrapped in her bearskins, stands alone at the window, looking out on the stockade.

"How do you know that?" Wiglaf asks the king, and Hrothgar sighs again and looks up at him.

"I *know* it, young man, because I have lived in this land all my life and know its ways. I *know* it because it is something that I know."

"Fine," says Wiglaf, glancing toward Beowulf. "But if it is not Grendel, then *who* is it? *What* is it, if not Grendel?"

Hrothgar taps the end of his sword lightly against the stone and grimaces.

"We would have an answer, *old* man," Beowulf says. "They are carrying the bodies of my men from your mead hall, and I would know why."

"Grendel's mother," replies Hrothgar. "It was the son you killed. I had . . . I had hoped that she had left this land long ago."

Wiglaf laughs a hollow, bitter sort of laugh and turns away. Beowulf frowns and kicks at the floor.

"How many monsters am I to slay?" he asks Hrothgar. "Grendel's mother? Father? Grendel's *fucking* uncle? Will I have to hack down an entire family *tree* of these demons before I am done?"

"No," says Hrothgar unconvincingly, and taps his sword against the floor a second time. "She is the last. I swear it. With her gone, that demonkind will finally slip into faerie lore forever."

"And you neglected to mention her before now because . . . ?"

"I have already said, I believed that she had deserted these hills and gone back down to trouble the sea from whence she came. I did not *know*, Beowulf. I did not know."

"Listen," says Wiglaf to Beowulf. "Let us take our dead and take our leave and have no more part in these evil doings. If he is not lying," and Wiglaf pauses to glare at Hrothgar, "then Grendel's dam has claimed her wergild and has no further grievance or claim upon this hall. We can sail on the next tide."

"And what of her mate?" Beowulf asks Hrothgar, ignoring Wiglaf. "Where *is* Grendel's father?"

And now Wealthow turns away from the window, her hands clasped so tightly together that her knuckles have gone white. "Yes, my dear husband," she says. "Pray tell, where *is* Grendel's sire?" But as she speaks, her eyes go to Beowulf, not King Hrothgar.

"Gone," says the king, then wipes at his mouth and glances up at Beowulf. "Grendel's father is *gone*, faded like twilight, not even a ghost. He can do no harm to man."

"Beowulf, he has already lied to us once."

"I *never* lied to you," snaps Hrothgar, his face gone red, his cloudy eyes suddenly livid, and he raises his sword. But Wiglaf easily bats the blade aside, and it clatters to the floor.

"Nay, I suppose you did not," he says. "You merely neglected to mention that once we'd slain her *son*—"

"Stop," Beowulf says, and he lays a firm hand on Wiglaf's shoulder. "You will not speak this way to the King of the Danes."

Exasperated, Wiglaf motions toward the window, toward the sea beyond. "Beowulf, please. Think about this. It is time we took our leave of these cursed shores. We have *done* what we came here to do."

Before Beowulf can reply, there are loud footsteps in the hallway outside the bedchamber, and Unferth enters the room. "Beowulf," he says.

"What now?" Wiglaf asks Hrothgar's advisor. "Have you come here to gloat, Ferret Kinslayer?"

Unferth takes a deep breath, disregarding Wiglaf's taunt. "I was wrong," he says. "I was wrong to doubt you before, Beowulf, son of Ecgtheow. And I shall not do so again. For truly yours is the blood of courage. I beg your forgiveness."

"Clearly, there is to be no end to this farce," sneers Wiglaf, and he turns his back on Unferth.

"Then I accept your apology," Beowulf says quietly, and Wiglaf laughs to himself. "And you must forgive my man Wiglaf, as we have seen many terrible things this morning, and it has sickened our hearts."

"If you will take it," Unferth says, "then I have a gift," and he turns to his slave, Cain, who has been standing just behind him. The boy is holding a great sword, which Unferth takes from him.

"This is Hrunting," Unferth says, and holds the weapon up for Beowulf to see. "It belonged to my father Ecglaf and to my father's father before him." The blade glints in the dim lights of the bedchamber, and Beowulf can see that it is an old and noble weapon. Unferth holds it out to him.

"Please," he says. "It is my gift to you. Take my sword, Beowulf."

Beowulf nods and accepts the blade, inspecting the ornate grip and pommel, gilded and jeweled and graven with scenes of battle. A prominent fuller runs the length of the sword, lightening the weapon. "It is fine, and I am grateful for your gift. But a sword like this . . . it will be no fit match for demon magic."

"Still," says Unferth, "Hrunting may be more than it seems. My father told me the blade was tempered in blood, and he boasted it had never failed anyone who carried it into battle."

"A shame he cannot speak of its might from personal *experience*," Wiglaf says, and Beowulf tells him to be quiet.

"Something given with a good heart," Beowulf says to Unferth, "that has its own magic. And it has a good weight to it, friend Unferth"

"I'm sorry I ever doubted you."

"And I am sorry I mentioned that you murdered your brothers . . . they were hasty words."

Wiglaf snorts. "The truth spoken in haste remains the truth."

Beowulf holds the sword Hrunting up before him, admiring the ancient weapon, the runes worked into its iron blade.

"You know, Unferth," he says, "if I track Grendel's dam to her lair, I may not return. Your ancestral sword might be lost with me."

Unferth nods once and folds his arms. "As long as it is with you, it will never be lost."

And now Beowulf turns to face Wiglaf. "And you, mighty Wiglaf. Are you still with me?"

"You are a damned *fool* to follow this creature back to whatever fetid hole serves as its burrow," he says, instead of answering the question put to him.

"Undoubtedly," replies Beowulf. "But are you *with* me."

Wiglaf laughs again, a laugh with no joy or hope to it. "To the bloody end," he says.

"And where are we to seek the demon?" Beowulf asks the king. At first Hrothgar only shrugs and scrapes the blade of his sword across the floor, but then he clears his throat and raises his head to look Beowulf in the eyes.

"There is perhaps one living who knows," says Hrothgar. "A man from the uplands. I have heard him speak of them, Grendel and its mother, and he has told stories of the places where they dwell. Unferth, he can take you to speak with this man."

"Will you stay behind, my king?" asks Wealthow, still standing at the window, speaking with her back to the room and all assembled there. "While Lord Beowulf once more seeks his death that *your* kingdom might be saved, will you stay behind with the women and children and the old men?"

Hrothgar coughs and wipes his mouth on the back of his right hand. "I *am* an old man," he says. "I would be no more to Beowulf than a burden. And I doubt there remains a horse in all my lands with the heart and strong back needed to bear me across the moorlands. I am sorry, Beowulf—"

"Do not apologize," says Beowulf, holding up a hand and interrupting Hrothgar before he can finish. "It is not necessary, my lord. In your day, you fought wars, and you slew dragons. Now your place is here, with your people. With your *queen*."

At this, Wealthow shakes her head and mumbles something under her breath but does not turn from the window.

"For my part," continues Beowulf, "I'd rather die avenging my thanes than live only to grieve the loss of them. If the Fates decree that I shall ever return to my homeland, better I can assure my kinsmen that I sought vengeance against this murderer than left that work to other men."

"A fool throws his life away," says Wealthow very softly, and Hrothgar sighs, shaking his head.

"All those who live await the moment of their death," Beowulf says, turning toward the Queen of Heorot Hall, wishing that she would likewise turn to face him, wanting to see her violet eyes once more before he takes his leave. "That is the *meaning* of this life. The long wait for death to claim us. A warrior's only solace is that he might find glory before death finds him. When I am gone, what else shall remain of me, my lady, *except* the stories men tell of my deeds?"

But she does not make reply, and she does not turn to look at Beowulf.

"We should not tarry," says Wiglaf. "I'd rather do this thing by daylight than by dark."

So Hrothgar bids them farewell and promises new riches upon their return, coffers of silver and gold. And then Beowulf and Wiglaf follow Unferth from the bedchamber and back down to the muddy stockade.

13

The Pact

They find the uplander of whom Hrothgar spoke tending to his horse in the stables, not far from the village gates. He is named Agnarr, tall and wiry and old enough to be Beowulf's own father, and his beard is almost as white as freshly fallen snow. Only by the sheerest happenstance did he escape the slaughter of the previous evening, having business elsewhere in the village, and now he is readying for the hard ride back to his farm. At first, when Unferth asks him to tell all he knows of the monsters and the whereabouts of their lair, the man is suspicious and reluctant to speak of the matter.

"Are these days not evil enough without such talk?" he asks, and lays a heavy wool blanket across the back of his piebald mare. The horse is nervous and snorts and stamps her hooves in the hay. "You see? *She* knows what visited us in the night."

"If these days be evil," says Beowulf, handing Agnarr his saddle, a heavy contraption of leather and wood, "then is it not our place to make them less so?"

The old man takes the saddle from Beowulf and stands staring indecisively back at Unferth and the two Geats. "Have you seen the tracks?" he asks. "They are everywhere this morning. I do not doubt the spoor would be easy enough to follow back across the moors."

"There is the forest," Unferth says, "and bogs, and many stony places where we might lose the trail."

"Are you Beowulf?" asks Agnarr. "The one who took the monster Grendel's arm?"

"One and the same," replies Beowulf. "But it seems I did not finish the job I came here to do. Tell me what you know, and I may yet put an end to this terror."

Agnarr stares at the Geat a very long while, his hesitancy plain to see, but at last he takes a deep breath and then begins to speak.

"It is an *ancient* terror," the old man sighs, then saddles the mare. "In my day, I have glimpsed them from afar, the pair of them, if indeed they *be* what troubles the King's hall. They might be trolls, I have supposed, or they might be something that has no proper name. The one you fought, Grendel, and another, which looked almost like a woman. It moved like a woman moves. It had breasts—"

"We know what they *are*," says Unferth impatiently, and he glances toward the stable doors. "We would have you tell us where we might *find* them."

"As I have said, I cannot say for certain that it was she who visited Heorot last night and did this murder. I only know what I have seen."

"Where?" asks Beowulf a second time, more brusquely than before.

"I am coming to that," replies Agnarr, and he ties a heavy cloth sack onto the saddle, looping it through an iron ring. "I just wanted to be clear what I *know* and what I *do not* know."

The old man pauses, stroking his horse's mane, then continues. "These two you ask after," he says, "they do not live together, I think. Not many leagues from here, east, then north toward the coast, and past the forest, there is a tarn. Deep, it is. So deep that no man has ever sounded its bottom. But you will know it by three gnarled trees—three oaks—that grow above it, clustered upon an overhanging bank, their roots intertwined." The old man tangles his fingers tightly together to demonstrate.

"A tarn beneath three oak trees," says Beowulf.

"Aye, and the roots of those trees, they all but hide the entrance to a grotto. The tarn flows into that fell hole in the earth. I could not tell you where it reemerges, if indeed it ever does. For all I know, it flows to the sea or all the way down to Niflheim. And another thing, I have heard it told that at night something strange happens here. They say the water *burns*."

"The water burns," says Wiglaf skeptically. "And what is that supposed to mean?"

"It is only what I have heard *told*," replies Agnarr, shaking his head. He frowns and glares at Wiglaf. "I have not ever *seen* that fire for myself, nor have I any wish to do so. This is a foul place of which you have me speak. Such tales I have heard, and the things I've seen with my own eyes. Once, I stalked a hart across the bog, a mighty stag," and the old man holds his hands above his head, fingers out in imitation of the rack of a stag's antlers.

"Three of my arrows in him, *three*, and yet still he led me from the forest and right out into the marches. With my hounds, I tracked him as far as the tarn and those oaks. It was winter, you see, and we had great need of the meat, or I *never* would have followed him to that place. The hart, it might have escaped me then. It had only to plunge into those waters, where I could not follow it across to the other side. But it dared not. It *knew* about that place, whatever dwells there. Rather than face the tarn, it turned back toward my dogs and me and so found its death."

"You spin a good yarn, uplander," mutters Unferth, and he gives the man two pieces of gold. "Perhaps you should have sought your fortune as a scop instead of a farmer."

"Do not mock me." Agnarr frowns and pockets the gold. "You ask, so I tell you what I know. Seek you the merewife if you dare, if you think her your killer, seek her in her hall below the tarn. Perhaps she'll even come out, to meet *you*," and the man points at Beowulf. "The foreign hero who slew her son."

"You have told us what we need to know," says Unferth. "Now be on about your way."

"So I shall, my good lord," replies Agnarr. "But you take care, Geat. That one, Grendel's dam, the merewife, they say her son was never more than her pale shadow." And then he goes back to loading bags onto his saddle, and his piebald horse whinnies and shuffles about in its narrow stall.

"He's mad as a drunken crow," mutters Wiglaf, as the three men leave the stables, leading their own ponies out into the dim winter sunlight. "And you're mad as well, Beowulf, if you still mean to go through with this."

"You will never tire of reminding me of that, will you?" says Beowulf.

"Nay," replies Wiglaf, forcing a smile. "The painfully obvious amuses me no end."

"The tarn the old man spoke of," says Unferth, mounting his pony. "I think I know this place."

"You've seen it?" ask Beowulf.

"No, but I have heard stories. Since I was a child. I have heard there is a lake, somewhere on the far side of the wood, which was once known as *Weormgræf*, the dragon's tomb."

"I hope we're not off hunting a *dragon* now," says Wiglaf, gripping the saddlebow and pulling himself up. "I should have thought an ordinary sea troll was nuisance enough for one day."

"There is a story," continues Wiglaf. "It is said that Hrothgar's grandfather, Beow, was plagued by a *fyrweorm*, and that he tracked it to a bottomless lake across the moors, where he wounded it mortally with a golden spear. The dying dragon sank into the lake, which steamed and bubbled from its flames, and was never seen again. The story says that the waters still burn at night, poisoned by the *fyrweorm*'s blood."

Beowulf is still leading his pony by the reins. They are not far from the gates and guardhouse now. "You think Agnarr's tarn is *Weormgræf*?" he asks Unferth.

"Fire on water," replies Unferth, and shrugs. "You think perhaps that's a coincidence? Or maybe these lands are fair teeming with combustible tarns?"

"We shall see for ourselves soon enough," says Beowulf, and before long they are outside the gates of Heorot and riding swiftly across the moors toward a dark and distant line of trees.

It is late day by the time the three riders at last find their way out of the shadow of the old forest beyond the moorlands and begin searching for some way across the bog. A low mist lies over everything, and the air here stinks of marsh gas and pungent herbs and the stagnant, brackish water. The ponies, which gave them no trouble either on the moors or beneath those ominous trees, have become skittish and timid, flaring their nostrils and shying away from many of the pools.

There are flocks of crows here, and Beowulf wonders if they are perhaps the merewife's spies. She might have other spies, as well, he thinks, for there must surely be some vile magic about her. No doubt she may command lesser beasts to do her bidding. The crows circle overhead and caw loudly, or they watch from the limbs and stumps of blighted trees that have sunk in the mire.

"It is hopeless," despairs Wiglaf. "We will not find a way across, not on horseback. The ground here is too soft."

"What ground," says Beowulf, looking out across the marches. "There is hardly a solid hillock to be seen. I fear you are right, Wiglaf. From here we will have to continue on foot."

"I am not so great a swimmer as you," Wiglaf reminds him. "I'm no sort of swimmer at all."

"Don't worry. I will not let you drown," says Beowulf, who then turns to Unferth. "Someone should stay behind with the horses. There are wolves about, and bears, too. I've seen their tracks."

"I'm actually very good with horses," says Wiglaf, and Beowulf ignores him.

Unferth gazes out across the bog, then back toward the dark forest, not yet so very far behind them. Beowulf can see the indecision in his eyes, the fear and also the relief that he has gone this far and will be expected to go no farther.

"I would not have it said I was a coward," Unferth tells Beowulf. "But I agree it's no use trying to force our mounts across that dismal morass. They might bolt. They could become mired and drown."

"I could drown," says Wiglaf.

"Then you will wait for us, Unferth," says Beowulf, as he slides off the back of his pony and sinks up past his ankles in the bog. "Ride back to where the forest ends and wait there. Do not let the ponies wander or be eaten, as I do not fancy walking all the way back to Heorot."

Unferth takes the reins of Beowulf's pony. "If you think that the wisest course," he says.

"I do. I will carry Hrunting, and so men will say it was the sword of Unferth that cut the demon's head from off her shoulders."

"Aye," mutters Wiglaf, dismounting with a loud splash. "His sword, if *not* his hands."

"I think there's already a fish in my boot," moans Wiglaf, and kicks at a thick tuft of weeds.

"If you do not return—" begins Unferth.

"Give us until the morning," says Beowulf, frowning at Wiglaf. "If we have not returned by first light, ride back to Hrothgar and prepare what defenses you may against the return of Grendel's mother. If we fail to kill her, we may yet succeed in doubling her wrath."

"And *there's* a cheery thought," adds Wiglaf.

And without another word, Unferth pulls back on his pony's reins, and soon he is leading the three ponies back the way they've come, toward the western edge of the bog. Beowulf and Wiglaf do not linger to watch him go, but press on eastward, locating what few substantial footholds they can among the thickets of bracken and the tall clumps of grass. Often their feet drop straight through what had seemed like firm earth, swallowed up to the knees by the mud and muck. Then much effort is required to struggle free of the sucking, squelching peat, only to find themselves hip deep a few steps later.

To take his mind off the possibility of drowning or the slimy things that might be waiting in the wide, still pools, Wiglaf talks, as much to himself as to Beowulf. He first relates what he can recall of a saga he heard from one of Hrothgar's scops—how a Danish princess, Hildeburh, married Finn, a Frisian king, and how much grief and bloodshed inevitably followed. But then Wiglaf forgets exactly how the tale ends—though he knows it has something or another to do with Jutland—and so switches to the daring feats of Sigurd Dragonslayer and his sword, Gram, and how, by tasting the heart's blood of a slain *fyrweorm*, Sigurd came to know the language of birds.

"If I but had the heart of a dragon," says Beowulf, "then perhaps I could learn what all these blasted crows are squawking about." And he points at three of them perched on a flat stone at the center of one of the pools.

"Oh, that's easy," replies Wiglaf. "They're only telling us we are imbeciles and fools, and that we will taste very good, once the maggots find us and we've ripened a day or three."

"You speak birdish?" asks Beowulf, stopping and peering ahead into the fog.

"No," says Wiglaf. "Only crow. And a little raven. It is a skill peculiar to the doomed sons of fishwives."

At that moment there is a sudden gust of sea-scented wind, one of the few the two Geats have felt since beginning their long slog across the marches, and it briefly opens up a gap in the mists before them.

"Look there," says Wiglaf, pointing north. Only fifty yards or so in that direction, the bog breaks off, as the land grows abruptly higher. And there is a steep bank at the edge of a steaming tarn, and atop the bank grow three enormous oaks, their gnarled roots tangled together like serpents slithering down to meet the water's edge. There is a dark gap in the roots, and even from this distance, Beowulf can see that the water is flowing sluggishly into the gap and vanishing under the bank. Before much longer, they've reached the nearer shore of the tarn and can see that there is an oily scum floating on its surface, an iridescent sheen that seems to twist and writhe in the fading daylight.

"Dragon's blood?" asks Wiglaf.

"The old man spoke true," Beowulf replies and then begins picking his way along the edge of the pool toward the bank and the opening in the tree roots.

"A damn shame, that," sighs Wiglaf. "I was starting to hope he'd made the whole thing up."

Beowulf is the first to gain solid ground, a barren hump of rocky soil near the entrance of the cave. There is still a patch of snow here, blackened by frozen blood. The corpse of one of Hrothgar's men lies half-in the tarn, half-out, mauled and stiff. It has attracted a hungry swarm of fish and crabs, and one of the crows is perched on its broken back.

"This must be the place," says Beowulf, and he curses and throws a stone at the crow. He misses, but the bird caws and flies away. Beowulf draws Hrunting from its scabbard and turns away from the dead man, toward the entrance to the merewife's den.

"Poor bastard," says Wiglaf, when he sees the corpse. "Beowulf, you do not want to meet this water demon in her own element."

"I know."

"Do you want me to go in with you?"

"No," Beowulf replies. "I should do this alone. That's how she wants it."

"Yes," says Wiglaf, drawing his own sword and coming to stand at Beowulf's side. "Which seems to me ample reason for me to go with you. You know that I will. You have but to ask."

"I know," Beowulf tells him.

Then neither of them says anything more for a time. They stand there watching the constantly shifting rainbow patterns playing across the dark water flowing into the cave, its entrance starkly framed by a snarl of oaken roots. *Almost anything might be waiting for me in there,* thinks Beowulf. *Almost anything at all.*

"It's getting dark," Wiglaf says finally. "You'll need a torch. I wouldn't mind having one of my own, to tell you the gods' own truth."

"Do you still have your tinderbox?" asks Beowulf. "Is it still dry?"

Wiglaf fumbles about inside his cloak and pulls a small bronze box from one pocket. The lid is engraved with a single rune, Sôwilô, the sun's rune. He opens the box, inspecting the flint and tiny bundle of straw tucked inside. "Seems that way," he tells Beowulf.

"The farmer, he said the water burns," and Beowulf nods toward the oily tarn.

"Well, old Agnarr's been right about everything else. Let me find a dry bough and we'll see." And Wiglaf climbs the bank to higher ground and hunts about beneath the oaks, returning with a sturdy bit of branch about as long as his forearm. Next he tears a strip of wool from the inside of his cloak and squats down beside the pool to soak it in the water.

"You're a handy fellow," says Beowulf.

"So they tell me," laughs Wiglaf, but then there's a loud splash from the tarn, and by the time he and Beowulf look up, there are only ripples spreading out across the surface. Wiglaf glances up at Beowulf. "Care for a swim?" he asks.

"A *funny* handy fellow," Beowulf replies, keeping both his eyes on the pool. "Grendel's dam is not the only monster haunting this lake," he says, for now he can see sinuous forms moving about just beneath the surface, the coils of something like an eel, but grown almost large as a whale. Wiglaf sees it, too, and he takes the strip of wool from the water and scrambles quickly away from the shore.

One of the coils rises slowly from the water, its green-black hide glistening in the twilight before it slips back into the deep.

"Maybe Hrothgar's grandfather lied about killing the dragon," says Wiglaf. "Could be he only wounded it."

"Finish the torch," Beowulf tells him.

"Could be it had babies."

"Finish the torch," Beowulf says again, and he reaches for the golden horn of Hrothgar, still dangling from a loop on his belt. "You can keep the wee dragons busy while I take care of the she-troll."

"I'll make a lovely morsel," snorts Wiglaf, tying the damp wool securely about one end of the branch. Soon, with a few sparks from his flint, the bough has become a roaring torch. "The water burns," he says, and forces a smile, passing the brand to Beowulf.

"I will see you again, my friend Wiglaf, and soon," Beowulf tells him, then, before Wiglaf can reply, Beowulf wades into the pool and disappears through the opening in the tangle of roots. Briefly, the hollow place beneath the trees glows yellow-orange with the torch's light. When the entrance has grown dark again, Wiglaf moves farther away from the tarn, climbing back up the bank to sit out of the wind among the oaks. He lays his sword across his lap and watches the water and the things moving about just beneath it, and tries to remember the end of the story of Hildeburh and the Frisian king.

The passage below the trees is narrow, and Beowulf stands near the entrance for a time, the cold water from the tarn flowing slowly about his knees. The ceiling of the tunnel is high enough that he does not have to stoop or worry about striking his head. He holds the brand in his left hand, Hrunting in his right, and the torchlight causes the walls of the cave to glitter and gleam brilliantly. Never before has he seen stone quite like this, neither granite nor limestone, something the color of slate, yet pocked with clusters of quartz crystals, and where the roots of the trees have pushed through from above, they have been covered over the countless centuries with a glossy coating of dripstone, entombed though they might yet be alive.

Don't tarry here, he thinks. *Do this thing quick as you can, and be done with it.* And so Beowulf follows the glittering tunnel deeper into the hillside, and when he has gone only a hundred or so steps, it opens out into a great chamber or cavern. Here the water spilling in from the tarn has formed an underground lake. He can only guess at its dimensions, as the torchlight is insufficient to penetrate very far into that gloom there below the earth. But he thinks it must be very wide, and he tries not to consider what creatures might lurk within its secret depths. The waters are black and still, and rimmed all about with elaborate stalactite and stalagmite formations.

The teeth of the dragon, thinks Beowulf, but he pushes the unpleasant thought aside. They are only stone, and he has seen the likes of them before. He takes a few steps into the cavern, playing the torchlight out across the pool, when suddenly it gutters and goes out, as though it has been snuffed by a breath both unseen and unfelt. The blackness rushes in about him, and it's little consolation that a lesser man might now retreat and relight the torch.

The oil from the tarn has burned out, he tells himself. *It was no more than that. I am alone in the dark, but it is only the dark of any cave.*

But then, suddenly, an eldritch glow comes to take the place of the extinguished torch, a bright chartreuse light like the shine of a thousand fireflies sparking all at once. And Beowulf realizes that this new illumination is coming from Hrothgar's golden horn, hanging on his belt. He reaches for it cautiously, for surely anything that shines with such radiance must be hot to the touch. But the metal is as cool as ever. Cold, in fact. He tosses the useless torch aside and unhooks the horn from his belt. There is nothing healthy in this new light, nothing natural, though he cannot deny it holds a fascination and that there is some unnerving beauty about it.

"So the demon shuns the light of the world," he says, speaking only half to himself, captivated by the horn's unearthly splendor. "But it also knows I cannot find my way down to it without some lamp to guide me, so I am given *this*, a ghostly beacon fit only for dwarves, that I may arrive and yet not offend her eyes."

For a moment, he stares out across the lake, seeing nothing, hearing nothing but the steady drip of water from the cavern's roof and the indistinct babble of the stream from the tunnel flowing gently about his legs into the pool.

"Show yourself, *aeglaeca!*" he shouts, expecting if not her answer at least the company of his own echo. But there comes neither. Only the sounds of water, which seem to make the silence that much more absolute.

"This is not *like* you!" Beowulf shouts, much louder than before. "You were bold enough when you stole into Heorot to murder sleeping men! Have you now lost your *nerve*, she-troll?" But once again there is no reply and no echo.

"*Then I shall come down to you!*" he bellows as loudly as he can. And Beowulf begins to undress, for his iron breastplate and mail are heavy and would surely drag him straight to the muddy bottom of the subterranean lake. "We will meet in whatever dank place you now cower," he cries out across the water, "if that is how you would have it!"

Does she hear me? Is she listening? Is she crouched out there somewhere, biding her time, laughing at me?

Beowulf leaves his armor and belt, his tunic and breeches and boots, bundled together and lying in a dry place at the edge of the pool. Carrying only Hrunting and the golden horn, which is glowing even more brightly than before, he wades out into the icy water. The floor of the lake is slimy underneath his bare feet, and once or twice he slips, almost losing his balance. When the water has risen as high as his chest, Beowulf draws as deep a breath as he may and slips below the surface. Holding the horn out before him like a lantern, he swims along the bottom. The pool is stained with peat from the tarn and by silt, and the glow of Hrothgar's horn reaches only a few feet into the red-brown murk. But soon he can see the bottom, strewn with the bones of men and many sorts of animals jumbled together—horses and wild boars, deer and auroch, the toothsome skulls of great bears and the wide, pronged antlers of bull moose. Her dining hall, then, this lake below the hill, and for long ages must she have returned to this place with her victims, feeding where none will disturb her.

Nestled in among the bones are gigantic white crayfish, their spiny shells gone as pale as milk down here in the eternal night, and they wave their huge pincers menacingly as Beowulf passes. There are other things, as well, eels as white as the crayfish and large as sharks, their long jaws armed with row upon row of needle-sharp teeth. Whenever they come too near, he fends them off with Unferth's sword. Only once does the blade find its mark, carving a long gash in a serpentine body and sending the eel slithering away to safety. Blood clouds the water, making it still harder for Beowulf to find his way.

He rises for another gulp of air, only to discover that this far out the ceiling of the cave has grown unexpectedly low, now mere inches above the pool. He can see that it slopes down to meet the water only a few feet ahead, so this will be his last breath unless he chooses to turn back.

"If the Norns decree I should survive this ordeal," he says, wiping water from his eyes, "then by the gods, I *will* teach you to swim, Wiglaf." And then he takes another breath and submerges again.

Below him, the grisly carpet of bones has thinned out, and Beowulf soon comes upon an immense cleft in the lake's floor, a wide black chasm beckoning him on to still-greater and more terrible depths. A weak but persistent current flowing into the hole tugs at him, and he hesitates only a moment, sensing this must surely be the path that will lead him to Grendel's mother. There is no knowing how far it might extend, if it will ever come to another pocket of air, but he pushes on, regardless.

And before Beowulf has gone very far, the current has grown markedly stronger, so that he hardly has to swim at all. The chasm narrows, becoming another tunnel, and the current sucks him helplessly along its moss-slicked course. The golden horn glows more brightly than ever, but it is cold comfort indeed that he will not die in utter darkness. The spent air filling his lungs is aching to escape, and his heart pounds loudly in his ears. The tunnel becomes narrower still, so that he is dragged roughly along this stone gullet, his flesh cut and battered by the pockets of quartz crystals and by every irregularity in the rock. And still the tunnel grows narrower. Soon, he thinks, he will be able to go no farther, so constricted will be this passageway, and as he lacks the strength and air to fight his way back against the current, he will drown here. This will be his grave, and the mother of the demon Grendel will have won. He feels his grip on Hrunting growing slack, and the golden horn almost slips from his fingers. Oblivion begins to press in at the edges of his mind, and Beowulf closes his eyes and waits to die.

But then the tunnel releases its hold on him, and he is buoyed suddenly upward, and Beowulf finds himself gasping at the surface of another underground pool. The current carries him onto a rocky shore, where he lies coughing and vomiting gouts of salty water, coming slowly back to himself. He opens his stinging eyes, blinking and squinting, trying to force them into focus.

"Where have you brought me to, demon?" he croaks, then begins to cough again.

"To me," replies a voice from somewhere overhead, a voice that is at once beautiful and loathsome and fearsome to hear. "Is that not where you wished to find yourself, here with me?"

Beowulf rises slowly onto hands and knees, rough bits of gravel biting into his exposed skin. "You are the mother of the monster Grendel?" he asks the voice, then coughs up more water.

"He was my son," the voice says. "But, I assure you, he was no monster."

"Your voice," says Beowulf, rolling over onto his back, turning to face the voice and brandishing Hrunting. "Your voice . . . it's not what I would have expected of a sea hag and the mother of a troll."

"He was no troll," the voice replies, and now Beowulf thinks that there's a hint of anger there.

"*Show* yourself, beast!" Beowulf calls out as best he can, his voice still raw from having swallowed, then spat up so much of the pool. "Let me *see* you."

"In time. Do not hurry so to meet your doom."

"Bitch," he hisses and spits into the mud. Sitting upright, fighting back dizziness and nausea, his vision begins to clear. And at last Beowulf looks for the first time upon the strange realm into which the current has delivered him. At once he knows this can be no ordinary cavern, but instead the belly of some colossus. The *fyrweorm* slain by Beow, perhaps, just as Unferth said, and now its calcified ribs rise toward the ceiling like the arches of Hel's own hall. They glow blue-green with an unearthly phosphorescence, as do the walls, and Beowulf sees that there is a mighty hoard of treasure heaped all about the floor and banked high along the walls. In some places, the stones and those titan ribs are encrusted with a dazzling mantle of gold and gemstones.

Slowly, he gets to his feet, clutching Hrunting and holding Hrothgar's horn out before him. Its shine illuminates more of the cavern floor before him, and Beowulf can see one corner heaped high with the rotting corpses of recently dead thanes, their armor ripped apart as though it had been no more than birch bark, their bellies gutted, their faces obliterated by claws and teeth. And Beowulf also sees the stone slab where the body of Grendel now rests. The monster's severed arm lies propped in place against its mangled shoulder. The corpse is a shriveled, pitiable thing, a gray husk devoid of any of its former threat, and Beowulf finds it hard to believe this could be the same creature he battled two nights before. Above the corpse and the slab hangs a broadsword, sheathed and mounted on iron brackets, a sword so large and heavy no mortal man could ever hope to lift it, a sword that might well have been forged in the furnaces of the Frost Giants.

"Does it *pain* you," Beowulf says, taking a single cautious step toward the altar, "to see him dead? To see him lying broken and so diminished?"

"You do not yet *know* pain," the voice says. "As yet, that word means *nothing* to you, little man." And then there's a scrabbling, scratching sound from somewhere close behind him, and Beowulf turns quickly about, peering into the shadows and the eerie blue-green light of the cavern for its source. But there's no sign of whatever might have made the noise, no evidence except the taunting voice to say he's not alone. Beowulf holds the golden horn still higher.

"I see you brought me *treasure*," the voice says.

"I have brought you nothing but death," he replies.

And now Beowulf catches sight of something there amongst the hoarded riches, what appears to be a golden statue, though a statue of what he cannot say. Perhaps it was an idol, long ago, for he has heard stories of ancient cults and the old religion once practiced by the Danes, of blood sacrifices made by men and women who did not hold Odin as the highest among the Æsir. Sacrifices to goddesses said to inhabit especially deep lakes, though this statue surely resembles no goddess. It is a grotesque thing, as though its creators had in mind some hideous amalgam of a lizard and a sea beast. Its eyes are lapis lazuli, and its coarse mane seems to have been woven from a golden thread. Beowulf turns back toward the altar, and he gazes in awe at the giant sword hanging there above Grendel's body.

"Your beautiful horn," the voice says. "It glows so . . . delightfully."

And once again he hears that scurrying from somewhere close behind him, and this time Beowulf does not turn, but only glances back over his shoulder. Light reflecting off the pool dances across the walls of the cave and across the statue. Something seems different about it, as though it subtly shifted position—the angle of its head, the arrangement of its reptilian limbs—when he looked away. But this must be only some trick of the cave's peculiar lighting, some deceit his eyes have played upon his mind.

"Show yourself," he says. "I have not come so far, through flood and muck, to bandy words with a shade."

"You have come because I have *called* for you," the voice replies, and now Beowulf does turn to face the statue once again. But it is vanished, gone. Before he can long ponder its disappearance, there's a loud splash from the pool, as though something has fallen from the wall into the water. Only a loose stone, perhaps, but he raises Hrunting and watches the pool.

"I have come to avenge those who were slain while they slept," he says. "I have come to seek justice for the thirteen good men who sailed the whale's-road and fought with me."

Ripples begin spreading out across the surface, creating small waves that lap against the shore, and from the shimmering water rises the likeness of a woman, entirely naked and more beautiful than any Beowulf has ever before beheld or imagined. There is an odd metallic glint to her complexion, as though her skin has been dusted with gold, and all about her there is a glow like the rising sun after a long and bitter night. Her flaxen hair is pulled back into a single braid, so long that it reaches almost to her feet. Her pale blue eyes shine bright and pure, as though blazing with some inner fire. And then she speaks, and it is the same voice that has mocked him since he entered the dragon's belly.

"Are you the one they call Beowulf?" she asks. "The wolf of the bees? The *bear*? Such a strong man you are. A man with the strength of a king in him. The king you will one day become."

"What do you want of me, demon?"

She moves gracefully, fearlessly, toward him, somehow treading on the *surface* of the water. Her long braid swings from side to side, seeming almost to undulate with a life all its own, flicking like a serpent or the tail of an excited animal.

"I know that underneath your glamour you're as much a monster as my son Grendel. Perhaps more so."

Beowulf takes a step back from the edge of the pool.

"My glamour?" he asks.

"One needs a glamour to become a king," she replies. "That men will follow you. That they will *fear* you."

And now, in hardly the time it takes to draw a breath, she has reached the shore and is standing before him, her lustrous skin and twitching braid dripping onto the stones at her feet.

"You will not bewitch me," he growls, and slashes at her throat with Hrunting, expecting to see her head parted cleanly from her shoulders and toppling back into the pool from whence she has risen. But she grabs the blade, moving more quickly than his eyes can follow. She holds it fast, and try though he might, Beowulf cannot wrest it from her grip. She smiles, and dark blood oozes from her palm, flowing onto the blade of Unferth's ancestral sword.

"And I know," she says, gazing directly into Beowulf's eyes. "A man like you could own the greatest tale ever sung. The story of your bravery, your greatness, would live on when everything now alive is gone to dust."

And now Beowulf sees that where her blood has touched the iron blade it has begun to steam and dissolve, the way icicles melt in bright sunshine.

"Beowulf," she says, "it has been a *long* time since a man has come to visit me."

And then she pushes hard against Hrunting, shedding more of her corrosive blood, and the entire blade is liquefied in an instant, spilling onto the ground between them in dull spatters of silver. The hilt falls from Beowulf's hand and clatters loudly against the rocks, and his fingers have begun to tingle. And he feels her inside his head, her thoughts moving in amongst his own. He gasps and shakes his head, trying to force her out.

"I don't need . . . a sword . . . to kill you."

"Of course you don't, my love."

"I slew your son . . . without a sword."

"I know," she purrs. "You are so very strong."

She reaches out, her fingertips brushing gently, lovingly, against his cheek, and already the gash in her palm has healed. Beowulf can see himself reflected in her blue eyes, and his pupils have swollen until his own eyes seem almost black.

"You took a son from me," she says, and she leans forward, whispering into his ear. "Give me a son, brave thane, wolf of the bees, first born of Ecgtheow. *Stay* with me. *Love* me."

"I *know* what you are," mumbles Beowulf breathlessly, lost and wandering in her now. Somehow, she has swallowed him alive, and like Hrunting, he is melting, undone by magic and the acid flowing in her demon's veins.

"Shhhhh," she whispers, and strokes his face. "Do not be afraid. There is no need to fear me. Love me . . . and I shall weave you riches beyond imagination. I shall make you the greatest king of men who has ever lived."

"You lie," says Beowulf, and it requires all his strength to manage those two words. They are only a wisp passing across his lips, a death rattle, an ill-defined echo of himself. He struggles to remember what has brought him to this devil's lair. He tries to recall Wiglaf's voice, the sight of dead men dangling from the rafters of Heorot and the screams of women, the sea hag that visited him in a dream, disguised as Queen Wealthow. But they are all flimsy, fading scraps, those memories, nothing so urgent they could ever distract him from *her*.

The merewife reaches down and runs her fingers along the golden horn, Hrothgar's prize, Beowulf's reward, then she slips her arms around Beowulf's waist and draws him nearer to her. She kisses his bare chest and the soft flesh of his throat.

"To you I swear, as long as this golden horn remains in my keeping, you will forever be King of the Danes. I do not *lie*. I have *ever* kept my promises and I ever shall."

And then she takes the horn from him. He doesn't try to stop her. And she holds him tighter still.

"Forever strong, mighty . . . and all-powerful. Men will bow before you and serve you loyally, even unto death. This I promise."

Her skin is sweating gold, and her eyes gnaw their way deeper into his soul, and Beowulf remembers when he swam against Brecca and something he first mistook for a herald of the Valkyries pulled him under the waves . . .

"This I *swear*," the merewife whispers.

"I remember you," he says.

"Yes," she replies. "You do." And her lips find his, and all he has ever desired in all his life is for this kiss to never end.

14

Hero

It is only an hour or so past dawn when Beowulf reemerges from the tangled curtain of roots and the tunnel below the three oaks growing there on the high bank beside the tarn. There is a gentle but persistent tug about his legs from the languid current, all that water draining away, flowing down the dragon's throat, gurgling down to its innards. He stands watching the white morning mists rising lazily from the tarn, this dark lake so long ago named *Weormgræf* by people who had heard the lay of Beow's triumph here or by travelers who had glimpsed for themselves its awful inhabitants. And at first, Beowulf thinks that he's alone, that Wiglaf has given him up for dead, that Wiglaf and Unferth have ridden together back to Heorot to give the king and queen the news of his demise beneath the hill and to prepare for the merewife's inevitable return. But then he hears footsteps and sees Wiglaf coming quickly across the rocky shore toward him.

"You bastard!" shouts Wiglaf happily, and there is relief in his voice and sleepless exhaustion in his eyes. "I thought you'd swum away home without me!"

"The thought crossed my mind but briefly," Beowulf calls back, and then he splashes to the muddy edge of the tarn and hauls himself out of the oily water. He drops the heavy wool sack at his feet, the obscene lading he's carried all the way back up from the merewife's hall, and sits down beside it. It's colder above ground than it was below, and there is the raw wind, as well, and he rubs his hands together for warmth.

"I thought sure you had drowned," Wiglaf says, standing over him. "The trees said no, you'd been eaten. There was a crow who swore you'd only lost your way and died of fright."

"And here I've disappointed the lot of you."

"I'm sure it couldn't be helped."

Wiglaf squats in front of Beowulf, eyeing the woolen sack, which has begun to leak some sticky black substance onto the stones.

"Is it done, then?" he asks.

"It's done," Beowulf replies, and Wiglaf, yet more relieved, nods his head.

"We're going to have to walk back, you know," Wiglaf sighs and turns to gaze out across the bog toward the distant forest. "You told him to wait until first light and no longer."

"A slight miscalculation," says Beowulf. "Ah, well. Likely, it will not kill us. And think how surprised they will be to see us, after Unferth has told them we have perished in the night."

"Aye," replies Unferth. "But I'll not be carrying *that*," and he points at the leaking sack.

"You've become an old woman, Wiglaf," Beowulf tells him. "But I think we'd already established that."

"There are no more of them? No more monsters?"

"It is done," Beowulf says again, and rubs at his eyes. "Heorot Hall is safe."

"And we can sail for home?"

"Unless you've a better idea," says Beowulf, and he gets to his feet again. Staring out over the still, black lake and its rainbow shimmer, he wonders if Wiglaf could get another fire going, and if the water truly *would* burn, as Agnarr said it has in times past, and if the flames might find the path down to the belly of the beast.

"We should get going," Wiglaf says. "With luck, we can make it back before nightfall."

"With luck," Beowulf agrees, and soon they have left the tarn far behind and are picking their way back across the bog toward the ancient forest and the wide moorlands beyond.

* * *

And, indeed, the sun has not yet set when the two Geats step wearily across the threshold of Hrothgar's mead hall. They find Hrothgar there with his queen and Unferth and the small number of able-bodied men who yet remain in the king's service. The corpses have been taken down from the rafters, and some of the blood has been scrubbed away. But the hall still stinks of the slaughter.

"It is a miracle!" bellows the old man on his throne. "Unferth, he said—"

"—only what he was bidden to tell you, my lord," says Beowulf, and he unties the wool sack and dumps its contents out upon the floor. The head of Grendel thuds loudly against the flagstones and rolls a few feet, coming to a stop at the edge of the dais. Its eyes bulge from their sockets, clouded and empty, and its mouth is agape, the swollen tongue lolling from withered lips and cracked yellow fangs. Wealthow gasps and turns her face away.

"It is *dead*, my lady," says Beowulf. "Do not fear to look upon the face of Grendel, for it will bring no more harm to you or your people. When I'd finished with the demon's mother, I cut off the brute's head that none here could doubt his undoing."

"It is over," says Wiglaf, standing directly behind Beowulf. "True to his word, my lord has slain the fiends."

Hrothgar's disbelieving eyes dart from Wealthow to Unferth, then to Beowulf and back to the severed head, his face betraying equal parts astonishment and horror, awe and joy at the gruesome prize the Geat has laid at his feet.

"Our curse . . . it has been lifted?" he asks, and glances back to Wealthow again.

"You see here before you the unquestionable proof," answers Beowulf, and he nudges Grendel's head with the toe of his boot. "I tracked the mother of Grendel to her filthy burrow, far below earth and water, and there we fought. All night we struggled. She was ferocious, and it might easily have gone another way. *She* might have emerged the victor, for such was her fury. But the Fates weaving their skein beneath the roots of the World Ash decreed otherwise, that I should triumph and return to you this day with these glad tidings."

And now a cheer rises from those few of Hrothgar's thanes there in the hall who have survived the attacks, and also from the women who have come to clean away the blood.

"Son of Healfdene," continues Beowulf, raising his voice to be heard, "Lord of the Scyldings, I pledge that you may now sleep safe with your warriors here beneath the roof of Heorot Hall. There is no more need of fear, no more threat of harm to you or your people. It is over."

"I see," says Hrothgar, speaking hardly above a whisper. "Yes, I can see this." But to Beowulf, the king seems lost in some secret inner turmoil, and the happiness on the old man's face appears little more than a poorly constructed mask. There is a madness in his eyes, and Beowulf looks to Queen Wealthow, but she has turned away.

"For fifty years," says Hrothgar, "did I rule this country, the Ring-Danes' land. I have defended it in time of war . . . and I have fought with the sword and with ax and spear against many invading tribes. Indeed . . . I had come to believe that all my foes were vanquished. But then Grendel struck . . . and I believed at last there had come among us an enemy that *no man* would ever defeat." And Hrothgar leans forward in his seat and raises his voice.

"I despaired . . . and my heart . . . my savaged heart abandoned all hope. And now I praise Odin Allfather that I have lived to see this head, torn from off that hateful demon and dripping gore . . . and to hear that his foul dam has been slain as well." And then he turns to Unferth. "Take it from my sight, Unferth! Nail it up *high*, that *all* will see—"

"*No*," says Wealthow, turning to face her husband once more. "No, not again. Once already has this hall been profaned by such a hideous trophy, and I will *not* see it done again."

"Wealthow, my love—" Hrothgar begins, but she cuts him off a second time.

"No. I will *not* invite some new horror into our midst by flaunting Lord Beowulf's victory over the fiends. No one among us can say that there may not yet be others, watching and waiting their turn, and we will not provoke them. I will not have it, husband."

Hrothgar frowns and furrows his brow, running his fingers through his gray beard. He stares deep into the dead eyes of Grendel, as if seeking there some hindmost spark of life, some ghost that might yet linger, undetected by the others. But then the king takes a deep breath and nods, conceding to the will of his queen.

"So be it." He sighs and leans back on his throne. "Take it away . . . hurl it into the sea. Let us be *done* with it. Never let us look upon that face again."

Unferth nods to two of his thanes, and soon the severed head has been speared on long pikes and carried off to a balcony. Another cheer rises from the hall when the head of Grendel is flung over the railing to tumble and bounce down the cliff face and at last be swallowed by the sea.

And the next evening, though the blood of those slain by Grendel's dam has not yet been washed completely from the walls and floors and roof beams of Heorot Hall—and likely it never shall be—the feasting begins. The world has been rid of monsters, and finally the horned hall can serve the purpose for which it was built. Finally, the men of Hrothgar's land can feast and drink there and forget the hardships and dangers of the hard world beyond those walls. And the feast honors Beowulf, son of Ecgtheow, and Wiglaf and the thirteen Geats who have died that this might be so. A long table has been carried onto the throne dais, and there the two men who braved the marches to slay the merewife and return with the head of Grendel sit in a place of distinction. The hall is alive with the boisterous din of merrymaking, with laughter and bawdy jokes and drunken curses, with song and the harpestry, with carefree, blissful celebration untainted by dread or trepidation. The cooking fire sends smoke and delicious smells up the chimney and out into the cold night. The fattest hog that could be found is hefted onto the king's table, its skin steaming and crisp.

Unferth is seated on Beowulf's left, and he leans close, summoning the confidence to ask a question that has been on his mind since the Geat's return from the wilderness, for the mead has given him courage.

"Beowulf, mighty monster-killer. There is something I must ask. Hrunting, my father's sword, did it help you to destroy the hag?"

Beowulf lifts his mead cup, surprised only the question did not come sooner. "It . . . it did," he replies, faltering but a little as he shapes the story he will tell Unferth. "Indeed, I believe the demon hag would not be dead *without* it."

Unferth looks pleased, so Beowulf takes up the knife from his plate and continues.

"I *plunged* Hrunting into the chest of Grendel's mother," and he demonstrates by sticking his knife deeply into the ribs of the roast pig. "When I drew it free from her corpse"—and here he pulls the knife from the pig—"the creature sprang back to life . . . so I plunged it once *more* into the she-troll's chest . . ."

Again Beowulf stabs the roast pig. "And there it will *stay*, friend Unferth, even until Ragnarök."

"Until Ragnarök," whispers Unferth, a note of awe in his voice, and he nods his head, then takes Beowulf's hand and kisses it. "Our people shall be grateful until the end of time," he says.

Beowulf finishes off the mead in his cup; Unferth's gratitude at his easy, convincing lie has provoked a sudden and unexpected pang of guilt, an emotion with which Beowulf is more or less unfamiliar.

Better to tell them what they need to hear, he thinks, then catches Wiglaf watching him from across the table. And now Queen Wealthow is refilling his cup, and he smiles for her. She is seated at his right, and pours from a large wooden jug carved to resemble a boar.

"I thought you might need some more drink," she says.

"Aye," replies Beowulf. "Always."

"And the golden drinking horn. Do you still have it?"

So now there's need of another lie, but this time he has it at the ready and doesn't miss a beat.

"No," he tells her. "I knew the greedy witch desired it, so I threw the horn into the bog, and she followed after it. And that's where I struck . . ." Unferth is still watching him, and Beowulf nods in his direction. ". . . with the mighty sword Hrunting," he adds, then takes a deep breath. "Once she was dead, I searched for it, but it was gone forever."

There is a faint glint of uncertainty in the queen's violet eyes, and Beowulf sees that she is perhaps not so eager to believe as Unferth, that she might have ideas of her own about what happened at the tarn. But then Hrothgar is on his feet, coming suddenly up behind Beowulf and snatching away his plain cup, dashing its contents to the floor. He seizes Beowulf by the arm.

"Then, my good wife," bellows Hrothgar, "find our hero another cup, one *befitting* so great a man. Meanwhile, the hero and I must talk."

Hrothgar, already drunken and slurring his speech, guides Beowulf away from the table and into the anteroom behind the dais. He shuts the door behind him and locks it, then drains his cup and wipes his lips on his sleeve.

"Tell me," he begins, then pauses to belch. He wipes at his mouth again and continues. "You brought back the head of Grendel. But what about the head of the *mother*?"

Beowulf scowls and plays at looking confused. "With her dead and cold, lying at the bottom on the tarn. Is it not enough to return with *one* monster's head?"

Hrothgar stares discontentedly into his empty mead cup, then tosses it aside. It bounces across the floor and rolls to a stop against the double doors leading out to the balcony overlooking the sea.

"Did you *kill* her?" he asks Beowulf. "And speak true, for I will know if you lie."

"My lord, would you like to hear the story *again*, how I struggled with that monstrous hag—"

"She is no hag, Beowulf. A demon, yes, yes, to be sure, but not a hag. We *both* know that. Now, *answer me*, damn you! *Did you kill her?*"

And Beowulf takes a step back, wishing he were anywhere but this small room, facing anyone but the King of the Danes.

I know that underneath your glamour you're as much a monster as my son Grendel, the merewife purred.

One needs a glamour to become a king. . .

"I would have an answer now," says Hrothgar.

"Would I have been allowed to escape her had I not?" asks Beowulf, answering with a question, and he suspects that Hrothgar knows the answer—the *true* answer. The old man backs away, hugging himself now and shuddering. Hrothgar wrings his hands and glances at Beowulf.

"Grendel is dead, and with my own eyes have I seen the proof," he says, and shudders again. "Not even that fiend could live on without his head. Yes, Grendel is dead. That's all that matters to me. Grendel will trouble me no more. The hag, she is *not* my curse. Not anymore."

To Beowulf, these are the words of a man fighting to convince himself of something he knows to be otherwise. They stare at each other in silence for a long moment, then Hrothgar takes the golden circlet from off his head and frowns down at it.

"They think this band of gold is all there is to being king. They think because I wear this, I am somehow wiser than they. Braver. *Better*. Is that what you believe?" he asks Beowulf.

"I could not say, my lord."

"One day," says Hrothgar, placing the crown once more on his head, "one day you will, I think. One day, you will understand the price—the *terrible* price—to be paid for her favors, and for the throne. You will *know* how a puppet feels, dangling on its strings . . ." Then he trails off and chews at his lower lip.

"My Lord Hrothgar—" Beowulf begins, but the king raises a hand to silence him. There's a mad gleam shining in the old man's eyes, and it frightens Beowulf more than the sight of any terror that might yet lurk in bogs or over foggy moors.

"No, I will speak no more of this," Hrothgar says, and he turns and unlocks the door and steps back out into the mead hall, and Beowulf follows him. When Hrothgar reaches the feasting table on the dais, he takes a place behind Wealthow's chair, and at the top of his voice, he addresses the hall.

"Listen!" he roars. "Listen to me, all of you! Because Lord Beowulf is a mighty hero. Because he killed the demon Grendel, and laid its mother in her grave. Because he lifted the curse from off this accursed, beleaguered land. And because I have no heir . . ."

Hrothgar pauses to take a breath, beads of sweat standing out on his forehead. The harpist has stopped playing, and the scop has stopped singing. Most of the hall has fallen silent and turned toward the dais. Beowulf glances at Wealthow, and she wears the mien of a frightened woman.

"Because . . ." continues Hrothgar, even louder than before. "Because all these things *are* true—and *no one* here among you may dare to say otherwise—I declare that on my death I leave all that I possess—my kingdom, my riches, my hall . . . and even my queen . . . It *all* goes to Beowulf."

Unferth rises, confused, and he glances nervously from Beowulf to Hrothgar. "But," he stammers, "my lord, *surely* you—"

"I have spoken!" bellows Hrothgar, and Unferth sits down again. "There will be no *argument.* When I am gone, Beowulf, son of Ecgtheow, shall be your king!"

And then, for the space occupied by no more than half a dozen heartbeats, a shocked silence lies heavy over the hall, a silence like storm clouds, but then it breaks apart and all those assembled under Heorot begin to cheer.

"My husband," says Queen Wealthow, her voice almost lost in the throng's hurrahs and hoorays, the cries of "Long live Hrothgar" and "All hail Beowulf," the whistling and clapping of hands. "Are you sure you know what it is you've done?"

But the king of the horned hall does not reply, only winks knowingly at her as though they share some secret. And so she glances to Unferth, who sits, hands folded on the table before him, silent, his jaw set, his teeth clenched. She knows that in earlier times, before Grendel and the coming of the Geats, that Unferth, son of Ecglaf, had believed with good cause that he would one day wear the crown and rule the kingdom of the Ring-Danes. She, too, had believed he would be Hrothgar's successor to the throne.

Hrothgar bends down and whispers in his lady's ear. His voice is thin, like high mountain air or old paper.

"I have had *my* days in the sun," he tells Wealthow. "I have had my nights with you, sweet queen, and taken my pleasures. Now, I would see another in my stead. And in my bed, as well. One who is truly worthy of these honors. One you may find both more suitable and less loathsome."

Many of the people in the hall have begun to climb onto the dais, crowding in around Beowulf, offering their congratulations and generous tributes to his bravery and future reign. He smiles, but it's an uneasy, uncertain smile, too filled up with the dizzying shock one feels when events turn too quickly, when dreams seem as real as waking thought. He glances to Wiglaf, but Wiglaf is staring deep into his mead cup, some peculiar sadness on his face, and he does not see Beowulf. And now the merewife's promises come back to him again, and might not *that* have only been a dream? Her hands upon him, her lips so cold against his?

Love me, and I shall weave you riches beyond

imagination. I shall make you the greatest king of men who has ever lived.

And now Hrothgar, son of Healfdene, grandson of Beow, turns to face him, and the old king bows, but only very slightly, and there is another deafening cheer from the hall. Then Hrothgar turns away and walks back toward the door leading to the anteroom behind the dais and then to the balcony beyond.

Queen Wealthow, feeling a sudden chill, a peculiar unease, turns to watch her husband as he takes his leave of the celebration. But she tells herself that whatever disquiet she feels is only a natural reaction to Hrothgar's startling abdication and nothing more. She watches him pass through the fire-lit anteroom and out onto the balcony, and Wealthow tells herself he needs some time alone, and so she keeps her seat and does not follow him.

Out on the balcony, the north gale whips at the old man's beard and at his robes, the breath of a giant to fuel high white waves. He faces the sea, and at his back lies his home and wife, all his lands, his kingdom and everything that he has ever done. All brave deeds and every act of cowardice, all his strengths and weaknesses, his victories and defeats. All he has loved and hated.

"Enough," he says. "I will go no farther." But the wind takes the words away and scatters them like ash. Hrothgar reaches up, removing the circlet from his head, that crown of hammered gold first worn by his great-grandfather, Shield Sheafson. He sets it safely in the lee of the low balustrade, so the wind will not carry it away.

"I will not see Ásgard," he says. "It is not meant for the eyes of men like me," and then Hrothgar steps over the balustrade and lets the abyss take him. Perhaps he hears Wealthow screaming and perhaps it is only the wind in his ears.

And in the instant before the fall has ended and he strikes the rocks, Hrothgar glimpses with watering eyes something slithering about beneath the fast-approaching waves, something plated round with glittering scales, a gilded woman with the sinuous tail of an eel, the unmistakable form of the merewife.

And only seconds later, Wealthow stands at the edge of the balcony, staring down at his body shattered there on the sea-licked granite boulders far below. By the time Beowulf reaches her side, by the time Unferth and Wiglaf and others from the hall have seen for themselves that Hrothgar is gone, she's stopped screaming. She has stuffed the knuckles of one fist into her mouth and is biting down on them to choke the sound in her throat.

And then all the sea appears to draw back, gathering itself into a towering, whitecapped surge, a wave high enough to reach the fallen king's body. It rushes forward, a crashing, frothing shroud for a broken corpse, and when it retreats, it takes Hrothgar away with it, and he passes forever from the eyes of man. Then the waves are only waves again, and the wind is only wind.

Wealthow takes her hand from her mouth. There's blood on her knuckles, tiny wounds born of her own teeth. The wind is freezing her tears upon her cheeks. "He must have fallen," she says, knowing it's a lie. "He was drunk, and he must have fallen."

Unferth has put one arm protectively about her shoulders, as though he fears she will follow her husband over the ledge. But now he sees the circlet lying where Hrothgar set it, and he releases her and stoops to pick it up. It seems unnaturally heavy in his hands, this dull ring of gold that might have been his, that he might have worn had Grendel's assault upon Heorot never begun. If he had been the man who slew the monster and its mother. But it is so very heavy, heavier than it has any right to be. Unferth turns to Beowulf and Wiglaf and the thanes who have shoved their way through the anteroom and out onto the balcony. They are all watching him, wide-eyed and silent. Unferth holds the crown up so all can see, and he looks Beowulf in the eye.

"All hail," he says, and swallows, the words sticking like dust in his throat. "All hail *King Beowulf!*"

And he places the golden circlet on Beowulf's head, glad to be rid of the crown. In years to come, he will recall the way it felt in his fingers, the weight of it, the peculiar sense that it was somehow *unclean.* For a time there is only the howling of the winter wind, the waves battering themselves against the rocky shore. But then Wealthow turns and looks upon her new king.

"You wear it well, my lord," she says, forcing a smile, and she pushes her way through the crowd, back toward the shelter of Heorot Hall. By the time she's reached the throne dais, the thanes have begun to cheer.

PART TWO

The Dragon

15

King Beowulf

And so the skein of years unwinds, the lone white eye of the moon trailing always on the heels of Sól's flaming, wolf-harried chariot—day after day and year after year, season following season as it ever has since the gods raised Midgard long ago. And even as the passage of time is constant, so are the ways of men, and so it is that on this cold day in the month of Frermánudr, but two days remaining before Yule, Beowulf, King of the Ring-Danes, sits astride his horse looking out upon the battle raging where the sea touches his land. Thirty years older than the night he killed Grendel, this Beowulf, and greedy time reckons its toll upon all things under Midgard, even heroes and the kings of men. His hair and beard are streaked with the frost that stains any long life, and his face is creased and wizened. But he might easily be mistaken for a man ten years younger, if only because his eyes still burn as brightly and his body is still strong and straight. He wears the scars of a hundred battles, but he wears them no differently than he wears the golden circlet that once crowned King Hrothgar's head.

Wiglaf, son of Weohstan, sits upon his own mount to Beowulf's right, and together, from this small bluff at the end of the moorlands, they watch the men fighting down on the shore. The Frisian invaders made landfall in the night, but in only a few hours Beowulf's archers and swordsmen, his thanes bearing axes and spears, have driven them back to the beaches. The Frisian force is in tatters, and there can be no hope left among them of victory. Even retreat seems unlikely, unless the man who commands these warriors should deign to call back his hounds. From the start, the Frisians were too few and too poorly trained to succeed in this attack, and any man still left alive among them will be fortunate to escape with his skin.

Beowulf shakes his head and shuts his eyes, wishing to see no more of this shameful, bloody scene.

"This is no longer a battle, Wiglaf," he says. "It's slaughter."

Wiglaf, also marked by age and also yet a strong man, nods toward the battle.

"The Frisians want to make themselves heroes,

my lord. They would have the bards sing of *their* deeds."

"It's going to be a short song," sighs Beowulf, opening his eyes again.

"Aye," says Wiglaf. "But can you blame them? Your legend is known from the high seas and the snow barriers to the great island kingdom. The whole world knows the lay of Beowulf and Grendel. You are the *monster slayer*."

Beowulf shakes his head again and laughs, but there is not the least trace of humor in the sound.

"*We* are the monsters now," he says, making no effort to hide his disdain and self-loathing. "We are become the trolls and demons."

"They come to find the hero," says Wiglaf, and he points to the handful of Frisian invaders who have not yet fallen.

"The time of heroes is dead, Wiglaf. The Christ God has killed it . . . leaving mankind nothing but weeping martyrs and fear . . . and shame."

And now a voice comes from the beach, rising free of the clash and clamor of battle. "Show me to King Beowulf!" it demands. "I would die by *his* sword and *his* alone! Show me to Beowulf!"

Wiglaf glances nervously to Beowulf, who has tightened his grip on the reins.

"You *cannot*," says Wiglaf firmly. "He means only to taunt you into delivering his own glory, my lord. You *know* that. Do not reward him."

"Leave him!" shouts Beowulf, ignoring Wiglaf's

counsel. He spurs his horse forward, riding swiftly along the sandy bluff and into the midst of his warriors, most of whom have gathered about one of the last of the Frisians remaining alive. They have stripped away his helmet and much of his armor, forcing him down onto the bloodied sand. They kick at his bare head and unprotected belly, laughing and cursing the man, denying him the honor of death. Beowulf recognizes the Frisian as the leader of this invasion.

"*Stop!*" cries Beowulf, bringing his horse to a halt, its hooves spraying sand in all directions. The men do as they're told, turning and gazing up at their king scowling down at them.

"What *is* this?" asks Beowulf to his thanes. "You think it *sport* to mock your opponent in this fashion? To kick and bully an unarmed man, then make jest of his pain? No. Let him die quickly, with some measure of dignity left intact. You are *soldiers* . . . behaving like a mob."

And then Beowulf pulls tight on the reins, turning his horse about and almost colliding with Wiglaf, who has only just gained the foot of the bluff.

"Kill me *yourself*!" shouts the leader of the Frisians, getting slowly, painfully to his feet. "If you would have me dead, then kill me yourself, coward."

And Beowulf sits there on his horse, staring ahead at Wiglaf, his back turned to both the Frisian and his own thanes. He can clearly read the warning in Wiglaf's eyes, the caution that never seems to leave them for very long. The waves are loud upon the shore, the waves and the wind and the pounding of Beowulf's heart in his ears.

"Kill me yourself," the Frisian says again, sounding bolder now and taking a step nearer the king.

"Hold your tongue, bastard," Wiglaf tells the man. "The king can never engage in direct battle." And then to Beowulf's thanes he says, "Kill the invader now. Do it quickly, and put his head on a spear. Plant it high on the bluff as a *warning* to others who would come to our land seeking their immortality."

There's a low murmur of disappointment from the Danes, as if they are being cheated of some rightful and well-deserved prize. But a number of the men raise their swords to do as Wiglaf has ordered.

"Stop!" Beowulf commands, turning his horse to face the Frisian once again. The thanes look confused, but immediately lower their weapons and begin to back away.

"You think me a coward?" Beowulf asks the leader of the Frisians as he nudges his horse forward, until he is looming over the battered man.

"I think you are an *old man*," replies the Frisian, standing up as straight as he can manage and looking Beowulf directly in the eyes. He has retrieved his weapon from the sand, a bearded ax, its iron head rusty and pitted but keen and slick with blood. "I think you've forgotten which end of an ax is sharp and how to wield a sword in battle. You *watch* from a safe distance, squatting on your pony, and then call the battle won by your own hand."

Beowulf draws his sword and dismounts, never taking his eyes off the Frisian.

"Hear me, my lord," says Wiglaf. "The king can *never* engage in direct battle."

"And whose rule is that, anyway?" Beowulf asks without turning to face his advisor, and Wiglaf does not reply. The thanes have begun to form a loose circle, with Beowulf and the Frisian at its center.

"So," says Beowulf to the Frisian, "you want *your* name added to the song of Beowulf? You think maybe that ballad should end with me slain by the blade of some netherland halfwit with no name that I have yet heard?"

"I am called *Finn*," the man replies. "And I am a prince among my people. And my name shall be remembered forever."

Beowulf nods and smiles, holding the pommel of his sword between thumb and forefinger, letting it swing this way and that like the arm of a deadly pendulum, the tip of the blade barely grazing the sand.

"Only if you kill me," he tells the man. "Otherwise, you are nothing." And Beowulf drives his sword into the sand at his feet, burying it halfway to the hilt, and he walks unarmed toward the Frisian.

"Give the king a weapon!" orders Wiglaf, and there are eager cries from the thanes:

"Take mine, Lord Beowulf!"

"No, take mine!"

"Kill the bastard with *my* sword!"

At least a dozen good blades are offered, but Beowulf waves them all away. He closes the space between himself and the Frisian, who stands his ground, gripping his ax and smiling as though this is a fight he has already won. Beowulf stops with scarcely ten feet remaining between them and begins loosening the leather straps on his breastplate. Still advancing on the Frisian warrior, he removes his mail and gauntlets and both leather greaves. Now less than five feet remains between him and Finn, and Beowulf is within reach of the warrior's ax. Beowulf rips open his white woolen tunic and strikes his chest hard with his right fist.

"What are you doing?" asks Finn, staring at Beowulf's naked torso, at the awful tapestry of scars there, the marks left by more battles than Beowulf could ever recall. The Frisian's smile has faded, and he clutches his ax so tight his hands have gone white and bloodless.

"You think you're the *first* to try to kill me, Finn, Prince of Frisia?" asks Beowulf. "Or even the *hundredth*?"

When Finn does not reply, Beowulf continues.

"Then let me tell you something, netherlander. Perhaps it is something you have not heard. The gods won't *allow* me to find death at the head of your feeble ax. Neither will Odin Allfather let me die by a sword or lance or arrow . . . or be taken by the sea," and Beowulf motions toward the waves behind Finn. "The gods will not even allow me to pass in my *sleep* . . . ripe as I am with age." Then Beowulf strikes his bare chest again, harder than before.

"Plant your ax *here*, Finn of Frisia. Take my life."

"Are you a madman?" asks the Frisian, and he begins to back away, holding his ax up in front of him. "Has some animal or demon spirit taken your mind? Are you bersërkr?"

"That may well be so," replies Beowulf. "Am I not called the Wolf of the Bees, the bear who slays giant-kin and sea hags."

"Take a sword and fight me like a man!"

"I don't *need* a sword. I don't need an ax. I need *no* weapon to lay you in your grave."

"Someone give him a fucking sword," Finn says to the Danish thanes. He's sweating now, and his hands have begun to shake. "Give him a blade, or I'll . . . I'll . . ."

"*You'll what?*" growls Beowulf. "*Kill* me? Then *do* it! Stop talking and cowering and fucking *kill me*!"

Finn looks down and is surprised to find the ocean lapping at his ankles; Beowulf has driven him all the way back to the sea. The Frisian grits his teeth, raises the ax above his left shoulder, and tries to raise it higher still. But he's shaking so badly now that the weapon slips from his fingers and lands with a dull splash at his feet.

"Do you know *why* you can't kill me, friend?" asks Beowulf. "Because I died *years* ago . . . when I was still a young man." And Beowulf pulls the edges of his torn tunic closed, hiding his scarred chest from view, and when he looks once again at Finn there is pity in Beowulf's gaze.

"It is as simple as that," he says. "You cannot kill a ghost." Then to his war captain, Beowulf says, "Give the prince a piece of gold and send him home to his kin. He has a story to tell." And Beowulf, King of the Danes, climbs onto his horse and follows Wiglaf back up the slope, leaving the battlefield behind. Overhead, the winter sky is filled with black and gray wings, a riotous host of crows and gulls, vultures and ravens, already gathering to take their fill of the dead and dying.

And as time changes men and whittles away at the mountains themselves, so must men, trapped *within* time, change themselves and the world around them. So, too, have the fortifications begun in the distant days when the great-grandfather of Hrothgar ruled the Danes been changed by the will of King Beowulf. Using stone quarried from open pits along the high sea cliffs, fine new towers and stronger walls have been erected, a bulwark against foreign armies and the elements and anything else that might wish to do the people of this kingdom harm. Where once stood little more than a shabby cluster of thatched huts and muddy footpaths, there now rises a castle keep that might be the envy of any Roman or Byzantine general, that Persian or Arab rulers might look upon and know that the Northmen have also learned something of the arts of warfare and defense, of architecture and the mathematics needed to raise a stronghold to impress even the gods in Ásgard. And on this day, after the battle on the shore and the routing of the Frisians, Beowulf stands alone on the great stone causeway connecting the two turrets of Heorot. A hundred feet below him, in a snow-covered courtyard paved with granite and slate flagstones, Wiglaf is preparing to address the villagers who have begun to gather there.

Beowulf turns away, pulling his furs tighter and turning instead to face the sea, that vast gray-green expanse reaching away to the horizon. The frigid wind bites at any bit of exposed skin, but the bite is clean. After the beach and the things he saw there, the things he said and did and those things that were said and done in his name, he greatly desires to feel clean.

Perhaps, he thinks, *this is why so many men are turning from Odin and his brethren to the murdered Roman Christ and the nameless god who is held to be his father. That promise, that they will be made somehow pure and clean again and freed from the weight and consequences of the choices they have made.*

Beowulf sighs and leans forward on the rough-hewn merion, watching as countless snowflakes swirl lazily down to the waves, where they melt and lose themselves in the heaving sea. He tries hard to recall how it was in the days before he left Geatland and the service of Hygelac and came to Hrothgar's aid, when he welcomed rather than dreaded the sight of the sea and the thought of all the hidden terrors of that deep.

He hears someone behind him and turns to find Ursula, a young girl he has taken for his mistress, or who has perhaps taken him as her lover. She is exquisite, even to eyes wearied by so much bloodshed and destruction, her fair skin and freckles and her hair like wheat spun into some fine silken thread. She stands, wrapped in the pelt of foxes and bears and silhouetted by the winter sky, and her expression is part concern and part relief.

"My lord?" she asks. "Are you hurt?"

"Not a scratch," Beowulf replies, and kisses her. "You know, Ursula, when I was young, I thought being king would be about battling every morning, counting the golden loot in the afternoon, and bedding beautiful women every night. And now . . . well, nothing's as good as it should have been."

Ursula gives him half a frown. "Not even the 'bedding a beautiful woman' part, my lord?"

Beowulf laughs, trying to summon up an honest laugh for her. "Well, some nights, Ursula. Some nights."

"Perhaps *this* night?" she asks hopefully, and tugs at the collar of his robes.

"No," Beowulf tells her, and he laughs again, but this time it's a rueful sort of laugh. "Tonight I feel my age upon me. But tomorrow, after the celebration. We can't forget what tomorrow is, can we now?"

And now Ursula grows very serious. "Your day, my lord," she says. "When the Saga of Beowulf is told, the tale of how you lifted the darkness from the land. And the day after, we celebrate the birth of Christ Jesus."

Beowulf smiles for her and wipes hair from her face.

"Christmond," he says, making no attempt to hide his feelings about this new religion, embraced now by fully half his kingdom, even by his own Queen Wealthow. "Is Yule no longer good enough?"

"Yule is the old way," Ursula replies. "Christmond is the *new* way."

"There is much yet to be said for the old ways, my dear," Beowulf tells her. And now he hears footsteps, and when he looks up, the king finds Wealthow and a priest coming across the causeway toward them. The priest wears long robes of wool dyed red as blood and a large cross of gilded wood dangles from about his neck. When Wealthow speaks, her voice is as icy as her violet eyes.

"I see that you've survived, *husband*," she says.

"Alas, my queen," replies Beowulf, the sarcasm thick in his voice. "The Frisian invaders have been pushed back into the sea from whence they came. And *you*, my good lady, are not a widow . . . yet."

Wealthow smiles, a smile that only looks sweet, and exchanges glances with the priest.

"How comforting, my husband."

And then, feeling confrontational but having no desire to argue with Wealthow, Beowulf shifts his gaze to the priest. He is a gaunt man beneath his robes, a thin man from some Irish longphort or another, his face the color of goat's cheese except for the broken veins on his hooked nose and the angry boil nestled in the wrinkles of his protruding chin. Beowulf grins at the priest, and the priest acknowledges him with a curt nod.

"You," says Beowulf. "Father. I have a question that vexes me terribly. Perhaps you can answer it for me."

"I can try," the priest replies nervously, and Wealthow glares at her king.

"Good. Fine. Then tell me this, *Father*, if your god is now the *only* god, then what has he done with all the rest, the Æsir and the Vanir? Is he so mighty a warrior that he has bested them one and all, even Odin?"

The priest blinks and bows his head, gazing down at the stones at his feet. "There is but *one* God," he says patiently, "and there has never been any other."

Beowulf moves to stand nearer the priest, who is at least a full head shorter than he. "Then he must be an awfully busy fellow, your god, doing the work of so many. How, for example, does he contend with the giants, keep Loki's children in check, prepare his troops at Ásgard, and yet *still* find time each day to dispense so much love and grace and forgiveness upon his people?"

"I will not be mocked, my lord," the priest says very softly.

"Mocked?" chuckles Beowulf, looking first to Ursula, then to Wealthow and feigning innocence. "I am not trying to *mock* you, good priest. These questions vex me, truly, and I believed that you must surely know the answers, as you say this unnamed god *speaks* to you."

"When you mock Him," the priest says, "you do so at the risk of your own immortal soul."

"Well, then, I suppose I must strive to be more careful."

"*Beowulf*," says Wealthow, stepping between the priest and her husband. "Stop it this minute."

"But I haven't yet asked him about Ragnarök," Beowulf protests.

At last, the priest lifts his head and dares to meet Beowulf's gaze from behind the protective barrier of the queen. "It is a heathen faerie story, this *Ragnarök*," and then to Wealthow he adds, "Your husband is an *infidel*, and I will not be ridiculed—"

"I only *asked*—" begins Beowulf, but the cold fire in Wealthow's eyes silences him.

"Forgive him, Father," she says. "He is a difficult old man and too set in his ways."

"That's right," mumbles Beowulf. "I'm hopeless. Please, do not mind me." And Beowulf puts an arm tight about Ursula and holds her close to him, but she tries to pull away.

"We will speak later, husband," Wealthow says.

"Of that I am certain," Beowulf replies, and Queen Wealthow and the priest turn away and head back across the causeway toward the east tower. The snow is falling harder now, becoming a storm, and soon

Beowulf loses sight of them in the mist and swirling snowfall.

"She frightens me," says Ursula. "One day, she will kill me, I think."

Beowulf laughs and hugs her again. "Nay, my pretty little thing. She will not touch a hair upon your head. Wealthow, she has her new Roman god now, so what need has she of an old warhorse like me? Do not fear her. She is all thunder and no lightning, if you catch my meaning."

"We should get inside, my lord," Ursula says, sounding no less worried for Beowulf's reassurances. "I do not like this wind." Beowulf does not argue, because the wind is cold and his need to wrangle words has been spent on the priest. He kisses Ursula atop her head.

"Indeed. It shall blow us all away," he laughs. "It shall grab us up and blow us to the ends of the earth."

"Yes, my lord," she says, and then she takes Beowulf's hand and leads her king along the causeway high above Heorot and into the sanctuary and comparative warmth of the western tower.

16

The Golden Horn

The storm ended sometime before dawn, and morning finds a glittering mantle of fresh snow laid thick over the rooftops and streets and courtyards of the keep. The giant eagle Hræsvelg, squatting high atop his perch in the uppermost limbs of Yggdrasil, beats mighty wings, and a vicious north wind howls across the world, whistling between the towers and moaning beneath the eaves. And Wiglaf, remembering the days when winter did not make his bones ache and his muscles stiffen, trudges through the deep snow to the granite platform where he delivers the king's decrees and news of battle and other such important proclamations. He stands there in the shadow of the two great turrets, and his breath comes out like mouthfuls of smoke. Already, a large number of people have gathered about the plinth, awaiting his announcement. He acknowledges them with a nod, their pink cheeks and red noses, then slowly climbs the four steps leading up onto the platform. They are slick with ice and snow, and Wiglaf does not wish to spend the rest of his days crippled by broken bones his body has grown too old to heal properly or completely. He stands with his back to the towers and clears his throat, spits, then clears his throat again, wishing he were back inside, sitting comfortably before a roaring fire and awaiting his breakfast.

"On this day," says Wiglaf, speaking loudly enough that all may hear him, "in honor of our glorious Lord of Heorot, let us tell the saga of King Beowulf." He pauses to get his breath and spit again, then continues. "How he so fearlessly slew the murderous demon Grendel *and* the demon's hag mother."

And the wind from under Hræsvelg's wings lifts Wiglaf's words and carries them out beyond the inner fortifications and the confines of the keep, to echo through the village and off the walls of the horned hall. Those who hear stop to listen—men busy with ponies, women busy with their stewpots and baking, children making a game of the snow.

"Let his deeds of valor inspire us all. On this day, let fires be lit and the sagas told, tales of the gods and of giants, of warriors who have fallen in battle and who now ride the fields of Idavoll."

And near the outermost wall of Beowulf's stronghold, at the edges of the village, stands the house of Unferth, son of Ecglaf, who once served Hrothgar, son of Healfdene, in the days when the horned hall was new and monsters stalked the land. The house a sturdy and imposing manor, fashioned of stone and from timber hauled here from the forest beyond the moors. The steeple at the front of its pitched roof has lately been decorated with an enormous cross, the symbol of Christ Jesus, for lately has Lord Unferth forsaken the old ways for the new religion. And even this far out, Wiglaf's words are still audible.

"I declare this day to be *Beowulf's Day*!" he shouts, delivering the last two words with all the force and enthusiasm he can muster, before a coughing fit takes him.

Unferth stands shivering in the shade cast by the cross on his roof, and a little farther along, his son, Guthric and his son's wife and Unferth's six grandchildren wait impatiently in the sleigh, which has not yet been hitched to the ponies that will pull it through the village to the keep. The long years have not been even half so kind to Unferth as to Wiglaf and Beowulf, and he is stoop-shouldered and crooked, bracing himself on a staff of carved oak. He glares toward the towers and the sound of Wiglaf's voice, then back at the sleigh and his family.

"Where the hell is that fool with the horses?" he calls out to Guthric. Then he turns and shouts in the direction of his stables, "Cain? Hurry it up!"

It has begun to snow again.

In the sleigh, Guthric—who might easily pass in both appearance and demeanor for his father in Unferth's younger days—fiddles restlessly with the large cross hung about his neck. He looks at his wife and frowns.

"Beowulf Day," he mutters. "Bloody, stupid old *fool's* day, more like. He's as senile as Father."

Lady Guthric hugs herself and glances at the ominous sky. "He is the king," she reminds her husband.

"Then he is the *senile* king."

"The snow's starting again," frets Lady Guthric, wishing her husband would not speak so about Lord Beowulf, whether or not she might agree. She fears what might happen if the king were to learn of Guthric's opinions of him, and she also fears that the storm is not yet over.

"Wife," says Guthric, "do you *know* how bloody sick I am of hearing about bloody Grendel and bloody Grendel's bloody mother?"

"I should," she says, "for you have told me now a thousand times, at least."

"What the hell *was* Grendel, anyway? Some kind of giant *dog* or something?"

"I'm sure I could not tell you, dear," she replies, then tells the oldest of the children to settle down and stop picking on the others.

"And what the bloody hell was Grendel's mother supposed to be? She doesn't even have a bloody *name*!"

"I believe she was a demon of some sort," his wife says, and looks worriedly at the sky again.

"A *demon*? You'd have me believe that broken-down old Geat bastard slew a goddamned bloody *demon*?"

"Guthric, you must learn not to blaspheme . . . at least not in front of the children."

"A demon, my ass," grumbles Guthric, watching his father now. "A toothless old bear, maybe. Or—"

"Can we just *go*?" his wife asks wearily, and dusts snow from her furs.

And now Unferth approaches the sleigh, shouting as loudly as he still may. "Cain! *Cain*, where are you!"

Guthric stands up, and, cupping his hands about his mouth, takes up his father's cry. "*Cain!*" he yells, with much more vigor than the old man. "*Where the bloody Christ are you?*"

And Unferth strikes him with his walking stick, catching him hard on the rump, and Unferth immediately sits down again beside Guthric's wife.

"Don't you *dare* blaspheme in my presence!" growls Unferth, brandishing the stick as if he means to land a second blow, this time across his son's skull. "I will *not* have you speak of the One *True* God, father of Our Lord Jesus, in such a manner!"

Guthric flinches and looks to his wife for support or defense against the old man's wrath, but she ignores him, an expression of self-righteous vindication on her round pink face.

"You will *learn*," Unferth tells the cowering Guthric, and his six grandchildren watch wide-eyed and eager, wondering just how bad a thrashing their father's going to get this time.

There's a sudden commotion, then, from the direction of the village gates, and Unferth turns away from the sleigh and his insolent, impious son to find two of his house guards approaching, dragging Cain roughly through the snow and frozen mud. One of the guards raises his free hand and jabs a finger at the slave—filthy and bedraggled, clothed only in a tattered hemp tunic and a wool blanket, rags wrapped tightly about his hands and feet to stave off frostbite.

"He ran off again, my lord," says the guard. "We found him hiding in a hollow log at the edge of the moors. A wonder the fool didn't freeze to death."

The guards shove Cain roughly forward, and he stumbles and lands in a sprawling heap at Unferth's feet. His woolen blanket has slipped off his skinny shoulders, revealing the glint of gold among the slave's castoff garments.

"What have you got there?" Unferth asks, and bends down for a closer look, but Cain clutches something to his chest and curls up like a frightened hedgehog. Unferth raises his stick again. "*Show* it to me, damn you!" he snarls. "You know well enough I do not waste my breath on idle threats."

Cain hesitates only a moment longer, something desperate in his cloudy, sickly eyes, and then he produces his golden treasure. It shines dimly in the overcast daylight, and Unferth gasps and drops his walking stick.

He has begun to tremble uncontrollably and he leans against the sleigh for support.

"Father," asks Guthric. "What's wrong?"

"Do you not *see* it?" Unferth whispers, taking the golden drinking horn from Cain's rag-swaddled hands. "My Lord Hrothgar's most precious . . ." and he trails off, dumbstruck by the sight of the horn, lost so long ago.

"Is it gold?" asks Guthric as he turns about for a better view, his interest piqued.

"Yes, yes," hisses Unferth. "Of course it is *gold*. This . . . this is the drinking horn King Beowulf was given by King Hrothgar in return for slaying Grendel . . ."

"But that was lost, wasn't it?" asks Guthric.

His eyes wide with disbelief, Unferth looks from the golden horn to Cain, shivering on the ground, then back to the horn.

"Yes," he tells his son. "It was lost. Beowulf cast it into the tarn, into the burning waters of *Weormgræf*, for the merewife greatly desired it. When she was slain . . . he said that he searched for it, but could not discover where it had come to rest in the mud and peat."

"It must be worth a fortune," says Guthric, climbing down from the sleigh and reaching for the drinking horn. But Unferth slaps his hand away.

"How came you by this?" he asks Cain, and when the slave doesn't answer, Unferth kicks him in the belly.

"Shall I have a go at him?" one of the guards asks.

"A few lashes, and the rat will start talking, sure enough."

"No," Unferth replies, shaking his head. "This is the *king's* horn, and now it will *go* to the king. And so will Cain. Perhaps he will tell Lord Beowulf how he came upon it. Perhaps the questions of our king mean more to him than the questions of his *master*." And Unferth kicks Cain again, harder than before. The slave gags and coughs a crimson spatter onto the snow.

"Bring out my ponies," he tells the two guards. "And Guthric, you help them."

"But *Father*—"

"Do not *argue* with me," Unferth says without looking at his son. "Consider it fair penance due for your earlier transgression."

And when the guards and his son have gone, Unferth kneels in the snow beside Cain and wipes blood from the slave's lips and nostrils.

"You *will* tell where you came upon it," Unferth tells him. "Or I shall have the pleasure of killing you myself."

And far across the village, beyond the walls of the keep, Wiglaf descends the four steps leading down from the granite platform. The crowd is breaking up, going on about their business, and he has much left to do before the celebration begins. He glares up at the leaden sky and curses the falling snow, then adds another curse for his aching joints. Then he spies a lone figure watching from the causeway connecting the two towers and thinks it must be Beowulf. Wiglaf waves to him, but the figure does not wave back.

"What's on your mind now, old man?" Wiglaf asks, uncertain if the question was meant for himself or for the figure standing on the causeway. And then he begins picking his way carefully back through the snow and ice, and his only thoughts are of hot food and a crackling hearth fire.

Unferth's sleigh has almost reached the gates of the keep when Guthric tugs at the reins and brings the ponies to a halt. Despite the day's foul weather, the streets are crowded with travelers who have journeyed to Heorot from other, outlying villages and farmsteads to celebrate Beowulf's Day and the Yuletide. Too many unfamiliar faces for Unferth's liking, too many wagons and horses and beggars slowing them down, and now that Guthric has stopped the sleigh, the unfamiliar faces stare back at Unferth as though it is *he* who should not be here. Cain sits behind his master, on the bench that Guthric's wife and children occupied until he ordered them to remain at home. And Cain gazes disconsolately at all the men and women and children on the streets. The slave's feet have been manacled so he cannot run again.

"What are you *doing*?" Unferth asks his son, and tries unsuccessfully to take the reins from Guthric. "We have to see our king. We must see him *at once*. We may have taken too long already!"

Guthric winds the reins tightly about his fists and

stares up at the two towers of Beowulf's castle, the one built straight and the other spiraling upwards like the shell of some gargantuan snail. His entire life has been lived in the shadow of those towers and in the knowledge that his father would have been king had not some adventurer from the east shown up to defeat monsters Guthric has come to doubt ever even existed. Some dark plot, more likely, some intrigue by which a foreign interloper might dupe doddering old Hrothgar and steal the throne for himself. Years ago it first occurred to him that "the demon Grendel" and the demon's nameless mother might only have been fictions concocted *by* Beowulf in a campaign to wrest control of Denmark from the Danes. Perhaps the Geat and his thanes merely set some wild beast loose upon the unsuspecting countryside, some bloodthirsty animal that would not be recognized and so would be believed by the gullible and superstitious to constitute a sort of monster or otherworldly demon, a troll or even the spawn of giants. In the end, by whatever means the deception was carried out, his father was robbed of his kingship and Guthric of his own birthright. And now there is this horn, this relic from that faerie tale, supposedly lost forever.

"Father," he says, "I would have you tell me why this horn is so very important. Clearly, it must be valuable, but there's something else, isn't there?"

"This is none of your concern," snaps Unferth. "But we must *hurry*. We must—"

"*Why*, Father? Why must we hurry? What is so

damned important about a bloody drinking horn that it has you so excited?"

Unferth wrings his hands anxiously and stares at the flanks of the two snow-dappled ponies, as though he might spur them to move by dint of will alone.

"Some things are not for you to *know*," he tells Guthric. "Some things—"

"If the tale is to be believed, Hrothgar's horn was lost at the bottom of a deep tarn. Tell me, how then might an idiot like Cain have come upon it. I do not even think he knows how to *swim*."

"There is not *time* for this impertinence," growls Unferth, going for his walking stick, but Guthric kicks it from the sleigh before his father can reach it. Then he turns and looks at Cain.

"*Can* you swim?" he asks the slave.

Cain looks confused for a moment, then he shakes his head.

"You see, Father? He cannot even swim, so how could he have possibly found a drinking horn lost at the bottom of a bottomless lake. Unless, of course, it was never lost there at all. Perchance, it was only *hidden*."

Unferth glares furiously back at his son, then down at his staff, lying in the snow beside the sleigh. "Why," he asks, "would King Beowulf hide his own drinking horn? You're being a *dolt*, Guthric, which comes as no surprise whatsoever. You have as little sense as that bitch who gave birth to you."

Guthric ignores the slight and continues, giving voice

to thoughts he has so long kept to himself. "He would have needed it to appear as though he had bested this demon hag at great personal loss. So, he loses the prize he won for killing Grendel. *And* your ancestral sword, I might add. He gives up a horn and gains a kingdom. It seems a fair enough trade to me."

"The horn was his *already*," insists Unferth, clutching tight to the golden horn, now that he has lost his stick. "I keep *telling* you that. Are you deaf as well as a fool?"

"Father, listen to me. We will do as you wish. We will take this thing to King Beowulf, but first I would like to show it to someone else."

"Who?" asks Unferth, raising one bushy gray eyebrow suspiciously.

Guthric takes a deep breath of the freezing air and glances about at the crowd moving slowly toward the mead hall and the night's coming celebration. There is a troupe of actors, mostly dwarves, and they're carrying a grotesque contraption made of furs and bones and leather, and Guthric realizes it's meant to be the monster Grendel. A puppet or costume the actors will use to reenact that glorious battle between Beowulf and the fiend.

"A seer," says Guthric. "A wisewoman I have spoken with before."

Unferth looks horrified, then begins to scrabble out of the wagon to retrieve his walking stick.

"A seer? A *witch* is what you mean!" he says. "Have you learned *nothing* from the teachings of our

Christ Jesus, that you would traffic with witches and have me do likewise!"

"I wear your cross," replies Guthric.

"It is not my cross, and it means *nothing*, if you do not *believe* in what it represents. You profane God, wearing the cross and meeting with witches."

Guthric scowls and lets go of the reins. He grabs his father's cloak, hauling him back into the sleigh. "She is *not* a witch," he tells Unferth. "She is only an old woman—older even than *you*, Father—who knows many things."

"Because she consorts with spirits and demons," sneers Unferth, still without his staff. "Because she keeps counsel with evil beings who wish to deceive us all."

"I only want to *show* her the horn," says Unferth. "Then we will go to the king, as you wish."

"This is *madness*," hisses Unferth. "We are *wasting* time, and now you would have me seek out the company of a witch and let *her* look upon this treasure which should be seen by Beowulf and *none other*." Unferth has begun excitedly waving the horn about, and several passersby have stopped to gawk at the old man.

"*You* seem to think everyone in Heorot deserves a good look," says Guthric, and Unferth immediately hides the horn beneath his robes once more.

"There is not time for this madness," Unferth says again, though he seems to have exhausted himself, and much of his anger and panic seem to have drained away.

"Father, the damned thing has been lost for thirty years. I suspect another few hours will make no difference, one way or the other."

"You do not know," sighs Unferth.

Guthric glances back at Cain again. "Retrieve your master's staff," he says. "It has fallen from the sleigh." When Cain nods forlornly at the iron shackles about his ankles, Guthric merely snorts. "You cannot run, but you can walk well enough to do as I have asked. Now, Cain, do as I have said and get Father's staff, or I swear that *I* shall beat you myself."

"Yes, my lord," mumbles Cain, managing to clamber down from the sleigh.

"I knew you were never a *true* convert," says Unferth. "But I did *not* know that you consorted with sorcerers and witches."

"I consort with those who can tell me what I need to know," replies Guthric, and again he looks toward the troupe of dwarf actors and their hideous Grendel suit. Something to frighten children and old men, an offense to thinking men and nothing more. One of the dwarves has set the immense head down upon the snow and is busy with the straps that seem to work its fierce jaws, which appear to Guthric to be nothing more than an absurd composite of bear teeth and boar tusks. A child points at the head and runs back to its mother, sobbing. The dwarves laugh and roar at the child. One of them works the phony jaws up and down, up and down, chewing at the air.

Better be a good boy, Guthric. Better be good and say your prayers, or Grendel will come in the night and gobble you up! How many nights had he lain awake, fearing the sound of Grendel's footsteps or a misshapen face leering in at the window of his bedchamber?

And all at once Guthric is seized with a desire to put an end to this pathetic charade, to draw his sword and hack away at the dwarves' puppet until nothing remains but dust and string and tatters. Nothing that can frighten children or keep alive the falsehoods that put a foreigner upon the Danish throne.

"Cain!" he shouts. "What the bloody hell is taking you so long?" but when he turns back toward his father, he sees that Unferth is holding on to his oaken staff and that Cain has already climbed back into the sleigh.

"How can I persuade you not to do this?" asks Unferth, staring down at the stick in his wrinkled hands.

"You cannot, Father. Do not waste your breath trying. You shall see, it's for the best. And *then*, when my questions have been answered, we will go to see King Beowulf in his horned hall." Unferth gives the reins a hard tug and shake, and he guides the sleigh away from the main thoroughfare and down a narrow side street.

* * *

And so it is that the old man and his son find themselves standing outside a very small and cluttered hovel wedged in between the village wall and the muddy sprawl of a piggery. At first, Unferth refused to enter the rickety shack, fearing for both his immortal soul and the welfare of his mortal flesh. The whole structure seems hardly more than a deadfall in which someone has unwisely chosen to take up residence, a precarious jumble of timber and thatch that might well shift or simply collapse in upon itself at the slightest gust of wind. But Guthric was persistent, and the snow was coming down much too hard for Unferth to remain behind in the sleigh with Cain (covered now with a blanket and tied fast to his seat).

The crooked front door is carved with all manner of runes and symbols, some of which Unferth recognizes and some of which he doesn't, and a wolf's skull—also decorated with runes—has been nailed to the cornice. When Unferth knocks, the entire hovel shudders very slightly, and he takes a cautious step back toward the sleigh. But then the door swings open wide and they are greeted by a slender woman of indeterminate age, neither particularly old nor particularly young, dressed in a nappy patchwork of fur and a long leather skirt that appears to have been stained and smeared with every sort of filth imaginable. Her black hair, speckled with gray, is pulled in braids, and her eyes are a bright and startling shade of green that makes Unferth think of mossy rocks at the edge of the sea.

"Father," says Guthric, "this is Sigga, the seer of whom I spoke. She was born in Iceland."

"Iceland?" mutters Unferth, and he takes another step back toward the sleigh. "Then what the hell is she doing here?"

"I often ask myself the same thing," says Sigga, fixing Unferth with her too-green eyes.

"Well, then tell me *this*, outlander," growls Unferth. "Are you some heathen *witch*, or are you a Christian? Do you offer your body up to evil spirits in exchange for the secrets you sell?"

Hearing this, Sigga grunts, some unintelligible curse, and shakes her head.

"I'm sorry," Guthric says, frowning at his father. "My father takes his conversion very seriously."

"I keep to the old ways," Sigga tells Unferth, standing straighter and her eyes seeming to flash more brightly still. "And what I do with my body is no concern of yours, old man. I *know* you, Unferth, Ecglaf's son, though you do not now seem to remember me. I midwifed at the birth of your son, and I did my best to save his mother's life."

"Then you *are* a witch!" snarls Unferth, and spits into the snow. "You admit it!"

Sigga clicks her tongue loudly against the roof of her mouth and glances at Guthric, then back to Unferth. She points a long finger at the old man, and says, "State your business with me, Ecglaf's son, for I have better things to do this day than stand here in the cold and be insulted by Hrothgar's forgotten lapdog."

Unferth makes an angry blustering noise and shakes his staff at the woman. "Witch, I have *no* business here," he sputters. "Ask my infidel son why we've come, for this was all *his* doing, I assure you."

"Sigga, there is something I wish you to see," says Guthric. "Our slave found it out on the moorlands, and—"

"Then come inside," Sigga says to Guthric, interrupting him. "I will not catch my own death standing in the snow. As for you, Ecglaf's son, you may come in where there is a fire or you may stand there shivering, if that's what pleases you."

"Father, show it to her," says Guthric. "Let her see the golden horn."

"*Inside*," Sigga says again, and vanishes into the hovel. Unferth is still mumbling about demons and sorcery, whores and succubae, but when Guthric takes him by the arm and leads him over the threshold of Sigga's house, he doesn't resist. Inside, the air stinks much less of the piggery, redolent instead with the scent of dried herbs and beeswax candles, cooking and the smoky peat fire burning in the small hearth. In places, weak daylight shows through chinks in the walls. There are several benches and tables crowded with all manner of jars and bowls, a large mortar and pestle, dried fish and the bones of many sorts of animals. Bundles of dried plants hang from the low ceiling and rustle softly one against the other. Guthric takes a seat before the fire, warming his hands, but Unferth hangs back, taking great care to touch nothing in the place, for, he thinks, anything here—anything at all—might be tainted with some perilous malfeasance.

"A golden horn?" Sigga asks, sitting down on the dirt floor beside the hearth. "Is that what you said, Guthric? A golden horn?"

"Show it to her, Father," says Guthric impatiently, then to Sigga, "Surely you have heard of the golden drinking horn that Hrothgar gave to King Beowulf, the one Hrothgar always claimed to have taken from a slain dragon's hoard?"

"I know the story," Sigga replies. "The golden horn is said to have been lost when Beowulf the Geat fought with the merewife after Grendel's death. But . . . I do not set much store in the boasting of men. I say if Hrothgar ever *saw* a dragon, he'd have run the other way."

"Insolent crone," mutters Unferth. "Hrothgar was a *great* man, a great *warrior*."

Sigga stares at him a moment, then asks, "So, have you come to argue politics and the worth of kings?"

Unferth glares back at her and his son, sitting there together like confidants or coconspirators, his one and only son keeping company with the likes of her. He grips his staff more tightly and says a silent prayer.

"What is it you have brought me?" Sigga asks Unferth. "I trust in my eyes. Now, *show* me this golden horn, and I will tell you what I *see*."

"I once saw a drawing of Hrothgar's horn, years

ago," says Guthric. "It was identical to the one found by our slave."

"*Shut up*," barks Unferth, producing the golden horn from a fold of his robes. It glistens in the firelight, and Sigga's eyes grow very wide and she quickly turns away, staring into the hearth flames. "So now you *see*," sneers Unferth. "The prize that Beowulf won thirty years ago, lost all these years in the black depths of *Weormgræf* when he battled the demon hag."

"Is that true?" Unferth asks Sigga, his voice trembling now with excitement. "Is that what this is, Hrothgar's royal drinking horn?"

"Please," says Sigga. "Put it away." She licks her lips and swallows, and though there are beads of sweat standing out on her forehead and cheeks, she tosses another block of peat onto the fire and stirs at the embers with an iron poker.

Guthric looks confused, but motions for his father to hide the horn once more beneath his robes. Unferth ignores him and takes a step nearer the place where Sigga sits.

"Is something wrong, witch?" he asks. "Does it so upset you to be *wrong* about the boasts of men?"

"Sigga, *is* this Hrothgar's horn?" Guthric asks again, and she glances at him uneasily.

"She does not know," snickers Unferth. "This bitch does not know *what* she sees. Let us take our leave, my son, and never again darken this vile doorstep."

And now Sigga turns slowly toward Unferth, but she keeps her green eyes downcast, staring at the dirty straw covering the floor so she won't see the glimmering object clasped in the old man's hands.

"You listen to me, Unferth Ecglaf's son, and heed my words. I cannot say for certain *what* that thing is, for there is a glamour upon it. The most powerful glamour I have ever glimpsed. There is *dökkálfar* magic at work here, I believe. I have seen their handiwork before. I have felt them near, when I was yet only a child."

"*Dökkálfar*?" asks Guthric, his tongue fumbling at the unfamiliar word.

"Aye, the Nidafjöll dark elves," Sigga replies, and wipes sweat from her face. "People of Svartálfheim, hillfolk, the dwellers in the Dark Fells."

"Heathen nonsense," scoffs Unferth. "Faerie tales. I thought you had no use for faerie stories, Guthric, but you bring me to hear them uttered by a lunatic."

"Hear me," whispers Sigga, her voice gone dry and hoarse. "I do not say these things lightly. Whatever it is, this horn you hold, it was not *meant* to be found. Or, it was meant to be found by something that harbors an ancient hatred and would see the world of men suffer."

"She's insane," Unferth chuckles. "Come now, my son, let's leave this wicked place. It should be razed and the earth here salted. And this witch should be stoned to death or burned at the stake."

Sigga clenches her fists and smiles, and now the

sweat from her face has begun to drip to the straw and dirt at her feet.

"Do not trouble yourself, Ecglaf's son, for you hold this kingdom's doom there in your hands. The one from whom that horn was stolen, she will soon come to reclaim it, her or one very like her, for it has been brought to Heorot in violation of some blood pact. A binding has been broken, and I would have you know that I will try to be far away from this village *and* our King Beowulf ere its owner misses it and comes calling."

"A pact?" asks Guthric, his curiosity piqued. "What manner of pact?" And Sigga turns and stares at him a moment, then looks back to the fire.

"I do not know, Guthric, why you come here. You do not believe—"

"I believe all is not what it seems with our king," Guthric tells her. "I believe there are secrets, secrets that have robbed my father of the throne and myself of princedom. And I would *know* these secrets."

Sigga takes a deep breath and exhales with a shudder. "Child, you come always asking questions, but ever you seek only the answers that would make you happy, the answers which you *believe* you know already. And I ask you, please take this accursed thing from my home."

"I will, Sigga. My father and I will take our leave and never come here again, but *first*, you will tell me of this pact."

"She knows nothing," grumbles Unferth, tucking

the golden horn away. "Leave her be. I have business with the king."

"She knows *something*, Father. She would not be so *frightened* if she knew nothing."

Sigga stirs at the fire and shakes her head. "I listen to the trees," she says. "The trees tell me things. The rocks speak to me. I speak with bogs and birds and squirrels. They tell me what men have forgotten or have never known."

"Guthric, do not be a fool. She talks to rocks," says Unferth, tapping at the floor with his staff. "She talks to *squirrels*."

But Guthric ignores his father and leans closer to Sigga. "And what do they tell you?" he asks. "What have they told you of King Beowulf?"

"It is your death, that horn," she says, almost too quietly for Guthric to hear. "And still, you care only for your question. Fine. Then I will tell you this," and she sets the poker aside, leaning it against the hearth.

"She is a madwoman," says Unferth. "Leave her be."

"There is a tale," says Sigga, "a story that the spruces growing at the edge of the bog whisper among themselves at the new moon. That Lord Beowulf made a pact with the merewife that he would become King of the Ring Danes and Lord of Heorot, and that this same pact was made with King Hrothgar before him.

"What is this *merewife*?" asks Guthric, and Sigga makes a whistling sound between her teeth.

"That I do not know. She has many names. She may have been worshipped as a goddess, once. Some have called her Njördr, wife of Njord, and others have named her Nerthus, earth mother. I do not believe that. She is something crawled up from the sea, I think, a terrible haunt from Ægir's halls. Long has she dwelled in the tarn your father calls *Weormgraef*, and in unseen caverns leading back to the sea. By her, Hrothgar sired his only son."

"How much more of this nonsense must we listen to? Have you not heard enough?" asks Unferth, stalking back and forth near the door, but Guthric shushes him.

"Hrothgar sired no sons," says Guthric. "This is why the kingdom could be passed to the Geat so readily."

"He sired *one*," Sigga replies. "The monster Grendel, whom Beowulf slew. That was Hrothgar's *gift* to the merewife, in exchange for his crown."

"You cannot believe this," says Guthric, looking toward his father, who has opened the cottage door and is staring out at the snow and the sleigh, Cain and the darkening sky.

"I tell you what the trees tell me," she answers. "Grendel was Hrothgar's child. But the pact was broken when Hrothgar allowed Beowulf to slay the merewife's son. So, she took her revenge on *both* men—"

"I've heard enough," says Guthric, standing and stepping away from the hearth. "I'm sure there is some speck of truth in this, somewhere. I have always known that Beowulf could not have come by the throne honestly. But I cannot believe in sea demons, nor that Hrothgar sired a monster."

"You hear that which you *wish* to hear," Sigga sighs. "Your ears are closed to all else. But I will *show* you something, Unferth's son, before you take your leave." And at that she reaches one hand into the red-hot coals and pulls out a glowing lump of peat. It lies in her palm, and her flesh does not blister or burn. "I brought you into Midgard, and I would have you know the danger that is now upon us all."

The ember in her hand sparks, then seems to unfold like the petals of a heather flower. "Watch," she says, and the flames become golden wings and glittering scales, angry red eyes and razor talons. "He is coming," she says. "Even as we speak, he is on his way." And then Sigga tilts her hand, and the coal tumbles back into the fire. "If you care for your wife and children, Guthric, you will take them and run. You will leave Heorot and not look back."

Then the head of Unferth's staff comes down hard against the back of Sigga's skull, and there's a sickening *crunch* before she slumps from the stool and lies dead before the hearth.

"Will you leave her now?" Unferth asks his son. "Or do you wish to remain here and keep her corpse from getting lonely?"

"Father . . ." gasps Guthric, the image of the dragon still dancing before his eyes. "What she said. I saw it."

"Fine," growls Unferth, wiping the blood from his staff. "Then go home to your wife and children. Run away, if cowardice suits you so well. Hide somewhere and cower from the lies this witch whore has told you. But I have business at the keep, and I will wait no longer. Already, the day is fading, and you have cost me hours I did not have to spare."

"You saw it, too," Guthric says.

"I saw a sorcerer's trickery," replies Unferth, and he turns and walks back to the sleigh as quickly as his bent and aching bones will allow. Later, he thinks, he will send men to feed the woman's carcass to the pigs and burn the hovel. Cain sits shivering pitifully beneath his blanket and does not say a word as Unferth climbs aboard the sleigh and takes up the reins in both his hands. When he looks up, Guthric is watching him from the doorway of the witch's foul abode.

"Are you coming with me?" Unferth asks.

"You *saw* it," Guthric says again. "Maybe it was something you knew all along. Either way, I must go to my wife and to my children now. We must leave Heorot while there is still time."

"I thought you did not *believe* in stories of monsters and demons," laughs Unferth as he turns the ponies around in the narrow alleyway outside the hovel. "I thought you even doubted the God and savior whose cross you wear there round about your neck. But *now*, now you will flee from a *dragon*? Fine. Do as you will, son." And then Unferth whips at the ponies' backs with the reins, and they neigh and champ at their bits and carry him and Cain and the golden horn away into the white storm.

This near to midwinter, the days are almost as short as Danish days may be, hardly six hours from dawn until dusk, and by the time Unferth has secured an audience in the antechamber behind the king's dais, the sun has set, and night has fallen. Already, the celebration in the horned hall has begun in earnest, and from the other side of the door come drunken shouts and music, the songs of scops and the rowdy laughter of thanes and their women. There is but a single table in the room and a single empty chair. Unferth pushes back the hood of his cloak and stomps his feet against the stone floor, dislodging muddy clumps of melting snow. Behind him, Cain stands shivering and staring out at the balcony and the dark sea beyond. There is a small fire burning in the fireplace, but the room is still so cold that their breath fogs.

Then the door leading out to the dais and the mead hall opens, and the noise of the celebration grows suddenly louder, but it is not King Beowulf come to speak with him, only Wiglaf, and Unferth curses silently.

"Unferth, you're not celebrating your king's glory tonight?" Wiglaf asks, and Unferth glares at the open door until Wiglaf shuts it again. "You and your family are missed in the hall," adds Wiglaf.

"I have brought something for the king," Wiglaf says, and he holds up the golden horn, wrapped in a fold of his robes.

Wiglaf extends his hand. "Then you'll show it to *me* first."

"Bollocks, Wiglaf. I'll show it first to Beowulf. Believe what I say. *The king needs to see it!*"

The door opens again, and now Beowulf stands in the entryway, glaring at Unferth. "The king needs to see what?" he asks, and narrows his eyes.

Unferth steadies himself against that steely gaze and takes a deep breath. His frown melts into a smirk. "A gift fit for a king," he says. "Lost and now found."

Unferth unwraps the golden horn, and once again its curves and the ruby set into the dragon's throat glitter in the firelight. At the sight of it, Beowulf's eyes widen with an expression of astonishment and also what Unferth hopes is fear.

"Do you *recognize* it, my lord?" asks Unferth, already certain of the answer.

Beowulf stares at the horn, and for a time there is only the muffled noise from Heorot Hall, the wind howling around the corners of the balcony, the sea slamming itself against the cliffs far, far below.

"Where did you *find* . . . this?" Beowulf asks at last.

Unferth moves to stand nearer the king, holding the horn up so that Beowulf might have a better view of it.

"Somewhere in the wilderness beyond the village

walls. My slave, Cain . . . *he* found it, if the truth be told. He will not say exactly where. I have beaten him, my lord, and still he will not say where it was he came upon it. My lord, isn't *this*—"

"It is *nothing*!" roars Beowulf, and with a sweep of his arms, he knocks the horn from Unferth's hands and sends it skidding, end over end, across the floor of the anteroom. The golden horn comes to rest at the feet of Queen Wealthow, who stands in the doorway, behind her husband. She reaches down and lifts the horn, once the finest prize in all King Hrothgar's treasury.

"So," she says. "I see it has come back to you . . . after all these years." And she passes the horn to her husband; he takes it from her, but holds it the way a man might hold a venomous serpent.

"Where is he?" asks Beowulf, and there is a tremor in his voice. "The slave. The slave who *found* it. Is that him?" And he points toward Cain.

"Indeed, I have brought him here to you," replies Unferth, and he turns and seizes Cain by the shoulders, forcing him roughly down upon the floor at Beowulf's feet.

"Please," Cain begs, "please don't kill me, my king."

Beowulf kneels beside Cain and shows him the horn. "Where did you find this treasure?" he asks.

Cain shakes his head and looks away, staring instead at the floor. "I . . . I'm sorry I ran away, my lord. Please . . . don't hurt me anymore."

At that, Unferth kicks Cain as hard as he can, and

the slave cries out in pain and terror. "Answer your king!" snarls Unferth.

"Stop!" orders Beowulf, glaring up at Unferth. "He will tell us *nothing* if you beat him senseless."

Cain gasps, and now his lips are flecked with blood. "I didn't steal it," he says. "I swear, I didn't steal it."

"Where?" asks Beowulf, lowering his voice and speaking as calmly as he can manage. "*Where* did you find it?"

"The bogs," answers Cain, his voice barely louder than a whisper. "Through the forest and down to the bogs."

"The bogs," says Beowulf, getting to his feet again.

"I was *lost*," Cain continues, rubbing his hands together, then wiping at his bloody lips. "Lost in the bog, and I thought I would never find my way out again. But I found a cave . . ."

"A cave?" asks Beowulf. "That's where you found the horn, inside a cave?"

"Aye," mutters Cain, nodding and looking at the bloodstain and snot smeared across the back of his left hand. He sniffles loudly. "I found it in the cave. There was so *much* treasure in the cave, my lord. So many pretty rings and bracelets, so much *gold* and *silver* and so many pretty stones. Such riches. Oh, and there were statues—"

"And you *took* this from the cave?"

"I did, my lord. But there was so *much* treasure. And I only took this one small thing."

"And that's *all* you saw there?" asks Beowulf, glancing toward Wealthow, who's watching the slave and so doesn't notice. "Only treasure? No *demon*? No *witch*?"

Cain looks up and shakes his head. "I was going to take it back," he says. "I swear. I only meant to keep it for a time, then return it."

"There was no woman there?" asks Queen Wealthow.

"No woman, my lady," Cain tells her. "Only treasure."

And now Wealthow does look toward Beowulf, and her violet eyes seem to flash in the dim room.

"No woman was there," Cain repeats, and sniffles again.

"Listen to me, Beowulf," Unferth says, and takes a step nearer Beowulf and Wealthow. "While there is yet time, hear me. I *know* what this means."

"You know nothing," Beowulf replies. "It is only some trinket, some bauble misplaced a thousand years ago."

"My lord, I have seen this horn before. I have held it, as have you and my lady Wealthow. This is no lost bauble. This is the very horn that Hrothgar gave to you."

"My king," Unferth continues, looking anxiously from Beowulf to Wealthow, then back to Beowulf, "you have no heir. But I have a son. I have a *strong* son. Now, while there is *time*, name Guthric heir to your throne."

"Truly, it saddens me . . . how age has robbed you of your *wits*, friend Unferth," says Beowulf. "But I will hear no more of this madness tonight or ever. Your slave found a *trinket* and nothing more."

"A trinket from a dragon's lair," hisses Unferth. "*Goddamn* you, Beowulf, I *know*—" But before he can finish, Beowulf turns around and leaves the anteroom, disappearing through the doorway, swallowed alive by the noise and smoke of the celebration and Heorot Hall.

"I did not think you a man who *spoke* in blasphemies," Wealthow says. Then she takes two gold coins from a pocket of her dress and holds them out to Unferth. "And please, take these in exchange for this man's freedom." She looks down at Cain, cowering on the floor. "I will not stand by and watch again while he is beaten like a cur for your amusement, old man."

Unferth blinks at the coins and laughs, a sick and cheated sort of laugh, a laugh tinged through and through with bitterness and regret. He taps his staff smartly against the flagstones and jabs a crooked finger at the queen.

"I would take no gold from out this cursed house," he sneers. "But if you wish a *dog*, my queen, then he is yours. Bid my lord to keep the golden horn for his own. I feel quite certain it has been trying to find its way back to him these last thirty years. Pray that none come seeking it, Queen Wealthow."

"Show him out, Wiglaf," says Wealthow, returning the coins to her pocket. "Then please care for this poor man. Find him some decent clothes." Then she sets her back to Unferth and follows her husband, shutting the door to the dais behind her.

"I *know* the way," Unferth tells Wiglaf, and as he hobbles slowly down the long hallway leading back out to the snowy night and his sleigh, the son of Ecglaf tries not to think about what he might or might not have seen dancing on a witch's palm.

17

Fire in the Night

Sleeping safe beside King Beowulf, Ursula is dreaming of the very first time she laid eyes on Heorot. She was still only a child when her family gave up their farm on the hinterlands. Her brother had been taken by wolves one summer, and thereafter her mother's mind became unhinged. She would wander alone at night across the moorlands, risking her own life, and nothing her husband could do or say would persuade her that the dead boy would never be found. So they came to Heorot, where Ursula's father found work in the stables and, in time, her mother accepted the loss of her son. In the shadow of the keep towers, behind walls no wolf could breach, Ursula grew to be a woman.

In the dream, she is standing in the back of her father's rickety wagon as it bumps and shudders along the rocky road leading to the village gates. She beholds the world with a child's eyes, and though she has heard tales of Heorot and the mead hall of mighty King Beowulf, she did not imagine anything half so grand as this. Surely even the gods and goddesses in Ásgard must envy such a magnificent edifice, and, as the keep looms nearer, it seems as though she is slipping out of the world she has always known and into the sagas and bedtime stories her mother has told her.

"Papa, are there trolls here?" she asked.

"No trolls," he replied. "There was one, long time ago, when I was still a young man. But it met its end in the coming of King Beowulf from Geatland."

"Are there witches?"

"No witches, either," said her father. "There was one, an evil hag from the bogs, but she, too, was slain by good King Beowulf."

"What about dragons, Papa? Are there dragons here?"

And upon hearing this third question, her father shrugs and glances up at the leaden sky. "I am only a farmer," he tells her. "What would I know of dragons? But I wouldn't worry, child. Hrothgar, who was king before Beowulf, he slew the last dragon in these lands before I was born, or so my *own* father always said."

And then she turns to her mother. In the dream, her mother's eyes are bleeding, and there are black tufts of feathers sprouting from her arms.

"What about the wolves, Mama?" she asks.

"No wolves," replies her mother. "Not here, for the walls are too high, and the warriors kill any wolves that come too near."

"What if the wolves grew wings?" Ursula asks her mother, who scowls and grinds her teeth.

"Wolves cannot grow wings," her mother answers. "Don't be such a silly child."

"They might dig tunnels deep below the ground," Ursula suggests. "The dwarves might *help* them dig tunnels under the walls of Heorot."

"The dwarves are no friends to the wolves," her mother says. "Do not forget how they forged the chain Gleipnir, thin as a blade of grass, yet stronger than any iron. And the wolves could never do such a thing all on their own." And then her mother coughs out a mouthful of black feathers and blood.

"What if the wolves came by *sea*?" asks Ursula. "What if the wolves built ships and learned how to sail the whale's-road?"

"The cliffs are too steep," her mother says, spitting more feathers. "And Lord Beowulf's archers are always watchful of the sea for invaders and wolves in boats."

"You worry about dragons," says her father, giving the reins a sudden tug. "Worry about trolls and witches, girl, but say no more this day of wolves."

"Then may I worry about *bears*?" she asks her father.

"You *are* a bear," he says. "You are *Ursula*, our little bear, and bears should not fear their own."

"I am a bear," she says very softly, speaking only to herself, and her mother, who has become a raven, caws and flies away toward the sea. Her black wings seem to slice the edges of the sky, so that soon it has begun to rain. Not drops of water, though, but drops of blood that spatter on the fields and road. Her father tells her not to worry, that her mother will be better soon.

But then the dream has changed, as dreams are wont to do, and Ursula is grown and wandering the moorlands alone, just as her mother did years before, searching in vain for a stolen boy. The sky above her has been torn asunder, ripped to hang in blue-gray strips, and she knows that the time of Ragnarök must at last be upon Midgard. The monster wolf Fenrisulfr has at last grown so large that when he opens his mouth, his snout brushes the stars aside and his chin drags upon the earth. He has broken free of the dwarves' chain and escaped his island prison of Lyngvi, and soon will the son of Loki devour Odin Allfather, before it is cut down by Odin's son, the silent god Viðar. Ursula wants to look away, wants to turn and run back to the keep, but she cannot take her eyes from the sight of the Fenrisulfr, filling up all the tattered sky. His teeth are as mountains and his shaggy silhouette blocks out even the light of the sun. His jaws drip steaming rivers to scorch the world.

"I don't want to see the end," whispers Ursula, wishing now that the wolves had also taken her when they took her brother, that she would not have to live to see the Twilight of the Gods and Loki's children set free to bring about the end of all things. The ground shakes beneath her feet, and everywhere she looks, the heather and bracken writhes with serpents and worms and maggots.

"It is only a golden drinking horn," Beowulf tells her, but he sounds frightened, and never before has Ursula heard fear in his voice. "Something I lost. That is all."

"My father," she says, "told me that Hrothgar took it as a trophy when he defeated the dragon Fafnir."

"That may be so," Beowulf sighs. "I could not say."

All around her, there is the terrible rending and splintering of the brittle spine of the world, wracked by the thunderous footsteps of Fenrisulfr as he marches past Heorot to keep his appointment with Viðar. The two towers of Beowulf's keep crumble and fall into the sea, and the sky has begun to rain liquid fire.

"It is very beautiful," Ursula says, admiring the golden horn in Beowulf's hands.

"The gods always knew that chain would never

hold the beast," her father mutters as the gates of the village come into view. "The beard of a woman, a mountain's roots, a fish's breath . . . such a waste."

"It means nothing to me," says Beowulf.

"It was your prize for killing Grendel," Ursula replies. "It was your reward."

"My reward," Beowulf whispers. "No, my reward was to die an old man and never ride the fields of Idavoll with the glorious dead. My reward was a frigid, Christ-worshipping wife and a pile of stones beside the sea."

Fenrisulfr turns and stares down at her, and his eyes are gaping caverns filled up with fire and thick, billowing smoke. He sees her and flares his nostrils.

"Father," she says. "Look. He is eating the sky alive."

"No wolves," he replies. "Worry about your dragons, little bear. Or you'll end up like your poor mother."

And she stares up into the furnace eyes of Fenrisulfr, seeing how little difference there is between a wolf and a dragon, on this last day, that they may as well be one and the same. A dragon devoured her brother, and King Hrothgar raided a wolf's golden hoard.

King Beowulf places a dagger to the soft spot beneath his chin, but *she* feels the blade pressing against her own throat. And then the dream breaks apart in the instant before Ursula can scream, the final instant before she dreams her death and her king's suicide, before Fenrisulfr swallows her and all of Heorot with her.

She lies naked and sweating and breathless beside Beowulf, and when she looks at him, he's clutching the golden horn to his chest, muttering in his sleep, lost somewhere in the labyrinth of his own secret nightmares. She watches his restless sleep and slowly remembers what is real and what is not. When she is finally certain that she is awake, Ursula rises from the bed and pulls on her furs and fleece-lined boots and very quietly leaves the king's bedchamber.

A spiral stairway leads up to the causeway connecting the two towers of the keep, and Ursula hugs herself against the chill air and climbs the granite steps. After the dream, she needs to see the sky and the sea and the moonlight falling silver on rooftops and the land beyond the village walls. She reaches the landing, a short hallway leading out to the causeway, and the air here is even colder than it was in the stairwell, and Ursula wishes she were wearing something beneath her furs.

She passes a tapestry, very old and neglected, torn in places and in need of mending. But even in the dim hallway, she can recognize the scene depicted there, Beowulf tearing the monster Grendel's arm from its shoulder. She keeps walking, and soon she has reached the place where the hall opens out onto the causeway and the winter night. She takes one step out into the moonlight, then she stops. Queen Wealthow is standing on the bridge, only a dozen or so yards away, clothed in her own fur cloak. She does not turn toward Ursula, but stares up at the twinkling stars.

"Another restless night?" she asks Ursula.

Terrified, Ursula can only manage to nod, and then the queen turns toward her. In the darkness, Ursula cannot be certain of Wealthow's expression, but there is no anger in her voice.

"It's all right, girl," the queen says. "I'm not an ogre. I'm not going to eat you."

Ursula takes a few hesitant steps nearer Queen Wealthow. In the light of the moon and stars, the queen's hair seems to glow like spun silver.

"He has bad dreams," says Ursula. "They've been coming more often, and tonight they are very bad."

Wealthow sighs and her breath steams.

"He is a king," she says. "Kings have a lot on their conscience. They do not have easy dreams."

Neither do I, thinks Ursula, wondering what sort of dreams queens have, what private demons might have brought Wealthow out into the night. Ursula glances at Wealthow, at the stars spread out overhead, then down at the stones beneath her feet. She wishes she could turn and flee back into the tower, back down to Beowulf's bed. The air smells like salt, and she can hear the waves against the rocks.

"Sometimes," she says, "he calls your name in his sleep, my Lady."

"Does he?" asks Queen Wealthow, sounding distant and unimpressed.

"Yes, my Lady," replies Ursula, trying not to stammer. "I believe he still holds you in his heart."

Wealthow cocks one eyebrow and stares skeptically at her husband's mistress. "Do you indeed?" she asks. Ursula catches the bitter note of condescension, and for a moment neither of them says anything else. The silence lies like ice between them, like the empty spaces between the stars, until Ursula finds her voice.

"I often wonder. What happened . . ."

". . . to us?" asks Wealthow, finishing the question.

Ursula only nods, wishing she could take back the question, dreading the answer.

Wealthow watches her a second or two, then turns back to the stars. "Too many secrets," she says.

And then, from somewhere across the moorlands, there is a low rumble, and at first Ursula thinks that it is only thunder, though there is not a single wisp of cloud anywhere in the sky.

"Did you hear—" she begins, but Wealthow raises a hand, silencing her. And only a heartbeat later, the southern sky is lit by a brilliant flash, a hundred times brighter than the brightest flash of lightning, brighter than the sun at midsummer noon. Ursula squints and blinks, her eyes beginning to smart and water.

It's only the dream, she thinks. *I'm still asleep, and this is only the dream*, for after the white flash, a brilliant yellow-red-orange stream of flame erupts and rains down upon the homesteads beyond the gates of Heorot. The fire pours across the landscape like a flood, and the causeway rumbles and sways.

"God help us," says Wealthow, and then she takes Ursula roughly by the arm and leads her back into the tower.

18

Scorched Earth

In his dreams, Beowulf has watched the fire fall, the sizzling gouts spewed forth from fanged jaws and splashing across the roofs and winter-brown moors. Everything become only tinder for the dragon's breath, everything only fuel for the greedy flames. Sleeping, he has been shown the burning of homes and fields and livestock, has seen the outermost walls of the village seared and *still* the fire came surging forward, coming on like the tide, enveloping and devouring everything it touched. *She* has shown him everything, so much more than Beowulf could have possibly seen with waking eyes. He has seen the night split wide by this holocaust, and he has looked deep into the eyes of Death.

In the courtyard below the two grand towers of Heorot, King Beowulf stands and watches the stream of refugees fleeing the smoldering wreckage of the village, believing there may yet be some sanctuary to be found within the castle keep. But she has shown him *everything*, and he knows there will be no place to hide when next the sky begins to burn. The lucky ones have died in the night. Beyond the walls of the keep, an immense gray-black column of smoke and ash rises high into the sky to meet the winter clouds.

"By the gods," whispers Wiglaf. "I have seen war, and I have seen murder and atrocities, but never have I seen such a thing as this."

Beowulf does not answer, and he would shut his eyes if he thought it would drive these desperate, hurting faces from his mind. The freezing air reeks of smoke and brimstone and cooked flesh, and what snow still lies within the courtyard has been sullied with a thick covering of sticky black soot.

"I have even seen the work of demons," says Wiglaf, "but *this* . . ."

"How many?" asks Beowulf, his mouth gone almost too dry to speak. "How many are dead?"

"I cannot say," replies Wiglaf, shaking his head. "I have been all the way to the village gates and back, but . . . I just don't know, my lord. Too many."

The procession of the burned and bleeding, the broken and maimed, files slowly past, and most are silent, struck dumb by their pain or grief or the horrors they have witnessed. Others cry out, giving voice to their losses or injuries or dismay, and still others pause to look up into the face of their king. Faces slick with blood and fever and seeping blisters, faces filled with questions he does not know how to answer. Those who can yet walk stagger or shuffle or stumble along, but many more are carried into the keep by thanes or by the strongest of the survivors.

"It came out of the night sky," a wide-eyed woman says. There's a baby clutched tight in her arms, and Beowulf can plainly see the child is dead. "Our houses and farms, it burnt everything."

He knows no words to comfort her. He has no words to comfort any of them. Wealthow is nearby, moving among the wounded, handing out wool blankets. The red-robed priest is with her, but he seems lost, and his lips mouth a prayer that seems to have no end. Beowulf wonders what consolation Christ Jesus and the god of the Romans has to offer, what salvation they might bring to bear against this wanton terror and destruction.

As much as any god watching on from Ásgard, he thinks. *Little, or none at all.*

Then Wiglaf takes hold of his shoulder and is saying something, simple words that Beowulf should understand but can't quite wring the meaning from. And then he sees for himself and so does not need to be told—old Unferth in the arms of one of his guards, Unferth scorched and steaming in the cold morning air, his charred robes almost indistinguishable from his flesh. His beard and almost all his hair have been singed away, and there is only a crimson welt where his left eye used to be. The wooden cross still hangs about his neck, gone as black as the scalded, swollen hand that clings to it.

"My son," murmurs Unferth, and so Beowulf knows that he is alive. "His wife and my grandchildren. All of them dead. All of them burned in the night. But not me, Beowulf. Not me."

"You saw what did this?" Beowulf asks him, and Unferth grimaces, exposing the jagged stubs of teeth reduced almost to charcoal.

"The dragon," replies Unferth. "I saw . . . the dragon. *Your* dragon, my lord."

Beowulf glances up at Unferth's guard. There's a wide gash on the man's forehead, and his face is bloodied, but he seems otherwise unharmed. "Did you see it, as well?" Beowulf asks the guard.

"I cannot say what I saw," the guard replies. "But they are all dead, my sire, just as my Lord Unferth has said. I do not know how we alone escaped."

"My *son*," Unferth says again, then he coughs and there's a sickening rattle in his chest. "Because that wretch Cain *found* the golden horn, yes? You had an . . . *agreement* with her. But now . . . now, *you* have the horn again, don't you? Now . . . the pact is *broken*."

"He is delirious," says the guard, and Beowulf sees that the man is weeping now. "His reason is overthrown. I can make no sense of the things he says."

"You have the *damned* horn," snarls Unferth and a fat blister at one corner of his mouth bursts and oozes down his chin. "So the agreement is now *ended* . . . and my son . . . my son is dead."

"What agreement?" asks Wiglaf. "Unferth, who *said* these things?"

Unferth's remaining eye swings about wildly for a moment, then comes to rest on Wiglaf. "You *must* know . . . surely *you* know, good Wiglaf. Or has the King kept his secrets from you . . . all these years."

"He is delirious," the guard says again. "He does not know what he's saying. Lord Unferth is dying, my king, and I should find the priest."

"*Sin*," sneers Unferth, and now that one eye, cloudy and bloodshot, glistening with pain, comes to rest on Beowulf. "Sins of the *fathers*. That's the last thing I heard . . . before my family was burned alive, the very last thing I heard . . . before their screams. The *sins*, Beowulf. The sins of the *fathers*."

"*Who* said this?" Beowulf asks. "Tell me, Unferth. Who said these things?"

"*He* did," Unferth whispers, his voice shrunken now to hardly the faintest whisper, and Beowulf has to lean close to hear. "The pretty man with golden wings. *He* said it. You have a fine son, my king." And then Unferth closes that mad and rolling eye, and Wiglaf points the guard toward the priest, still standing with Queen Wealthow and still muttering his futile pleas and supplications. When the guard has carried Unferth away, Wiglaf runs his fingers through his hair and takes a deep breath.

"He was insane, my lord," says Wiglaf. "To have seen what he's seen, the death of his house—*any* man would lose his wits. When I went down to the gates, I saw all that now remains of Unferth Hall. Slag and cinder, Beowulf, a glowing hole in the ground, and little else." Wiglaf sighs and stares up at the column of smoke rising from the ruins of the village. "A dragon," he says and swallows. "Do you believe that, my lord, that a dragon is abroad, that a *fyrweorm* has come among us."

The pretty man with golden wings.

"What does it matter what I believe. What any of us *believe*. Unferth believed his crosses kept him safe from evil. I believed the age of monsters was behind us. Do not trouble yourself with belief, Wiglaf. Trust only what your eyes now see," and he motions toward the village. "This was not the work of man."

"But a *dragon*?"

"Or something near enough," says Beowulf. "Call my officers. Have them meet me in the armory."

"Some have surely died," says Wiglaf. "Others are unaccounted for."

"Then gather those who still draw breath, however many you can find. There is not much time, I fear. We must try and discover this fiend's lair *before* it returns to finish what it began last night. And we must make such defenses as we are still able, to protect those who have so long looked to us for protection. I have failed them all, Wiglaf."

"I will not believe that," Wiglaf says. "No king has ever guarded the land of the Danes as you have. If this thing . . . if it *is* a dragon . . ."

"Then perhaps we will have one last chance to seek our place in Valhalla," Beowulf tells him, watching Wealthow moving among the refugees. "Maybe we shall not die in our beds, sick old men fit only for Hel's gray realm."

You have a fine son, my king.

Wiglaf nods, but there is nothing like certainty or hope in his eyes. "This is not a troll and its mother," he says. "Whatever it is."

"Enough talk, Wiglaf. Make haste. The day will not be long, and we do not know what our enemy intends."

And so Wiglaf leaves him there, surrounded by the dead and the soon to be dead, and Beowulf can still hear the firestorm from his dreams, and the screams, and the fearful sound of vast wings bruising the night sky.

The day shines dimly through the narrow windows set into the thick stone walls of the king's bedchamber, but there is neither warmth nor joy nor even solace in that wan light. Beyond the walls of Beowulf's keep, the village still burns, and the king's warriors have reported that all their efforts to extinguish the blaze have been in vain. The breath of the great *weorm* has poisoned everything it touched, some strange incendiary substance that continues to burn even when doused with water and earth. The ground itself is burning. They have managed only to keep the flames from spreading inside the walls of the keep, and that pillar of smoke and ash still rises into the winter sky above the ruins of Heorot. It has turned the afternoon to twilight.

King Beowulf tugs at the straps of his breastplate, adjusting the fit of armor he has not worn since he was a younger man. Then he chooses a sword and shield from off the wall, and his longbow, too. He glances toward the windows, that hazy light falling across the bed he once shared with Wealthow, the bed he now shares with another woman—no, a *girl*, a girl young enough to be his own granddaughter. But it hardly seems to matter now, for surely he will not survive this day to ever again bed any girl or woman. It is waiting for him out there, what poor, mad, dying Unferth has named "the sins of the fathers." The price of the life he has lived.

The life she gave me, he thinks, and takes a great ax down from the wall. *It was never more than that.*

Beowulf has already given Wiglaf and the officers of his thanes their orders, to take up positions along the northern rim of the gorge dividing Heorot from the moorlands. If he cannot defeat this beast, they will be all that stands between the dragon and the keep's uttermost destruction. He could clearly see the doubt in Wiglaf's eyes, doubt that any man or army of men might stand against such a calamity, but Beowulf also saw in Wiglaf's eyes a grim determination.

The king lifts his heavy cape from an iron hook set into the wall, a great cloak sewn from wolf and bear pelts, and he drapes it around his shoulders. When he looks up again, Ursula is watching him from the doorway, and her cheeks are streaked with tears.

"I beg you," she says, her voice hardly more than a sobbed whisper. "Do not leave me. Please . . ."

"You are free to go," he tells her. "I release you. Find a good man, if one still lives when this day is done. Bear him children . . . bear him a son, Ursula."

She crosses the room to stand beside him, and Beowulf sighs and gently cradles her face in his scarred and callused hands.

"Please, child. Do as I've asked," Beowulf says. "Let me go down to this battle knowing that you will not waste your life grieving for an old man."

She shakes her head. "I don't want anyone else. I want you, my lord."

"I'm not the man you think me to be, Ursula."

"You are King Beowulf," she replies. "You're a great man, and a hero. This I *know* to be true."

"You know a legend," sighs Beowulf. "You know only the stories told by scops."

"I believe—" Ursula begins, but Beowulf places his hand firmly over her mouth, for he will hear no more of this, not today, not ever.

"Then you are as much a fool as all the rest of them," he tells her, making his voice as hard and unfeeling as he can manage. Confusion and fury flash bright in Ursula's wet eyes. She pushes him away and runs from the room.

Beowulf turns back toward the wall and catches his reflection in a shield still hanging there. "You are a tired old man," he says, speaking to that haggard image of himself trapped in the polished metal. "You go to seek your death in the wilderness."

"Indeed you do," says Queen Wealthow, and he turns about to find her standing in the open doorway. Her gown and furs, her face and hair, are smeared with black soot and stained with the blood of the dying and wounded whom she has helped to tend. "And indeed, husband, you *are* a tired old man. Cladding yourself in the armor of a younger Beowulf will not change that in the least."

"Woman, have you nothing better to do this day," he says, "than to trouble yourself mocking me? Shouldn't you be with your priest, doing the holy works of your weeping, merciful Christ Jesus?"

Wealthow steps into the room, pulling the door shut behind her.

"Why don't you take that poor girl and live out your remaining years in peace. You are an old man,

Beowulf. Let some young hero save us. Some wanderer from a far shore, a Frisian, perhaps . . . or a Swede. Some callow fool come looking for gold and glory and a crown."

Beowulf glares at her for a moment. He can smell the stink of burning seeping from her clothing.

"And start the whole nightmare all over again?" he asks, then shakes his head. "No. I have visited this horror upon my kingdom, like Hrothgar before me. And so I must be the one to make an end to it. Now. Today. I must be the one to finish *her*."

Wealthow's startling violet eyes, hardly dimmed by age, match his glare, match it and double it, and she walks quickly from the closed door to stand before him.

"Was she so beautiful?" Wealthow asks, and now there is anger in her voice. "Beowulf, is there in all the world *any* beauty so costly, any mere earthly beauty worth what you have seen today?"

"I could *lie*," Beowulf says. "I could tell you, my queen, that in the wisdom of my many years I have learned there is *no* beauty worth this terrible price. I could tell you she was only a hideous sea hag who bewitched me, casting a wicked glamour that only caused me to *think* her so beautiful a being. But how would that profit either of us? Yes, Wealthow, she *is* beautiful, a beauty beyond reckoning and beyond mere words and almost beyond imagining. A beauty the gods in Ásgard would themselves die for."

"The gods," scoffs Wealthow.

"Or even your ghostly Jesus," adds Beowulf. "Even *he* would have climbed down off his Roman cross for the love of such beauty."

"That is heathen blasphemy," Wealthow mutters.

Beowulf tries to laugh, but it's a dry and humorless sound. "Aye," he says. "For I am still a *heathen* king, and so I have not yet learned proper Christian blasphemy."

"It is not too late. You do not have to go to meet this fiend as an unbeliever and unbaptized. The priest—"

"—will get *none* of me," cuts in Beowulf. "Oh no, not that Irish sheepfucker. It is enough, I should think, that he has duped the better part of my kingdom with his talk of sin and salvation and heavenly life eternal. No, I will keep the gods of my father and his fathers before him. If there is any life awaiting me beyond this one, then I will be content to take my seat in Odin's hall, should I earn that honor. Else I will find myself with Loki's daughter in her foul hall on the banks of the Gjöll."

"You still *believe* these things?" asks Wealthow.

"In more than sixty years, I have heard nothing better. Certainly not the ravings of your dear sheepfucking Irish priest."

Wealthow takes a deep, resigned breath.

Beowulf swallows and scratches at his beard. "My lady, I do not wish to leave you with anger and bitter words," he says. "I would have you know, Wealthow, that I *am* sorry, that I do regret the suffering I have visited upon you and my people. I was a fool."

"You were a *young* fool," she tells him, still trying to sound angry, but her voice has softened, losing its keen self-righteous edge.

"Now I am a sorry *old* fool," Beowulf says. Then he pauses, lost for a moment in those eyes, lost in the memories of this strong woman who was herself only a girl when first he came to Heorot. "You should know, I have always loved you, my queen."

"And I have always loved you," she whispers, and smiles a sad and weary smile, then looks away so that he will not see the tears brimming in her eyes.

"She is only a child," Beowulf says. "Do not be unkind to her when I am gone."

"She is much more than a child," Wealthow replies. "You should have recognized that by now. But do not worry yourself, husband. I mean her no harm. *She* knows that. She will always have a place here, if she so wishes it."

"That is very gracious of you."

Wealthow shrugs, then glances back to her king.

"I will miss you," she says. "May you find whatever it is you seek."

Beowulf smiles, wishing that he might know one last night with the woman he took as his wife and queen so many long years ago, that he might hold her and know the peace he once knew in the sanctuary of her arms.

"Keep a memory of me," he says. "Not as a king and a hero, not as a demon slayer, but only as a man, fallible and flawed as any man. That is how I would be remembered." And then the King of Heorot kisses his wife for what he knows will be the final time, and she does not flinch and does not pull away.

19

Dark Harrower and Hoard-Guard

In truth, Beowulf is glad for Wiglaf's company. The king had ordered his herald and oldest friend, Weohstan's son, to remain behind with those warriors charged with defending the keep and what little remained of the village, the thanes commanded to protect the lives of those who survived the dragon's night raid. But Wiglaf protested, saying that the king should not ride out across the moorlands alone, and that one old man more or less would make little difference if Beowulf should fail and the *fyrweorm* return to Heorot. Better I ride at your side, Wiglaf said, and in the end Beowulf had relented. It is a grim prospect, to face death, but grimmer by far is the prospect of facing it in the wilderness alone. By the time the Geats rode out, the fires that had engulfed the village had mostly burned themselves out, leaving behind little to show that only the day before had stood a living, breathing town of men.

And now, looking once more out across the oily tarn, the peat-stained waters of *Weormgræf*, Beowulf is thankful he did not come here alone. In three decades, the place has changed in no way that he can detect. The poisoned surface of the lake still dances with that same unclean iridescent sheen. The grass still grows thick and brown around its boggy shores, and at this spot where the mist-bound land rises up into a steep bank crowned with three mighty oaks, the steaming lake still flows down beneath the earth, gurgling softly as it passes between the knotty roots of the three oaks. The air stinks of rotting vegetation and fungi, mud and peat and dead fish.

But this time, Beowulf and Wiglaf did not cross the ancient forest beyond the moorlands and then the wide and treacherous marches, picking their way on foot. There is another route, one not known in those faraway days when Grendel and its dam terrified the men and women of the horned hall. And so the two men have come on horseback, wandering bleak and rocky paths down to the lake and the three trees and the cave leading deep below ground. But as they near the trees and the water's edge, their mounts whinny piteously and stamp their hooves against the gravelly soil and shy away from the *Weormgræf*.

"You cannot blame them," Wiglaf says, then he leans forward and whispers something comforting into his horse's right ear.

"This is the place," says Beowulf, tugging hard at the reins of his own mount, pressing his heels lightly into the frightened horse's ribs. "Long years has it haunted my dreams, Wiglaf. In nightmares, I've come here a thousand times. But never once did I suspect I'd have need to visit it again awake."

Wiglaf pats the horse's neck, then sits up straight in his saddle and stares out across the tarn. "It hasn't changed," he says. "It's the same sorry piss hole it was the day you killed Grendel's mother, a blighted waste fit only for demons and their kin."

"But I have changed. I am no longer a boastful young man," Beowulf mutters, half to himself. "Once, I might have called this night-ravager out to face me in the open. I might have faced *it* as I faced Grendel, naked and without any weapon but my own strength."

Wiglaf turns his head and looks to Beowulf, who is staring at the three trees and the entrance to the cavern. His eyes are distant, and to Wiglaf he seems lost in unpleasant thoughts. For a while, there are only the sounds of the skittish horses, the wind, and a noisy flock of ravens watching from the oaks. When the King of the Ring-Danes speaks again, his voice seems to Wiglaf to have grown heavy as the cold air, as though every word is an effort.

"There is something I must say, my Wiglaf."

"Yes, my lord?"

Beowulf takes a bracing, deep breath and exhales fog. Some part of him had wished that they would reach this place and find that the grasping, probing roots of the trees had long ago sealed the entryway, that the ground itself had collapsed, closing off the path leading down to those haunted subterranean pools.

"I have no heir," he says. If I should be slain by this creature . . ." and he pauses and takes another deep breath. ". . . if I should *die* this day," Beowulf continues, "then you shall be king, Wiglaf. I have arranged it with the heralds. They have been given my instructions."

Wiglaf turns away, looking back out across the tarn. "Don't speak of such things, my lord," he tells Beowulf.

Beowulf sighs loudly and stares at the grim opening waiting for him there between the oaken roots. A sorrow has come over him, and he has never been a man at ease with sadness. He is holding the golden drinking horn, Hrothgar's horn returned to Heorot by Unferth's slave.

"Wiglaf, there is something I would have you know. Something you *must* know."

"There's a story about this place," Wiglaf says, as though he has not heard Beowulf. "It was told by a woman in the village, an Icelander wench called Sigga. Some say she is a witch and a seer. I expect she's dead now, dead or dying. She said this hill"—and Wiglaf motions toward the trees and the steep bank—"did not begin as a dragon's hoard or as a demon's den. She said that it's the barrow of the last man of a long-forgotten race. The name of that man and his people has been lost to the world for three hundred years."

"Wiglaf," Beowulf begins, but Wiglaf shakes his head and points up at the trees, their limbs heavy with raven feathers.

"Sigga said that the three oaks were planted by that last man, and that they are meant to represent the three Norns—Urd, Skuld, and Verdandi. The roots of the trees are the great tapestry of fate that the Norns have woven. I have heard it said that the witch called this place—"

"*Wiglaf*!" Beowulf cuts in impatiently, as his voice draws a raucous new chorus of caws from the ravens. "There is something I *have* to say to you. And you have to *listen*."

Wiglaf turns suddenly about to face his king, and Beowulf has never seen such fury in the Geat's eyes as he sees there now, some desperate wrath boiling up, wild and hot. Wiglaf's cheeks are flushed an angry scarlet, and he narrows his eyes.

"*Nay*," he says, raising his voice to a shout. "There is *nothing* I must know I do not know already! You are *Beowulf*. Beowulf the *mighty*! Beowulf the *hero*! *King* Beowulf, the slayer of and destroyer of trolls and sea hags and demon spawn! *That* is what I know, my lord, and *all* I need to know, this day or any other. Now . . . let's do what we *came* here to do. Let's *kill* this bloody flying devil where it sleeps and get on with our bloody lives!"

For a moment, Beowulf stares back at him in stunned silence, while the ravens caw and flutter their wings in the trees. He thinks that maybe he has never truly *seen* Wiglaf before now, that he has only ever glimpsed some shadow of the man, and he knows, at least, that he has done the right thing, naming Wiglaf his successor to the throne.

"Now," says Wiglaf, then pauses to get his breath. Already, the anger is draining from his face. "Do you want me to go in with you?" he asks his king.

Beowulf merely shakes his head.

"Good, I will wait here," replies Wiglaf, eyeing the ravens in the three oaks. "Perhaps I can make some decent sport of our blustering friends up there," and he reaches for his longbow.

King Beowulf has not forgotten the path down to the merewife's lair, for too many nights has he retraced it in his fitful sleep. The path below the trees, the first pool there below the hill—still infested with white eels and its muddy bottom still strewn with bleached bones and skulls—then the treacherous underground river spilling into some ancient chasm that the she-demon took for her home long ages ago. Beowulf doesn't fight the current, though the rocks batter and bruise his flesh. And in time he emerges once more from that lowest pool, from the icy water accumulated there in a void left when a buried monster rotted away—another dragon, perhaps—leaving only its bones to become the caverns walls, its massive spine to form a roof. Beowulf stands shivering and dripping a few feet away from the icy shore.

Unlike the tarn, this place has changed somehow since last he came here. It seems to have *grown*, the distances between the cavern's walls, from its floor to the stalactite-draped ceiling, increasing by hundreds of feet. The sickly blue elfin light that lit the chamber thirty years ago has dimmed, and the pool is black as pitch. There does not seem to be nearly so much golden treasure as before, as though the slave Cain is not the only man who has found his way here and plundered the hoard. Beowulf takes Hrothgar's drinking horn from beneath his mail and sodden robes, and it glows, casting a warm light across the rocks at his feet and pushing back some of the stifling darkness. The sound of dripping water is very loud, and Beowulf imagines if he stood here long, that dripping might come to sound as loud as the blows of Thor's hammer.

Beowulf holds the horn high above his head, and shouts into the gloom, "Come forth! Show yourself!" But by some peculiar property of this accursed place, some aural trick, a long and eerie silence falls between the act of speaking and the sound of his own voice. When his delayed utterance does finally greet Beowulf's ears, it seems to roll back as little more than an echo, diminished by the darkness and distance of the place.

Come forth! Show yourself!
Come forth! Show yourself!
Come forth! Show yourself!

He takes another step toward the edge of the pool, moving nearer the pebbly, muddy shore, but the moment seems to stretch itself into long minutes. So, thinks Beowulf, the sorcery shrouding this fetid grotto has been fashioned to twist sound *and* time, and that thought takes at least as long as a single footstep, fifteen minutes, ten, half an hour. His left boot sends up a crystal spray, each droplet rising so slowly from the pool, every one of them a perfect liquid gem reflecting and refracting the red-orange glow of the drinking horn or the soft blue phosphorescence of the cavern walls. Beowulf looks down, and there's his face gazing back up at him from the pool. But it's the face of his younger self, not the visage of the old man he's become. Those eyes are still bright with the vigor of his lost youth, and the beard that face wears has not yet gone gray. Then the sluggish arc of the droplets brings them back down across the water, and they strike the pool like deafening thunderclaps. Each drop creates a perfect ring of ripples that languidly radiate across the surface, intersecting with other ripples, and for some period of time he cannot judge, he stands there transfixed, watching them. When the water is finally still again, the face looking up at him from the pool is only that of a battle-scarred old man.

And then he feels dizzy and sick to his stomach and

feels something else, as well—an odd, unwinding sensation, as though time is suddenly catching up with itself again. His next footstep toward the shore takes no more or less time than any footstep should.

"I have not come to play games," he mutters, climbing out onto the shore, the rocks shifting and crunching noisily beneath his feet. Breathless, he pauses at the edge of the pool, exhausted by the arduous journey down from the tarn and the three oaks. There's a stitch in his side and the faint coppery taste of blood on his tongue, and Beowulf wonders if maybe he cracked a tooth as he was tossed and pummeled along the underground river connecting the two subterranean pools. He spits pink foam onto the ground at his feet.

"I no longer have the *patience* for such games," Beowulf says. "So show yourself, and save the trickery for someone who hasn't seen it all before."

There is a rattling, clanging sound from the shadows to his right, and Beowulf turns to see half a dozen figures shambling toward him across the stony beach. They are little more than skeletons, held together by desiccated scraps of sinew and shriveled bits of skin, wrapped up in rusty armor and rags. Some of them have lost an arm or a leg, and Beowulf sees that the nearest is missing his lower jaw bone. The figures glare back at him from eyeless skulls, dazzling cerulean orbs of the cave's faerie light shining out from otherwise-empty sockets. Beowulf reaches for his sword, but immediately the skeletal figures stop their staggering advance and stand very still, still as stone or mortar, all of them watching him.

"Hail Beowulf," the nearest says, its voice like iron scraping dry bone. And Beowulf realizes that this wraith was once the Geat Hondshew, one of the boldest and bravest of all his thanes. "Great Beowulf, who killed the monster Grendel."

To Hondshew's left, another thane, this one unrecognizable as its face is far too decomposed to bear resemblance to any living man, raises a bony finger and jabs it in Beowulf's direction.

"Hail Beowulf," it croaks. "Great Beowulf, who slew Grendel's demon mother."

Behind it, another of the dead thanes makes an awful, choking sound that might be laughter. "Hail mighty Beowulf," it says. "The wisest king, and the mightiest who ever ruled the Ring-Danes."

Now Beowulf takes several steps backward, retreating to the edge of the wide black pool. His hand still rests firmly on the pommel of his sword, but he does not draw it from out its sheath.

"This is but some deceit!" shouts Beowulf. "Some poor jest to throw me off my guard, to weaken my resolve!"

"Hail Beowulf," mumbles another of the fallen thanes, and Beowulf thinks this one might have once been Afvaldr who all the men called Afi. There is a dreadful commotion of rattling vertebrae and ribs, and Afi grinds his decaying teeth and points at Beowulf. "Good and faithful Beowulf," he says, "who left us all for *dead.*"

"You fell in battle," Beowulf replies. "I know my eyes have been deceived, for this day you ride the battlefields of Idavoll—"

"I was *murdered* by the monster's mother while I slept," snarls the apparition. "*That* is no glorious death. I will *never* have a seat in Valhalla."

"This is not *real,*" says Beowulf. "I cannot be fooled by such shoddy witchcraft."

Another of the shamblers has made its way to the front of the pack, and right away Beowulf recognizes him. The once-corpulent Olaf is now little more than a scarecrow.

"Hail the guh-great King Beowulf," snarls Olaf. "Liar and muh-muh-*monster.* Lecher and fuh-fuh-fool."

"You built your kingdom with our spilled blood," says the thing that wants Beowulf to believe it was once Hondshew and scurrying black beetles and albino spiders dribble from its lipless mouth. "You built your glorious keep from our *bones.*"

And now all the dead men raise their arms and cry out in unison, "Hail! Hail! Hail! Hail!"

"I will not *see* this," Beowulf hisses. "I will not *hear* this filthy coward's lie. Show yourself!"

And like a handful of dust in a strong gale, the wraiths come apart in some unfelt gust, vanishing back into the half-light and murk from whence they came. At once there is a new disturbance in the mere-wife's cavern, the din of great, leathery wings from somewhere directly overhead. And before Beowulf can draw his weapon, he is assailed by a violent blast of hot wind that almost knocks him off his feet. The air now reeks of brimstone and carrion rot. He hears footsteps and turns toward the ledge of ancient granite altar stone where, thirty years before, Grendel's corpse lay. The enormous sword, surely a giant's blade, is still mounted on the wall above the stone. Near the altar is a tunnel, yet another tributary of this underground waterway, and from that tunnel comes the disquieting echo of a soft male voice.

"How strange," says the voice. "When I listened at windows and from rooftops to the talk of the mighty King Beowulf, all the talk I heard was of a hero, valiant and wise, courageous and noble. But here, now I see . . . you're *nothing*, a pathetic, empty *nothing*."

Beowulf tries to push the images of the wraiths from his mind, steeling himself for this new horror, whatever it might be.

"I am Beowulf," he says.

Now, the water in the tunnel has begun to burn, whirling sheets of flame racing across it and licking at the travertine and granite walls. And in that flickering light Beowulf can clearly see the speaker, the image of a slender, well-muscled young man, and he is not standing *in* the water but walking *upon* it, as though he might weigh no more than a feather. The man's skin is golden, as golden as the drinking horn, and he is clothed only in a strapwork harness of curled leather. Except for his glistening, gilded skin, this young man might well be Beowulf, as he was in his twentieth or twenty-fifth year. There is a sinking, sour realization growing in Beowulf's mind, and he shudders and forces himself not to look away.

Give me a child, Beowulf. Enter me now and give me a beautiful, beautiful son.

You have a fine son, my king.

"I am Beowulf," the Lord of the Ring-Danes says again.

"You are *shit*," replies the golden man. Those three words bite at Beowulf's heart like the iron heads of an archer's shaft.

"Who," begins Beowulf, then stops and swallows, his mouth gone dry as dust. "*What* are you?"

The golden man, wreathed all in flame yet unburning, smiles a vicious smile. "I'm only something you left behind . . . Father."

Beowulf feels a weakness in his knees, and his heart begins to race and skips a beat.

"*Here*," he says, holding out the golden horn. "Take back your damned, precious bauble. The man who stole it has been punished. *Have* it, demon, and leave my land in peace." And with those words, Beowulf hurls the drinking horn toward the golden man and the fiery tunnel entrance. It lands at his feet with an audible splash, but also does not sink into the water as it should. The golden man looks down at the horn and shakes his head.

"It is much too late for that," he says, and raises one bare foot and gently presses it down upon the horn, crushing it flat against the water in an instant. Where the horn had been, there is only a bubbling puddle of molten metal. It floats on the steaming water for a second or two, then Beowulf watches in disbelief as it flows up over the foot and ankle that crushed it, melding seamlessly with the golden man's skin.

"How will you hurt me, Father?" he asks, stepping through a curtain of flame to stand on the stone floor of the cave, between Beowulf and the altar ledge. "With your fingers, your teeth . . . your *bare hands*?"

Beowulf licks his parched lips, and he can feel the heat from the flames against his face.

"Where is your mother?" he asks. "Where is she hiding?" And then, shouting toward the cave's ceiling. "Show yourself, bitch!"

The golden man laughs, a sound like rain and a handful of coins scattered across cobbles. "Nobody ever sees my mother," he tells Beowulf. "Unless, of course, she wishes. Not even me."

"This is madness," mutters Beowulf.

"You have a wonderful land, my Father," the golden man says and takes another step toward Beowulf. "A beautiful home. Oh, and *women*. Such beautiful, frail women. When I came and listened at windows, sometimes they *spoke* of your women. Your wise Queen Wealthow. Your pretty bed warmer, Ursula.

I wonder—which of them do you think I should kill first?"

"Why? Tell me, please, why are you *doing* this?"

The golden man raises a shimmering eyebrow and pretends not to understand the question. "Why am I offering you a choice?" he asks Beowulf.

"No, you bastard," snarls Beowulf. "Why would you harm *either* of them?"

The golden man nods his pretty head, and the smile returns to his face. "Oh, I see. Because you love them both so much, Father. And because I hate you."

"Your mother, she *asked* me for a son. I only gave her what she asked for."

Now the golden man is striding confidently toward Beowulf, trailing a mantle of flame in his wake. And with each step he takes, he seems to grow larger. At first Beowulf thinks it's only some other enchantment or guile of the cavern, but then he remembers how he watched the mortally wounded Grendel grow *smaller*.

"And she gave *you* a kingdom and crown," the golden man says. "And you have them still, your lands and your treasure . . . your glory *and* your women. But what have *I*, dear Father? Where do *I* fit in your grand scheme?"

"You are your *mother's* son," Beowulf replies. "She never *asked*—"

"Never asked? Haven't you ever *wondered*? You, an old man without an heir to his throne, have you never lain awake in the stillness of the night and wondered about the son whom you used to *barter* for power and riches? That he might have dreams and aspirations, that he might wish to be something more than a phantom and a bad memory?"

"My heir? You are an *abomination.*"

The golden man, taller than Beowulf now by a head, is standing only ten or twenty feet away, and he smirks and glances at the ground.

"An abomination," says the golden man. "Like poor Grendel, you mean? Grendel, the ill-made and misbegotten son of good King Hrothgar—"

"The *son* of Hrothgar?" asks Beowulf, disbelieving. "Can you speak nothing but lies?"

"You did not *know*? Did you truly think you were my mother's first dalliance with a son of Odin? Your Queen Wealthow knew, even before you met her—"

"I did *not* know it, and I do *not* know it now, for there is naught in you but bitter guile and deception."

"Say what you will, Father. My skin is thick, and you cannot make me hate you any more than I already do. Indeed, if you were to engrave my hatred on every star in the sky, upon every grain of sand on every beach from now until the end of time, you would still not possess the smallest *inkling* of just how *much* I hate you."

"How could I have known?" asks Beowulf.

"What matter? I am, as you say, an *abomination*, a *demon* born of an abominable union and unfit to sit upon your throne or upon any throne of man."

And now the golden man, the son of Beowulf, has grown to such a great height that he stands easily twice as tall as his father, almost as tall as the monster Grendel. And his gleaming body has begun another and far more terrible sort of transformation, that smooth metallic skin suddenly becoming rough and scaled. The flourishes and whorls of the curled leather strapwork he was wearing have vanished, leaving only their intricate patterns behind, spirals of buff and amber on his gilded hide. From his face and skull, an assortment of horns and other bony nodules and excrescences have begun to sprout. Where a moment before towered a man of unearthly, incomparable beauty, now there stands some equally unearthly but hideous creature, neither quite reptile nor man.

"How *will* you kill me, Father?" the thing asks, but its dulcet voice has become an ugly, guttural rumble as lips and cheeks fold back and shrink away, tissue retracting to reveal a mouthful of uneven yellowed fangs and a purplish forked tongue. Its thick saliva drips to the cavern floor and spatters across the stones where it instantly flashes to puddles of blue-white flame. "*Crush* my arm in a door and *tear* it off? Do you think that will be enough? Or will you cut off my *head* and take it back to your *pretty women* as a trophy?"

Beowulf draws his sword, and the creature sneers and laughs at him. Its hands have become talons, and its arms have grown so long they reach the ground.

"Last night, you visited unspeakable suffering upon

my people," Beowulf says, holding the blade out before him, horrified by the metamorphosis he is witnessing, but incapable of looking away. "You have *murdered*—women and children, old men in their sleep. You are as much a coward as was your foul half brother, Grendel. You rain death upon those you despise and never do you look them in the face."

"I am looking *you* in the face, Father." But its bristling, venomous mouth is no longer suited to human speech, and Beowulf can only just make out the slurred and garbled words.

"Then fight *me* and leave the others be, for they have *never* done you harm."

"But you *love* them, Father. Or so you *profess*, so you would have them *believe*. And I *do* hate you, so what better way might I ever harm you than by harming them? How better to take my vengeance?" More fire leaks from its jaws and spreads across the cobbles; Beowulf takes a quick step backward to avoid the flames.

There is a loud splash from the pool behind him, but Beowulf does not look away from the grinning dragon thing to see what might have made the sound.

"*Enough*," the creature snorts, and now it has grown enormous, its horned skull brushing against the stalactites, breaking off bits of the smaller dripstone formations. Its neck is long and ripples with serpentine muscles, and where its arms were but a moment before there are gigantic leathery wings. A spiked and spiny tail lashes from side to side, and with one blow it smashes the altar stone to rubble. The beast is gigantic, the size of a small whale at least, almost as large as the sea monsters Beowulf fought when he swam against Brecca so long ago. It shakes its massive head from side to side, and scalding air washes over Beowulf.

"THERE WILL BE NO MORE TALK!" it bellows. "NOW, FATHER, YOU WILL *WATCH* AS I BURN YOUR WORLD TO CINDERS!"

And as the dragon opens its jaws wide, belching blinding gouts of liquid fire, Beowulf turns and dives headlong into the deep black pool. The cold water closes around him, soothing his blistered skin, and he lets himself sink to the muddy bottom bathed in the red-orange light from above. He looks back up at the roiling inferno writhing across the surface, wondering how long before the entire pool is turned to steam. Then there is a gentle but insistent tug at his arm, and when Beowulf looks down again, the merewife is floating before him. Even more beautiful than his memories of her, and he thinks if only Wealthow could see her, surely then his wife would understand why he has done the things he has done. Her yellow hair drifts like a wreath about her face, and her blue eyes seem brighter than any dragon's fire. Her lips do not move, but he plainly hears her voice inside his head.

At last, you have met our son? she asks, and smiles, then raises a hand and lightly brushes his cheek with long, webbed fingers. *He is so very much more than my poor idiot Grendel, but then his father . . . his father is so much more than that fat dullard Hrothgar ever was.*

"Stop him," Beowulf says, mouthing the words, and precious air rushes from his throat, rising in silvery bubbles toward the fire overhead.

Why would I do that? she replies. *He is his father's son, dear Beowulf. He is a willful being, a veritable wolf of the bees.*

She drifts forward to kiss him, but now Beowulf can see the jagged, serrate teeth set into her blue-gray gums, the shimmer of scales between her breasts, and the Geat King is gripped by a powerful wave of revulsion. He raises his sword between them.

You will not hurt me, she whispers without speaking. *You could not, even if you tried. Now, go and witness the grand deeds our beautiful son has come to work upon this land. He will be disappointed if you are not there to see.* And she motions toward the surface of the pool.

On the hill overlooking the tarn, Wiglaf leans against one of the three oaks as the earth continues to shudder and roll beneath him. He has lashed both the horses to one of the lower limbs, and is grateful for having taken that precaution, for they would have fled in terror as soon as these convulsions began. Ripples spread out across the iridescent mirror of *Weormgræf*, and small waves have begun to lap at the shore. The horses snort and neigh. Their eyes roll, and they buck and pull at their restraints.

"You old fool," Wiglaf mutters. "What in the name of Odin's hairy scrotum have you gone and stirred up in there?"

And then Beowulf comes crashing through the tangled curtain of roots where the lake flows away under the hill. He flings himself down flat against the shore, and before Wiglaf can call out to him, the hill itself seems to exhale a white-hot burst of fire that incinerates the roots and then spreads out over the tarn, setting the oily, combustible water aflame. Beowulf rolls away from the edge of the tarn, and Wiglaf scrambles down the slope to help him. But then the earth heaves as though the last day of all has arrived, as though the Midgard serpent itself has awakened, and Fenrir is abroad and loosed upon the world. Wiglaf loses his footing and tumbles over on top of Beowulf.

"What have you *done*?" he asks, and the king glances back at the lake, squinting at the intensity of the flames.

"Be patient," Beowulf tells him. "I fear you will soon enough see that for yourself."

One last time the hillside heaves and shudders, and there's a deafening crack as the oak farthest from the reined horses splinters, its roots tearing free of the rocky soil, and it topples over into the tarn with a tremendous splash. Only a moment later, the fallen tree is brushed aside by the horror that comes clawing its way up from the caverns below, and Wiglaf stares speechless at the golden dragon as it erupts from the earth, scattering a fusillade of dirt and stone, mud and glowing embers. It unfurls its mighty wings and sails out across the burning lake.

Beowulf is already on his feet again, moving swiftly up the hill toward the terrified horses.

"It's a bloody damned dragon," says Wiglaf, pointing at the beast soaring across the bog.

"And it's heading for Heorot!" Beowulf shouts back at him. "Now, get up off your arse and stop gawking like you've never seen a monster before!"

"I've never seen a swifan *dragon*," mutters Wiglaf, standing up, but still watching the *fyrweorm* as it hammers at the air with its wings, silhouetted against the winter sky and rising ever higher, moving out across the marches toward the old forest and the moorlands beyond.

20

Fire Worm

If Wiglaf hadn't stopped him, Beowulf would have set out on horseback across the marches. And by now his mount would likely be hopelessly mired, leaving him to make the long, slow crossing on foot. Beowulf thinks it might have been his last idiotic mistake. Instead, he and Wiglaf have ridden back toward the moors by the same route that carried them to the poisoned, haunted tarn, a winding, rocky path skirting the bogs and the edges of the forest. And though they have ridden as fast as the horses can carry them along this craggy, treacherous path, it almost seems to Beowulf that he is back in the cavern again, caught once more in the merewife's time-bending spell so that each second takes an eternity to come and go. He cannot imagine that they will reach Heorot ahead of the monster, that they will return to find anything remaining but blazing debris where the keep once stood. And then Wiglaf shouts and points to the sky above the ancient trees, and Beowulf sees that the dragon is soaring in wide circles beyond the highest limbs.

"What's it doing?" asks Wiglaf.

"The bastard's *waiting* on me," replies Beowulf.

. . . what better way might I ever harm you than by harming them? How better to take my vengeance?

Beowulf tugs back hard on the reins, and his horse skids to a stop in a cloud of dust and grit. Wiglaf rides past, then slows his own mount and circles back.

"Ride on to the keep," Beowulf tells him, not taking his eyes off the dragon. "Warn them. Tell the archers to be ready. I'll see what I can do to slow it down."

"No," Wiglaf says. "I'll not leave you to face that beast alone, my lord. We'll face it together. The archers already have their orders."

"You will *do* as I have said, Wiglaf. We will not argue. I know what has to happen now."

"Oh," snorts Wiglaf. "So, it's not enough to kill demons and be crowned King of Denmark and bed a queen. *Now* you'd have me believing you know the weaving of the Norns and have seen their skein for yourself."

"Only a glimpse," Beowulf replies. "Now, do what I need you to do. Make haste for Heorot. Ride as though Loki's wargs were on your ass, and do not look back."

Wiglaf lingers a few seconds more at his king's side, peering through the settling dust as the dragon wheels and dips just above the tops of the tallest trees. There is a dreadful majesty in the rise and fall of those vast wings, a fearful grace in the motions of its unhurried flight.

"He's going to kill you," Wiglaf sighs. "You know that, right?"

"There is an old score to be settled this day," Beowulf says. "An old debt, friend Wiglaf, and it is none of yours. Now *ride*. Do not make me ask you a third time."

"Very well. But I'm warning you, there'll be Hel to pay if you reach the gates of Valhalla before me. How's that going to look to Hondshew and Afi and the rest, me staggering in last of all?"

"I'll be along soon," Beowulf tells him, and Wiglaf frowns and gives the reins a firm shake, urging his horse forward again. Soon, Beowulf is alone at the edge of the shadowy wood, and Wiglaf is only a distant, dusty smudge.

Riding along beneath the canopy of the old trees, it isn't difficult for Beowulf to keep an eye on the slowly circling dragon. There are enough gaps in between the boughs, and so many of them are completely bare of leaves in this dead month of Frermánudr that he only occasionally loses sight of the creature. His horse's hooves seem to clop unnaturally loud against the forest floor as Beowulf picks his way between the immense boles of ash and spruce and oak, larch and birch and fir. There is no trail here, except the indistinct paths made by deer and auroch and wild boars, and more than once he has to backtrack to get around a deadfall. He fears that the dragon might choose to follow Wiglaf, that it might take note of his dash back to Heorot and choose to pursue instead of waiting for Beowulf to catch up. But no, the dragon is waiting. This has been its plan all along. Beowulf understands that it, and its wicked mother, want him to miss none of the coming devastation. And were it to gain the keep before him, Beowulf might arrive too late and only see the aftermath. Overhead, the *fyrweorm* beats its wings, a sound that reminds the Geat of a storm wind whipping at canvas sails, and Beowulf glances up at the beast.

"Be patient," he says. "I am coming, worm. Do not fear that your previous hatred will be misspent."

Before very much longer, Beowulf has ridden far enough into the wood that the dragon passes directly overhead. His horse whinnies and staunchly refuses to go any farther.

"Fair enough," he tells the horse, and pats its withers and the strong crest of its neck. Then, very carefully, he gets to his feet and stands upright in the saddle, a trick he learned when he was still a boy in Geatland. Though his balance isn't what it once was, he only wobbles a little. There's a low oak limb within reach, and he uses it to pull himself into the tree. Beowulf straddles the limb and stares up as the dragon soars past once again, trailing smoke and embers. Below him, the horse snorts.

"Aye, it *is* a long damn climb," he says to the horse. And then Beowulf claps his hands together loudly, and the startled animal turns and gallops back toward the moors. Beowulf sits on the limb a moment, watching the horse go and getting his breath, then he begins to climb the oak. The limbs are large and spaced closely together, and it proves an easier undertaking than expected. Halfway up the tree, he remembers that this day is Yule, the day after Beowulf's Day, and that it is also Christmond, the day the followers of the Roman Christ Jesus have claimed as their own. Either way, he should by rights be sitting on his throne in the horned hall, feasting on roast pig and drinking mead and marking the turning of the wheel of the year toward spring, *not* climbing this bloody huge tree to confront a dragon intent upon destroying his kingdom. He's certain that it's no accident that the dragon—this creature born of his union with the merewife thirty years ago—has chosen this day over all others to make itself known.

When he has climbed more than halfway up the

oak, higher now than the tops of most of the trees in the forest, there's a horrendous screeching from the sky. Beowulf looks up to see the dragon swooping low, coming in close this time around, its jaws agape and steaming with noxious vitriol. He wraps one arm tightly about the tree, then uses his free hand to tug the bearded ax from his belt.

"Let's make an end to this!" he shouts, as the monster comes skimming across the treetops, decapitating a spruce with the leading edge of its left wing. But at the last possible moment, it veers sharply away, and Beowulf realizes that it means to make a game of this, to toy with him as long as possible. On its next pass, however, he's ready, and when the dragon swoops down, he pushes off from the tree, lunging toward the monster and managing to snag the spiked blade of his ax upon one of its hooked talons. An instant later and Beowulf is soaring above the forest, carried aloft below the beast's armored belly. He clings tightly to the ax handle and tries not to think about how far the fall would be if he loses his grip.

"So be it," growls Beowulf. "If it's sport you're after, you'll have sport. But know *this*, bastard, that the game will end in your death."

When the dragon realizes what Beowulf has done, it roars and spits rivers of fire into the trees, setting them alight. Its gigantic wings rise and fall more swiftly now and with more force, gathering speed, and its barbed tail whips viciously from side to side, tearing away many of the uppermost branches in its path and scattering them like so much kindling. Once or twice, Beowulf is very nearly dashed against those tallest limbs, but then, suddenly, the forest is behind them, and the dragon is racing out over the moorlands. In the distance, through the fog, Beowulf can make out the charcoal column of smoke rising from the ruined village coming into view, and he can also see the two spires of the keep and the causeway connecting them.

"*No!*" he says. "You will *not* have them, you ugly son of a whore, not this day nor any other," and he cranes his head to get a better view of the monster's gleaming underside. However, it resembles nothing so much as a heavily cobbled street paved over with gold, and Beowulf can scarcely imagine the blade has been forged that might pierce that hide.

But then the dragon belches flame again, scorching the grass and bracken far below, and this time Beowulf sees a distinct reddish glow from a fist-sized patch of skin near the base of its long neck. And he recalls the ruby set into the throat of the dragon on the golden drinking horn, also he remembers what Hrothgar once told him—*There's a soft spot just under the neck, you know. You go in close with a knife or a dagger . . . it's the only way you can kill one of the bastards.*

The dragon dives lower, and when Beowulf looks down again he can see the deep gorge dividing Heorot from the moors and the wooden bridge that spans it. The dragon is making for the bridge, he realizes, and a moment later he hears a man shouting from somewhere below, one of his commanders giving his archers the order to fire. And then Beowulf sees the soldiers rising up from the tall grass near the edge of the gorge, their longbows charged.

"*Now!*" cries the commander, and a volley of arrows is loosed and rises up, whistling through the cold evening air to greet the creature. But it incinerates most of them with another blast of its incandescent breath, and the rest bounce harmlessly off their target. The dragon sprays bright fire toward the archers, even as they release a second hail of arrows. One whizzes past Beowulf's right ear and another grazes his left leg just below the knee, and he wonders if this is how he shall die, slain by his own soldiers.

Then, abruptly, the dragon banks and dips, diving headlong toward the bridge. The archers break ranks and scatter this way and that as the screeching monster bears down on them, and Beowulf can feel his hold on the ax handle finally beginning to slip. The gorge lies directly below him now, a precipitous, boulder-filled chasm leading down to the sea, and a fall that no man could ever hope to survive. But already his aching, sweat-slicked hands are sliding down the shaft, and he knows that only seconds remain before he loses his grip. When the dragon spreads its wings and glides over the trestle, Beowulf lets go of the ax, dropping only a scant five or six feet to the surface of the wooden bridge. He lands hard and rolls along the deck and is back up on his feet in time to see the dragon's tail scraping along the walls of the gorge, digging ragged furrows in the earth and uprooting one of the small trees growing along the steep walls. The monster banks to the south, and Beowulf guesses that it's turning, coming around for another pass at the bridge. The Danish warriors stationed on the bridge watch the great beast's approach, as though they are too stunned by the monster's proximity and Beowulf's sudden appearance among them to do more than stare.

"Ready the wagons!" Beowulf shouts, and the sound of his voice is enough to startle the men from their awestruck stillness and get them moving again. More arrows are nocked by the archers, and several of the thanes roll two great wagons out onto the bridge. Inside one cart is a tremendous catapult, and in the other a crossbow, constructed after the fashion of a Roman ballista—a solid oak structure held together with iron plates and nails. At the back of the weapon, two thanes hastily work the twin winches, ratcheting the taut bowstring into the firing position. He might have no use for the religion of the Romans, but the son of Ecgtheow has learned much from their war craft.

"*Wait* for him," says Beowulf to his men, not daring to take his eyes off the dragon as it speeds back toward the bridge. When the creature is near enough that Beowulf can spot his axe still dangling from its talon, he gives the signal and the men in the wagons open fire. The bolt flies from the crossbow, but rebounds impotently off the dragon's adamantine hide. But from the catapult is launched an enormous net woven of braided hemp and strong enough to haul a small whale from out the sea. Beowulf watches as the net arcs up and over the gorge, unfolding directly in the creature's path. There is not time for the dragon to avoid the net, and a moment later its head, neck, and shoulders are ensnared, tangled in the weave.

A joyous cheer rises from the men, but Beowulf knows it is too soon to claim victory, and at once the dragon proves him to be right. With a single gout of flame, it effortlessly burns away most of the hemp, and as the beast soars by over the heads of the thanes, the ruined net falls away in a heap to lie smoking upon the deck of the bridge. Beowulf turns and watches as the dragon turns for another pass.

"Come on, then!" cries Beowulf, unsheathing his sword as the dragon wheels about in a wide arc. There is not time to reload the crossbow or the catapult, and the men who armed them make a dash for shelter. A few of the archers are still huddled there on the bridge, and they call out to their king, begging him to take cover while there is yet time. But Beowulf ignores their pleas and warnings. He will not cower and watch while this demon lays waste to his land, while it burns his keep and murders his thanes. The dragon turns back toward Heorot and the bridge, bellowing and spraying flame as it dives, and now Beowulf sees that this time it means to fly directly *beneath* the span.

"So it *is* a game," he whispers, and as the thing races toward him between the sheer granite walls of the gorge, the King of Heorot Hall turns and vaults deftly over the bridge's low railing, timing his leap perfectly so as to land on the monster's broad and scabrous shoulders. Beowulf brings the blade of his sword down, putting all his weight behind the thrust. But when the iron blade strikes the dragon's flesh it shatters like glass, and he's left holding little more than the weapon's hilt. The dragon flaps its wings once and rises from the gorge, and as it does so, it turns its head to glare back at Beowulf with furious amber eyes, eyes that shine and spark with a hateful, vengeful intensity.

"Are you ready to *die*, you filthy piece of *shit*?" Beowulf howls, but the cold wind whipping past snatches at the words, and he hardly even hears the question himself. Before the dragon turns its head away again, Beowulf imagines that it tries to smile, some smirking expression on those toothsome, lipless jaws half-approximating a smile.

The dragon shrieks and whirls back toward the trestle a fourth time, banking so abruptly and with such force that Beowulf is almost thrown off its back.

It opens its mouth wide and vomits an inferno across the timber bridge. The same thanes who only moments before had begged Beowulf to take cover with them are engulfed in fire, as are the two wagons. For some, death is instantaneous, but others somehow manage to rise and stagger a little ways through the flames before collapsing. Three or four men nearest either end of the bridge drop and roll in the snow banked high there, but this is no earthly fire that can be extinguished with melted snow.

Satisfied with the carnage, the dragon turns away from the blazing bridge, spying a ragtag troop of thanes retreating to the east along the cliff's crumbling edge. Once more, the fading day is rent by the monster's hideous shrieks, a sound to shame even the mighty cries of Odin Allfather's ravens. It folds its wings against its ribs and drops from the sky, falling upon the hapless men. Some are crushed beneath its belly and the living bulwark of its chest, and others are impaled upon talons and snatched up in those jaws and flung screaming into the gorge.

When every one of the thanes is dead, the dragon looks back at Beowulf again with that same smirking grimace as before. But now Beowulf can hear the golden man's voice, even though no voice comes from that slavering maw.

You see? it asks. *You see how easily men die? You see how none may stand against me, Father?*

"I will have your lizard's head on a spike!" snarls

Beowulf, and his head is filled with the golden man's laughter.

Will you, Father? Will you do that? No, I think not.

And then the dragon is airborne again, pitching and rolling in an attempt to dislodge Beowulf. But the Geat king digs his strong fingers deep into the grooves between bony plates and scales and holds on.

Wiglaf has ridden hard from the edge of the forest and across the moors, but it is no small distance, and by the time he reaches the gorge leading back to Heorot, the bridge is ablaze, and the air reeks of burning human flesh. He yanks back on the reins, and his horse rears and kicks. To Wiglaf's left, the ridge is scattered with the bodies of thanes who have simply been pulverized or torn asunder. The stone is smeared with blood and gore, and he can see where the monster's talons gouged deep grooves into the rock itself. He spares a quick glance at the heavens, and there's the dragon, maybe a hundred feet overhead. And there's King Beowulf, clinging to its back.

"Well," Wiglaf says to the horse, "at least it'll make a fine tale . . . if either of us lives to *tell* it," and he wraps the reins tightly in his hands. He starts to urge the horse forward, but just then there's a low rumble from the bridge, a loud crack, and one side of the burning structure breaks apart and tumbles into the gorge. Only a narrow section of the deck remains, three feet wide at most. And all of it is on fire, the flames rising above the shattered bridge to form a whirlwind and a twisting pillar of black smoke and red-orange cinders.

Wiglaf takes a deep breath, then spurs his horse forward and together they dash through the flames and out across the remains of the bridge, even as more planks pull free and fall away behind them. Squinting through the heat and blinding glare, Wiglaf thinks he's made it, that in only another second he will have gained the far side and Heorot. But the deck in front of him suddenly sags and collapses, plummeting into the gorge. He kicks the horse, driving his heels hard into its ribs. The terrified animal screams and leaps for the rocky edge of the gorge, carrying Wiglaf up and out of the flames.

Only just barely does the horse clear the chasm, landing at such an awkward angle and with such force that the animal's legs buckle beneath it and its rider is thrown. Wiglaf slides from his saddle, tumbling ass over tit, and comes down hard on the stones sticky with mud and ash. There is a terrible, uncertain instant, then, as the horse's hooves scrabble desperately at the slick rocks for purchase, and Wiglaf realizes that it's off balance and slipping backward toward the gorge. But the son of Weohstan still holds the reins wrapped tightly in his hands, and with all his might he pulls upon them.

"Oh no you don't, *hross*," Wiglaf grimaces, as he strains and the leather straps begin to slice through his gloves; the soles of his boots skid across the muck, dragging him forward. "If I have to go chasing after dragons, than *so do you*!" The horse slips another inch toward a long fall and certain death, before it neighs and gives a mighty kick with its hindquarters. Wiglaf feels the reins go slack as the beast at last finds its footing, and soon his feet are once again in the stirrups and the horse is galloping along the crooked road toward Heorot.

After its attack on the bridge, the dragon soars back out over the moorlands. Beowulf has succeeded in pulling himself forward onto the creature's spiny neck, and he lies there flat against its hide, contemplating his next move. The dragon twists its head madly from side to side, straining to see him, but Beowulf has found a blind spot.

"Don't worry," he says. "I'm still here. You haven't lost me yet."

Surely, Father, you cannot hope to win this battle, the golden man says, speaking from somewhere inside Beowulf's skull. *Here is the glorious warrior's death you have always wanted.*

"You will kill no more of my people."

I will do ever as I please, the dragon replies, the dragon and the golden man, two faces and one voice for the same nightmare. And now the dragon is banking sharply once again, turning back toward Heorot.

"It was no accident Unferth's slave found your

hoard and returned with the horn," says Beowulf, drawing his long dagger from its leather sheath.

There are no accidents, answers the golden man. *The skein was woven long ago, Father. We only move like spiders along its threads.*

Lying flat against the dragon's spine, Beowulf can almost reach down to that soft, glowing spot on the underside of its throat, that one fortunate chink in its otherwise-impenetrable armor. He grips the dagger and stretches his arm as far as he may. Only another few inches and he could easily plunge the blade into the unprotected patch of skin.

What do you think you're doing, Father?

"Something that someone should have done long ago," Beowulf replies, and the dragon ripples the muscles along its neck. The sudden, violent movement almost throws Beowulf off, almost causes him to drop the dagger as he struggles for a better purchase on the beast's knobby spine.

Look, Father. There's one of your pretty women now.

Beowulf raises his head, his eyes watering from the wind, but he sees that they've almost reached the keep, and he also sees Ursula standing alone on the causeway connecting the two spires. Already they have come so close that Beowulf can see the terror in her wide eyes.

She will die quickly, the golden man says, and the dragon dives for the causeway. The wind screams through its wings, and Beowulf imagines that it is Ursula screaming.

"*Run!*" he shouts at the girl, but she does not move, either because she cannot hear him or because she is too paralyzed with fear.

Again, the dragon's mouth gapes open very, very wide, its jaws distending and unhinging like those of some titanic adder. A sickening gurgle rises from someplace deep in its chest, and the monster spews forth a seething ball of fire. In his mind, Beowulf hears the golden man laughing triumphantly, and he can only watch helplessly as the deadly missile roars toward Ursula. But then he realizes that Queen Wealthow is running across the causeway toward her, and in the last moments before the dragon's breath strikes the keep, Wealthow knocks the girl aside, and both women roll out of harm's way. The flame splatters across slate and mortar, and as the dragon sails by between the towers, Beowulf sees Wealthow hauling Ursula to her feet before they run for the safety of the eastern tower.

Cheated of its kill, the enraged dragon bellows, and the golden man screams inside Beowulf's head. Immediately, it wheels back for another assault upon the women.

Beowulf can only hope that Ursula and Wealthow have had time to find shelter somewhere deep within the tower's thick stone walls. Holding tight to one of the spikes rising from the dragon's neck, Beowulf tries again to reach down and under its throat to plunge the dagger into the soft spot there, but it remains just out of reach.

If only your arm were a little longer, the golden man laughs. *They cannot escape me, Father. I will pull the castle down to its very foundations if need be, but I will have them, and I will have them now. I will taste their blood upon my tongue.*

"You will taste *nothing* this day, worm, but the sting of my blade," Beowulf growls, "and that is the last thing you will *ever* taste."

The dragon snarls, gnashing its rows of yellowed teeth, each almost as long as a grown man's forearm. It flares its cavernous nostrils and two greasy, fetid plumes of smoke stream back into Beowulf's face.

By the time Wiglaf finds himself once more before the gates of Heorot, the causeway far above him is shrouded all in flame. He guides his horse as quickly as he may through the blasted outer defenses and then onward, through the desolation where once the village and Hrothgar's mead hall stood. Everywhere are the corpses of the fallen, lying where the dragon's breath struck them down. But few are anything more than the roughest charcoal husks, only dimly suggesting the forms of vanished men and women, children and livestock. Here and there, blue-white tongues of flame still lick hungrily from the blackened, cratered earth. The stench is almost beyond bearing, and repeatedly

Wiglaf's horse tries to bolt, but he holds firmly to the reins and urges the terrified animal on until they have gained the keep. Above him, the causeway is in flame and the golden monster from Weormgræf seems to fill half the winter sky.

"Open these damned gates, you fools!" Wiglaf shouts as a handful of men struggle with the damaged mechanism meant to raise and lower the heavy iron portcullis grille. Beowulf ordered it closed behind them when he and Wiglaf left for the tarn many hours before, and the heat has since all but fused certain of the gears and counterweights. When the thanes have managed to raise it a foot or so, Wiglaf slides off his horse and scrambles beneath the metal pickets. Getting to his feet, he pauses again to stare up at the horror looming bright above the bailey.

One of the thanes, a man named Halli, rushes to Wiglaf's side. "The refugees have all been moved into the castle," he says. "Most of the men have also sought shelter, but . . ." and then Halli trails off and glances up toward the flaming causeway.

"But *what*?" asks Wiglaf, unable to look away from the dragon.

"My Lord, I am told the *queen* is up there," replies Halli and points toward the bridge between the towers. And an icy fist clenches Wiglaf's guts as the dragon releases another gout of fire.

"Get that bloody gate open and get my horse inside," he barks at Halli, then draws his sword and dashes across the courtyard toward the entrance to the east tower. Inside, he takes the steps two and three at a time, his heart slamming like Thor's own hammer inside his chest.

"*Faster*!" cries Wealthow, all but dragging her husband's lover toward the sanctuary of the keep's eastward tower. Behind them, the causeway has been completely swallowed by flame, and beneath her feet the bridge shudders ominously, as though the structure has sustained some mortal injury and might come apart at any moment, spilling them both to their deaths in the bailey far below. She does not dare look to see if the dragon is coming back. She already knows that it is, for Wealthow can hear the thunderous beating of its wings growing louder.

"But it's going to kill him," Ursula says breathlessly, trying to pull her hand free of Wealthow's grip.

"In all likelihood," replies the queen. "But that doesn't mean *we* have to die as well. Now shut up and *run*."

From his perch upon the dragon's neck, Beowulf can plainly see that there will not be sufficient time for the two women to gain the tower's entryway before the dragon is upon them once again, before they are within range of its fiery exhalations. He makes another futile attempt to reach around to the soft spot on the creature's underside. But his arm is simply too short, the dragon's neck too large around. Desperate, Beowulf glances over his shoulder at the great wings, fleshy membranes stretched taut between struts of bone, and to his eyes there does not appear to be any armor protecting them. Indeed, they are thin enough as to be translucent, and he can even make out the fine pattern of veins beneath the skin.

Shall I kiss them for you? the golden man whispers from somewhere inside Beowulf's head. *Shall I take them one at a time, or the both together?*

Beowulf stands up, letting the wind force him backward along the monster's spine until he is past its shoulder blades and come even with those membranous wings. *Perhaps,* he thinks, *Old Hrothgar was wrong. Perhaps there is more than one way to hurt the bastards.* And he dives for the right wing, plunging the dagger's blade into and through the tough but not inviolable flesh. The dragon shrieks in anger and surprise and unexpected pain. With one hand, Beowulf holds tight to the leading edge of the wing, and with the other he slices a long gash from front to back. Immediately, black blood seeps from the wound, and the air pressing from below rushes up through the wound, tearing it wider still.

"Does it *hurt*, worm?" Beowulf mutters, knowing now that he does not need to raise his voice to be heard by the dragon. There is no reply but for its shrill cry, and Beowulf pulls the dagger free and drives it in a second time, sawing another long slash in the wing, this one running parallel to the first. The monster tilts suddenly to the left, losing altitude and control, going into a spin as it struggles to stay aloft. Frantically, it flaps the damaged left wing, struggling to regain control and finally shakes Beowulf loose, tossing him high into the air. For several seconds, the King of the Ring-Danes is falling, watching as the dragon drops away below him, the creature rolling over and over again as the earth rushes up to meet them.

So, at last, this *is how I shall die,* thinks Beowulf, more amused than frightened of the end, much too tired and too relieved that Wealthow and Ursula have been spared to feel any fear at the thought of so unlikely a death as toppling from the back of a dragon.

But then, as the monster pitches forward and rolls completely over onto its back, it spreads its wings wide and the death spiral abruptly ends. Once more, the dragon is gliding, and a second later, Beowulf catches up, slamming hard into the low keel of its girded breastbone. Though stunned and gasping, the breath knocked from his lungs, he succeeds in digging his fingertips and the toes of his boots firmly between the armor scutes before the dragon rolls over again and rights itself.

Nice try, Father, the monster laughs bitterly, flapping hard and favoring its right wing now. It has begun a slow, steep climb, so that Beowulf finds himself standing upright, watching as they rise toward the causeway. *But not enough,* the golden man says. *Never quite enough.*

* * *

On the causeway, Wealthow has stopped running, certain for a moment that Beowulf has brought the dragon down, and she rushes to the balustrade and looks over the edge, expecting to see them both lying dead and broken on the flagstones below. Instead, she's greeted by the spiteful amber glare of the creature's roasting eyes staring up at her and by the sight of Beowulf clinging to its chest. The dragon flaps its wings again, and now it has risen level with the causeway, its eyes still fixed upon Wealthow, and it rears back and opens its jaws wide. Wealthow feels its breath on her, like a sulfurous, carrion wind blowing off some infernal battlefield.

"*Run!*" shouts Beowulf, but now she knows how the girl must have felt, unable to move or even look away from the awful grandeur of the thing. She is dimly aware of Ursula tugging hard at the sleeve of her gown.

"My queen," Ursula says, though her voice seems to come from someplace very distant, two words spoken from a half-forgotten dream or from the borders of a land beyond the walls of Midgard.

The dragon roars, its serpentine throat distending, filling up with flame, and the patch of skin just above Beowulf's head glows bright as a midsummer sun. And then Ursula is screaming and shoving Wealthow aside, both of them falling to the deck and rolling away as the air around them fills with fire.

* * *

It seems to Wiglaf that he spends at least a small eternity ascending the spiral stairwell, and when he has finally gained the uppermost level of the tower, a fierce burning pain rages within his chest as though the dragon has somehow found its way *inside* him, and Wiglaf is dizzy and nauseous and gasping for breath. Worse still, the landing and alcove at the top of the stairs is filled with smoke and the stench of the dragon's flame. He covers his mouth and nose with one arm and squints through the gloom with stinging, watering eyes, but sees at once that the causeway beyond is wreathed in flames. Even if Wealthow yet lives, there is no hope remaining that he may now reach her, for it seems the very furnaces of the fire giants, the forges of all Muspéllsheim, have been placed outside the tower. And yet he does not turn back, struggling to find some path through the flames and searing heat. And finally he is rewarded with a fleeting glimpse of the queen and also of his King's mistress, the woman Ursula. But once again the heat drives him back from the burning causeway, and his lungs fill with choking fumes as the tower begins to sway and shudder all around him.

"Twice now you've missed them," says Beowulf. "What kind of dragon is it cannot even kill two *women* caught out in the open?"

The fireball spilled from the creature's maw and surged across the causeway's span, but not before Ursula had pushed Wealthow out of the path of the blast, not before they were both safely out of range. Now, two pillars of flame spurt from the causeway, and his mistress and his queen are both trapped there between them. The dragon beats its wings, already preparing to unleash another attack, and this time there is nowhere left for the women to run.

"What manner of *son* are you, worm?" asks Beowulf, and then he answers his own question. "None of *mine*," he growls, and plunges his dagger into the soft, glowing spot at the base of the creature's throat. The blade and his fist punch straight through hide and sinew and into the hollow kiln of the monster's gullet.

Inside Beowulf's aching skull, the golden man screams, even as the dragon shrieks and coughs forth another gout of flame, searing most of the flesh from Beowulf's hand and arm and turning the dagger to molten slag. This blast misses the causeway, however, and momentarily billows overhead like an impossible, burning cloud. The king of the horned hall cries out, this pain greater by far than any he has ever felt in all his life, a long life that has been filled with so much pain. His right foot slips as the dragon's body is wracked by horrendous convulsions, and he almost falls. But Beowulf grits his teeth, tasting his own blood, and hangs on.

"It is *over*," he whispers, and the dragon's body trembles. "Take me, and let them be."

The golden man's voice has finally left his head, and Beowulf cranes his neck, gazing back over his shoulder at the causeway connecting the towers. Wealthow and Ursula are huddled together against the far balustrade. He can see that their gowns have been singed and their faces are stained with soot. They are bruised and terrified, but they are both *alive*, and even now Beowulf can feel the dragon's life ebbing away.

"By the gods, it is over," he says again, resting his cheek against the dragon's chest. "Die."

But the *fyrweorm* narrows its eyes and rears back again, cocking its head to one side as it prepares to send another blast of fire down upon the keep. This time, however, there is merely a labored, strangling sound from the depths of its mighty chest, and no flame erupts from out that maw. And Beowulf understands that he has punctured and destroyed some crucial part of its anatomy, some organ without which the monster cannot spark and make fire. Enraged, the dragon shrieks and hammers the air with its wings. It hisses and strikes at the causeway with only its jaws, shearing away a section of the balustrade and part of the deck, snapping off several of its fangs. Ursula screams and Wealthow hides her face, but the women remain out of the monster's reach. Again, it strikes and snaps its jaws, but this time they close on empty air. The beast is once more losing altitude, its left wing too torn to keep it airborne any longer. It is drifting back from the causeway.

And the golden man's words echo in Beowulf's mind.

How will you hurt me, my Father? Your fingers? Your teeth? Your bare hands?

And with the last of his strength, Beowulf forces the charred stump of his arm deeply into the beast's torn throat, pushing it in up to his shoulder, ripping through more of the soft muscle and organ meat beneath its golden armor. The dragon bellows, and from their place on the causeway, Ursula looks up to see its amber eyes roll back in its head.

"*Let go*," sighs Beowulf, unsure if he's speaking to the golden man or himself.

The dragon's chin slams down upon the deck of the causeway, the end of its snout only scant inches from the two women. It rests there for a moment, and then slips backward, its wings falling slack at its slides as the creature tumbles out of control. It seems to Beowulf that the long fall lasts almost forever, that last precious glimpse of Wealthow and Ursula before the endless descent down, down, down to the slate-gray sea crashing against the craggy rocks below the keep.

In the reckless frenzy of its death throes and its final savage assault upon the causeway, the dragon has dislodged keystones and rent the colossal pillars supporting the bridge. The very foundations of the causeway where it joins with the native granite have been broken by the force of the beast's attack, and though the dragon has fallen, the entire structure begins quickly to sag and collapse in upon itself. In only moments, the work of Heorot's engineers and architects has been undone, and Wealthow and Ursula hold tight to one another as the deck begins to list. They have somehow been so fortunate as to survive the creature's murderous and fiery onslaughts, only to find their deaths in the destruction of the bridge.

Wealthow glances desperately toward the eastern tower, where only moments before she saw Wiglaf trying to reach them. But the fire burns even more fiercely than before, as though the masonry itself is feeding the blaze. There is no sign of Wiglaf anywhere.

A nearby section of the causeway cracks apart suddenly, slinging bits of rock and mortar and raising a cloud of dust. Ursula screams and hides her faces in Wealthow's arms as the bridge begins to tilt toward the sea. And the Queen of Heorot Hall holds tight to the woman her husband bedded in her stead, the one he must have come to love more than her, for what profits anyone bitterness or spite, and Wealthow waits for the end.

"I am so sorry," the girl sobs, but Wealthow tells her there is nothing left now to be sorry for.

"But I took him from you."

"Child, you took nothing I did not first let slip away from me," says Wealthow.

And at that moment, the causeway cracks again, and this time a large portion of the flaming deck dividing them from the eastern tower and their escape pulls free and tumbles toward the crashing waves and jagged shingle far below. As it goes, it opens a narrow, crumbling pathway through the flames. And there is Wiglaf, still standing on the other side.

"*Get up*," Wealthow tells Ursula, all but lifting the girl to her feet, not knowing how long the path might endure or how soon until the entire structure drops away beneath them. "We have to run. We can *live*, but we have to run, and we have to run *fast*."

Through her tears, Ursula stares, uncertain and terrified, toward Wiglaf and the slight gap in the roaring wall of fire. "But . . ." Ursula begins.

"*Run*, damn you," Wealthow growls, pushing her ahead toward Wiglaf, who has begun picking his way toward them through the ruin. "Run, or I will throw you over the side myself and be done with it."

And then Ursula is running, with Wealthow close on her heels, the two women dashing toward deliverance as the causeway groans beneath them. But another explosion erupts from somewhere close behind them, and the deck abruptly leans away from the sea, pivoting on its columns and swaying instead in the direction of the eastern tower and Wiglaf. Wealthow loses her footing and begins sliding across the precipitously listing causeway toward a spot where the teeth of the dragon broke away the balustrade and so there's nothing there to stop her from slipping over the edge. Ursula shouts for Wiglaf and lunges for her queen, managing to grab hold of Wealthow's left hand. But Ursula is only strong enough to slow Wealthow's progress toward the causeway's shattered rim, and now both women are sliding nearer the edge.

"Wiglaf!" Ursula cries out, digging her heels into the quavering deck.

"Please, save yourself" Wealthow implores the girl. "It's too late for me, but we don't *both* have to die here." And with that, Queen Wealthow wrenches her hand free of Ursula's grasp. The girl screams, but in the last instant before Wealthow tumbles over the edge, Wiglaf catches her and straining, digging deep for the last of his strength, hauls her safely back onto the deck.

"What you ladies say we get the hell out of here?" he moans, and then the Geat leads them both to the eastern towers. Only moments after they have gained that harborage, the swaying causeway again changes its course, pulling free of the tower wall in a final, decisive lurch before plummeting toward the sea. It leaves behind only a wide gulf of smoky air to mark the space between the spires of Heorot.

Beowulf comes to on a small patch of sand in the lee of a boulder, awakened by the chill of the icy waves. For a second, it seems he lies atop the fallen dragon, but then as salt water and foam retreat, he sees that he lies beside the golden man from the merewife's cave. A terrible wound extends from the man's throat all the way down his chest to his belly. His eyelids flutter, and then he opens them and stares up at the winter clouds.

"Father?" he coughs. "Are you here? I can't see you."

"I'm here," Beowulf replies weakly. He ignores the pain that seems to radiate from every part of his body and drags himself closer, cradling his son's head in the crook of his good arm "I'm sorry . . ."

"Are we dead?" the golden man asks, and blood leaks from his lips.

"Almost," Beowulf replies, before another wave rushes forward and crashes over them both. Beowulf gasps at the cold, and when the sea recedes again, he is alone on the sand. The golden man is gone, returned to his mother. The King of the Ring-Danes lies back down on the beach, watching the clouds passing by overhead, dimly aware that he has begun to cry, but his tears seem of little consequence here beside the resounding ocean.

I will lie here just a little longer, thinks Beowulf, and then he hears footsteps, the crunch of boots on the pebble-strewn sand. He turns his head, and Wiglaf is walking toward him across the beach.

"You lucky bastard," mutters Beowulf.

Wiglaf kneels next to him, inspecting the cauterized stump of his right arm.

"I told you we were too old to be heroes," he says. "Let me get you to a healer."

"No," Beowulf tells him, and shakes his head. "Not this time, old friend."

"You're Beowulf, son of Ecgtheow," Wiglaf says. "The scops sing your deeds in all the lands of the world. No way a little thing like *this* is going to finish you off. That's not how this story will end."

"No," Beowulf tells him again. "I'm done, my Wiglaf. And it is not so bad an ending. It will be a fine enough tale for Gladsheim."

"Aye," replies Wiglaf, sitting down and brushing wet hair away from Beowulf's blood-streaked face. "It will make a fine tale for Odin's hall, but not *this* day, my lord. I have a fresh, strong horse, there, just beyond the rocks."

Beowulf smiles for Wiglaf and closes his eyes, listening to the waves and to something he hears woven in between the waves. It might be the voice of a woman singing, the most beautiful voice he has ever heard.

"Do you hear her?" he asks Wiglaf.

"I hear nothing my lord, but the sea and the wind and the gulls."

"The *song*, Wiglaf," says Beowulf. "It's Grendel's mother, the merewife . . . my son's mother . . . *my* . . ." but he trails off then, distracted by the pain and uncertain what word he was going to say next, whether it might have been *lover* or *mother*, *foe* or *destiny*.

He opens his eyes again, for now the song has grown so loud he does not have to try so hard to pick it free of the noise of the sea. Wiglaf is gazing down at him, and Beowulf has never seen Wiglaf look so frightened.

"No, lord. Don't say such things. You slew Grendel's mother. When we were yet young men. It's in the saga—"

"Then the saga is a *lie*," says Beowulf, raising his voice, angry and almost shouting, and he feels something pulling loose inside his chest. "A *lie*," he says again. "Wiglaf, you know it was a lie. You always knew."

Wiglaf does not say a word, and Beowulf shuts his eyes again, wanting only to listen to the song flowing up from the sea.

"And it is too late for lies," he whispers. "Too late . . ."

A wave rushes up the shore, soaking Wiglaf, and when he looks back down at Beowulf's pale face, Wiglaf realizes that he's alone on the beach. King Beowulf is dead.

Epilogue

The Passing of Beowulf

At the center of the world stands the ash Yggdrasil, the greatest and best of all trees, and below the roots of Yggdrasil dwell the three maidens—the Norns—who work always, busy at their looms, spinning and shaping the lives of every man and every woman, weaving what must be from chaos and infinite possibility. Even the gods in Ásgard are only threads in the handiwork of the Norns, and even they, like mortal men and the giants, may not glimpse the threads of their lives or know the judgment of those nimble, tireless fingers. The length of each thread is known only to these three maidens, there below the foundations of the World Ash. And so it was with Beowulf, who sought always the glory and the brave death that must be sought out by those who wish to enter Odin's hall and fight alongside the gods in the final battle when Ragnarök comes and the children of Loki Sky-walker and Shape-Changer are again loosed upon the cosmos. At the moment of his birth, the Norns had already woven the fate of Beowulf, and in all his struggles and on down to the day of his death, he has only ever followed the course of that thread.

Such are the thoughts of the new Lord of the Danes on this winter day, the day of Beowulf's burial. King Wiglaf, son of Weohstan, the son of a Geatish fish-wife, stands alone and apart from all the others who have come to bid the old king fare well. Today he wears the golden crown so recently worn by Beowulf and by King Hrothgar before him, by the line of Hrothgar's house all the way back to Scyld Sheafson. From his place upon the rocks above the edge of the sea, Wiglaf looks out at the whitecapped waves and setting sun and the funeral ship. It is the same dragon-prowed ship that he and Beowulf and the other Geats sailed across the stormy waters of Jótlandshaf to reach the shores of a demon-haunted land thirty long years ago, and now it will bear Beowulf away on this, his final journey from the walls of Midgard across the span of the Bilröst Bridge.

So many have come—the survivors of the worm's attack on Heorot and also outlanders from all the four corners of the kingdom of the Ring-Danes. They have gathered upon the rugged shore, silent or whispering among themselves. A young scop stands on the sea cliff not far away from Wiglaf, and his voice is high and clear and drifts out over the dusk-stained beach.

Across the whale's-road he came
And made our land his hearth and home . . .

Ten strong thanes take their places, five on either side of the funeral ship. The masts have been rigged full sail, and the evening wind whips and billows in the shrouds. Fourteen of the finest iron battle-shields ever made line both the starboard and larboard wales, and the burial vessel has been heaped with treasure, gold and silver and bronze, and with swords and axes and bows, with helmets and bright mail shirts. All these precious things Beowulf had asked be buried with him, that he might be properly prepared to ride out upon the wide fields of Idavoll. His oaken bier rises from the center of the hoard, and Beowulf lies there, dressed in his best furs and armor.

The thanes strain and heave and finally push the ship down the sand and into the icy surf. At once it is caught in a current that will carry it away from shore by way of a magnificent sea arch, an ancient granite vault carved by wind and rain and the sea herself. There is a company of thanes posted high upon the crest of the towering arch, tending the immense cedar bonfire built there.

Wiglaf takes a deep breath of the cold, salty air, silently saying his good-byes, and watches as the wind and the current ferry the ship beneath the arch of stone. The scop's voice rises, nearing the end of his song.

So much blood where so many have died
Washed ashore on a crimson tide.
Just as now there was no mercy then.
Dogs of war gnawed the bones of men.
Brave and strong as they fell in the fight,
Feeding Death's endless appetite.
Only one with the heart of a king
Set them free. It's of him we sing.

Wiglaf catches sight of the thin Christian priest in his red robes, lurking near the queen and bearing the standard of Christ Jesus, but the Irishman has no formal role in these proceedings. These are the old ways, already fading from the land as a strange new religion takes hold, but they were the ways of Beowulf, and the ways of King Wiglaf, as well, and so will be honored and observed on this day.

Queen Wealthow stands hand in hand with Ursula, and Wiglaf hopes that together they may find some solace from their grief and horror. Wealthow will remain the Lady of Heorot, the Scylding Queen, though Wiglaf will respect her wishes and not ask her to be his wife.

The funeral ship sails beneath the arch, and as it exits the far side and makes for the open sea, the thanes tending the pyre use long poles to force it over the cliff. A brilliant firefall of glowing embers and flaming brands spills down from the rocks and rains across the masts and the deck of the dragon-prowed ship. In only a moment more, the entire ship is burning.

The scop's song ends, and for a moment Wiglaf listens to the hungry roar of the flames, the waves and wind, the sad and gentle murmur from the crowd. The sun's chariot has reached the horizon, and it seems to Wiglaf like an enormous crimson eye gazing out across the sea toward the burning ship and the mourners lining the shore. The burning sails of the funeral ship are framed in stark silhouette against that blazing eye. And finally King Wiglaf speaks, calling out loud to be heard.

"He was the bravest of us. The prince of all warriors. His name will live forever. He—" But then the lump in Wiglaf's throat is too painful to say any more, and he turns away so no one will see the tears on his cheeks.

Now it is Wealthow's turn to speak, and she does so despite her own tears.

"His song," says the queen, "shall be sung forever. As long as the world endures, the tales of his brave deeds shall be told."

And then there is only the wind and the surf once again, and Beowulf's funeral ship has been carried out into the open water. Slowly, the mourners begin to turn away, filing along the road winding up through the cliffs to the keep. Wiglaf watches Wealthow and

Ursula go, but he remains behind, determined to stand vigil as long as the ship floats, as long as it burns. His mind drifts back to a day thirty years before, he and Beowulf standing together on the listing deck in a howling, storm-wracked sea.

The sea is my mother! declared a grinning Beowulf. *She spat me up years ago and will never take me back into her murky womb!*

Then Wiglaf hears something on the wind, a wordless keening, and he peers out across the sea, seeking the source of the sound. As he stares at the sea, bloodied now by the setting sun and the flames of the funeral ship, the keening begins to take another shape, becoming a beautiful song, a song more exquisite than any that has ever reached his ears or that he has ever before thought possible.

The song, *Wiglaf. Grendel's mother, the merewife . . .*

And then he sees her, the form of a woman astride the prow of the burning dragon ship. The sunset gleams off her naked skin, and then she slips silently into the sea. Relieved of its queer passenger, the boat lists to starboard and immediately begins to sink. Wiglaf leaves his place in the boulders and walks quickly down to the wet sand, where something metallic sparkles as it rolls to and fro in the foamy surf. At first he thinks it only some trinket that must have fallen from the dead king's ship, perhaps thrown free by the impact of the firefall. But when he stoops to pick it up, he finds the golden drinking horn, twice lost and now returned once more. He picks it up, though some more cautious part of his mind suggests he would be better off leaving it be, turning about, and following the others back up the cliff to the keep. Wiglaf stands there with the sea lapping at his feet and holds the horn, realizing that he has not until this second fully appreciated the elegance of its craftsmanship. He glances back toward the sea, which is quickly growing dark as the sun slips away.

She is rising from the water, the gilt-skinned mother of the demon Grendel, the mother of the dragon who was Beowulf's only son. She stops singing and smiles, beckoning Wiglaf with one long finger. Wiglaf takes a hesitant step toward her, the sea rushing about his ankles and seeming to draw him forward. He is only dimly aware of the burning funeral ship now, as its carved bow rises high into the air and lingers there a moment before sliding backward to be swallowed up by the ocean. The water hisses and steams as the deep accepts the mortal remains of Beowulf, son of Ecgtheow, into Ægir's gardens.

"A man like you," she says, "could own the greatest tale ever sung," and Wiglaf, son of Weohstan, gazes deeply into the honeyed eyes of this woman from the sea. His mind is filled with the siren lure of her promises, but also does he clearly see the price he would pay, the price that so many other men have paid before him.

"A man like *you*," she says again and extends a hand to the Geat.

"Might walk any road that pleases him," replies Wiglaf, and the icy sea slops at his feet. "I *know* you, she-demon, and I know you speak of glory and of wealth and renown, and but for what I've *seen*, it might appear the fairest gift ever offered a poor fish-monger's son."

"As you say," the merewife smiles, for she is ancient and skilled at waiting games, having yet more time before her than any mortal man might ever comprehend.

And the Norns—Urðr, Verðandi, and Skuld—the three fates busily weaving beneath the roots of Yggdrasil, watch the progress of another cord held tight within their looms. For every single thread is a wonder to them, and so they spin and wait with the patience of all immortal things.

A Glossary of Norse, Icelandic, Old English, and Anglo-Saxon Terms Appearing in the Novel

Ægir—in Norse mythology, the personification of the sea and husband of the goddess Rán, father to nine daughters (the billows, waves); a synonym for "sea" in skaldic poetry. Ægir is sometimes described as a giant, though this seems unlikely.

aeglaeca—in reference to Grendel's mother ("Grendles modor"); Anglo-Saxon, "awesome opponent," "ferocious fighter."

Æsir—the principal gods of the Norse pantheon, including Odin, Baldr, Bragi, Loki, Vé, Heimdall, etc.; excludes those gods referred to as the *Vanir*, with whom the Æsir do battle.

aglaec-wif—Anglo-Saxon, in reference to Grendel's mother ("Grendles modor"); some controversy surrounds the correct translation of this phrase. The *Dictionary of Old English* translates it as "female warrior, fearsome woman." Earlier authors translated it as "monster wife" and "monster woman," but those same translations of *Beowulf* translate *aglaeca* and *aeglaeca* as "hero" or "warrior" when referring to Beowulf himself.

Árvak—Norse, "early riser," one of the horses that draw the chariot of the sun goddess Sól.

Alsvin—Norse, "all swift," one of the two horses that draw the chariot of the sun; also *Alsvid*.

Ásgard—the home of the Æsir, literally "enclosure-of-the-Æsir."

Ásynja—feminine form of *Æsir*.

Audhumla—in the Norse creation myth, the first cow, who licked the first god, Búri, free from a block of salty ice.

Aurgelmir—"gravel-yeller," father of the race of Frost Giants; also known as *Ymir*.

Bestla—a Frost Giant, mother of the gods Odin, Vé, and Vili, wife of Borr (Burr), daughter of Bolthorn.

Bilröst Bridge—also known as Bifröst, the Bifrost Bridge, the Rainbow Bridge, etc.; a great bridge connecting the homes of the Æsir with Midgard, the realm of men, to be destroyed at Ragnarök.

Bragi—Norse god of poetry, son of Odin.

Bronding clan—a Germanic tribe, probably located on the Swedish island of Brännö, west of Västergötland in the Kattegatt (an embayment of the Baltic Sea); Beowulf's childhood friend, Brecca, was of the Bronding.

Búri—the primeval god in the Norse pantheon, father of Borr, grandfather to Odin.

Dark Fells—Nidafjöll, "fell mountains" of the Norse underworld, from whence came the great dragon *Nidhögg Rootnibbler*.

Dökkálfar—in Norse mythology, the subterranean "dark elves"; known also as the Svartálfar ("black elves"). Possibly synonymous with the dwarves (*dvergar*).

einherjar—in Norse mythology, the spirits of those who have died bravely in battle and so dwell with Odin in Valhalla, awaiting the coming of *Ragnarök*; also *einheriar*, singular *einheri*.

Éljudnir—*Hel*'s hall in the Norse underworld.

The Fates—(see *Norns*).

Fenrir, Fenrisulfr—in Norse mythology, a great wolf, son of Loki and the giantess Angrboda. Fenrir was bound by the Æsir, but will one day grow so large he will break his chains and devour Odin during *Ragnarök*, before being slain by Odin's son, Vidar.

Frermánudr—frost month, twelfth month of the Old Norse calendar, corresponding roughly to mid-November to Mid-December, Yule month; also known as Ylir.

Fyrweorm—literally, "fire worm"; dragon.

Gandvik—probably an old name for the Baltic Sea; also Grandvik in some translations.

Geat—Beowulf's tribe, a people who lived in what is now Sweden, in Götaland ("land of the Geats"); the Goths.

Ginnunga gap—a primordial void or chaos that existed before the world was ordered; also Ginnungagap.

Gjöll—in Norse mythology, one of eleven rivers (the Élivágar) whose sources are the Hvergelmir (the wellspring of all cold) in Niflheim. The Élivágar ("ice waves") flow through Ginnunga Gap; Gjöll is also a name used for the stone to which the wolf Fenrir is bound.

Gladsheim—Odin's great hall in Valhalla, located on the Plain of *Idavoll* within *Ásgard*, where sit the Æsir and the valiant einherjar.

Gleipnir—the binding force that holds the wolf Fenrir, said to be thin as a cloth ribbon and stronger than an iron chain; forged by the dwarves of Svartálfaheim from six ingredients: the sound of a cat's footfall; a mountain's roots, the sinews of a bear; a bird's spittle; the beard of a woman; and a fish's breath.

Gram—the sword wielded by Siegfried (also Sigurd) to slay the dragon Fafnir.

Gullinkambi—Norse, literally "golden comb," this is the name of the rooster who dwells at Gladsheim in Valhalla, whose crowing wakes the *einherjar* each dawn, and whose cry will also signal the start of *Ragnarök*.

Heathoreams—a Germanic tribe living near Oslo, Norway, in the fifth and sixth centuries.

Heimdall—the son of nine different mothers, Heimdall is the guardian of the gods and blows the Gjallarhorn ("ringing horn") should danger approach *Ásgard*; also Heimdallr.

Hertha—another name by which the goddess *Nerthus* is known (see *Nerthus*).

Hildeburh—daughter of the Danish King Hoc and the wife of the Frisian king Finn.

Hræsvelg, Hraæsvelg Corpse-swallowe—a giant eagle whose beating wings create the world's wind.

Hymir—a giant who owned a gigantic cauldron which was taken by *Thor* to brew mead for the *Æsir*.

Idavol—in Norse mythology, the plain upon which *Ásgard* is located.

Jörmungand, Jörmungand Loki-son, Jörmungandr—one of Loki's monstrous offspring by the giantess

Angrboda; the World Serpent or Midgard Serpent, this great snake was imprisoned in the seas by Odin, after which Jörmungandr grew so large that he encircles all the world.

Jótlandshaf—also Skagerrak; a strait between Norway, Sweden, and Denmark, connecting the North Sea with the Baltic.

Jötnar—the giants (singular *jötunn*).

Jotunheimr—the home of the giants, also known as Jotunheim, who dwell beyond the great wall of Midgard.

Loki, Loki Skywalker—son of the giants Fárbauti and Laufey and foster brother of Odin, Loki was responsible for the murder of the god Baldr. For this crime, the *Æsir* bound Loki to three stone slabs and placed above him a serpent, whose searing venom drips into Loki's eyes. When he writhes, the earth quakes. Loki will be freed at *Ragnarök*, where he will meet and slay *Heimdall*, but later die of his wounds.

Lyngvi—the island where the Æsir bound the wolf *Fenrir*. Lyngvi is located in a lake known as Ámsvartnir ("red-black").

Máni—son of the giants Mundilfæri and Glaur, Máni is the Norse god of the moon. Every night he pulls the moon across the sky, pursued by the wolf Hati. Come *Ragnarök*, Hati will finally catch Máni and attempt to devour the moon.

Menhirs—standing stones, megaliths.

merwif—Grendel's mother; Old English, literally "water woman" or "woman of the mere."

Midgard—in Norse mythology, the realm set aside for man by the *Æsir*, divided from the rest of the cosmos by a great wall constructed from the eyebrows of the giant Ymir. Midgard is an English transliteration of Old Norse *Miðgarðr* ("middle enclosure"). Middle English transforms Miðgarðr to Middellærd (or Middel-erde), or "middle-earth."

Midgard serpent—(see *Jörmungand*).

Mörsugur—in the Old Norse calendar, the midwinter month, following *Frermánudr*.

Mundilfæri—in Norse mythology, a giant, father of the sun goddess *Sól* and the moon god *Máni* by the giantess Glaur; also *Mundilfäri*.

Muspéll—a giant associated with *Ragnarök*, who dwelt in the primeval realm of fire bordering Ginnunga Gap. The sons of Muspéll will break Bilröst, signaling the final battle between the Æsir and the giants.

Nerthus—a Germanic fertility goddess associated with water; also known as *Nerpuz*, *Hertha*. Some *Beowulf* scholars believe that "Grendles modor" may have been intended as an incarnation of this goddess.

Nidafjöll—(see *Dark Fells*).

Nidhögg, Nidhögg Rootnibbler—the great dragon that dwells beneath the "World Ash" Yggdrasil, gnawing always at the roots of the great tree. Also *Níðhöggr* ("malice-striker").

Niflheim—the Norse "land of mists," to be found north of Ginnunga gap, home of the Frost Giants and Loki's daughter, *Hel*.

Njörd, Njördr—in Norse mythology, one of the *Vanir*, a god of wind and seacoasts, of fishermen and sailing. Njord has the power to calm either sea or fire. Husband of Skaði, father of Yngvi-Freyr and Freyja.

Norns—the women who spin the fate of the cosmos beneath the boughs of Yggdrasil. The three most prominent are Urðr ("fate"), Verðandi ("to become"), and Skuld ("shall"), who not only spin destiny but tend the roots of the World Ash lest they rot. The arrival of these three powerful giantesses from *Jötunheimr* heralded the end of the golden age of the *Æsir*.

Odin, Odin Allfather, Odin Hel-binder, Odin Langbard—the central god in the Norse pantheon. With his brothers, *Vili* and *Vé*, Odin slew the *ur*-giant *Ymir* and used the dead giant's corpse to order the cosmos. After hanging on the World Ash for nine days, pierced by his own spear, Odin won wisdom to rule the nine worlds. At the cost of his left eye, he drank from the Well of Wisdom and gained knowledge of the past, present, and future. With the other *Æsir*, Odin will fall at *Ragnarök*.

Ragnarök—Old Norse, "twilight" or "fate of the gods." Ragnarök is the final battle between the Æsir and the forces of chaos, including Loki and his monstrous offspring, along with the other giants. Ragnarök will destroy almost all the universe and will herald a new age.

Rán—wife of *Ægir* and mother of the nine daughters, Rán is a goddess of the sea. It is said that Rán had a net with which she sometimes snared unfortunate sailors. Indeed, Rán means "theft." All men who drown at sea are taken by Rán.

sahagin—"sea hag," a phrase applied to Grendel's mother.

Sigurd Dragonslayer—an heroic figure of Norse mythology, also figuring prominently in the Icelandic Völsunga saga. Foster son of the god *Regin*, Sigurd slays *Fafnir* (son of the dwarf king *Hreidmar* and brother of Regin), who has assumed the form of a dragon. Sigurd is known in Old Norse as *Sigurðr* and in Old German as *Siegfried*.

Skoll—the wolf that pursues the chariot of the goddess *Sól* across the sky each day.

skorsten—Swedish, a chimney.

Skuld—(see *Norns*).

Scylding—Old English (plural Scyldingas), Old Norse Skjöldung (plural Skjöldungar), translates as "shielding" and refers to members of a family of royal Danes and also to their people. The etymology of the word may be traced to King Scyld/Skjöld.

Sól—goddess of the sun, daughter of *Mundilfæri* and *Glaur*, wife of *Glen*; Sól bears the sun across the daytime sky in a golden chariot.

Svartálfheim—the subterranean realm of the dwarves.

Thor Giant-killer—the Norse god of thunder, son of *Odin* and *Jörd*. Thor wields the hammer *Mjolnir*, and at *Ragnarök*, he will die while slaying the World Serpent.

Twilight of the Gods—Ragnarök.

Urdarbrunn—the well from which the three *Norns* draw water to nourish the World Ash.

Urdines—the nine daughters of the sea god Ægir and the goddess Rán; the waves.

Valgrind—the gates of *Valhalla*.

Valhalla—in Old Norse, *Valhöll*, "hall of the slain." This is Odin's great hall in *Ásgard*, where those slain in battle feast and celebrate and await the coming of *Ragnarök*.

Valkyries—goddesses who serve *Odin* and may be synonymous with the Norns. The Valkyries welcome the *einherjar* to *Valhalla*, where they also serve as handmaidens. Odin sends the Valkyries to every battle, where they determine victory and death.

Vandals—an ancient Germanic tribe. Consisting of two groups, the Silingi and the Hasdingi, the Vandals were mighty warriors.

Vanir—a subgroup of the *Æsir*, including the gods *Njörd*, *Heimdall*, *Freyja*, and *Frey*. For a time, the Vanir warred with the other Æsir, until a hostage exchange brought an end to the fighting. The Vanir dwell in *Vanaheimr*.

Vé—brother of *Odin* and *Vili*, son of *Bestla* and *Bur*, and with his brothers he created the world from the remains of the slain giant *Ymir*.

Verdandi—the Norn Verðandi (see Norns).

Víðar—often known as the "silent god," *Víðar* is Odin's son by the giantess *Grid*. At *Ragnarök*, he will avenge his father's death, and is one of the few *Æsir* who will survive that final battle. A god of vengeance, and he who defines space (as *Heimdall* defines the boundaries of time).

Vili—Odin's brother. With Odin and *Vé*, he created *Midgard* and ordered the world.

warg—Old Norse, "wolf."

Weormgræf—"worm grave," "dragon's grave."

wergeld, wergild—payment, in the form of money or a human life, for murder and other very serious crimes.

World Serpent—(see *Jörmungand*).

Wylfings (also *Wulfings)*—an important tribe, perhaps the ruling clan of the Eastern Geats. *Wealthow*, wife of the Danish king Hrothgar was of the Wylfing clan, as was *Heatholaf*, slain by Beowulf's father, *Ecgtheow*.

Yggdrasil, World Ash—in Norse mythology, the tree that stands at the center of the cosmos, uniting the nine worlds. The only two humans who will survive *Ragnarök*—*Lif* and *Lifthrasir*—will do so by seeking shelter in the boughs of Yggdrasil and feeding off the dew on its leaves.

Ymir—the first giant, licked from a block of rime by the first cow *Audhumla*. Ymir was killed and dismembered by the Æsir Odin, Vé, and Vili (the sons of Bur), who used his remains to shape the cosmos.

Yule, Yuletide—a pre-Christian winter solstice celebration, including feasting and sacrifice, present in many Northern European cultures.

Author's Note: If a teacher or professor has assigned you *Beowulf*, this novelization doesn't count. Not even close. For readers who would like to learn more about Norse mythology, I strongly recommend John Lindow's *Norse Mythology: A Guide to the Gods, Heroes, Rituals, and Beliefs* (Oxford University Press, 2001).

Author's Note and Acknowledgments

Though in the writing of this novel I have generally and in the main followed the course set out for me by Neil Gaiman and Roger Avery's screenplay, there are a number of additional sources I would like to acknowledge here. John Lindow's *Norse Mythology: A Guide to the Gods, Heroes, Rituals, and Beliefs* (Oxford University Press, 2001) has been indispensable and is recommended to anyone with an interest in the beliefs and practices of the "Viking Age." Also, I should acknowledge a number of scholarly works which proved very helpful and were frequently consulted during the writing of this book: J. R. R. Tolkien's "*Beowulf*: The Monsters and the Critics" (1936); John Leyerle's "The Interlace Structure of

Beowulf" (1967); Ralph Arnold's "Royal Halls: The Sutton Hoo Ship Burial" (1967); Christine Alfano's "The Issue of Feminine Monstrosity: A Reevaluation of Grendel's Mother" (1992); Frank Battaglia's "The Germanic Earth Goddess in Beowulf" (1991); John Grigsby's *Beowulf & Grendel: The Truth Behind England's Oldest Legend* (2005); Kevin S. Kiernan's "Grendel's Heroic Mother" (1984); E. G. Stanley's "Did Beowulf Commit 'Feaxfeng' against Grendel's Mother" (1976); and Doreen M. Gilliam's "The Use of the Term 'Aeglaeca' in Beowulf at Lines 893 and 2592" (1961). While working on this book, I have also frequently consulted two translations of the anonymous *Beowulf* poem—E. Talbot Donaldson's classic prose translation of 1966 and Seamus Heaney's 2000 verse translation. When making my own translations from the original Anglo-Saxon, I have used *A Concise Anglo-Saxon Dictionary* by J. R. Clark-Hall (University of Toronto Press, 1984) and *Old English: A Historical Linguistic Companion* by Roger Lass (Cambridge University Press; 1994), among others.

I would also like to thank the following persons and institutions: Poppy Z. Brite, for lending an ear; Neil Gaiman, for trusting me with his vision; my literary agent, Merrilee Heifetz; my editor on this book, Will Hinton and Jennifer Brehl at HarperCollins; Jennifer Lee and James Shimkus; Sonya Taaffe, for Latin and commiseration; Byron White; the staff of the Robert W. Woodruff Library (Emory University); Claire Reilly-Shapiro and Albert Araneo at Writer's

House (NYC); David J. Schow, for encouraging my investigation of the striking parallels between Ridley Scott's *Alien* and *Beowulf*; and most of all, Kathryn A. Pollnac. This book was written on a Macintosh iBook and iMac.